Born in Lancashire, UK, Shahida Ahmed is a third-generation British-Asian, multimedia artist, creative director, educator and art consultant who has long loved entertaining her friends by telling them stories. "My friends were always encouraging me to write a book and, in the end, I decided to take them up on their dare," she says.

Shahida holds a BA in Visual Arts from University of Leeds and a BA (Hons) in Art and Design from University of Bradford. She gained a scholarship for an MA in Traditional Islamic Arts from the Royal College of Art, London, MA in Community Leadership from the University of Central Lancashire and an MA in Visual Arts from the University of Bradford, along with several other professional qualifications. Shahida currently divides her time between the UK and Qatar, where she lives and works. Throughout her career she has believed that art and creativity is a diverse form of dialogue that brings communities together. Although English was Shahida's second language, she followed her passion and wrote secretly, following her heart and having the right people around her enabled her to believe that anything is possible.

This book is dedicated to the three blessings in my life, Natasha, Azim and Maliha. Also to my beloved parents, Zohra Parveen and Maqbool Ahmed – may they rest in peace – and my beloved brother Imtiaz (Immy) Ahmed, who sadly passed away in September 2020. Immy left us with three words: love, peace and unity.

I also dedicate it to Ghafooran Begum, a wonderful woman who was like a second mother to us. Having sadly left us in February 2021, she is now reunited with my birth parents and brother. We will be forever indebted to her for her unconditional love.

I hope *Through Brown Eyes* will empower women and that proceeds from the sales will enable me to support women around the world who sadly still aren't able to benefit from the opportunities that are available to some of us.

I look forward to sharing updates with you on my next book, which is titled *Full Circle*.

Dear Nunu & Abi
I love you so much
and thank you for everything
you have done for me, the love
and care unconditionaly. my journey
Thank you for being part of

2nd copy
14th Oct 2021

Shahida Ahmed

THROUGH BROWN EYES

AUSTIN MACAULEY PUBLISHERS™

LONDON • CAMBRIDGE • NEW YORK • SHARJAH

ISBN – 9789948844884 – (Paperback)
ISBN – 9789948844877 – (E-Book)

Application Number: MC-10-01-9821762
Age Classification: E

Printer Name: Al Nisr Publishing LLC
Printer Address: Dubai, United Arab Emirates

First Published (2021)
AUSTIN MACAULEY PUBLISHERS FZE
Sharjah Publishing City
P.O Box [519201]
Sharjah, UAE
www.austinmacauley.ae
+971 655 95 202

I would like to thank all the people who have remained by my side throughout challenging times and given me the strength over the years to believe in myself. These include:

My mother and father, who gave me life and enabled me to become the person I am today. They also taught me that life is about giving and sharing. Despite being illiterate themselves, they were visionaries, with better leadership qualities than many, who recognised the importance of education and championed empowerment.

My three children who have been my rock over the years. Natasha, Azim and Maliha – I will forever be grateful for your patience, encouragement and support. You have my unconditional love and I pray that you will each find your own fulfilment as you journey through life.

I would also like to thank:

My dear friend and editor, Miriam Dunn, for giving me the confidence and self-belief to write a novel. Without this, I wouldn't have seen the project through.

Bano Murtaja and Helen Assaf for their painstaking editing and proofreading work.

Zeba Bakhtiar, the first person to suggest I should write a novel after I told her how much I enjoyed creating and sharing stories.

Noor Jehan Dhanani (Nunu) and Asgar Khan (Aki) for acting as parent figures, mentors and role models and keeping me on track.

My friends Nazya Khalid, Aisha Mirza, Tara Hussain, Mehr Mussarat and Sabah Bapir for being part of the journey.

My beloved friend Heather Alnuweiri, who sadly is no longer with us.

Douglas Jackson, who has been a ray of light, providing me with the encouragement I needed and the unconditional friendship of a brother.

Sabah Arbilli, for the Arabic calligraphy for name and logo; Mohamed Amine Serhane, for the cover design and Maryam Alwazzan for the cover photo.

Finally, thank you, Rumi, for your poetry, which has pierced my soul.
Life is a journey and you have all been part of it. I thank you all.

Life is beautiful when we understand that it's a gift of giving – living with your soul and being content.

The best stories are the ones that are put into words to make a book which then becomes a reality.

Table of contents

1
Darkness Is Your Candle

A steady stream of traffic was heading toward me. I could feel the speed of the vehicles as each one tore past, the vibrations almost knocking me off balance as they headed on their way. The sheer force and a giddiness I couldn't shake, shunted me over to the far side of the hard shoulder.

This was a spot I knew like the back of my hand: part of the M65 motorway that runs through East Lancashire. I'd been down this road daily and could pretty much navigate it on autopilot. But this time, something had gone catastrophically wrong. Today's journey had been different and unplanned. My mind was elsewhere, caught up in the raw pain of losing both my parents. I was grappling with having become an orphan, floundering and unable to think of anything other than how tough, dark and bleak my life seemed, just like the weather around me.

It had been two months since I'd lost my father. Though I was engulfed by lethargy, unable to function, time didn't stand still. It forced me into action, even though I was emotionally drained, my senses blunted.

I stared down at my cold, numb feet. It took me a few minutes to realize I was still wearing my house slippers and a flimsy georgette *salwar kameez*, with no cardigan or coat.

The rain came down in sheets, soaking my hair, cascading down my face and neck. Everything around me was a blur, pushed out of focus by the water in my eyes. A sixth sense made me keep track of the lights from each car, helping me stay on the verge. Thoughts slipped in and out of my mind, but I couldn't seem to hold on to them. Had I been thrown out of my car onto the motorway? Could that have even happened? It felt like it, but maybe this was a bad dream. I'd had many of those of late, hoping to wake up to a different reality, only for the dark clouds to re-emerge with the morning.

Yet reality was biting once again now, in the form of lashing rain on my skin, the stark rattling of my teeth and a shivering that I was unable to control. Barely able to walk, I staggered aimlessly onwards, but as my muscles tightened even this became too much. My legs burned with an excruciating pain that was eclipsing everything else.

That moment is etched in my memory: Tuesday, February 7, 2006, 6.30pm. It was a landmark day on so many levels; full of trauma and emotional upheaval but also the day that I was ultimately freed from prison, albeit self-inflicted and suddenly all the rules were of my own making.

This point of no return had been 10 years in the making. It marked the end of so many battles and the moment at which I knew I was too tired to fight any longer. In many ways, the nature and timing of how the events of that day unfolded provided the ideal setting for a tragedy in waiting. The flashbacks remain with me, as do the memories of the first day when it all really began.

2
The Journey
Nelson, Lancashire, 1996

Questions plagued me as I packed. Why was I really disrupting my final term of my first year of university to make the long journey to Karachi with my mother? Of course, it was because I loved my brother Fahad and I wanted to be sure he'd made a good choice with his wife-to-be. It felt like he'd only just met her on his fly-by-night trip to Pakistan. But more important than whether I agreed with the speed of his decision was making sure my mother didn't travel alone.

My Literature and Arts course leader was fine about me taking leave. I'd told him that my trip was for research on a first-hand study that would count towards my assignment. In effect, this would be no-hassle time off.

So off we set. After sitting for hours in the cramped airplane seat, I couldn't wait to disembark onto the tarmac. I guess everyone else felt the same way, because the minute we touched down the shuffling started and passengers began pushing each other to be the first ones to the door. My claustrophobia took over as the shoving worsened and I pushed and squeezed past the line of people so I could breathe in some fresh air. Outside, everything felt far from refreshing; the humidity caused beads of sweat to form and trickle, making my clothes damp and sticky. Aromas of sweat, perfumes and food pervaded. The sunlight was blinding, brighter than I had ever experienced. Squinting against it, I took a deep breath, excited to be entering uncharted territory.

As we stood in yet another queue at passport control, the lack of white faces was overwhelming. I was so used to seeing people of every colour, shade and hue in my hometown of Nelson. So many men here, almost all sporting moustaches, made me feel out of place.

While waiting at the baggage carousel, my thoughts were interrupted by a group of men heading toward us who began haggling about our luggage. I was ready for them. My mother had warned me that when we landed, people would try to take our things. She'd told me to look out for pickpockets and said we should carry our own suitcases rather than allow porters to take them. About 15 of these men crowded around us, chattering away in Urdu, demanding money and lifting our cases off the trolley even as we pushed them along saying no. It was impossible to persuade them to leave us alone, however hard we tried and eventually we gave in and let them carry our luggage.

Welcome to Pakistan, I thought, *the country that my parents' family had called home.* I once questioned Mum and Dad on why they said they were Pakistani and not Indian, since their parents were born and raised in India before the partition. I asked a lot of questions when younger and didn't always get answers, at least not satisfactory ones; I think this was one of those times.

The plan was for us to stay in Karachi for a few days and then get a connecting flight to Faisalabad, where Dad's family lived. Those first days in Karachi were spent with some of my father's more distant relatives. Truth be told, Pakistan was a very different place than I'd imagined. Based on the stereotypes I'd had planted in my head in England, I expected a poverty-stricken country with mud huts and an uncivilized, corrupt population. I was so wrong. There were signs of progress all around us, even though this was a country that had gained independence only a few decades ago.

As we stood in the overwhelming heat outside the airport, miraculously still in possession of our luggage, my cousin Imtiaz approached us. He'd come to take us to his home. I'd never met him before, but he seemed pleasant enough and made a concerted effort to speak English. *He doesn't think I speak Urdu,* I thought, amused.

Imtiaz's father, my uncle, was in the air force, so the house we were staying at was located in an air force complex. I was taken aback by the sheer scale of everything here; from the houses to the roads and paths, everything was so much bigger, longer and wider than what I was used to in Lancashire. As I sat taking everything in, I left my mum to do most of the socializing with the relatives who were putting us up. She was doing a valiant job with the small talk. After a while, a girl aged about 16, who wore her hair in a tight plait down her back, came in. "Salam, I'm Syma," she said.

Syma and her family lived next door to my uncle. "I have three sisters and three brothers, they are studying abroad," she said in her best basic English. I wondered why she didn't talk to me in Punjabi or Urdu, since I could speak both, but didn't want to interrupt her. She was full of praise for her siblings, telling me how wonderful they were, but mostly, she talked about her brothers. I wondered why she didn't tell me about her sisters.

I looked across to see how my mother was dealing with the relatives and realized the huge effort she was making to interact with them. I'd never witnessed her in a situation like this before, but I could tell from the colour in her nose and cheeks that she was feeling the heat. *What a brave woman,* I thought, *coming all these miles without my father, just to mingle and network with relatives.* I knew this trip was about finding marriage suitors for her kids, despite what she and Dad had said to us. I knew this was what she had to do for tradition's sake, but still it made no sense to me, the way you were expected to meet people, identify with them and get acquainted in such a short space of time.

My eldest sister Neelam was finishing university that year and Mum and Dad were focused on arranging a marriage for her, as well as the rest of us, 'back home.' Mum was handed the task of visiting family and relatives in Pakistan to see if there was any interest in us and potential proposals. Though the principle was certainly a cause for concern, I wasn't too worried about being married off. Neelam was older than me and I naively assumed that marriage went in order of age.

For now, this trip was about supporting my mother, something my father had made clear was the priority. But I was overwhelmed by the experience of visiting my parents' country of origin far more than I'd expected to be. Everything I'd heard about Pakistan was being challenged, enabling me to connect with my roots and explore my identity in a way I hadn't imagined.

Exhausted from a long day of travel and sweltering in the heat, I sat awkwardly with Syma in a large bedroom containing two sofas covered with white bedsheets. She was staring straight at me, a smile glued to her face, features fixed. I couldn't be sure whether her expression was natural or forced, or what was expected of me in return. The silence was deafening. To make it worse, there were mosquitos and insects everywhere and I was covered in small red lumps that were itching like mad.

We went out for dinner that night to a restaurant called Usmania, along the busy Shah Faisal Road. It was late, around 10pm, but everyone ate late here; they had to because of the heat. I was worn out from travelling and the time difference. I stifled my yawns, kept awake by the promise of visiting an ice cream parlour on the way home. Ice cream, especially coconut and chocolate chip mint, had always been my biggest weakness.

The next morning, we packed our bags and left for the airport, this time for a much shorter, 90-minute flight. Mum had warned me that Faisalabad would be different. Here, the roads were occupied by donkeys, buffalo, cows, goats and camels as much as they were by cars; dust seemed to fill the air like a fog. It was incredibly noisy, with the constant din of traffic, passers-by shouting out to each other and crowds that seemed to be chanting outside buildings.

We'd been met at the airport by my uncle, who was a doctor, the first one in our family. Dr Saif, as I called him out of respect, drove us to his house. He parked the car in his garage and, as we got out, a young boy who couldn't have been more than nine years old came to help us with our luggage. My insides filled with discomfort as I watched him carrying out my uncle's orders. *He should be in school,* I kept thinking. The boy, whose name was Imran, asked me if I wanted something to drink, but I refused. How could I possibly allow a child to wait on me?

15

3
The Path of Love

At my uncle's house we settled into a routine. Morning after morning, Mum would wake me up in the same way. "Get ready, Shama, we have to go out and meet people," she would say. Even though they were 'family,' albeit distantly related, they were simply strangers to me. On every visit, I had to go through the same motions, being polite and making small talk.

On one occasion, the mission was visiting Neelam's potential suitor. I knew that this required good behaviour on my part. Now more than ever, first impressions mattered. I got ready, put on the new *salwar kameez* that Mum had sewn for me and headed for the drawing room in my uncle's house. At that moment Imran came over to me hesitantly, as if he wanted to ask me something important. Instead, he asked me what I wanted for breakfast. I told him I'd come to the kitchen and help myself, but I could see from the frown appearing on his face that I'd upset him. "What do you mean?" he responded. "You can't come to the kitchen; they will scold me."

"How can my uncle tell you off just because I've gone into the kitchen?" I replied, incredulously. I couldn't understand why this poor kid would get in trouble for something so trivial. I felt bad for Imran. He was so young and working as a servant in a house belonging to my own uncle. At that moment, my mum appeared to see what all the noise was about. I told her I wouldn't allow Imran to cook me breakfast and, because of this, he was getting upset. She told me I had to learn to be less vocal with my opinions in someone else's house. I couldn't get my head 'round what she was saying. She'd raised me to always speak the truth. Wasn't it wrong for a young child who should be in school to be slaving away in someone's house? This was child labour; he was a kid who should be getting an education, not working at such a young age. I was deeply uncomfortable with the whole idea of having others do things for me, especially children. My uncle should have known better, I felt, especially since he was a doctor.

Later that day, on yet another social visit, our car pulled up at the main gate of a beautiful house. A group of people came out to greet us, looking friendly and welcoming. The men, including the elderly father figure, put a hand on my head as a sign of respect. One after the other, the ladies hugged me and kissed my face. This seemed to go on forever and was made worse by the fact that I didn't know any of them.

Mum was escorted into a separate room. Once again, I sat awkwardly surrounded by strangers who did nothing but stare and smile for no reason. It occurred to me that although we all had our origins in the same culture, theirs was still a different one from mine back home in England. I had to accept that I didn't belong in this group; I had always assumed I would comfortably adapt, given our common roots. The reality of being in a foreign country and completely out of my comfort zone suddenly hit me and, right then, I wanted nothing more than to return to England. To my horror, I felt a lump in my throat, a warning sign that I was about to cry. "Where's my mom?" I said under my breath.

Eventually, I asked Faheem, Neelam's potential future brother-in-law, where my mother was. He replied, rather curtly, that she was busy. Upset now, I told him that I needed to see her. When it became apparent he wasn't taking me seriously, I got up to go and find her myself. At that point, he relented and took me to her in the room next door where all the adults were. So that she alone would understand, I told Mum in English that I was upset and needed to get out of the house. If I thought she'd be sympathetic, I was wrong. She threw me an angry look and told Faheem to take me out for a bite to eat or to the bazaar to take my mind off feeling so homesick. I was horribly embarrassed. Now they all knew I was missing England and unhappy at being in an unfamiliar house.

For a minute, I felt pleased at the prospect of getting out, but I was in the company of a man I didn't know and couldn't talk to. He took me to a restaurant in D Ground, a popular shopping district and invited his friend to join us there. *Now I would be with two strangers rather than one,* I thought. When his friend came over to our table, I discovered to my joy that he spoke fluent English. He explained that he'd just come back from the UK and was visiting his family. Here was someone I could share my feelings with. I think Faheem was happy too, if only because I looked more cheerful. We ordered some soup and spent time talking about Faisalabad and the cultural differences between Pakistani children living in the UK and those born and raised in Pakistan. I thought British-Pakistani children were more naïve and less mature than kids in Pakistan. He agreed to a point and translated everything back to Faheem. I was, as always, very vocal with my thoughts. We chewed over a variety of topics relating to culture – differences and similarities – asking questions and putting forward answers. Time flew and I realized how late it was. I didn't want to go back to the house where I'd almost broken down in tears, but I was worried that my mum would be upset, thinking I was abusing the freedom she'd given me. Yet, when we arrived back, Mum was glowing with happiness. The discussions with the family had obviously gone well. She was being nice to me in front of everyone else, despite everything that had happened earlier; something adults often did when they'd achieved what they wanted. We had dinner and headed back to my uncle's.

In our family only Dr Saif had done well academically. Uncle told me the story of how, when his mother died, the family ended up staying with his and my father's maternal uncle. They were treated well because their mother had died and, as a result, were given the chance to go to school. After the partition, the family had gone through one challenge after another, uprooted from their home in India and coming to Pakistan and then moving again from their home to Faisalabad to live with their uncle.

Circumstances of the partition forced families, including mine, to leave their homes, work and belongings in India. My father's older brother, who had worked in the Crescent Mill factories in Faisalabad, was fortunate. He was offered a work permit visa to go to the UK. He took the opportunity, recognizing it as a solid career move and a way of earning the money he needed to survive. That's how we all ended up in the UK: from India to Pakistan to Lancashire. When my dad and uncle moved to England, they started out working in factories and then, after a few years, established their own business in textiles. These commitments meant they went for many years without visiting Pakistan. Grandma and Grandad also came to the UK, although they died just a few years after settling into their new life.

This was the context in which Mum faced the task of matchmaking and networking with my dad's relatives to marry us all off. I really felt for my mother, having to take on this challenging job of pleasing everyone, when she herself was returning to Pakistan for the first time in 20 years. I overheard my uncle ask Mum about the proposal. She told him it was agreed and the formal engagement would take place in December. Oh my! My sister was getting married and to someone from Pakistan!

The next morning, everyone had a day off for the congregational prayer that Muslims hold every Friday just after noon. Dad rang to ask how we were and Mum updated him on the engagement and the marriage proposal for Neelam. He seemed happy and in a way relieved. Mum chatted away for over an hour and I grew increasingly impatient, desperate to talk to him myself. The only way I could get a word in was to grab my mother's attention, so I started gesturing to her in sign language. My plan to distract her finally worked and she gave in, handing me the phone. Dad, his usual caring self, asked me about the trip and wanted to know how his relatives were treating me. "So far so good," I told him, "but there are still many places I want to visit." I asked him if he could persuade Mum to take me to Lahore now that the family matters were finally sorted, but he told me, in no uncertain terms, that Mum would decide the schedule for the trip and I had to accept her decisions.

It sounded like I had no say in the matter and that inevitably put me in a bad mood. Mum could see I was sulking when I came off the phone and immediately told me to straighten my face and get ready to go out. We were visiting relatives of the family we'd stayed with in Karachi, she said, and Syma and her family would also be there. Was this supposed to make me feel better? Letting me know that I'd be seeing someone I'd already met before was her way of asking me if I wanted to see Syma again without making it obvious.

I managed a weak smile, but with the prospect of more visits to relatives, I couldn't maintain it. Why should I be happy to see them? Because I'd already met them? Because we had something in common? I decided it was better than staying at my uncle's in an empty house. With him at work and my cousins at university, two studying medicine and one doing engineering, I knew I'd be bored. If any of them had been at home, at least I would have had someone to talk to.

When we were ready to leave, Imran went to get us a rickshaw, a three-wheel motorcycle taxi. I'd never seen one before and wanted to take photos, but I was told I couldn't, as it would look disrespectful. Women and girls didn't draw attention to themselves here. *Why?* I wondered. The rickshaw was open with no cover on it, so inside we were essentially exposed to the public; and yet I couldn't take photos. I found the whole thing confusing.

The rickshaw was uncomfortable, with seats as hard as rocks and made a sound like a motorbike in slow motion. Today's mission was to visit more relatives and, although I was excited about the trip farther afield, I was becoming increasingly fed up with having to introduce myself to new people and then socialize with them. The rickshaw moved through the larger streets to an area congested with narrower alleyways and drab houses. The smell of food cooking and rancid air became increasingly stronger. At last we arrived in a small neighbourhood, where buffalo wandered along the small streets. Seeing them tied up outside houses exposed me to an entirely new living environment. The stench was becoming unbearable. I tried my hardest not to make a fuss, but I felt horribly uncomfortable and was worried I might be sick. Embarrassed, Mum told me to control myself and have some respect for the people who were living there. She said I was being dramatic, although I certainly wasn't putting on an act.

As we got out of the rickshaw, I realized people were gathering around and staring at us. We clearly looked foreign here. Kids emerged from the small alleys and ran up to me as I got out of the rickshaw and walked alongside me through the tiny alleys, chatting and asking questions. Was I from America? they wanted to know. If not, where from? They were staring unashamedly, in a way that made me feel intimidated. Some were talking in broken English and attempting to make conversation, their innocence and curiosity overriding any shyness or fear of rudeness they might have felt.

Open sewers ran along the sides of the house, which we entered through a small door. The veranda was open, and, to my amazement, there was no roof on the house. While I was still digesting this, a crowd suddenly rushed toward us, with smiles and hugs. The greetings and small talk were as before, but this time people in another room were peering out. The other visitors, who were related to the family in Karachi, stared without shame and then asked if they could take photos. After this they kept mentioning Saleem, a name I'd heard before when we were in Karachi. They invited us to visit them at their home. I couldn't understand why they wanted us to pay them a visit, but Mum stepped in and said we'd go later that night. *Oh great,* I thought, heart sinking, *another house.*

So later that evening, we made yet another trip to visit this family. We sat in the drawing room as Mum paid her respects and I hung on in there as her support, trying to disguise my boredom. Then, out of nowhere a handsome man with a fair complexion and luxuriant, curled moustache walked in. He spoke to me in English with an American accent. *Wow, finally someone I might be able to talk to,* I thought. He was telling me about his studies in Malaysia and how, after graduating in computer science there, he'd returned to settle in Pakistan permanently and was now searching for a job. When he introduced himself as Saleem, I realized that his was the name I'd kept hearing at my relatives' houses.

We discussed university and I talked about my course and how I'd managed to get leave to visit on the grounds of research. Time flew and we ended up having dinner there, before going back to my uncle's place.

The time in Faisalabad continued with family meetings and shopping at the city's famous bazaars in the area formerly known as Lyallpur. At this point, I was feeling much more excited and motivated. I'd been waiting to go to Lahore, my mum's home city, since I got to Pakistan and that was where we were heading to next.

4
Goodness and Trust

In Pakistan there's a saying: if you haven't seen Lahore, you haven't lived. My first impressions of the city were dominated by the vast range of architecture and wealth of history, dating to the Mughal Empire, which greeted me. I was immediately struck by the sight of a large red dome that loomed in the background as we approached the city. Driving further into the city, the red-bricked building dwarfed everything around us. Of course, I realized, this was the famous Badshahi Mosque! I immediately started taking photos, before a loud noise made me jump. This was the call for noon prayers from the minarets, the first time I'd ever heard it live from a mosque on such a big scale. Hearing it in this way, so loud and proud, in a Muslim country, gave me a spiritual high.

We spent a week in Lahore, touring all the sights, such as Jahangir's tomb and Sheesh Mahal. I took hundreds of photos and found myself incredibly inspired by the artworks and architecture. The more I was drawn to them, the more I began questioning why I wasn't using them as themes in my own art. I was so grateful to have the opportunity to visit the sites, really study them and learn about the Mughal Empire and the rulers; the exquisite miniature paintings of this period particularly fascinated me.

Lahore transported me back to the past and made me appreciate history and humanity. The Mughals' contribution to architectural concepts and development was vast. People before us with limited resources and technology did all of this, I thought and I could only stand, admire, take a deep breath and say wow. Living in the UK I'd arrogantly thought we had some of the finest buildings in the world, without paying any attention to what existed elsewhere. The city I was in put me in my place, reminding me that people the world over, irrespective of colour, culture, or faith, have found the capacity to contribute hugely to the world in which we all live.

Comparing Lahore to Faisalabad, I thought how hard the community had worked to create a sewerage system. The smell and open troughs may have disgusted me, but these people had designed and created a system with what little they had and their initiative and resourcefulness deserved credit.

After an incredibly tiring but satisfying trip to Lahore, we returned to Faisalabad. That night, we were invited out for dinner and I met Saleem again, the relatable guy I could talk to. I was happy, as at least I'd have some common ground for conversation and be able to communicate with someone. My main challenge in all my time in Pakistan had been dealing with boredom and keeping myself entertained during the endless social occasions. There were so many cultural barriers when it came to humour, social background, upbringing and even language in some ways. Not being given permission to go out was another factor. I was constantly being warned that because I was from England, I ran the risk of being kidnapped. Fear and frustration fought for prominence as I struggled with not being able to enjoy the freedom of visiting and living in a place so rich in culture.

We had arrived for dinner, but before being seated we were guided into different rooms. I was told to go in one direction, while Mum was sent in another. Maybe that was a tradition I hadn't come across, I thought. I went into the part of the house where Saleem's brother Adnan and his wife Nazya lived. It was a bedsit room with a combined bedroom and sofa area. I felt awkward going into rooms belonging to others to use them as a lounge, but the locals found it routine. I couldn't help thinking about privacy and the idea of allowing strangers into my personal space. At home, I'd get really annoyed if my brothers even came into my room.

As I was being led to the room to be seated, my ears picked up a sound which felt out of place. Saleem's sister Asma kept talking to me in her squeaky, high-pitched voice, assuming I could follow what she was saying, but no matter how hard I tried, I couldn't focus on the conversation. I kept homing in on the gorgeous voice of Sinead O'Connor as she sang 'Nothing compares 2 U'; a strange song to hear in traditional Pakistan. Sinead was one of my favourite singers – her voice, her look, her feminism.

Saleem walked in, pulling me from my musings on Sinead. I breathed in sharply. This was culturally very out of place. While free mixing was encouraged in our home in the UK, I was alone, with no parents or siblings around, with a guy I hardly knew, in a bedroom-cum-lounge. It turned out Saleem was just passing through to get something from the room near where I was sitting. As he walked in, he looked at me and asked what I thought of the song and I told him I loved it. This was music that he'd been listening to while living abroad and he'd missed it. *Good taste,* I thought and someone who seemed to be a bit more my cup of tea to hang out with.

Enjoying Sinead O'Connor in a separate room from the adults was fun. As we headed out for dinner, Asma told me that she was surprised to see her brother chatting away to me, admitting that he didn't often talk to girls and certainly wasn't easily impressed. She told me that her brother had talked about me continually after my mother and I had left for Lahore. I wasn't sure what to make of this, or why I was being told. Looking back, I can't believe how naive and culturally unaware I was.

Talking to Asma had unnerved me and left me feeling very uncomfortable. At the dinner table, Saleem kept looking over and smiling. With Asma's words ringing in my head and at a very innocent 19 years old, I was flattered to be given so much attention. After dinner, Saleem asked his mother and Asma if we could go for a walk in the park behind his house and if my mother was OK with it. I was never allowed to go out with guys on my own, but surprisingly Mum agreed and told us to go. Something made me suspect that she was simply testing me to see what my response would be when put on the spot in front of other people, so I refused. Salem's mother stepped in, suggesting that we all go for a walk together, to burn off some calories.

Whilst in the park, I noticed that the others seemed to have contrived to ensure that Saleem and I were left alone, drifting away from the group until it was just the two of us. It was dark and humid, which only added to my nerves. The situation was causing me to clam up, to the point that I found it difficult to join in the conversation. I was feeling embarrassed and knew my cheeks were burning, but I could also feel something stirring inside. Some of his questions, like 'what were my plans for the future?' and 'what did I do in my spare time?' seemed weirdly out of place and left me struggling to answer. In the face of my silence he told me that he couldn't believe how boring I was. I felt mortified. He realized I was uncomfortable and to help break the tension, he insisted that we re-join the others. It was now very late and Mum said we should stay over, so as not to disturb my uncle. I didn't have my pyjamas or my toiletries, but Mum was adamant. Our hosts gave me some clothes to wear and bought toothbrushes from the local store for us, but nobody seemed to be planning on sleeping. Instead, they all congregated on the rooftop, the coolest part of the house and continued to talk.

Up on the rooftop, and with everyone else around, I felt more comfortable and able to talk to Saleem. Gradually, the others dispersed and went to bed, leaving just the two of us together; but this time I felt relaxed, rather than self-conscious. We chatted away about anything and everything, joking, laughing and sharing stories. Unaware of where the time had gone, we suddenly realized we could hear the first call of the day for prayer from the nearest mosque, meaning it was early morning. I told Saleem we had to leave and get some sleep. I slipped into my room, where my mum was snoring away, feeling content, happy and relaxed. Having changed into my night clothes, I cleansed my face and brushed my teeth. As I got into bed, I had an unfamiliar sensation of excitement. I decided it came from knowing that Saleem was attracted to me. I wasn't sure how I sensed this, but there was a definite feeling that I couldn't shift.

In the morning, we returned to my uncle's house after breakfast. Mum asked me what I thought of Saleem and I replied that he seemed nice, adding that since he spoke English, he was, at least, one Pakistani guy I could communicate with, in a country where many didn't know the language. My mother disappeared into the other room to phone my father and knowing she'd be on the phone for hours, I decided to head off for a nap.

Later that evening, my brother Sajjad called and said he needed to have a chat with me. He asked me first about my trip and then about Saleem and his family. He told me that Saleem's family were asking for my hand in marriage and that both my parents had discussed the matter with him. Sajjad always seemed to know more than us girls and was consulted by our parents on everything in life that involved decision-making.

My parents and Sajjad had several conversations with me that day. My only thought was that I was just 19 years old and studying; marriage was certainly not on my agenda. Yet, I genuinely believed that my family would make the right decision for me. It wasn't forced, simply conventional for the time and a culture where parents were concerned about finding good suitors for their daughters. Sajjad told me that the family were comfortably off, since although Saleem's mother was widowed, his father had been fairly high up in the army and that the sons were well travelled. A naïve teenager, I hesitantly replied, "Do what you think is best."

5
The Agony of Wishing

The following day, members of the family started congratulating each other and then me. The entire thing felt surreal; these people were all strangers and now they suddenly wanted to get close to me. *They don't know me and here they are, all emotional and expressive,* I thought. I found it a real challenge to respond. I couldn't reciprocate their outpourings of emotion.

Saleem's three sisters arrived with all his family in tow. There was a huge amount of hustle and bustle. I still hadn't seen Saleem and my eyes were darting around trying to spot him. I saw him walk past the veranda with a huge grin on his face, like the cat that had got the cream. I wanted his full attention, for his eyes to rest on me and remain there. Everybody else in the room seemed irrelevant. As the sun set and early evening approached, his eldest sister Shazia came to me and said Saleem was on the roof and wanted to see me. Embarrassed, I avoided making eye contact or responding, wondering whether she simply wanted to see how I reacted. Impatient, she repeated that her brother was waiting and that I was to go up to the roof with her. Something inside made me refuse to budge and to my horror her grandfather stepped in. He said, calmly, "Saleem is waiting for you on the roof, and you must go." I had no choice but to respect my elder, regardless of how horrified and embarrassed I was at such a public display of interaction between a man and woman.

I went to the bathroom first, my heart pounding faster than normal. I was excited; I very much wanted to see Saleem, but I was also scared, nervous and confused, my thoughts and feelings in turmoil. I looked at myself in the mirror, painfully conscious of my appearance and prepared myself to go up the stairs toward the roof, surreptitiously looking around to see if anyone had spotted me. My stomach was churning and my heart pounded in my ears. I found it impossible to look upward as I made the trip upstairs, thinking that Saleem would be there, gazing down at me.

When I reached the roof, I realized it was dark, making it difficult to find Saleem, however hard I tried. But then I heard a voice. "You finally came. Do you know how long I've been waiting for you?" Suddenly tongue-tied, I couldn't answer. "Let's sit. Come here," he said, walking toward a traditional handmade bed-cum-sofa called a *mangi*.

I felt vulnerable, obeying a male stranger, but I was also happy to listen to his instructions. I sat down, looking at him and waiting, searching his eyes for a signal of what he wanted from me. But rather than being romantic, he bluntly told me he wanted to marry me because he thought I was educated and could be a good mother to his children. He wanted children and his father had always wanted educated daughters-in-law, he explained. Suddenly, at the age of 19, I was having to think about being a mother! My shoulders slumped, feeling the burden of such an unexpected, heavy weight. Was I to become a mother before knowing what it even was to become a wife?

Looking back, many years later, I don't think I really understood the enormity of what was happening. Perhaps I felt that the concepts of marriage and of being a mum were everyday ones for women and naively, within our culture, I thought life was about being a mother and a wife.

My feelings for Saleem at the time were muddled; there wasn't that magnetism and I couldn't say I was hypnotized or shot through the heart with a dose of love. Yet, I convinced myself that this was an exciting time. After all, someone 'liked me' and was keen for me to be part of his life. This man wanted me, of all people, to be his wife; this was the source of my joy, rather than me being ready to get married and settle down, or that this man would make my life better or prove to be someone with whom I could carve out a future. Was this really love? Was this what it was all about? Unable to make sense of it all or comprehend what was happening, my mind fought more than a few battles. But the uncomfortable truth was, I suspect, that I didn't really want to understand what was happening, so I pushed the difficult questions to one side.

I looked at Saleem's lips as they moved, not listening to his words, but instead, inexplicably and suddenly, thinking about how my friend Lisa hadn't got into art school. How tragic it was and unfair that a kind, determined, hard-working girl had been rejected. The unfairness of it had made me sad. With a start, I realized that while I'd been thinking about art school, university and opportunities, Saleem was talking about me uprooting everything and moving to Pakistan.

As the significance of what was happening began to dawn, my thoughts were returning to England, even as my physical presence remained in Pakistan. Here I was, in a foreign country excited because I'd received a marriage proposal, but in the drama completely forgetting what I'd left behind in the UK, just like that.

I was about to take a huge, life-changing step, but I didn't feel scared. How could this be? Was this sudden change of direction part of life's big plan for me, I wondered. Or was it just fate?

Syma and her sisters came over from next door to put henna on my hands. They were happy and excited, cracking jokes in Urdu that I barely understood but that I could tell were a source of great amusement to them. I'd never had henna put on me before and was surprised by how strong the smell was, reminding me of burnt tea.

Waking up the next day, I was given a highly ornate *salwar kameez* in a brocade fabric called *keem khaab*, made from gold thread, together with a jewellery set of gold and pearls. Of course, the jewellery wasn't mine, it had been lent by Nazya.

An aunt, who was Dad's first cousin, arrived and asked if she could do my makeup and hair. I'd never had my makeup and hair done by someone else. It also involved having my face decorated, which was something else completely new. I sat there while a first layer of white foundation was put on my face. Being light-skinned was a sign of beauty for most South Asians and, although I wasn't dark, it was clear that the idea was to make me even fairer. My hair was then backcombed into a honeycomb style pin-up hair do, with a *tikka*, a jewelled headpiece and a headscarf to provide the finishing touch.

Some hours later, I was ready to be presented to the crowd. Everyone stared at me and took lots of pictures, but all I could think of was Mum and why couldn't I see her among the people. Where was she? After what seemed an eternity, she came into the room, led me out onto the veranda and sat me down on a sofa where Saleem and his grandfather were already sitting. Saleem looked over at me and, through his large moustache, gave me half a grin, while his grandfather peered at me through small squinted eyes. We sat together and Saleem's mum brought us a plate of sweets. She took one and popped it into her son's mouth then put 500 rupees in his hand. She then did exactly the same to me.

The veranda was full of Saleem's relatives, while from my side it was just my mum and the few people she knew. Saleem's brother Adnan came next, placing a necklace made of rupee notes and tinsel around Saleem's neck, before doing the same to me and giving us both sweets. One after another, the family followed the same process, with the closest relatives approaching us first and a photographer taking photos, asking us to smile each time, as if we were on a stage and in a show. It occurred to me at this point that Saleem and I hadn't exchanged a word. We hadn't even smiled at each other, only for the camera.

Saleem didn't compliment me on how I looked or ask how I was or how I felt. More than an hour passed, with the formal exchange of gifts and congratulations taking forever. Eventually, Saleem's three sisters came and took me to their brother's bedroom, sitting me on yet another sofa. They were followed by young girls who looked at me and said things to each other about my eyes, my hair and my complexion, as well as discussing my nationality and whether I could speak Urdu, unaware that I understood everything.

Nazya rushed in with a tray of food and fussed at me to eat. I was incredulous; the room was full of these annoying girls, sitting on the bed and beside me on the sofa. How could I eat with everyone watching me? My face was itching with all the makeup and the jewellery and clothes were annoying me. I wanted to remove the makeup and get changed, but it seemed that wasn't part of the plan.

Saleem's mum came into the room with Asma and his sister and told me to eat up, since I was expected to go back out again.

Needless to say, the occasion was hardly an enjoyable one and it seemed to take forever for night-time to arrive. Eventually, with everyone gone, I showered and happily removed the rainbow-colored eyeshadow and cream foundation from my face. I carefully returned the jewellery and gave the clothes to my mum so that she could pack them for me. Being able to relax and sip a coffee and finally be myself in my pyjamas was, I confess, the best part of that day.

6
The Door of Reality

With the vacation and the official engagement over, we flew back to England. Leaving was more of a relief than it was tearful goodbyes. I'd been missing aspects of life back home; the smell of fish and chips from the local chippy, the feel of rain, hearing English spoken with a Lancashire accent. Pakistan was okay, but it was certainly not home. Now, I felt as if I was going back to where I belonged, all I'd known since I first opened my eyes. England was the country in which a dear friend and my grandparents were buried, where I lived with my family, a land of greenery, full of people who were familiar to me and one in which I had a room containing my belongings.

I also had to get back to England to resume my studies, but my life had changed so much in just a matter of weeks, I felt caught between two worlds. I was questioning things more, wondering whether, if circumstance hadn't made me a Pakistani, Muslim, dark-skinned female, my life would've been the same.

It felt like there were pieces of a jigsaw missing within me. A somewhat daunting feeling, one I couldn't quite pinpoint, was growing, alongside the creeping realization that everything had happened far too quickly. Was it fate for this to happen in my life or was it just circumstance? I didn't know and couldn't find an answer. The only thing to do, I thought, was to carry on and see what happened.

Arriving in the UK, I was immediately taken by the shift from the bright, colourful tones of Pakistan that had made me squint to the dullness of the grey clouds and shadows staring back at me through the airport windows. We went through to the baggage reclaim area and waited for our luggage to arrive. As the bags went round, I looked at them and thought how each one was a compact story of a life. Every case contained an individual's personal belongings; the contents of a life in a case, which we each waited in turn to collect.

As we exited the airport, a sharp breeze hit my face and seeped down my neck, making me shudder. I hated the cold weather and I hadn't brought my scarf or hat. Along with the wind, the rain trickled down. While wet weather was common, something I'd missed even, this time I saw it differently, as if I was watching it as a visitor or a guest and it was temporary; as if I was looking at it through the eyes of someone who was moving away and getting married.

My dad and Sajjad came to pick us up from the airport. It was a Friday and I was thinking about university and what I needed to get packed for Sunday, when I would be returning to academic life. We arrived home and my siblings and the rest of the family were waiting for us with a delicious, freshly cooked meal in the dining room. We all sat down to eat, with my sisters going on about how weird it was that I was engaged. I didn't have an engagement ring as such. Saleem's mum had just given me an old antique gold ring, which had a huge circle and some little enamel dots on it. It wasn't especially valuable and I wasn't expected to wear it all the time.

Saleem's family didn't really understand the concept of engagement rings in the way we did in the West, where the ring was significant because it represented a commitment to a person and signalled that you were taken. Since my friends at university had no idea about my engagement, my thoughts turned to how surprised they'd be on hearing about it. Sunday came and I was getting ready to go to university. I'd already forgotten about my trip and Saleem, having refocused on university life, transported by my different surroundings and daily routine.

As Dad drove me to university though, my thoughts drifted back to my time in Pakistan and the notion that I really was engaged and committed to getting married. We were driving through Lancashire, reaching the Yorkshire moors with rain pouring down blurring the views and for some reason it reminded me of the day of the engagement.

Saleem was my partner now and that was it. He'd be in my life forever, a permanent fixture. I would go to university and then my life would change, beyond recognition, within a few years. But for now, he wasn't part of my university life or my circle of friends.

My father left and my flatmates came rushing into my room, desperate to find out how the holiday had been and what I'd thought of Pakistan. I told them I'd had a good time and recounted with enthusiasm everything I could think of about the country, its culture and Mughal history. But when it came time to share the biggest piece of news, the event that would change my life, I hesitated. I felt that as close friends they deserved to know, but part of me was tempted to just not tell them; after all, they most probably wouldn't believe what had happened anyway. The more I thought about it, the more I felt that they'd never believe I'd got engaged, knowing me the way they did. In fact, even I was beginning to doubt whether that had actually been me over there agreeing to get married.

After a while, we settled down with coffees and teas and I announced somewhat hesitantly, "I have something to tell you, girls... You know how I'm anti-marriage and believe in being career-minded?" Seeing their confused faces, I quickly spoke before they could say anything. "Well, I got engaged!"

"WHAT?! Shama, are you kidding us?"

"What do you mean, you got engaged?"

"I got engaged," I repeated, amidst the questions.

"You were forced to," concluded one of my friends, Emma.

Again, "What?"

"I'm serious. I got engaged. I met this guy who spoke English. He was charming and I thought it would be good to get engaged. It happened really quickly."

As I said this, I realized my words relayed zero happiness. I hadn't been forced into anything and I desperately didn't want my flatmates to think that this had been what happened, but I was acutely aware of how wrong it all sounded and the implications.

My friends were staring at me in astonishment. They had no idea what commitment and engagement meant at our age and the silence was heavy with the notion that I'd made a mistake.

My friends insisted on seeing some evidence, such as photos, a ring, anything, none of which I had. I sensed that perhaps they didn't believe me or were disappointed that I'd done something they felt was so out of character. Or was this my own thought? How I felt about myself, perhaps? There was little time, or willingness to dwell on things, so once again difficult questions were pushed to one side; I had lectures to attend and university work to do.

In the morning, I had my first lecture on the artist Turner on the Thames. After the whirlwind of the last few weeks, here was a chance to concentrate on something I should be able to relate to.

I was jetlagged though. Returning from Pakistan to Lancashire, then travelling to Yorkshire and managing the time difference was a lot. After the lecture, which made no sense to me, I met up with my flatmates at the university cafeteria. By this time, news had spread about my engagement and I began to feel a different vibe and attitude from most of my friends.

Not wanting to chat and feeling tired, I went back to my university accommodation and slept. I was so exhausted I slept right through until 8pm, roughly the time my parents usually called. Mum rang at exactly 8.16pm and said, excitedly that she'd organized an engagement party for me at the weekend back home. I wasn't allowed to stay at university over the weekends – my parents were worried I'd go out clubbing or worse – so I always went home from Friday to Sunday.

After I put the phone down, the reality of what Mum had just told me sunk in. I couldn't believe she'd organize something on this scale without my consent or giving thought to my university work. Yet, this was how things were done in our household – the adults made decisions, took care of all the arrangements and told us children later.

7
Among the Branches

Friday, the day of the week that to most people signals the beginning of a leisurely weekend, arrived quicker than I expected. In my case, the weekend marked a time of cultural shift and grounding in the home environment, rather than an opportunity to relax. Going back to my parents' house from university was like being transported from one universe to another.

They wanted every aspect of our home life to be extremely traditional, including language, clothes, faith and food. For me, it meant no break. Weekends were all about catching up with cooking, cleaning and ironing, along with other chores that we female siblings were expected to do. The daily routine was easily accommodated, although at times I questioned my place in this culture and society and whether I truly fitted in. If not, what was my place in this world? Were we a product of circumstance or did we have freedom of choice? I asked myself these questions over and over again, but rarely got satisfactory answers.

Whilst my university friends partied, went to libraries and enjoyed student life, I had to keep others happy. Home was a place in which my role was of a daughter and sister and where I now had to think of becoming a wife and mother. I'd never thought about myself in this space.

Dad picked me up as usual, as I wasn't allowed to use public transport. My mind was elsewhere on the journey home and we barely spoke. I was in a trance stepping back to my trip to Pakistan. Was I really engaged? I started to think about Saleem. He was a friendly, decent, polite man who also spoke English, which was important.

We arrived home and I took my bag and my laundry in, before going to find Mom. She greeted me with a warm hug as always, but she was happier than usual to see me and excitedly told me she had something to give me. Dashing to her room, she returned with a bag and took out five letters sealed with airmail stamps and featuring writing I recognized as Saleem's. I felt a rush of excitement and couldn't wait to open the letters. I could smell the aroma emanating from them, like they'd been sprayed with the same fragrance that Saleem wore. As I took the letters, Mum announced that the engagement party had been postponed to the following weekend because Dad was really busy. I just about managed to disguise my massive sigh of relief.

After a while, curiosity got the better of me and I was keen to be alone in my space. I went upstairs to my room, impatiently waiting for my sister Fatima to leave. After she'd gone, I checked the date stamps on each letter and opened the first with a beating heart, feeling tingly and weak.

Saleem had begun with the header '786', often used as an abbreviation for 'In the name of God.' (*Bismillah irahmaan iraheem*). As children, we used it to begin anything we wrote when we went to the mosque. He followed this with:

My dear,
I am blessed to have such a wonderful person who will be the future mother of my children and wife to me....

I paused for a second… Was this for me? Was I a future wife and mother? I was not even married yet and Saleem was writing to me like a mother and wife. Surely I was Shama? Me, before anything else?

I suddenly felt burdened with the potential responsibility of these roles. My mind span round like a whirlpool, leaving me confused about what was happening, who I was and what was about to happen. Where, who, what was I? I feared losing myself, my identity. There was a battle going on inside me that for once wasn't about culture, faith, colour, or anything else, but simply about who I was.

My musings were interrupted by Mom's voice from downstairs. "Pick up the phone from up there!" she called in a tone that told me it was important. "It's Saleem. He was waiting for you to come home so that he could speak to you." I picked up the phone and heard Saleem's voice.

"Hello, are you there?" He spoke in a smooth, soft, intimate way that I felt unable to reciprocate, given that I wasn't alone and had just arrived home.

"Yes, *Assalam alaikum*, how are you?"

"*Walaikum salam*, I've been waiting four hours for you to get home so that I can call you."

"Four hours? How come?"

"I left work early and went to my apartment. I was waiting because I knew you would be home at about 8pm. Did you get my letters?"

"Yes, thank you. I only opened one and was reading it when you called me."

"Do you miss me?"

All of a sudden, I went silent as I didn't know what to say or how to respond.

"Er, well, I've been really busy at university."

"I…I can't stop thinking about you. I want you to write to me every day. Everyone here misses you. What are you going to do today?"

"I think I need to sleep all weekend. I'm exhausted from travelling and going back to my studies," I answered.

"I can't sleep, I'm too excited. I've been writing and thinking about you all the time," was Saleem's reply.

I wasn't sure how to respond to this level of intensity and fatigue was catching up with me, making it difficult to hold a conversation. I didn't really know what I was babbling on about and I was aware that calling abroad was expensive.

"Can you call me back?" he asked.

"No," I answered. "I'm very tired and we can't make international calls from home. I think I'd better eat then sleep. Maybe we can speak tomorrow?"

"You're not excited to hear from me, are you?" came the accusation.

"I'm just tired," I said, barely stifling a yawn.

"OK, then I'll let you go."

I'd arrived home, been inundated with letters, then received a call. My space was being invaded and I felt as if someone was intruding into my life. But since I'd let that someone in, I could only ask myself why I'd done so.

As the evening progressed, I pondered over these questions and my state of mind. Dinner with the family was dominated by my siblings wanting to hear all the details of the trip, including everything about Saleem and his family. Unsure of why, I found myself portraying him as a high-flier, making out that our engagement was the best thing that could have happened to me.

The letters continued to arrive over the following days. I felt obliged to reply to them, but often wished I had the time to absorb and think about my feelings, given the whirlwind pace of change taking place, catapulting me into a new phase in my life.

Every Sunday, my sister Amina and I would pack all our bags with food and clean clothes to return to university. On Monday mornings my first lecture always began with a focus on philosophy.

My philosophy lecturer often referenced the Sufi mystic Jalaluddin Mevlana Rumi. One quote that stuck in my head was: "Your task is not to seek for love, but merely to seek and find all the barriers within yourself that you have built against it."

I loved the quote, but Rumi's words were too deep and meaningful for me to understand at the time and I was too embarrassed to admit that I couldn't grasp what he meant. After the lecture, I went and sat under my favourite sycamore tree outside my university accommodation and began writing down my thoughts. I wanted to expand my understanding, push the boundaries and try to sum up the beauty of love and feeling, not for the man I was engaged to, but from within.

I made some sketches and jotted down the thoughts that came to me as I pondered Rumi's words. My thoughts formed a poem that I signed with She, the signature I used for my artwork.

The Four Walls
The four walls
The walls surround her
Surrounding her body

She cries out aloud
She cries hard, not hard enough to be heard
The four walls bleed into her body
She cries, the walls bleed and bleed till they shatter
She is left in the OPEN
She can be seen beyond the four walls that penetrated through her
She can be heard
1996 Shama – The light!!!
She ©

My poem said it all. Was I hearing myself? Was I a woman of circumstance, born into a dark-skinned family? Born into a Muslim household, with South-Asian culture?

While I'd thought of myself as a woman who had all her rights and was free, I remained restricted by my roles of daughter and sister and now wife-to-be. I wasn't free at all and I'd had no say in choosing my background, colour, or faith.

On Monday evening, I cooked with my university flatmates and we had dinner together. As women, my friends and I bore many similarities, irrespective of colour and faith, but during the meal I couldn't stop thinking about all the differences between us, differences rooted in culture rather than anything else. I noticed that the type of food we had back home in Nelson and even how we ate was different. We didn't have alcohol and our meat was always halal. Even the way I was dressed was different: very Eastern compared to the clothes worn by my friends.

University meant being transported from a Muslim household with strict boundaries to an environment in which I was independent, respected for who I was, not having to obey adults. I could do anything I wanted, within reason. Curious, my friends were asking me about my relationship and since most of them had never known anyone involved in an arranged marriage, they had loads of questions.

Steph asked me how it could be an arranged marriage if I was speaking to him and writing letters. "I thought an arranged marriage meant that you meet for the first time on the day you got married," she said. We all started laughing, I told her I had thought so too, since I hadn't known what to expect or what to do. Then she asked me if I loved him.

I remembered the Rumi quote from the morning. I didn't know what love really was, I replied. Tasha jumped into the conversation, admitting that she, too, had always wondered the same thing, questioning whether she'd really loved a boyfriend when they broke up, since she'd often moved on quickly.

"You know what, girls?" Emma said. "Life is much more enjoyable without men."

"Having your heart broken is just a headache," Rachel agreed. "It's much better to focus on your studies and career."

"Shama, when you get married, will you stay at home and be a housewife?" Emma asked me.

"Emma, you know what I really want is a career. I don't want to just stay home, but we haven't discussed this at all. Saleem never asks me what I want to do, but he has mentioned me being a mom, wife and daughter-in-law," I replied without thinking.

"Are you serious?" Tasha asked, incredulous.

The room went silent as everyone, myself included, digested my words. I thought, once again, that my career and indeed, my life, were not really in my hands, rather I was going to be living my life for others. I lived for others growing up as a daughter and sister and now I would be taking on the new roles of wife, mother and daughter-in-law. That feeling of being burdened hit me again and my future suddenly felt incredibly claustrophobic.

I immersed myself in the busy term leading up to the summer break, hoping the weeks at university would drag on, giving me some breathing space and more time for myself, delaying the inevitable return to family commitments. The sycamore tree under which I sat was my only real confidant, providing me with a safe, non-judgmental space, where I could write about and draw my inner-most feelings freely. One evening, I carved 'Shama' into the tree bark and was immediately wracked with guilt. I'd damaged this living entity to satisfy my own needs. This tree and I had something in common; it couldn't express itself, we were both blessed with life yet unable to make our own choices or decisions.

At university, white British students accounted for 99 percent of the intake, meaning I was in the non-white one percent segment. If I married a white boy, I thought, would that be acceptable or would it destroy my mum and family? As the first generation that had come to the UK, Mum had a deep-rooted fear of the family losing its identity and culture, which was one of the reasons that she and my dad had embedded their roots in us so deeply. Although at university I had the freedom to do as I wished, deep down I felt I couldn't. The grounding that prevented me from breaking down that wall or barrier was within me.

Once again, my mind returned to Rumi's quote: "Your task is not to seek for love, but merely to seek and find all the barriers within yourself that you have built against it."

My days of being independent were numbered and the clock was ticking. While the other girls went out to bars, I would sit or lie down, reading Saleem's letters which I'd brought with me from home.

The world I inhabited felt strange and somehow foreign, while burning questions continued to haunt me. Why did my parents emigrate to England of all places? Why was I born in the North? How did I define my cultural roots? Was I Pakistani or British? Above all, who was I? Far from mature and with so many questions unanswered, here I was, about to enter into a marriage.

8
The Seeds of Devotion

Friday night came around once again, bringing with it my wonderful, committed, punctual father who would collect me and take me back home each weekend, without fail.

That night, over dinner my parents announced that they'd decided it would be best if I got married in summer, as everyone in the family would be able to book it as holiday. As usual, I didn't get any say in the matter; instead, everyone else was making the most important decisions of my life for me, including setting the date for my wedding. Mum and Dad spoke to my in-laws-to-be and the date was set.

July 19th. The date I'd go from Miss to Mrs. It would be a departure in more ways than one, since I'd be leaving the UK for Pakistan, making the same journey as my parents did all those years ago, but in reverse. Saleem didn't have a British passport and had no wish to acquire one. He had confided in me that he thought the UK was boring.

To be honest, I didn't mind; somehow the prospect of a new adventure seemed exciting and fun. Although my emotions were all over the place, at times I felt like I'd enjoy having new relatives, a different climate and a change of scenery.

Perhaps these feelings were prompted by a combination of recent events. My best friend since childhood, Lara, had lost her battle with cancer and Steph, my closest university flatmate, was beginning a new life away from the UK. The idea of living as someone's princess was becoming more and more appealing.

I wasn't mature enough to understand what marriage and all that it entailed meant. I was a sheltered 19-year-old with no experience. Was it about love and being swept off your feet? Or was it about compromise and accepting that you must do what it takes to spend the rest of your life with someone? My inquisitive mind was, as always, plagued by questions, most of which I couldn't answer. Many of them didn't even make any sense to me.

My mum and sister Neelam were busy planning and shopping for their clothes and shoes. They seemed to have forgotten that the bride needed to choose a dress too, but I kept this to myself. My father, on the other hand, being a practical man, decided that we'd fly to Pakistan one month early. He needed to make plans for the arrival of all the relatives and ensure everyone was catered for.

It was decided that my clothes would be ordered and made in Pakistan since none of the embroiderers in England met my mom's specifications and the fabrics she wanted to use were not available locally. The thought of having to visit bazaars for material and dressmakers for fittings was making me nervous. It would involve noisy streets, being pushed and shoved by crowds of passers-by and shopkeepers shouting, all the things that put me off on my first visit to Pakistan.

The next few months flew by quicker than I'd thought possible. A letter arrived from Saleem daily and I was expected to send one back in return. I lived in a fantasy bubble that was completely unrelated to the reality of everyday life. Even though I found them a bit overwhelming, the letters still made my heart skip a beat, if I was honest and gave me something to look forward to in my daily routine.

While my emotions were mixed about leaving my homeland and uprooting to a different country, the enormity of what was happening hadn't really registered. I was still surrounded by my family and living at home, so didn't yet know what to expect from my new life.

Weeks continued to pass in a haze that involved distancing myself from my friends, focusing on my studies and going home at weekends, where the sole topic of conversation seemed to be my wedding and the growing piles of letters from Saleem. The date for departing drew nearer and suddenly the doubts I'd been pushing to one side grew stronger. *Do I really want to move to Pakistan and become Pakistani?* I asked myself in a moment of panic. I was British, I thought. How could I move and live there?

Time flew by, even though I did my best to hold on to each moment and enjoy the precious weeks I had left in the UK. The days warmed, banishing the cold and bringing with them a brighter light that replaced the dull grey skies. Summer was on its way – the summer of my sacrifice in which I'd be leaving home, family, friends and university.

University was my refuge from cultural pressures, where I enjoyed the company of people my age. I was increasingly morose, overwhelmed by the sense of loss at having to say goodbye to my friends. I wouldn't hear their laughter or share precious moments with them again. But it was also about more than that; university had taught me a great deal about independence and freedom, about doing things for myself.

I wasn't sure if I'd be able to maintain these friendships abroad once I was married. Would Saleem and my in-laws be okay about me meeting my friends? We'd never talked about that sort of thing. My friends couldn't come for the wedding anyway, as the cost of flying was too high.

Looking back, the scale of the sacrifice seems difficult to imagine now. On my final day of university, I was picked up for the last time by my father. The image of that scene, of everything associated with my university life growing more distant and fading as we drove away, remains with me today. This route, so familiar, was not one I'd be taking again anytime soon. My friends had also been busy packing and gathering their belongings to go home, their thoughts turning to summer and spending time with their families. For the most part, they were too excited and preoccupied to consider in any detail that I was leaving for good and being sacrificed to a man for marriage.

Home, when I arrived, was pandemonium. Everyone was running round in a panic as they ticked off lists and moved from one packed bag to another, opening and closing them again at random. There was so much to do, it seemed. Standing in the midst of it all, I struggled to see where I fitted in. On one level nowhere, since I was leaving for good and starting a new phase in my life, but on another, right in the middle, since I was the central character in this charade.

In the evening, a blessing was held for the wedding, at which family and friends gathered together to recite the Qur'an and to wish me happiness and safety. My family always held gatherings like these for major occasions, but this one felt different.

As I joined in, it was dawning on me with greater clarity than ever before that my life had been handed to a man I didn't really know anything about, except that he spoke English and listened to Sinead O'Connor. But what could I do now? This was my last day at home and in a few hours, I'd have left England.

Saying goodbye to my friends at university and leaving that phase of my life behind had been something of a reality check. I was aware now that I would no longer be in a place where I had space to be myself, choose my friends and live my life, but instead I would be living for others. Even my home, where I'd grown up as a daughter and sister, where I had my own room and space, was soon to be a thing of the past. I'd always assumed my belongings and the four walls of my room would be permanent fixtures in my life. Instead, here I was, having given away all the clothes, jewellery and shoes that I wasn't taking with me.

As I sat alone in my room for the last time, I recalled the changes it had undergone over the years when we'd decorated it, the fights with my siblings, the memories of growing up, shifting from childhood to teens, from school to university. A room so rich in memories, I thought wistfully, that was now bare and empty. I already felt that I no longer belonged there. I was heading to the Serena, the hotel that was booked for us all in Pakistan. Built by the Agha Khan, red-bricked, shiny and new, the Serena hotel was "the best one in the city of Faisalabad," Dad had told us.

My father walked into my room and sat on the bed beside me. "Families in our culture are always sad when girls are born, since they know that daughters will eventually take their place in another family," he told me in his soft voice.

"What do you mean?" I asked, confused. "You are my family."

"I mean, when you get married, that's your family, Shama," he replied. "Our door will always be open, but now you'll enter it as someone's wife first and our daughter second."

Tears rolled down his face. I'd never seen my father cry before, but that day I saw him sob, distraught in the knowledge that he was losing his daughter to another family. He gave me a hug and we both cried together, before walking downstairs to where I'd say my final goodbyes. My sister Amina gave me my favourite cuddly toy – Ernie from Sesame Street – and my white teddy that was called Hakim. I'd had both of these for years and she assumed I'd be taking them with me.

My aunt was next. In true Asian style, she started crying loudly, saying, "Oh my, you're leaving us for good! We pray we won't have girls because they have to leave us and now that's happening to you! Your home, your life, you have to simply tolerate everything as it's for your marriage!" If I'd been hoping for compassion and wise words, I was disappointed. This was hardcore. I gave all the family members and friends who weren't coming with us a hug. Funnily enough, they cried more than me, even though I was the one leaving.

We headed for the airport, with everyone now excited about the flight and the trip, which helped to lift the mood and lighten the atmosphere. We were flying with Pakistan International Airlines to Karachi and from there we'd be getting a connecting flight to Faisalabad. I wasn't keen on flying. It was something about being in the air, unable to touch the ground, and not having a firm grip on my location. My family were oblivious. They were over-excited, going on endlessly about the wedding, their clothes and other details relating to the event. I had a new diary in my handbag that I planned to start from this flight. It began with my poem *The Four Walls*, then moved on to how I felt about leaving my birth country and uprooting to a different continent.

I wanted to be positive, but I couldn't prevent the negativity seeping in; after all, Pakistan wasn't California, Australia, or Italy. It was a place perceived as 'third world' and 'corrupt.' Most Pakistanis who lived in the UK loved visiting it, but they didn't want to live there. The thought kept entering my head that I was going backwards, but I shrugged it off, remembering that I'd really liked it when there and now I'd have Saleem, my partner for life, holding my hand, and treating me like a princess. This thought sent a spark of excitement through me and gave me hope for my new beginning.

The journey was going to be long, and just the thought of arriving in Karachi and having to change planes was exhausting. After completing the first page of my diary, I decided to try to sleep for the rest of the flight. As I curled into my seat and closed my eyes, I gave in to my feelings of isolation, pondering over how everyone else seemed caught up in their own concerns, too preoccupied to ask me how I was feeling about the big day and staying on in Pakistan afterwards.

We arrived in Karachi and were quickly chivvied onto the much smaller plane that would take all of us on the one-hour journey to Faisalabad. Someone did a headcount, which reminded me of Mum checking on us when we were kids going off to school. One by one we were all accounted for and took our seats.

The plane was full of the aromas of fresh spices and herbs. I recognized garam masala and coriander among them; we'd definitely arrived in Pakistan.

Landing in Faisalabad, the heat immediately hit me as we disembarked and made our way across the tarmac to the airport building under the glare of the burning sun. It was a small, stuffy place, with only one conveyor belt. The luggage was taken for us once we'd retrieved it, since Dad had arranged for several officials to look after us all to keep things hassle-free. My siblings were complaining about the heat and all the luggage we had to navigate.

As I was looking for one of my cases, I sensed someone behind me. Turning around, I found Saleem standing there. After all his letters in which he talked about counting the days until my arrival, here he was, at the airport, to meet me. He was freshly shaved and wore a striped polo shirt, looking quite handsome, I had to admit. I was trying to work out what scent he was wearing – *Dior's Poison for Women? I must be mistaken,* I thought.

"Hi," he said with a cheeky grin.

"Hi," I responded, more hesitantly and nervously, "how did you get in?"

"Protocol and connections – it is easy in this country if you have them," he replied with a shrug.

My nerves had kicked in and my thoughts were confused and muddled. I didn't know what to do, whether to move, talk, or walk. *Is this what happens when you see your fiancé after time apart?* I wondered.

"Do you want a drink?" Saleem asked, followed, more quietly, by, "You look nice."

I decided to pretend I hadn't heard him, asking, instead, "Are the cars here to take us to our hotel?"

Before he had a chance to reply, my sister Fatima came over to introduce herself. "Saleem *bhai*, you look so different in real life from the photos," she exclaimed.

"What do you mean?" Saleem asked.

"I mean you look much better and more handsome in real life. Shama is lucky her husband-to-be is so good looking!" she replied with a giggle.

Saleem laughed in return, "I am the lucky one, with such a beautiful bride," he said, smiling.

My cheeks started to burn, and I could sense myself blushing. I was incredibly flattered at being called beautiful in public by the man I was going to marry. At that moment, I honestly believed that Saleem was being genuine and truthful about how he felt.

We walked along together, following the men who were escorting us from the luggage area. Saleem did his best to engage me in conversation and make eye contact, but I was overcome with shyness and my siblings stepped in to entertain him. I slipped away quietly and caught up with my father and his friends. When Dad asked me how I felt, I replied that I was tired and wanted to go straight to the hotel. It had been incredibly stuffy in the airport and now, outdoors, the heat was scorching.

As we left the airport to get into the cars, Saleem's immediate family and other relatives were stood in a line, waiting to shower us with flowers and red rose petals in a traditional welcome. Then we embarked on a meet and greet with the family. Most of them were new faces and I had no idea who these people were or how they were related to Saleem.

Finally, we were led in groups to our cars, with Mum yelling at us to make sure we held onto our bags. Thankfully, our hotel was only a 20-minute drive from the airport. We were assigned drivers who would remain with us throughout the wedding. The hotel was beautiful, just as my father had said, from its majestic exterior to the fresco paintings on the ceilings, stunning décor and ornate wooden furniture, painted in rich hues of turquoise and red.

It was a great venue for a wedding. The organizer gave us information about dinner, breakfast and the hospitality lounge, which was available for our group. My father wanted everyone to meet for dinner in the Chinese restaurant at 7pm, after we'd freshened up and looked around.

My siblings were roaming around the hotel excitedly and taking loads of photos, so I slipped off to my room with my sister Amina to take a nap. As soon as I'd got changed, the phone rang. It was Saleem, asking to meet me. I told him I was tired and that we were meeting later anyway. Although he said okay, I suspected from his tone that he was annoyed. Mentally and physically exhausted, I pushed any concerns to one side and fell quickly asleep.

Both my family and Saleem's were to gather for dinner. The meal, which was set up as a buffet, was delicious, while the Chinese restaurant was decorated sumptuously in red and gold. At dinner, Saleem's sisters kept asking me about the trip and what plans I had for my wedding clothes. His sister Shazia said she needed to take me shopping to buy me clothes and gold for the reception scheduled for their side. She said they'd made plans, but had wanted to wait until I arrived, so I could choose them. Suddenly I heard Saleem's voice breaking into the conversation. Gently, he said he'd seen a dress that he thought I'd look beautiful in and had been waiting so he could take me to buy it. His sisters started giggling, repeating, with a smile, that their brother had already seen a dress he liked for me, prompting Saleem to shy away and turn back toward the men.

After dinner, we all went for a walk around the hotel gardens. The women and girls explored the grounds, while the men sat in the gardens, smoking and laughing. Saleem looked up every time we walked past, trying to grab my attention. The next day, I was told, we would visit Saleem's home for the *dholki*, a night of dinner and singing to kick off the celebrations.

The following morning, I woke up and began to get ready, planning my dress for the evening. Suddenly, things got hectic. First the seamstress arrived to take my measurements. Then came the beauticians to discuss my henna, makeup and hair for the wedding. After they'd left, we had lunch and started making our preparations for going over to Saleem's house for the first time since we'd arrived.

Saleem's family were waiting anxiously to meet the bride-to-be. The house was covered in lights and adorned with garlands, in the style typical of homes decorated ahead of a Pakistani wedding. We were showered again with rose petals on arrival, while my family carried gifts and sweets to give to our hosts.

We went out onto the large veranda, which had seats all around it and one particular area decorated with a stage and special seating. My three sisters, together with those of Saleem, escorted me to the special seating area and, once I'd sat down, all the women came up one by one to greet me and give me a hug. Saleem's mother came up to me with a squawking, black hen and started to swing it in circular movements around my head, prompting me to start screaming.

"What are you doing?" Mum hissed. "It's to protect you from the evil eye!"

I didn't even know what that was, but thought I'd better bite my lip as everyone was looking at me. Cringing, all I could think about was how I might now have hen droppings on my head.

Saleem's aunts began to tap a rhythm on a *dhol* and started to sing traditional wedding songs. I couldn't understand their accent or the Punjabi vocabulary, but it was fun. I noticed that Saleem kept his eyes on me, and, in the true spirit of a bride-to-be, I lowered my gaze and smiled coyly. This was real, I had to keep repeating to myself – I was getting married. Everybody seemed happy, dressed up in their finery and keen to celebrate our impending wedding.

The evening was fun, I decided, apart from the hen incident, with plenty of singing and dancing. Before I knew it, the music finished and it was time to head back to the hotel. I'd watched plenty of wedding scenes at the movies, but this one was not fiction; it was my life. On the way back, the following thoughts filled my head and which I later wrote down in my diary:

I wandered swiftly to the day I heard the music of the birds
The smell of the farms and the green carpet which surrounded me
My brothers and sisters chanting and playing and my mother calling my name
Today the time was full of colour and a variety of smells
Other than nature
The noise and sounds different
Decoding the noise to understand the meanings
She wandered fading away from the night.

9
Moving Water

We all headed back to the hotel before regrouping later in the evening for the wedding dinner. At dinner, my father went through the wedding itinerary, giving us details for each occasion and function, including logistics, money and security.

The next stage for me was to go and view my clothes, including the wedding dress, which I'd designed myself. I was keen to make sure everything was as it should be and would have appreciated the thoughts of my sisters, but they were preoccupied with their own outfits, makeup and jewellery. I wasn't allowed to go to the bazaars by myself and Saleem wanted to visit me each day anyway, so I found myself looking at the same walls much of the time. The hotel was seen as a safe place for us all to roam around freely and, while I appreciated my surroundings, I still felt removed from what was happening. Even though it was my wedding, it felt as if everyone else was doing all the planning.

The next morning, Saleem, his sister Shazia and her husband arrived to take me shopping. My mother insisted my brother Sajjad came along, so all five of us set off together to the bazaar.

As we browsed the stalls, we received a great deal of attention due to our accents and appearance. The bazaar was open plan with no air-conditioning and the effect of the heat and humidity soon became unbearable. As we walked through the crowds, I suddenly heard swearing and shouting. It took me a few seconds to realize that it was Saleem's voice. He'd noticed a group of guys looking at me and was asking them why they were staring at 'his wife.'

An audience had gathered to see what was going on and I grew scared. It was the first time I'd heard Saleem talk in such a harsh tone. I wasn't used to hearing any male member of my family or friend talk in this way.

For the rest of trip, Saleem was in a terrible mood and not in the least bit interested in shopping. Shazia became angry with him, insisting that we carry on. The streets were narrow and the stalls confined, manned by vendors shouting out to lure customers in. There were no female sellers or shop assistants. Everywhere we went, people stared at us.

My favourite stall was one that sold glass bangles. The display included hundreds of different designs coordinated to mix and match every outfit. My in-laws bought around 10 different sets to go with the clothes they'd had made for me.

Once we'd finished, we went to another stall selling hair accessories called *paranda* that I hadn't seen before. Shazia explained that it was traditional for brides to wear them and showed me how to braid one into my hair. There were different models, with some similar to tinsel and others adorned with beads and sequins. Shazia bought a few, but I didn't buy any of them as I had no idea what I was looking for or what colours to choose. Shazia explained that one part of the *paranda* is plaited into the hair, while the other part is ornamental, dangling down. I found it hard to take in all the detail; what with the heat and the crowds, it was all getting a bit too much.

I was ready to return to the hotel but Shazia had spotted a stall that was full of yellow accessories and motioned that we should head over there. Yellow was the colour used for the henna night, the *mehndi*, a joint, formal function that would take place in the hotel, with traditional singing and dancing while Saleem and I sat on a stage. The *mehndi* had its roots in Hindu, Indian heritage, so it was very much a cultural event, rather than a religious one.

For this occasion, I'd have to wear traditional yellow clothes, with a trimming called *gotta*, similar to appliqué and a scarf covering my head, to enable me to act like a shy bride-to-be.

We collected the yellow dress and matching accessories and, as we gathered our purchases together, I noticed out of the corner of my eye that Saleem was still sulking. He was looking directly at me, as if to say, 'how much longer is this going to take?' His stare made me feel uncomfortable and put me on edge. My heart began beating faster than normal and I realized that I was very conscious of how he was feeling. For some reason, I felt under pressure to do something about it. I turned to Shazia. "Can we leave now?" I asked. "I'm really tired."

She looked at me, surprised. "But we have a lot of shopping still to do!" she replied.

"Can't we come back another time or you get what's needed on your own?" I said, "I really I want to go home and rest."

Shazia was whispering something to her husband and I could sense from their body language and the change in their tone that they were unhappy with me. Still, we left the bazaar followed by young street vendors armed with combs, sweets, towels and hair clips. I really felt for them as they ran alongside us with their wares, yet I couldn't help thinking how happy and content they looked. Could I honestly say I was happy and content in the way that these innocent boys seemed to be?

Pushing these uncomfortable thoughts to one side, I took a deep breath and walked towards Saleem who was a little ahead of me. Once out of the bazaar, I returned to the hotel with Sajjad, while Saleem followed us on a motorbike and the rest of his family went home. Desperate for a shower after the heat and grime of the bazaar, I went straight up to my room. There were just two days to go until the first *mehndi* event.

When the day arrived, I was given my clothes and accessories, which included the bangles, shoes and *paranda* that I'd be wearing. In Saleem's family, there was a tradition that the in-laws provided this outfit, which is why I was obliged to wear what I'd been given. *Tough luck,* I thought, *if you were a bride-to-be and hated what you'd been told to wear!*

I changed into the clothes and, before long, the hotel beautician came to my room to braid my hair and pin my headscarf. I wore hardly any makeup, just a little eyeliner, although even that was applied much more heavily than I was used to in the UK.

I was glad the *mehndi* and wedding ceremony were being held in the hotel, as I could relax and get ready in my room before heading to the function room. Looking around, I took a moment to admire the beautiful furniture, with its turquoise upholstery and real chestnut wood frame. I was becoming quite attached to this hotel, which was my home for such a pivotal point in my life.

I sat in the armchair waiting for instructions, while everyone else frantically ran around, checking their outfits and doing their hair and makeup. The cameraman arrived at the door to do a photoshoot, so Mum started shooing everyone away. The female members of Saleem's family were due to come and collect me and hand me over to my brothers and male cousins, who would take me into the hall, Mum told me. In the meantime, everyone else lined up ready for the traditional filing into the function hall, where the ritual *mehndi* dances would take place. "Walk slowly and don't look directly up. Act shy," were my mom's parting instructions.

I heard loud *dhol* beats outside my room, signalling that the time had come for me to leave. The boys were holding a decorated red *dupatta* shawl up high for me to walk beneath. We followed the drummer, but my nerves quickened my pace, matching my heartbeat. "What are you doing? Slow down!" my mum shouted down the corridor. I had to force myself to walk slower.

The cameraman who was walking in front told me to keep looking at him. I could hear my brothers and cousins asking what they had to do, while the deafening drumbeat continued. The entire scene felt like organized chaos to me.

As we approached the grand hall, with its doors still closed, I realized that this was the moment when I was going to make my first entrance as the bride-to-be. My stomach lurched, I felt sick and fought the urge to run away. *What on earth am I doing?* I asked myself, my head spinning. *Is this really me, here, outside this door?*

The door opened, the lights dimmed and the drum became even louder. I was now exposed to the world in my role as Saleem's prospective wife. As we went in, I scanned the room. I was awestruck by how happy all the guests looked and how much time and effort had been put into the event. I kept focusing my thoughts on everyone around me, sparing myself from questioning what I wanted and whether my heart was in this marriage.

Saleem, the man whose life I was going to share, awaited. How had he come to be my destiny? The questions persisted, but no answers followed.

I was seated next to Saleem, but during the whole evening we didn't feel like a couple. I felt more like I was sat next to someone who'd walked into my life, was destined to play a huge part in it, but was still a stranger.

As the night went on, the music, dance and food flowed. My hands and feet were painted with henna. The colour would last for a few weeks, I'd been told and if I was honest, I didn't like either the smell or the stained look of my hands. I didn't say anything though, as I knew it was viewed as an attractive decoration, based on traditional designs.

The guests were having fun and sounds of laughter were everywhere. Most of them would have fond memories of this *mehndi*, even if my own were less kind. *I'm the bride, but I'm also the sacrifice,* I thought.

The following day, the seamstress's assistant arrived at the hotel carrying my wedding dress. We all sat around my bed, as he opened the box. I couldn't wait to see the dress I'd designed, a breath-taking mix of soft pink with a border in two colours of parrot green and magenta pink. The embroidery I'd opted for was done in sequins and glass beads, with a metal wire – subtle, refined and painstakingly crafted. But the dress in the box looked completely different. Confused, I asked the assistant whether this was my dress.

"Yes, madam, this is your dress," came the reply. "The dressmaker told me to deliver it."

Horrified, I told my parents that there'd been a mistake; the design, the colours and the material were not what we'd ordered. Knowing that there were only two days to go until the wedding, I started to cry with panic and anger, distraught that I might have to wear something that wasn't mine. Dad called the dressmaker on the landline in my room, shouting angrily at them. "We didn't order this dress. It's not what we paid for. We need the correct one urgently, she's getting married in two days!" he kept repeating. The mood had shifted from happiness and excitement to anger and worry. Eventually, Dad hung up, resigned. He told us they couldn't make a new one in two days and, since we'd already paid them, we had no option but to see if we could buy another dress at short notice.

In the middle of this crisis, Saleem rang. *He certainly picks his moments,* I thought sullenly. My sister Fatima answered and started signing at me to say he wanted to talk to me. "Tell him to go away," I retorted. The groom-to-be was the last person I wanted to talk to. As the tears rolled down my face, everyone tried to console me, but all I could think was that this was meant to be my dress and my day.

No doubt meaning well, Fatima turned and said, "When you wear your makeup and jewellery, nobody will notice your dress."

Predictably, this only made me angrier. Ever the practical one, my brother Sajjad suggested heading out to the bazaar to see if we could get anything ready-made, but deep down, I think even he knew that this was a long shot.

Eventually, and with a heavy heart, I realized I had no choice but to wear the dress they'd delivered. Just another compromise in a long list of compromises. Everyone told me the dress was amazing, but I knew they were simply trying to cheer me up, their smiles and reassurances fake. Imagine getting married, your once-in-a-lifetime day of being a princess having arrived, and then discovering that the dress delivered isn't the one you chose. That was me!

The beautician arrived early on the morning of the big day while I was having my breakfast. Mum said I was to get ready and prepare for the wedding ceremony with my sister Neelam, then our family would have photos taken. I put on the dress I hadn't chosen and had my makeup done, a layered rainbow of colours on my eyelids, which was the fashion at that time. I paced the room, knowing once my hair was pinned up and, as was the tradition, my headscarf pinned to my hair, I wouldn't be able to move around much.

I was getting married…this wasn't a dream, it was real. My wedding day, overseas, here in Faisalabad. Who would have ever thought it? Since none of my university friends could come over, I only had my family with me. My sisters, mom, and aunties all looked amazing with their makeup applied and hair all done up. Their clothes looked better than my wedding dress, I thought ruefully.

Thinking about my friends from the UK who were unable to make it, I wondered if they'd ever be in touch again or whether that part of my journey had ended there on the campus, under my tree, where I sat and thought about life and belonging. Under that tree, I'd discovered Rumi, his poetry and his understanding; his words painting a picture of my life and guiding me through it, all at the same time. How apt was his poem *Moving Water*? I thought.

When you do things from your soul, you feel a river moving in you, a joy.
–   Rumi

10
The Life's Soul

My relatives had all got ready at the hotel, while Saleem's family were due to arrive there with the guests. An entire team of cameramen and photographers had been hired to record the event. My room and the surrounding area felt like a film set. One photographer assigned to me was already busy taking photos as my hair and makeup were being done, while some were stationed with my family, and others filmed the rest of the proceedings. Once the photos were done, we patiently waited for the arrival of the groom and his party.

Saleem had designed a traditional *sherwani* outfit for himself with a matching turban, the fanned headpiece at the front starched to keep it stiff. It was an off-white colour and, even though I wasn't wearing the dress I'd ordered, I realized at least our colours would match.

In keeping with tradition, the groom would make a grand entrance and my family would line up to throw rose petals on him by way of a greeting and place garlands of flowers around his neck. The elders of each family would enter first, followed by the guests, to be greeted by the elders from my family.

Dad received the phone call in his suite telling him that the wedding procession was just around the corner and due to enter the hotel in about 10 minutes. He gathered everyone together and told them to get ready and be prepared to receive Saleem and his guests. My sisters were so glamorous in their wedding outfits and makeup that I hardly recognized them. They were evidently excited, looking forward to celebrating my day, or perhaps simply thrilled to be experiencing their first wedding in Pakistan. Having arrived at the wedding venue, Saleem's family would pause and gather their guests together, as was tradition, Dad said.

Saleem's family had brought an army band with them since Saleem's father, who had died a few years previously, had been in the army and the family wanted to pay tribute to him in the ceremony. I could hear the band from my room, where I sat waiting with my cousins Amina and Safina. Aged just 10 and 13, they were alternating between eating all the chocolates in the mini-fridge and running up and down the stairs to peep at the wedding hall entrance, to update me on the latest developments. I kept asking them how Saleem looked, but they just giggled and refused to say much. The band, which included bagpipes, had accompanied him as he entered the hall, they said, and the men were dancing, while guests were throwing rupee notes over the groom. On the way in, local beggars were running up and grabbing the money off the ground.

They told me the wedding hall looked incredible, with its décor and impressive stage beautifully offset by the ornate decorations. On their last journey back to my room, they said the guests were all seated now, with Saleem, the male members of his family, and the elders on the stage. Drinks were being served while they waited for the local Imam to arrive to conduct the wedding ceremony.

For the first time it dawned on me that I'd have to walk through the main aisle of the hall with guests on both sides. The function room was divided, with men on one side and the female guests on the other. Panic was setting in. What if I fell? My heels were pretty high and the dress was heavily embroidered. Would I be able to see properly with my headscarf on?

Before long, my father, brother Sajjad and uncle came to collect me, signalling that the Imam had arrived, meaning it was time for the official ceremony to begin. As we walked toward the hall, I could just make out my mum in the distance, crying. I knew that most mothers became tearful and dramatic in this, the official *nikah* ceremony, the moment they lose their daughter to another family. I was asked to fully cover my hair and the service began. The Imam recited his words in Arabic, then asked me to sign the papers that meant I'd been given away to Saleem.

My father, Sajjad, and uncle were all called on to sign the legal documents, as my guardian and witnesses. The Imam said a prayer to bless our marriage and moved into the main hall with the witnesses, where Saleem was waiting to complete his part of ceremony.

A cacophony of sound erupted, as guests all began saying the congratulatory word *mubarak*, hugging one another and our families and eating sweets to mark the celebration. This was it: the moment I had to walk into the main hall to meet my husband. I walked down the aisle in the dress that wasn't made for me. I'd decided the dress was symbolic in some way, but I hadn't quite worked out why. I tilted my head upward a little, trying to sneak a look at the people around and, as I scanned the room, I noticed Saleem's female relatives turn their heads toward me.

Walking past them, I caught snatches of their conversation in Punjabi:

"Wow, look at her jewellery."

"She has all those jewels because the family are from London."

"Saleem's lucky he got married to someone from the UK. He won the lottery."

I walked toward where Saleem stood waiting to greet me and take my hand to lead me onto the stage. His expression was everything I'd imagined; he looked captivated and I was convinced that this was the moment I'd been waiting for, my happy ever after. As our eyes met, suddenly filled with emotion, I thought to myself, *...for his one glance turns me to ashes.*

I felt happy and excited, loved and desired. Someone was taking me and would keep me forever. But was this what I wanted? My inquisitiveness was off again, forcing me to question so many things. There were times when I really wanted to turn it off like a switch and this was one of them.

The wedding day rolled on with more rituals and photos that seemed to last forever. By the end of the day, heavy with exhaustion, I could no longer even smile. The queue of people coming onto the stage, wishing us well, giving us money and taking pictures seemed to be endless.

Then it was time for another ritual, the drinking of the milk by the groom, known as *dhood paliyee*. As part of this fun tradition, the bride's sisters give milk to the groom and demand money in return, threatening to take his shoe and hide it if he doesn't comply.

All the youngsters gathered on the stage and began haggling with Saleem. He dutifully joined in, joking and teasing the girls by offering them peanuts, which they loudly refused and continued trying to remove his shoe. In the end and because my mum was getting mad, he gave in and handed them 1000 rupees. I was surprised. This was less than I expected him to hand them, roughly converting to just £10, which wouldn't go far once shared among them.

As everyone returned to their places, my uncle took to the stage. He was going to recite a poem and a prayer so the *rukhsati* could take place, the time I officially left my parent's hearth for another's. This was a poignant part of every Pakistani wedding, focused on giving away the daughter to her husband and his family. Mum said that as part of the tradition I needed to grab a fistful of rice and throw it above my head, to symbolize that I was leaving everything behind and starting a new life afresh. It was certainly different to throwing a bouquet and looking to see which bride-to-be had caught it, I thought.

The rice tray came, and I was asked to begin. Scooping up the rice proved something of a challenge since my false nails kept hitting the bottom of the tray. Mom's eyes were full of tears and, in a voice cracking with emotion, she spoke of losing me and having to let me go. All my family joined in, crying and hugging me, telling me to take care and to look after myself. Then it was time to leave for Saleem's house. Together with his family, Saleem and I headed down to the reception area of the hotel, where the car was parked, covered in fresh flowers. I'd seen this scene in movies, but this time it was *my* wedding car, I thought excitedly. Saleem and his sister Asma sat next to me in the car as we drove off. I was still very emotional, having just said goodbye to my family and thought Saleem might take my hand or comfort me, but he didn't. Maybe this was a cultural thing, I thought.

When we arrived at Saleem's house, his mother got a black hen out and, once again, started to swing it around Saleem and me. I backed away, screaming and grabbed hold of Saleem, much to everyone's amusement. Saleem explained that this was a ritual and a sacrifice to protect us, the couple. She also rotated a jug of water around before drinking it and finally poured oil on the steps. Only then was I allowed to enter the house. I went in, still reeling from the strange unfamiliar rituals and exhausted from the day.

We were escorted to the bedroom, where my first few hours of married life were to begin. Everything felt strange, even more so since we had been given the bedroom that Adnan and Nazya usually slept in. I was shocked to discover there was a photographer here too! The photographer wanted to take pictures of the bride and groom, complete with flowers and garlands across the bed.

Children kept coming in to sneak a look, while Saleem's female relatives were busy telling us how to pose. I found the whole thing uncomfortable in front of an audience. Nazya came in with a glass of milk and fruit for Saleem, but nothing for me. My stomach rumbled, a reminder that I hadn't eaten for hours, since I'd lost my appetite through nerves during the day. I was exhausted and desperate to get out of my uncomfortable dress and heavy jewellery. Right then, all I wanted to do was to shower and change.

After what felt like an age, everyone filtered out and I was left alone with Saleem. He took out a small box from a drawer and said, "This is a gift for you. It was given to my brother Adnan to give to his first wife, but when he got divorced, she returned it. I was told to give it to you."

It was a gold, fan-shaped locket. Saleem explained that the chain had been swapped with one of his sister's because it weighed more. The first gift from my husband was second-hand! Hardly the princess-like treatment I had been hoping for! Something stirred inside me: disappointment or regret? There was a hollow feeling where happiness should have been and I felt cheated.

It wasn't just the second-hand gift; there was also the lack of compliments. Nothing was said about how I looked in my dress, my appearance, or about the effort I'd made with my clothes and accessories. I realized, unhappily, that these words weren't going to materialize. It was my wedding day and my husband was showing no sign of emotion or tenderness toward me.

There was more fruit, milk and drinks in the room. Saleem took the milk without even asking me if I wanted anything to eat or drink. He told me that if I wanted to change, the shower and bathroom were in the right-hand corner. I paused, wondering how on earth I was going to manage to remove all my accessories and get out of my dress, given that it had taken three women to get me ready, pin my hair, zip me in, and help carry everything. Here I was, in a strange room, a bathroom I'd never used, weighed down with hair accessories and caked in heavy makeup.

I slipped into the bathroom with my night bag, removed my headscarf that had been held in place with a full box of pins, and managed to extract the sausage-shaped roll which had kept my backcombed hair in shape. Facing the mirror, the rainbow-colored eyeshadow looked tired and tacky now. Perhaps it was the harsh light that made it look garish or perhaps it was simply reflecting how I felt.

I removed my jewellery from around my neck, breathing a sigh of relief as the weight lifted. I splashed some water on my face, trying to buy some time before the inevitable. Stomach churning, I knew Saleem would be waiting for me in the bedroom. My first encounter with a man and one who hadn't even told me I looked beautiful on my wedding day…need I say more about that night?

The morning after, I woke to the sound of screaming and shouting, first in the distance and then much nearer. Still coming around, it took me a few seconds to realize that the person making all the noise was Saleem, his voice now deafening. He'd just got out of the shower and was dripping wet, and I came to with a start as he bellowed in my ear, "***Kutey kee bachee*** – *tum nay bathroom my towleeyah nahee rakah?*" (Daughter of a dog, did you not put a towel in the bathroom?).

Could he really be talking to me, his wife, in that tone and using that language? I double-checked to see if there was someone else in the room he was speaking with, but there wasn't. Why was he yelling and swearing about a towel and asking me about it? I started to shake. I'd never heard language like this. Surely this man wasn't getting so worked up about a towel? Yet, not just any man…my husband.

I leapt out of bed and just as I did, Saleem's mother and Asma, his sister, banged on the door, asking to come in. I wanted to get dressed first, but they came in anyway, asking what the matter was.

"This pathetic woman knows that her husband is going to be having a shower, so why didn't she put a towel in the bathroom?" he said.

Unbelievably, the two women didn't jump to my defence; they simply began to placate Saleem, "You shouldn't speak like that, Saleem, you're scaring her," they said, in bright, false tones.

Turning to me, Asma gave me clothes from their gift bundle and told me to put them on and get ready since guests were coming for breakfast. There was no "How are you?", not even an explanation. Saleem left the room and, all alone, I burst into tears, feeling confused, miserable, and shattered. As I showered, my only consolation was that my family would be arriving today to visit.

When I was ready, Asma came in and asked me why I hadn't put on any jewellery or makeup. "The bride is supposed to wear both," she said.

Resigned to doing as I was told, I tried to make an effort. I desperately wanted to go home, away from these people who were strangers, not my family, and very different in their ways.

I was told to come to the dining room since guests had arrived and wanted to see me. I went into the room and the crowd that had assembled greeted me and gave me money as a gift. I was served breakfast by Nazya, but, despite my hunger from the previous night, I couldn't swallow any of the food. Saleem didn't look at me once. Amid my disillusionment, the same words wormed their way into my mind, *…for his one glance turns me to ashes…*

I had a lump in my throat and desperately willed myself not to cry. These people all knew each other and were talking, joking, and laughing. I sat in silence, overwhelmed by a sense of being entirely alone. I didn't belong here. I may be Saleem's wife, but I didn't even know my husband. He was a total stranger, the man who once wrote letters to me every day and wouldn't leave me alone was not even making eye contact with me, talking only to his family.

As midday approached and most of the household went for a nap, Saleem started up a conversation with me for the first time that day.

"Do you know why I did that this morning?" he said. I didn't answer. "Because I wanted my mother and sister to feel sorry for you," he went on. "In this culture I have to be a man and can't show that I love my wife. It's not accepted here, since it makes people think their sons and brothers are weak and under the thumb of their wives. That's why I acted in that way."

I didn't reply. I couldn't get my head around what he was saying. If this was true, the culture and the way women were treated was too much for me to comprehend.

Saleem continued to explain away his action, and, as he did, his powers of persuasion began to take effect. Perhaps Saleem had genuinely acted as he did to protect me and show how much he cared, I began to think. It never occurred to me to question his actions or that I was being manipulated. I knew something wasn't right and that I was pushing my doubts away, out of reach. After all, although I'd led a sheltered life, hadn't I always been curious and constantly sought answers? Yet here I was, believing and trusting this person, my husband, blindly.

By the afternoon, my spirits had lifted, knowing I'd soon see my family. We were due to go back with them for a few days, as was tradition.

Mum arrived with my three sisters and, as soon as they saw me, they started to cry. I, too, got emotional on seeing them, unable to control my feelings. I felt safe and secure when they arrived and Saleem's mum was being extra nice to me in front of them.

I went to my room to gather a few things to take back to the hotel while also asking Saleem what he wanted to bring with him and whether he'd already packed a bag. To my astonishment, he replied that he wasn't coming. "You go and spend time with your family, I'll stay here," he said.

"But we've just got married and we're supposed to go together," I answered.

I knew that my family had made plans and would be extremely upset. Dad was due to fly back to the UK the following day.

"I have things to do. I'll come and collect you," was his response.

I went to find my mother and let her know. I could tell from her face that she was surprised and disappointed. "But it's tradition for the bride and groom to come to see the parents of the bride the day after the wedding," she said. "He and his family should know better."

When Saleem's mother joined us, my mum raised the subject straightaway. "So Saleem isn't coming with us?" she asked.

"I don't know," his mother replied, feigning ignorance. "Should he be going with Shama?"

"Well, traditionally it's customary for the groom to accompany the bride on a visit straight after the wedding and my husband is leaving tomorrow," Mum said, somehow managing to keep calm, "then they will go to the north for their honeymoon."

"Well, it's up to Saleem," she shrugged, "I don't interfere."

With that my mother turned to me. "Just get ready then, we have to leave," she said, "we're not going to change our side of the arrangements as we agreed them ages ago." I could tell she was extremely annoyed at the response from Saleem's mother and, once we were in the car, she let her anger out. "These people have changed since you got married and very quickly," she snapped. "We haven't sold our daughter to them. Who do they think we are to treat us like this? Your dad leaves tomorrow and he will be very upset."

To make things worse, Saleem hadn't even been at home when we left, as he'd gone to sort out the payments to the car-hire firm. I didn't get the chance to say goodbye or see him before leaving.

We arrived at the hotel and my spirits lifted when I saw the rest of my family. I was pleased to hear that they'd planned plenty of activities, but my thoughts kept returning to Saleem. I wondered where he was, what he was doing and whether he would be angry because I never got to say goodbye.

The day passed and the next morning my father was due to leave. He came to find me for a chat before leaving for the airport. "Remember the values your mum and I have instilled in you. Be good and be honest," he said. "It's important to tolerate and respect your mother-in-law in the same way you would your mom, as she won't be with you forever." His parting words were wise and spoken from the heart. As his daughter, all I could do was to promise to do my best to stay true to them.

Before we knew it, the taxi arrived to take Dad away from me. There were tears in my father's eyes. Our parting hug was tight, as neither of us knew when we'd next meet. Shortly after, Saleem arrived to take me back home, telling me to collect my things, since we had to go and get ready to set off on our honeymoon.

When we got back to his house, Saleem's mother asked me where the wedding gift money was. "It's in my purse, in my handbag," I answered.

"It's customary to hand it over to the mother-in-law, who will then decide what to spend it on," she said to me.

With no idea of whether what she said was truth or fiction and with my father's parting advice fresh in my mind, I immediately went into the bedroom, took the money out of my bag and gave it all to my mother-in-law, without even counting it. She took it without hesitation.

Saleem and I had one more day at his family's home before we were due to set off on our honeymoon. I'd heard from many Pakistanis that the northern parts of the country were the most beautiful, with echoes of Switzerland. I was looking forward to getting there, thinking that perhaps this would be the start of a truly positive chapter in our lives.

11
No Walls

Our bags were packed and the car was outside, with the driver ready to take us to the airport at Islamabad, from where we'd be flying off for our honeymoon. After the confinement of the family home, I was finally going to have some time alone with my husband, a thought that filled me with excitement.

I'd packed my walking boots, sweaters and some scarves, as I'd been told it was going to be quite cold there. Unsure what to do with my jewellery and other valuables, I left everything with Saleem's mother for safekeeping.

On our way to the airport, Saleem seemed to revert to the man that I'd first met: entertaining, fun, informed and attentive. He chatted about everything under the sun and I felt that perhaps we could find a way forward as a married couple after all, if given a bit of space. However, even here, on our way to our honeymoon, we had to keep parts of the conversation low key in case the driver eavesdropped.

The roads were nothing like as smooth as the motorways in the UK and, along with the bumps, we were surrounded en route by crazy drivers overtaking us with no concept of fear. The vehicles themselves were also a sight to behold, ranging from rusty cars to huge trucks overloaded with cotton sacks that hung down either side like an over-sized belly. I'd come to recognize the particular smell of raw, dry cotton and still would today.

While somewhat scary, the journey also took us past some beautiful scenery and provided glimpses of rural life. Women walked barefoot along the roads, carrying pots and other items on their head effortlessly. Each village, town and city we drove past had a different vibe and its own identity, which I found fascinating.

After four uncomfortable hours of bumping up and down in the car, we arrived at the airport and took our flight to Swat, our destination. The plane was much smaller than any I'd ever been in before, which was nerve-wracking in itself, and, to make matters worse, our route took us through mountainous territory. My heart was thumping in my chest and, fearful of crashing, I squeezed Saleem's hand tightly for most of the flight.

Once we'd landed and I saw how scenic our surroundings were, I quickly began to relax. We were staying at the Hotel White Palace, a delightful getaway that was once a royal residence and sat nestled majestically in the mountains, enveloped in lush greenery.

The hotel was staffed by locals, who greeted us warmly and took our luggage up to our room. I noticed that they seemed to have fairer skin and different features than the city folk I'd met since arriving in Pakistan.

Saleem and I both gave thanks for our safe arrival by praying on the prayer mats that were in our room, before showering and getting ready for dinner.

The ambience at the hotel was incredibly romantic; there was an open log fire in the hotel grounds, flickering to a backdrop of mellow music. Most of the guests were newlyweds, like us, including the couple sat at the next table. I also realized, with a start, that the woman was from the UK. Hearing English spoken with that accent was disorientating and, for a moment, catapulted me back home.

After dinner, we decided to go for a walk in the grounds. Maybe it was the tranquil surroundings or having our own space, but Saleem suddenly seemed keener to begin opening up to me and the conversation turned to our childhood memories.

Back at the hotel, I opened the door of our room and was delighted to find that a log fire had been lit for us. Catching my smile, Saleem seemed both pleased and amused at this display of happiness. "Your face looks so vibrant, really glowing," he said. I was glad that he'd noticed how I felt, but a little disappointed that he hadn't yet paid me the type of compliments I'd hoped for. After all, what bride doesn't want to be described as pretty and beautiful by her husband? Maybe he simply hadn't got around to it yet, I thought, dismissing my doubts. "Your eyes really talk. They show every expression. Through those brown eyes I can really see you clearly," he continued.

I'd been complimented on my eyes in the past, but this was different. The words really meant something because they were being spoken by the man that I thought I loved. Somehow, Saleem expressing how he felt in these intimate surroundings and at this important point in our relationship just felt right. A Rumi quote came to my mind at that moment, 'They say there is a doorway from heart to heart, but what is the use of a door when there are no walls?'

I was feeling light-hearted and excited, anticipating how things would progress now that Saleem was expressing himself more. True, he was still reticent and didn't seem to be a tactile person, not being one for cuddles and linking arms, but all in good time, I decided. I was also hesitant about how to react, given that Saleem was the first man in my life, but I was certainly feeling more optimistic.

The next morning, we went for a stroll along the river and the topic of Westernization came up. Saleem asked me if Muslim Pakistanis in England had girlfriends and boyfriends. He also openly admitted that he had dated a lot of women and drank alcohol. I told him that my sisters and I had been raised in a fairly sheltered, traditional way, with no exposure to clubbing, drinking, or dating. When I asked Saleem why he drank and dated even though he was raised in Pakistan, he replied that it was common to behave in this way here. I was surprised, given that I'd never been around alcohol and my brothers and father were always respectful toward women.

Although these were sensitive issues, I was pleased that we were breaking down barriers and discussing our pasts. But then Saleem suddenly changed tack. "I heard your cousin Waqqas was upset that you married me because he wanted to marry you himself," he said. "You're so beautiful...how come when he was visiting England, you never dated him?"

"Sorry?!" I exclaimed, alarmed. "Waqqas is like my brother! How can you think that?"

"I find it very hard to believe that your cousin stayed at your parents' house and you two didn't have a relationship," he continued, doggedly.

"Saleem, are you crazy? What makes you think that?" I responded, incredulously. "And if we had, I assure you I'd tell you!"

Heart sinking, I realized that Saleem's mood was slowly changing. Where had this jealous, possessive streak come from? I hadn't seen this in him before, assuming him to be open-minded. "We have male friends at uni and school, and talk to our cousins, that's normal, but it not like we are dating," I insisted. But he wasn't prepared to let it go.

"On the one hand you say you're traditional, but then you say that you have male friends," he said. I felt I was being unjustifiably challenged and criticized.

"I'm your wife, aren't I?" I retorted, defensively. "What else do you want?"

After that, Saleem was in a foul mood and went on and on about girls who pretend to lead a modest life but are secretly off out partying. I couldn't be bothered to get embroiled in what seemed to me to be idiotic mind games and accusations. We went back to the hotel room and the picturesque view across the river and mountains calmed me a little. Tired from the walk, I decided to have a nap and then wake up for brunch.

Our room had tea and coffee facilities, including a kettle. "What would you do, darling, if I threw this boiling water from the kettle on you?" Saleem asked, playfully.

"Hahaha! Very funny!" I answered, pleased that his mood appeared to be lifting and thinking I'd join in the joke. "You'd never do that. First, because you're not crazy and second, because you love me, so stop messing about!"

I stretched out on the bed and closed my eyes, relaxed, enjoying the welcome breeze created by the ceiling fan, with the glorious mountain view from our window still vivid in my mind. Sleep came easily...then suddenly: "Owwwww, oh my God, oh my God! Oh God, arghhhhhhhhh!" I leapt out of bed screaming with shock, disorientated, and aware of nothing other than being in excruciating pain.

Stumbling around the room, I realized the unbearable stinging and burning sensation was coming from the right side of my chest. Now fully awake, I put my hand to my chest, only to find that my black nylon slip had burnt into my flesh. Instinctively, I tried to pull it off, with the result that both fabric and skin came away in my fingers.

In a state of shock, I felt like I was watching a horror movie. Was this really my skin? Yes, the pulsating pain confirmed it. What was going on? I couldn't take anything in, other than the crippling, scalding sensation down my chest. I became aware that Saleem was standing in front of me and I continued screaming. "What the hell happened?" I yelled.

"I am so sorry, darling, I cannot bear anyone to have you or see your beautiful body," he said.

"What?" I managed to reply. "Who the hell is going to see me other than you?"

Still screaming, I ran into the bathroom and locked the door behind me. Rummaging around, I managed to find some cotton wool I'd brought with me to cleanse my face and placed it over my weeping, peeling skin. However, where the wound was weeping, the cotton wool simply stuck to my skin, making matters worse and exacerbating the pain.

I lay on the bathroom floor in shock, trying to register and understand what had just happened. Then I grabbed the notepad and pen that were on the unit and started writing a note to my parents. 'Forgive me,' I wrote, 'but Saleem is an animal and I can't continue in this marriage…' Then I paused, thinking of the money they'd spent on the wedding and their expectations. I decided I'd prefer to die than face them again. 'I am very sorry,' I finished.

I put as many dissolvable paracetamol tablets as I had with me into a glass of water and gulped it down, hoping I would die, after which I wrote one more letter, this time to Saleem, saying, 'I only ever loved one man and that was you. But I can't be with a man who burns me.'

As I willed death to take me, there was a banging on the door. The housekeepers and Saleem were urging me to open up. I could also hear Saleem telling them that I wasn't feeling well. "Go away," I shouted back. "I'm not unlocking the door." Here I was, on my honeymoon, supposedly a time of immense happiness, in terrible pain, with scalded skin peeling off my chest, having overdosed in the hope of leaving this world.

Saleem was just the other side of the door, talking to me. "Shama, open the door. I love you and I care about you," he said. "I am crazy because I miss my father. I need you."

"Go away, and tell my parents I died in an accident," I answered.

I came round to the sensation of water being splashed on my face and slowly realized I was in Saleem's arms. Somehow, he'd got into the bathroom.

So, I didn't die, I thought grimly.

"Wake up. What are you doing?" he asked. "I know I'm crazy. It's only because you're so beautiful and I can't bear the thought of anyone else seeing you. That's why I behaved like this, because I love you. I haven't got much time to live and I think about my father all the time."

At that moment I felt a wave of sorrow for Saleem, who was clearly suffering. Why was he saying he didn't have much time? Was he dying? I wanted to ask him, but was still in agony myself, unable to think or speak clearly.

Saleem helped me up. Noticing the cotton wool on my chest, he told me to remove it by washing the wound with water. I poured water onto my chest, crying out in agony as it made contact with my raw flesh, but the cotton wool refused to budge. Saleem told me to try showering it off and, finally, after I thought I'd pass out with pain, the cotton wool came away, revealing several open wounds. At this point, Saleem promptly took a tube of toothpaste from the sink and squirted it over the damaged skin, explaining that it would help the burn heal and prevent it from becoming infected.

While the tablets were taking the edge off the pain, the wound was still weeping, so I covered it with a flannel. The realization of what had taken place was now beginning to sink in. I said I wanted to see a doctor, but Saleem told me there were no medical practitioners where we were staying, so I grabbed a blanket and tried to sleep it off. But the pain made this almost impossible. All I could think was that I wanted to get away and return to Faisalabad.

As my body ached, my mind went over and over the events of that morning. Traumatized, I still couldn't quite believe what had happened, but the stabbing sensation down my right side told me otherwise. I'd been wounded and disfigured by the man I loved, or at least, thought I loved. Worse, I could feel the seeds of acceptance taking root within me. Would I have to tolerate this kind of behaviour in my marriage? Was this part and parcel of the package?

I couldn't help feeling that the turn my life had taken echoed the film *Sleeping with the Enemy*; the strong woman who advised others to fight for equality and to stand up for justice was now suffering herself, reduced to a pathetic character who tolerated nonsense at best and domestic violence at worst.

Is this really me? This person? I asked myself. *Is this what I've become?* I knew that if any of my friends were to confide in me that their husbands had done this to them, I'd tell them to leave, without a second thought. Yet here I was, accepting this abuse. Could I really be allowing this to happen?

I wanted to get away from Swat; beautiful though it was, I'd always think of it as the place that I'd discovered my husband's true colours. I wanted to see my mom, or at least familiar faces, people with whom I felt safe. Yet Saleem did his best to persuade me to stay for a little longer, clearly afraid that his actions might be exposed while my wounds were so raw.

The atmosphere was tense, however, and conversation stilted. Saleem's unspeakable act had driven a wedge between us and somehow confirmed something I'd suspected. Intuition, or my sixth sense, had been niggling away at me for a while, telling me that something wasn't right, but I'd been unable to say what that was. Did this terrible event mean things were beginning to fall into place?

"Shall we go out for breakfast and walk along the river?" Saleem's voice interrupted my thoughts the following morning.

"I don't feel well enough to leave the room, I'm still in a lot of pain," I answered.

"OK. You rest and I'll order you room service for breakfast," he said and left.

Saleem had decided to find a driver and car to take us back to Faisalabad, rather than do part of the journey by plane. I was happy to be going, but the thought of travelling by car along those bumpy roads in excruciating pain for more than 10 hours filled me with dread.

We were scheduled to leave the following morning, so I slowly packed my bag, leaving aside some towels for my wounds and extra painkillers to keep handy for the journey.

What a different vibe heading back! I thought back to how happy and hopeful I'd been on the journey here. Life really can change in an instant, in one action, I mused. As I wrestled with the pain, other questions were whirling around in my head. Should I tell my mother and the rest of my family what had happened or not?

As if sensing my thoughts, Saleem chose this moment to begin opening up about how his life had been affected by his father's death, all while repeating that he was not going to live that long. I knew that he was making me feel sorry about what had happened to him before we met, yet lurking in the back of my mind was a growing awareness that he was also manipulating me.

But I also wanted to be a good wife and help him however I could. "Saleem, I want you to know I will always be here for you by your side," I said. "Please don't think I will judge you or make you feel bad. I'm sorry if I wasn't able to understand you." As I spoke, it dawned on me that while I'd apologized, Saleem hadn't really seemed remorseful for what he'd done to me. Instead, he had made excuses or given explanations for his actions.

Halfway through the journey, we made a stop at a makeshift service area so I could change the towel I was using as an impromptu dressing. As I wrung out the soaking towel, it was beginning to dawn on me that these wounds were going to scar, both psychologically and physically.

When I returned to the car, I took some more painkillers in the hope that they'd knock me out for the rest of the ride. The tablets did their job, but the sleep wasn't restful; instead I ended up drifting in and out of nightmares, against the drone of the engine and bumps along the road, in which I relived the horrendous events of my honeymoon.

Finally, we arrived home. If I was worried his mother might notice my injuries, I had no cause to be; all her attention was reserved for Saleem. "I hope you are happy to be home. I'm so grateful that my son came back safely. I prayed that he'd return safe and sound to his mother," she said, hugging him and turning to me with a cold smile.

I asked her where I should put my bag and she told me to leave it on the veranda.

"I need to lie down," I said to Saleem in English. He replied that he wasn't sure which room was ours, as when we'd first arrived, we'd been given Adnan and Nazya's room. There was only one other bedroom, which his mother shared with Asma. As I digested these facts I felt more out of place and bereft than ever. My immediate thought was that all I wanted to do was go home. But what did that mean? This certainly wasn't any home of mine.

We sat and spoke to Saleem's mother for what seemed like hours until I couldn't keep my eyes open. Finally, I interrupted him to say that I really needed to go into a room and get changed and sleep. To my surprise, Saleem took me out to the veranda. "Can't you see that my mum needs me?" he hissed. "And instead of accepting that, you're just going on and on."

"I'm hurt and need to rest," I replied. "If it's too much effort, then call my mother and I'll go there instead."

"How dare you threaten me!" he exploded.

"What?" I replied, astonished. "What are you going on about? I need to sort myself out and rest. We've just done an entire day's drive!"

Our argument was interrupted by the sound of the front doorbell, followed by the voice of Saleem's mother telling him to go and open the gate. Unwillingly, I returned to the lounge and sat across from my mother-in-law. The atmosphere was tense to say the least, as she fixed me with a cold stare. There we remained, in stony silence.

Saleem could be heard walking up the steps and I realized that he had other people with him. To my delight, my mum and my two brothers came in, all smiles. I was so relieved and excited to see them that I made straight for my mother and buried myself in her arms. Instinctively she embraced me in a bear hug, which sent a sharp jab of pain down my chest, causing me to scream out.

"Are you okay?" she asked, concerned, looking into my eyes.

"Yes, just aching from sitting in the car for so long," I replied, lowering my gaze and trying to hide my tears. Was this how life was going to be? Having to lie to my darling mom? Saleem and his mother were all smiles and friendliness, I noticed, in the presence of my family. My mum then asked my mother-in-law if I could spend a few days with them before they returned to England.

"Saleem will come back to you on that," she replied pleasantly. The words made my heart sink.

12
A New World

The next day, I waited anxiously for Saleem to decide whether I could go and stay with my family, doing my best to disguise how desperate I was to visit them. Instead, I focused on trying to keep everyone happy and, as I saw it, earning my reward of spending precious time with my mom.

When I could bear it no longer, I put the silver tray on the table, poured his tea and plucked up the courage to ask him if he'd call my mum and organize the visit.

He turned around and answered, casually, "Sure, we can both go and stay there for a few days."

What? Both of us? I thought to myself, in dismay. I didn't want him there! I wanted to be alone with my family. Yet, even as his response was sinking in, I realized I had no choice but to agree to what he was proposing if I wanted to see my loved ones. *At least I'd get to meet up with Mum and the others,* I thought, my mood lightening again. I began packing my bag, keen to leave as quickly as possible and went to get my money which I'd put in my handbag, only to find it wasn't there. After checking again, I turned to Saleem. "Do you know where the money is that I had in my bag?" I asked him, innocently.

His face immediately twisted with rage and he spat his response out. "*Kutey kee bachee,*" he snarled. "Are you saying that I took it?"

I was shocked, both by the insult hurled at me and the spiteful tone used. Perhaps it was routine for him to use these words, the same way people swore habitually in English back home, but I certainly wasn't used to hearing people talk to family in this way.

"I was just asking where my money was," I answered, still in shock. "I never meant to accuse you."

"*Kutey kee bachee,*" he repeated, with just as much venom. "Are you saying my family took it then?"

"Of course not. I just don't know where my money is…" I trailed off, realizing that anything I said was futile and would be met with the same rancour.

I made for the bathroom, which was quickly becoming my place of refuge and allowed the tears to fall freely. Reminding myself that I would, at least, get to see my mum soon, I washed my face and put on some lipstick, like any new bride would before visiting relatives, before returning to my packing.

Soon I was ready and itching to go, but Saleem, aware that I wanted to leave and still in a thunderous mood, had decided to play a waiting game as a form of punishment. I didn't dare ask him what time he planned for us to leave out of fear of sparking another temper tantrum, so instead I tried to keep myself busy. But what did that even mean? Back home I'd have plenty to amuse myself, but I didn't even know what I should be doing here, I realized, with a sigh.

Eventually, I changed out of my outfit and back into comfy, casual clothes for around the house. Almost immediately, Saleem appeared. "Why have you changed when we're about to leave?" he asked brusquely.

I decided it was better to keep quiet rather than risk antagonizing him again, so I said nothing and went off to fetch my bag, which I had put on the veranda.

"Where's my bag?" came Saleem's voice. Panic began rising inside me as I realized I'd annoyed him yet again.

"I wasn't sure what you wanted to pack or where you keep your things," I replied, hesitantly.

Nazya looked over in amusement. "What? Your wife hasn't packed your bag and doesn't know where your things are?" she said, mockingly. "Well, you know how it is with these girls from the West – especially girls from America and the UK – they have no idea how to look after and keep a husband!"

I couldn't believe how insulting she was being toward me and the fact that Saleem simply sat there allowing her to talk in that way only added to my feelings of inadequacy. What was it that Mum had said to me in her 'wife-to-be' lectures? Something about remembering my upbringing, whatever my in-laws said and reminding myself that I wouldn't be living with them forever. I knew my mum meant well, but I was beginning to doubt the wisdom of these words.

Saleem called me into the room. "Why do you have to embarrass me in front of my family by causing these dramas, changing out of your clothes and then coming in here with a bag just for yourself?" he hissed. "Go and pack me a bag as well!"

"What shall I pack?" I asked wearily.

"Don't you even know what a husband needs for a few days away?" he snarled. "Are you that dumb?"

Deciding yet again that it was best not to respond, I went to the wardrobe and took out three shirts in different colours, two pairs of trousers, underwear, socks, toiletries and slippers. Despite the fact that he and his family had hurt my feelings, I was happy to fold his clothes and prepare his bag. Deep down, I genuinely wanted to be a good wife to him.

Saleem hailed a rickshaw and we were on our way. The atmosphere was tense, with barely a word exchanged between us during the journey, but for once I didn't care. All I wanted to do was to see my family. The only dampener was that Saleem was there too.

After what seemed like an eternity, we arrived at my uncle's house where my family were staying before returning to the UK. Before we'd even got out of the rickshaw, my family came rushing out of the house in excitement. In a welcoming gesture that had its roots in Hinduism, but had also been adopted by Punjabis, they showered us with rose petals and poured oil on the steps.

We tumbled into the lounge, talking over each other excitedly and laughing, before moving into the dining room. Dinner was a fantastic mix of cuisine, from local dishes to Chinese and Italian platters. As we ate, I was reminded of just how hospitable the South Asian people were.

Saleem was socializing with characteristic ease, holding everyone's attention with his entertaining anecdotes and impressive knowledge on a range of subjects. Like the others, I found myself spellbound by his charisma. I knew the other people gathered around the table would be thinking that I'd found the perfect husband and told myself how lucky I was to be married to this charming, attractive and intelligent man.

My mother had decorated our bedroom with garlands of fresh flowers, which immediately lifted my spirits. I breathed in the fragrant bouquet and felt more relaxed than I had for days.

She and my sisters followed me into the room, whilst the men remained in the lounge, chatting.

"You look exhausted," Mum said, concerned. "Have a lie-in tomorrow and I'll arrange for you to have a massage later in the day."

My sisters and cousins were keen to hear all about the trip to Swat. Was it really like Switzerland? Did I have the photos I'd taken with me? Instinctively, I leant forward to fish the photos out of my bag, but in doing so caught the burns to my chest on my shirt. The pain was excruciating and I was desperate to get some air to my skin, aware that the wound was weeping once again, but I did my best to talk my excited relatives through the photos.

Sensing I was tired, Mum eventually herded the girls out of the room. I couldn't wait to remove my top and clean the wound, which showed no signs of healing. If anything, it was becoming more inflamed and beginning to smell. I was desperate to get some ice from the freezer to cool it down, but knew my sharp-eyed mum would ask questions, so had to make do with water and the cream I'd brought with me.

Saleem came into the room as I was doing my best to clean the wound. Making no comment, he stretched out on the bed, having announced that he was tired, turned his back on me and went to sleep.

Applying the cream and makeshift bandages from a cut-up t-shirt was a lengthy process. Somehow it was made worse knowing that the perpetrator was lying in bed next to me sleeping soundly.

The first call to prayer in the morning woke me with a start, reverberating around the house, since the mosque was just a few doors away. I rose, performed my ablutions and got myself ready for *fajar*, the first prayer of the morning.

Mum and Dad had always got us up for morning prayers. On this particular occasion, I prayed for my marriage to work, for Saleem to change into a caring human being and for God to look after me at this time of need. Afterwards, I went back to sleep.

I woke up later to Saleem complaining about feeling cold because the air conditioning had been on all night. Heart sinking, I wondered if he was going to blame that on me too.

We got dressed and went downstairs to the drawing room, where my uncle sat reading the local newspaper. I could hear my mum and aunt in the kitchen preparing breakfast. The sounds of familiar domesticity filled me with love for them both. The conversation with my uncle turned to Swat, a topic I'd already discussed in detail with my sisters and cousins and a place I'd have preferred to erase from my memory. We also talked about my father and his childhood and our family tree while Saleem read the paper. Before long, Mum came in to greet us, asking if we'd slept well. She said breakfast was almost ready and went off to wake my sisters and cousins who hadn't yet emerged. Mum hated anyone sleeping in!

The clink and clatter of cutlery and plates told me that my aunt was setting the table and at the same time, the appetizing smell of *paratha* (flatbreads) wafted into the room. As we all gathered around the table for breakfast, I felt happier than I had for some time, surrounded by my family and delicious food.

I was immersed in conversation with my sisters when Saleem suddenly chimed in with an announcement that we'd have to leave that evening because his sister Sadia was planning to visit the family. Everyone around the table expressed their disappointment at this news, including my mom, who said they'd made plans for that night and the following evening. Since this was the first that I'd heard of Saleem's plans, I, too, was knocked sideways, having assumed we'd stay for a few more days. I was desperate to see more of my mum and the others. Perhaps he'd return alone and I could follow on, I thought.

After much persuading, Saleem agreed that we'd stay one more night. We were booked to have lunch at a Chinese restaurant, which was well known for serving great food. In keeping with tradition, the men got ready separately, which meant I had some precious time with my mom, sisters and cousins. We laughed and joked together as we put on our *salwar kameez* and did our hair and makeup. The only grey cloud was Saleem's looming presence; somehow knowing he was here amongst the people I loved and with whom I felt safe and secure unnerved me.

I was asked to dress once again as the bride, complete with makeup and off we set. The wedding was in fact the main topic of conversation, with the girls keen to go back over every detail, from their hairstyles and makeup to their outfits. After we'd eaten, my sisters and cousins produced a selection of gifts, which they presented to me and Saleem. Ever the perfect gentleman, my husband thanked everyone around the table so graciously and with such charm that I could see why they'd fallen under his spell. I could tell they thought I was incredibly lucky to have married this well-mannered, articulate and handsome man. Perhaps only I was aware that he hadn't even made eye contact with me during the meal, let alone started a conversation. I sat at the table, a newlywed, supposedly one half of a happy couple, yet feeling totally alone.

After lunch, we all returned to the house for a nap and, before long, it was time to start packing. Mum came into the room for a chat before we left. I could tell she was desperate to talk to me on my own, but Saleem didn't seem to take the hint, or perhaps chose to ignore it. Time wasn't on our side, so in the end she simply pulled me to her. "Stay happy and look after Saleem and his family. You're part of their family now," she whispered, hugging me tightly.

Tears rolled down my cheeks. I couldn't help feeling that the future I faced was an uncertain one. Not only that, but, instinctively, I had a real sense of foreboding ahead of our return to his family's home.

It was time to say goodbye. I hugged my family as never before. Had it taken this new chapter in my life to make me truly appreciate how lucky I'd been to have such wonderful relatives? Yes, I thought, it had.

I was relieved that at least we'd be making the journey back to Saleem's home by car rather than in the uncomfortable rickshaw, but the sadness I felt at leaving my loved ones behind was still overwhelming. I knew that the only time I'd see them in the near future would be to say goodbye at the airport, and, only then, if my husband agreed to the trip. I'd hoped that Saleem would be on hand to console me, but instead he sat in the front with the driver, discussing politics with him while ignoring me.

When we arrived at the house, the driver helped us to carry our bags inside, a gesture which I thought we should acknowledge. "Can you tip him 100 rupees?" I asked Saleem.

"I haven't got any change on me," was his reply. I turned away embarrassed. My mother had always told us to help others and show manners, but there was nothing I could do for the driver there and then. When we went inside, I was relieved to discover that Saleem's mother was having a nap. We were sleeping in the lounge for now and had been given a cupboard in Saleem's brother's bedroom to use as a wardrobe. I tried to remind myself that these arrangements were temporary, but still it felt a little like living in a hotel. I was desperate for Saleem to talk to me, but I could sense that his mood was dark, so after asking him if he wanted some tea, decided it was best to get on with the unpacking.

Saleem had taken himself off to bed, but my head was too full of questions to allow sleep. How had I ended up in this house, with these people? The fact that they were all sleeping soundly as I walked around their veranda restlessly seemed to accentuate the differences between us. Where did I fit into their lives? What role would I be expected to fill? And what would happen to my own hopes and dreams now that I had another part to play? The questions came thick and fast, but, as usual, no answers followed.

Later that evening, the call for *maghrib* prayers rang out from the mosques around us, stirring Saleem's family. My mother-in-law rushed to the corner bathroom on the veranda to perform her ablutions for one of the five daily prayers we were expected to perform.

Her favourite activity was spending time with her sons in the lounge. Seeing them sitting together after prayers, it was evident that nobody else was welcome. I wandered around the house idly, unsure what to do with myself. In the end, I decided to go and tend to my burns, which were finally showing signs of healing. But before I knew it, my mother-in-law called out, asking for some green tea.

As I served the tea, Saleem caught my eye for the first time that day.

"Adnan is taking Nazya to the doctor, so why don't you join my mother and me?" he asked.

Me? Invited to be part of a conversation with his mother? Could this be a turning point? I sat down, my spirits rising. The conversation soon turned to the topic of the wedding.

"*Kush kaber*? (Is there any good news?)," his mother asked. I wasn't sure what she was getting at. Did she mean Saleem's search for work? I knew he was looking for a new job.

"Mum wants to know if you are pregnant," Saleem explained to me.

"What? Are you serious? We've only just got married!" I replied, shocked.

Then Saleem's mother told us the story of how her neighbour's daughter-in-law had been trying for a baby for eight months without success.

Oh my! I hadn't even given this a moment's thought, yet already I was under pressure to conceive! Having been immersed in my own thoughts, I tried to pick up the thread of what she was now saying.

"Of course, a lot of women can't have babies, sadly," she mused, throwing me a look. "It's a shame, but it's only fair that they allow their husbands to remarry."

Was this a hint? It certainly felt like one!

Next morning, Saleem's sister Sadia arrived from Multan with her family. She was clearly close to Saleem and Adnan and spent most of the time sharing jokes and chatting in a way that made me feel like an outsider. I decided to take myself off to the veranda to pass the time.

Then, in a voice that she made sure was loud enough for me to hear, Sadia said, "Of course, *bhabhi* (my sister-in-law) is from the UK. I bet she doesn't know how to do the *jaroo ponchach* (sweeping and mopping)."

Back in England, we'd had a dishwasher and vacuum cleaner, so I'd never needed to learn how to clean hard floors like the ones in Pakistan. Her jibe made me feel nervous, as if I was being set up to fail.

Saleem chimed in, telling me to go and get some Pepsi for everyone and prepare dinner, as Sadia was tired from her journey. Pepsi was a special treat in Pakistan. I loved the glass bottles it came in and still think of them with nostalgia.

I went to the kitchen and started making lunch. Before long, Nazya came to lend a hand. While we were working, she talked about how Sadia would start bossing everyone around when she visited. I asked why she was like this, but Nazya simply shrugged and said she'd always been this way.

We put out a sheet on the floor for everyone to sit on to eat, since there wasn't enough room around the dining table and then popped to the tandoor nearby to buy naan bread. The food, a mutton dish with side accompaniments, looked wonderful when laid out and I was especially proud when Saleem commented on how good it tasted.

After a pause, Nazya admitted, seemingly reluctantly, that I'd done most of the cooking. I hadn't wanted to appear boastful, but the way she'd hesitated made me feel as if she didn't want me to receive the credit for my hard work.

After lunch, we cleared up and then tried to sort out everyone's sleeping arrangements for an afternoon nap. I ended up in the lounge with his sister, mother and two nieces, while the men disappeared into another room. My mother-in-law and Sadia were chatting for what seemed like an age, making it impossible for me to get any sleep. It felt like I'd only just drifted off when the call to prayer sounded again. The rest of the day was spent rushing around after Sadia and her family, leaving me exhausted and desperate to know how long they'd be staying. Later, I was secretly relieved to discover that the siblings had decided to go out for dinner and leave us in-laws behind.

The next morning, I woke up to be informed by my mother-in-law that the woman who usually washed the floors and cleaned was sick and would be unable to work for the next few weeks.

"I guess I'll have to clean now, won't I?" she said, holding my gaze long enough for me to know what she was implying and within earshot of Asma, who was hovering outside.

"Why should my mother have to clean when my two sisters-in-law are living in the house?" Asma asked, appearing at the doorway before I'd even had time to respond.

After breakfast I cleared up for the third time in less than 24 hours and then went out to the bathroom on the veranda, where I filled a bucket with water and found the broom used for sweeping the floor. I knew there was a special technique for sweeping to ensure I collected as much of the dust as possible without it getting in my eyes, but I had no idea what that involved. Nazya stood behind me, laughing. "Don't you know how to do this?" she asked. "You have to sit down for starters, not stand."

I looked at my hands that were still adorned with the bridal henna decorations, yet fast becoming red raw from the cleaning and clearing I'd done since yesterday. Here I was, sitting on the floor, trying to clean in the way I'd been told to – struggling, but determined to prove to these people that I could do what was asked of me, even though I'd lived in the UK all of my life.

The burns on my chest had rubbed where I'd been crouched on the floor and I suspected the wounds were weeping again, but I gritted my teeth and pressed on, pride alone preventing me from shedding tears. I desperately hoped that Sadia and her family would be leaving that evening, freeing up the room I'd been sharing with Saleem so I'd have a bit more privacy. To my dismay, I soon learned that they'd decided to stay on for two more days. It had become evident during this visit that when Saleem and his siblings were together, there was little time or space for us in-laws. He might be my husband, but he was clearly a son and brother first.

On the day of Sadia's departure, my mother-in-law told me that it was traditional to give the daughters gifts when they visited the family home and that I should therefore offer Sadia some of my new clothes.

I could hardly believe what I was hearing and hated the thought of giving this rude woman anything that my parents had gifted me, but Sadia was already making her selection. Saleem must have caught my look of dismay as she rummaged through the beautiful outfits.

"Let her have whatever she wants," he said, tersely.

Wearily, I left the room. It had occurred to me that, given my apparent role as skivvy, I was unlikely to need many of the gorgeous dresses Sadia had her eye on, but the injustice of it still burned.

We waved the visitors off, my mother-in-law in tears, while I secretly rejoiced at their departure. That evening was the first I'd spent alone with Saleem since we'd returned. As soon as we had some time to ourselves, I told him that my burns were still causing me problems. "I really need to see a doctor, I'm worried the wound might become infected," I said.

"A doctor's too expensive," he replied, dismissively. "Just look after it yourself."

I was hit by a wave of despair and loneliness. Here I was, aged 19, having to tend to wounds inflicted by a husband given to unpredictable temper outbursts and a slave to his family.

It was Friday, the day my loved ones were leaving Pakistan and heading home to England. As I wandered through the house, allowing the significance of their approaching departure to sink in, I realized that my mother-in-law was talking on the phone to my mom, unaware I was within earshot.

"Saleem's out," she was saying.

That's a complete lie! I thought, incredulous. *He's standing right next to you! Why are you lying to my mom?!*

"If he has time, he'll bring her to the airport to see you off," she continued down the phone.

I realized from the next part of the conversation that my darling mother was offering to come and visit me at the house to ensure we said a proper goodbye to each other.

Once Saleem's mother hung up, she turned to Saleem. "Take her to the airport," she said. "If they all come here, we'll have to give them Pepsi and snacks."

Saleem came to find me, unaware I'd heard any of the conversation and told me we were heading to the airport to see my family off. We went by motorbike, since his family didn't have a car. I spotted them all immediately, waiting impatiently to see us before they went airside. There was very little time, since they were being hurried along, so I hugged them all quickly, tears rolling down our faces. My mum gave me and Saleem 20,000 rupees each as a parting gift. "Until next time, God willing, look after yourself," she whispered in my ear.

My sisters and cousins were playfully lecturing Saleem, telling him to look after their 'precious gem' and saying how much they'd miss me.

70

"She's my life and my responsibility," he replied, solemnly. "I'll never let you down."

As they walked away and then turned with a final wave at the gate, I felt wracked with grief, as if my family had died there and then. Riding home on the motorbike, I held on tightly to Saleem, allowing my tears to fall freely and be blown away on the wind. Aside from the pain of being separated from my family, I had other, deeper concerns. Would Saleem allow me to see my family in the future? And if so, how often?

When we arrived back at the house, Saleem seemed uncharacteristically sympathetic. "Don't feel sad. You've got me, haven't you?" he said, gently, as we went out onto the veranda. His compassion was incredibly comforting and I thought that spending time with my husband was probably the best way to take my mind off the earlier farewells. Yet, before I could respond, his mother, who was seated in her usual place, interrupted by starting up a conversation with her son. It was nothing important, but enough to command his attention and leave me yet again feeling excluded. As they hugged, she shot me a cold, yet triumphant look.

I knew there'd be adjustments to make when swapping families, but the stifling relationship between my mother-in-law and her son, which inevitably made me an outsider, was something I hadn't been prepared for. My own mother loved my brothers dearly, but this was different, I felt, to the point of being suffocating. It also dented any hopes I had of working on my own relationship with my husband.

I was fast becoming resigned to the fact that my life would be one of daily chores and looking after the family while seizing whatever time my mother-in-law decided to allow me with my husband. On one level, I patted myself on the back for making such a major adjustment with just a few teething problems, aged just 19. Yet these were lonely days, spent cooking and cleaning, thousands of miles away from my family. The phone was only to be used by Saleem's family members; we in-laws were only allowed to answer if no one else was in.

From being a student at a British university and a member of a loving family, I'd become a woman in a third-world country, taking orders from her in-laws. My clothes, valuables and belongings had been removed, leaving me with limited resources and I didn't even have a room to call my own.

This was to be my reality, my life and my new routine, I thought, in a foreign country without my loved ones and amongst people that were only family in name.

13
A Ray of God

Over the next two months, I fell into a routine of cleaning and cooking on weekdays while waiting for Saleem to come home at the weekends from Lahore, where he was looking for a job. I felt like I was living out the fairy-tale life of Cinderella, a story I'd read as a child – being a skivvy, but without the happy-ever-after ending. Saleem's family showed me no respect, viewing me as nothing more than someone who was there to take instructions, cook, clean and change bedsheets. I knew deep down that this was, at least in part, due to the way he treated me.

My daily chores, which started immediately after morning prayers, were taking their toll on my health. I knew I'd lost a lot of weight, since my clothes were loose and my cheeks were much hollower than before. In fact, I'd always been teased about having a round face, unable to shake off the affectionate nickname 'moon-face' back home.

My parents and siblings telephoned regularly, but Saleem's family made sure I didn't get to talk to them by pretending I was out with Saleem, fearing that I might let them know what my life there was really like. Letters, which my siblings wrote to me and my new family handed over, were the only form of contact I had with my loved ones back in the UK. I waited anxiously for them to arrive and then dashed to the bathroom, where I could read them in privacy and cry freely. These pieces of paper were a lifeline during those dark days, with only happy memories and hope that things might improve, keeping me going.

I certainly didn't feel like I belonged in this family or that Saleem and I were a team. In fact, he remained a stranger, coming into my life as and when he pleased and mostly when he needed a woman. The relationship was a million miles away from the one I'd envisaged from the hundreds of letters he wrote to me before I arrived in Pakistan or the calls he made, eager to hear my voice and see me. Now that I was his, he no longer cared. Had he ever loved me or even liked me? I honestly didn't know. I spent lonely hours going over and over events that had brought me to this point in my life. Had I missed clues or chosen to ignore them? Was this outcome obvious to outsiders looking in?

One morning, Saleem came in at 4am and woke me up, demanding I make him something to eat. Although it was past 6am by the time I finished cooking for him and managed to fall back asleep, around an hour later I heard my mother-in-law banging on my door asking why I hadn't got up to pray and make breakfast. I looked up at Saleem, pleadingly, hoping that he'd come to my defence, but he didn't say a word. It was left to me to explain that I needed to catch up on some sleep.

I could hear my mother-in-law huffing and puffing, making sure I could hear her complaints as she wandered around. "Look at the time," she grumbled loudly. "In her world, mothers-in-law wake up to make breakfast, whilst the daughters-in-law sleep."

That morning, I was told to make an omelette with fresh coriander and onion for Saleem when he woke up. As I was chopping and the smell of the ingredients reached my nostrils, I was suddenly overcome by a wave of nausea, which sent me dashing to the bathroom, where I threw up. Still feeling sick, I returned to the kitchen and struggled on with the meal.

Saleem was sitting in the lounge with his mother, as usual, chatting to her and acting as if I didn't exist. I walked in and told him his breakfast was ready, at which point his mother invited me to sit and eat with them. I followed them through to the table, although I could barely hide my surprise and suspicion at this out-of-character offer.

However, as soon as I began to eat, another wave of nausea hit me and I began retching. My mother-in-law followed me out to the bathroom and asked me where I was in my monthly cycle. While I was still trying to process her question, she turned to Saleem and told him to take me straight round to the local clinic.

Busy and dirty, the clinic certainly didn't help my nausea. I was told to take a seat with several other women and wait until a nurse or doctor was available. To my horror, there were stray cats wandering in and out of the room, while the heat made it impossible to breathe. I wanted to leave, but was stranded there, since, with it being a women-only facility, Saleem had already left.

Eventually, a nurse emerged and asked me if I was 'the girl from London.' I said yes, deciding there was no point in correcting her geography and she instructed me to go into a room housing an old, metal bed. "Lie down here, please," said the nurse.

I took one look at the bed and resolved to stand firm. "Sorry, no way, it's not clean." I could tell from the way she glared at me that she thought I was a snob.

Once the nurse realized that I was not prepared to lie down, she asked me whether my periods were regular and then made me go off into a bathroom to provide a urine sample. Before long, she returned with the news that I was pregnant.

Shell-shocked, I collapsed into a chair; yet another life-changing moment, from wife to mother-to-be and in such quick succession. I couldn't really take in the news, although, fleetingly, I felt a sense of relief knowing Saleem's mother would be satisfied that I was fit and healthy. In her eyes, women who didn't conceive in the first month or so of marriage were ill.

With my emotions reeling, I paid the 200 rupees at the desk, having gone to get the money from Saleem outside. As soon as we began the journey home, I told him that I'd taken a pregnancy test, which had come back positive. Saleem's face lit up. "That's great," he said. "I can't wait to see my son."

Son? What if it's a girl? I thought. In fact, I'd already begun secretly hoping the baby was a girl, although I couldn't say why.

Saleem rushed into the house to share the good news with his mother and family, exclaiming "*Ami jaan, ami jaan*, you're going to be a grandma! Shama is having a baby!"

His mother looked at me and, for once, her smile was genuine; I was on the way to fulfilling my role – I was going to have her son's baby.

"Sit down," she said and started peeling me an apple. However, keeping any food down was a problem, although my mother-in-law reassured me that the nausea would pass.

Saleem decided to take me out to the park that evening for a walk. It was so rare for me to leave the house that only now did I realize I had no clothes to change into, as his mother had stored all my belongings. I had just four outfits, one of which was for bed. Only later would I discover that she had, in fact, given all my clothes to her daughters.

I found this aspect of my life very difficult to deal with, having been used to an extensive wardrobe of clothes back in the UK. As a child, I'd been thoroughly spoilt by my father, whose indulgence was the cause of many a light-hearted argument between him and my mother. We siblings were lucky in that we all grew up in Lancashire at a time when the region was a thriving hub for textiles – our line of business – especially amongst South Asian families.

Eventually, I dressed in my only casual outfit and couldn't help noticing how loose it was on me, due to the amount of weight I'd lost. I was also aware that Saleem was being much more attentive than usual as we walked through the park, but somehow I knew that this show of affection was only due to the fact that I was now going to give him a child. He wanted an heir, as he called the baby, to show the world that he was a real man, I suspected and I was simply the tool to make this happen.

As we walked, we talked, with pregnancy and parenthood inevitably dominating the conversation. Saleem said that he wanted his son to join the army, an ambition that was shared by many other Pakistanis. Somehow his words heightened the ache I had for my family back in the UK, the people with whom I truly wanted to share my happiness, especially my mother. I visualized the soft blanket she always wrapped around herself at home, her bright red lipstick, the noise of her shoes on the hard floors, the sound of her voice and her sweet smell. I was in no doubt now that my husband couldn't give me the comfort I craved. Only my loved ones far away could provide that affection and warmth. Saleem was still talking, but I was no longer listening to his words. I'd somehow managed to distance myself from the conversation and, instead, sought solace in a world of my own, one where I felt safe and happy.

I was desperate to let my family know about the baby and asked Saleem if we could call the UK, at which point his manner abruptly changed. "Why do they need to know?" he asked. "This is our life now, our happiness. You are part of this family, not their family." His voice had become significantly louder as he spoke. "You need to forget them and concentrate on your life here." His words were like a knife through my heart. "You know that in Pakistan women get married and give up their life and their family, right? In the West, girls have no respect for their husbands and prefer to become disgusting divorcees," he continued.

I couldn't believe how offensive and sexist Saleem was being, or that he was making such sweeping statements. I realized that what had begun as an enjoyable walk of celebration had quickly turned sour, but figured it was better to keep quiet than challenge him and risk incurring his wrath.

Days passed and the nausea persisted. I woke up vomiting and was unable to keep down any food throughout the day. I went back to the local clinic, even though I hated the place. This time, the doctor said I was dehydrated and would need a drip. The thought of having a needle inserted filled me with terror, although Saleem's mother told me it was not that unusual and would help to put some fluids back into my system.

I was beginning to feel grateful, until I heard her mutter under her breath, "My God, so now we have to pay for her treatment as well?" I couldn't believe she was complaining about the medical fees, which I'd worked out were negligible. Knowing I needed to focus on my health somehow helped me to find the strength to push the negativity around me to one side and breathe in whatever positivity I could find.

One of the doctor's assistants came along and began prodding my arm, looking for a vein that was suitable for the needle. The process was difficult and painful, made worse by the fact that I was lying on a stretcher surrounded by other female patients the entire time, but eventually the assistant managed to insert the glucose drip in my sore, bruised arm.

As I lay there trying to blot out the scene around me, my thoughts returned to my beloved sycamore tree on campus at university and the Rumi poem I used to read when sitting underneath its branches; the tree that had shared the wisdom of its years, I realized and was now helping me to understand some of the harsh realities of life's journey. I closed my eyes and allowed the words to swim to the surface:

You cannot hide love
Love will get on its way
To the heart of someone you love
Far or near, it goes home
To where it belongs
To the heart of lovers.

As I contemplated Rumi's words, it suddenly dawned on me that the great poet appeared to be referring to pure, unconditional love rather than feelings for a lover. I knew I'd stumbled upon something important, something that might help me in my search for answers, the definition of genuine, fulfilling love, perhaps.

Focusing on the poem helped me to while away the two hours I was kept at the clinic. Eventually, I was allowed home, under strict orders to rest. However, no sooner was I in bed than my mother-in-law began walking in and out of my room, banging the door, muttering about how in her day women were so strong that they gave birth without their husbands even knowing.

"These days, girls are so fragile, pretending they need bed rest," she said.

I knew she was making a dig, but I was determined to not let it wash over me. I also reminded myself that she'd paid my doctor's fees, even though she'd made a fuss about it. Only later did I discover that she'd settled the bill by using money she'd taken from my bag.

After some time of hearing her moving noisily around the rooms and muttering under her breath as she whipped off sheets, I could bear it no longer and dragged myself out of bed. Weak and barely able to put one foot in front of the other, I walked across to the veranda, where I found the entire household's sheets piled up for washing. Sighing, I went off to find the large bucket we used for the washing and began mixing the soap with cold water, ready to soak the sheets. I shifted around, trying to find a position in which I could work that wasn't painful, eventually squatting, with my back wedged against a wooden log.

As I worked, my mother-in-law watched me, a smug smile of satisfaction on her face that I was up and taking care of the chores. Then the phone rang, causing her to rush off to answer it. I could tell from her voice that it was Saleem. Relieved, I waited for her to call me over so I could speak to him and tell him I was feeling unwell. However, his mother chatted for what felt like an age, before handing the phone over to Asma while I hovered in the background like a spare part. Finally, I'd had enough and made a point of walking toward them. Reluctantly and after giving me one of their looks, they handed me the phone.

"How are you?" I asked him.

"I'm fine," he replied. "Mum was saying you've been resting and asleep most days."

"What?!" I exclaimed, before I could stop myself. "I haven't been sleeping! I've been sick non-stop and today I've washed the bedsheets! Did your mother tell you I had to go to the clinic and have a drip inserted because I was dehydrated?"

"Shama, what are you saying?" Saleem answered, an urgency in his voice. "They told me you were fine? Hand the phone back to Mom."

Hesitantly, I passed the phone to his mother and, although I was unable to hear her words, I could tell that her tone had now switched from light-hearted to defensive. Eventually, she handed the phone back to me.

"Shama, Mum says she didn't want to worry me, as I was away from home and looking for a job, so she'd decided not to tell me that you weren't feeling well," he said. "She's upset that you've told me."

"What about me?" I replied, desperately. "I have no one here to talk to about my feelings."

There was a pause. "My mother is going out of her way to look after you and this is how you repay her?" Saleem said, cold and calm now. "How can you be so unappreciative? Why do you always have to bend my ears with your complaining?"

However, I wasn't prepared to back down today. "I'm ill and nobody is supporting me," I retorted. "What do you expect me to do?"

"I don't want to hear another word. Mum is right," he cut in, before slamming the phone down on me. As I replaced the handset and turned to leave the room, I caught my mother-in-law's eye and her triumphant expression, a look that said 'I won!'

Once again, a wave of disappointment and despair washed over me, but I reminded myself of my mother's words before my wedding. "Your mother-in-law will not live with you forever. Be patient, one day you will have your freedom."

However, I had no idea how long I'd have to wait for that time to come and in the meantime life was proving to be unbearable. And now I had to adjust to being responsible for a new life. I was bringing a child into this world.

Three days later, Saleem arrived for a visit. I was pleased to see him, but couldn't understand why I had to stay in Faisalabad looking after his family while he was searching for a job in Lahore. Yet, it was evident that this was the expectation.

When he walked in, he found me hard at work, washing the veranda. I got up and rushed toward him, but before I could even make contact his mother and Asma had beaten me to it and were engulfed in a group hug. I was told to go to the kitchen and fetch my husband some water. As I picked up a glass and prepared to fill it, I stared at it for a second, thinking that I too was empty, starved of affection. I returned to the lounge to hear Saleem's mother telling him that she was taking great care of me and that he could surely see how well I looked.

I found her lies deeply disturbing, having been brought up in a household where transparency was practised and honesty taught. 'Never lie and always share your feelings' was part of my parents' code of conduct, but here the rules of the game seemed to be reversed.

Toward the end of the day, I found myself alone with Saleem. "So, how's the pregnancy going?" he asked.

"I feel sick and I can't keep food down," I answered. "The doctor said I need to rest and be careful, as I'm losing weight."

"Mum thinks you're panicking because it's your first pregnancy," he replied. "She said it's best to carry on as usual, especially since you're not even three months' gone yet."

I was incredulous – did this woman think she knew better than the doctors? "But the doctor said to take bed rest and that the first three months are the riskiest," I replied, in despair. But there was no convincing Saleem.

"Shama, you have to be strong and not panic," he said. "It's good to keep busy and not get bored. You need to have positive thoughts in your head, otherwise it might affect the baby."

At this point, I gave up and took myself off to bed. Yet, no sooner had I fallen asleep than I woke up to find myself soaked in blood. Screaming, I shook Saleem awake. "Look! See?" I shouted. "You wouldn't listen and now I'm losing the baby!"

Saleem leapt out of bed and said we'd rush to the emergency department. I covered myself with a large shawl and followed Saleem out into the street, where he waved down a rickshaw. With tears streaming down my face, I barely noticed Saleem's expression – one of fear.

As soon as we arrived at the hospital, I was whisked away for tests while a group of doctors stood talking amongst themselves in hushed tones. Saleem hovered next to me, both of us united by our feelings of helplessness.

When the medics approached us, Saleem asked that we be given a female doctor, although this was the last thing on my mind. I was taken into a room, where a nurse and doctor performed an ultrasound. After what seemed like an age, they turned to us. "We've picked up a heartbeat," the nurse said, smiling.

Relief swept over me, but it was interrupted by the arrival of another doctor, holding the results of my tests. "Your wife is in a very fragile state and needs bed rest," she told Saleem, in an American accent. "The ultrasound shows that the bleeding is being caused by the umbilical cord, which has moved and is putting pressure on the womb. If she doesn't take it easy, she could lose the baby."

I was overcome with fury. "Didn't I tell you I was ill and needed bed rest?" I hissed at Saleem. "Yet you told me to keep busy. Did you want to kill my baby? Are you happy now?"

For once, Saleem didn't reply, shocked at the idea that he'd almost lost the son he imagined I was carrying and upset that the advice he'd given me had been so misguided.

The doctors suggested that I remain in hospital for a week, until my weight was stable. They could give me something for the sickness, they explained, but I'd need to lie flat with my legs elevated. Saleem nodded, struggling to take everything in and went off to reception to call his family and tell them where we were. Craning my neck, I could just make out his face as he explained the situation to his mother. There was a lot of gesticulating, but I had the impression that he was doing his best to convince her that the doctors knew best.

When Saleem came back, he said he had to return to Lahore, but that his mother would stay with me at the hospital. He then left to get my medication from the pharmacy, leaving me to digest this bombshell. As soon as he'd gone, I turned to the doctor. Something made me feel I could confide in her – perhaps it was her accent. "Please, don't let my mother-in-law stay in my room. She's made my life hell," I begged, tearfully.

The doctor eyed me with sympathy. "You wouldn't believe how many similar requests we get," she said. "Where's your own family?"

"They're all back in the UK," I answered. "My husband's family won't even tell them I'm pregnant. I have my father's relatives here, although no one knows I've been ill."

"Let me see what I can do to help," the doctor said gently. "It really is important that you don't have any stress or upset."

Later that evening, Saleem's mother and Asma came to the hospital with fruit and soup for me and Saleem. I was astonished at my mother-in-law's reaction, which seemed extreme. She was sobbing incessantly, dabbing her eyes in between conversation. I also noticed that Saleem's mother had already brought her overnight bag. However, I couldn't see any of my own things.

"Did you bring my toiletries and clothes?" I asked.

"No, I wasn't sure where they were," she replied.

Desperate to clean up, I immediately asked Saleem to go home and get them. As they were making their arrangements in Urdu, I picked up that the subject of the hospital fees was also being discussed. "We should tell her parents that she's in hospital, maybe they'll send money," I heard my mother-in-law say in a hushed tone.

Saleem went off to call my mother, relaying the good news – that I was pregnant – followed by the more worrying part, which was that I was in hospital and unable to speak to them. When he came back, he admitted that my mother was very upset, that she'd told me to eat lots of fruit and rest and then asked to be kept up-to-date.

Saleem decided to stay and told his mother to go home. I wondered how much of his decision was down to the fact that the room was comfortable, with a lounge area and a spare bedroom, since the hospital was a private facility.

The following morning, my three uncles arrived with fruit, flowers and food, happy to see me, but very concerned to find me lying in a hospital bed, looking pale and thin. Seeing these blood relatives for the first time since my wedding was a breath of fresh air. Here were people that really cared about me and were genuinely concerned for my wellbeing. However, I noticed that they also seemed slightly uncomfortable around Saleem.

We had a fantastic time catching up. Before they left, I told them to call my mum and let her know that my in-laws wouldn't let me speak to them. I felt bad about sharing this fact, but also relieved that my mum would finally know the truth.

The next day, Saleem came into the room with some food and announced that he was leaving for Lahore but would be back in a few days. I felt a twinge of regret, since he'd been more attentive lately than any time since the wedding. Unaware of the conversation I'd had with the doctor, he told me that his mother would come and sit with me in his absence. Saleem also informed me that my brother Fahad was planning to get married in England in January and that my parents wanted to send over money for tickets so we could attend.

Just at that moment, Saleem's mother walked in. As she hugged her son, I picked up some of her conversation, complaints about how difficult it was for her to get to the hospital and also manage the house, along with another about finding the money to pay the hospital bill. I closed my eyes briefly and willed the doctor to come into the room.

Then I heard Saleem tell his mother about the wedding invitation. "How can we let her go to a wedding when we have so much happening here?" she retorted. I honestly couldn't understand what this woman wanted from me, other than to inflict endless misery.

Saleem set off for Lahore, leaving his mother in charge of my care. When the doctor arrived to check me over, I asked in English for a notepad and pen and, as soon as they were handed to me, I scrawled on the paper, 'Please get her out of here, she is making my life hell.'

Immediately, the doctor took my mother-in-law to one side and explained that I wasn't allowed any visitors.

"She has to be on her own to rest – the only person permitted to be here is her husband," the doctor said politely. Unbelievably, Saleem's mother threw a tantrum, shouting at the doctor about everything, from the cost of the rickshaw to the attitude of the staff. Finally, she left, cursing the doctor and, under her breath, me. As the door slammed, I smiled to myself, relishing the prospect of a few days of peace and quiet, away from the daily grind of housework and abuse. Bliss!

The following day, my mother telephoned and, as I walked to the reception area to take the call, I realized this would be the first time I'd hear her voice since she'd returned to the UK after the wedding. I was so thankful to my uncles for making this happen that I wanted to hug them all over again.

My heart was thumping in my chest and the tears were trickling down my face as I took the call.

"Hello?"

There it was, the voice of unconditional love.

"How are you?"

At first the lump in my throat made it impossible for me to answer, but eventually, I found my voice: "I'm fine. Just battling a bit of morning sickness and weak."

"I'm so happy that you're having a baby and we are going to be grandparents," she gushed. "We're all excited. Don't worry, I had a lot of morning sickness too. Shall we come to see you?"

"No, no, I'm fine, don't worry," I said quickly.

"Let's see if you can come to the wedding," she continued. "But wait for your in-laws to approve it first. We'll call Saleem and ask him too."

"How is everyone?" I asked, desperate to hear everything about my family and be a part of their lives again.

"They're all good, busy with everyday life and we're busy with the first UK wedding ceremony," she explained. "It's not like Pakistan. Here you have to arrange everything. It's good you have all your clothes and jewellery with you, so that's not a headache." I didn't want the conversation to end. I wanted to hear my mother's voice for as long as possible.

"How's Dad?" I asked, my voice trembling with emotion.

"He's fine, he misses you a lot. You were always the loudest in the family and used to drive him mad," Mum said fondly. "But he's happy that you're settled and enjoying married life with Saleem."

There was a pause as I resisted the temptation to tell Mum the truth, knowing that I couldn't burden them. Before I knew it, the call was over and I was walking slowly back to my bed, trying to hold onto her words and retain the warmth of her voice.

The phone call had heightened the huge difference between my mum and mother-in-law. Both had been born in the same subcontinent, yet their attitudes and approaches were poles apart. Was it due to their culture, faith, upbringing or a little of each? Still, speaking to my mum had brought a grain of comfort.

By the end of the week, I was past the riskiest, three-month stage of my pregnancy. However, while relieved, I was also dreading returning home to the supervision of my in-laws. Saleem came to collect me and paid the bill, without even a murmur of complaint, to my surprise. He also booked a car, since the doctor warned him that I wasn't to travel in a rickshaw due to the bumps in the roads.

"Do you fancy some Chinese food?" he asked on the way home.

I was delighted to be asked, especially since my appetite was beginning to return.

While at the Chinese restaurant, Saleem began telling me that I needed to take better care of both myself and the baby and also that he planned to take me to Lahore for a week. My spirits rose at this news. He then also explained that since his mother was a widow, it was our job to give her plenty of attention and keep her happy. "I know it's hard, but my mother will always come first," he said, looking straight at me.

"I get that," I replied. "But when you're not around, she treats me differently."

Saleem cut in before I'd finished, telling me that he didn't want to hear any more. "Shama, I can't listen to this and I will never be able to say anything to her. I hope you understand," he said. "We will go to Lahore next week."

When we arrived home, Saleem's sister Shazia was sitting with her family. She asked after me, voicing concern and hugging us both. But instinct and things I'd heard her say and seen her do in the past made me suspect that it was an act. Out of all of them, Shazia had proved to be a real disappointment, given that she had married into my father's side of the family.

After we'd all caught up with each other, Shazia and Nazya went into the kitchen to prepare dinner, with me, for once, spared the chore. Over dinner, Saleem told everyone that he planned to take me to Lahore. His mother immediately raised her eyes from her plate and looked straight at him. "Are you crazy?" she shouted. "She isn't well, she needs bed rest."

"Mother, she's fine," he replied, patiently. "The doctor said she could do with a change. It will also be good for the baby."

I didn't say a word but sensed the tension in the air.

"What do you mean?" Shazia joined in. "What if anything happens in Lahore?"

"The hospital is nearby and it's a good one," he answered. "I've booked the car and the room now."

"Shall I come with you?"

It took a few seconds for me to realize that the person asking this question was my mother-in-law. Horrified, I turned to Saleem, waiting for his response.

"No, Mother," he answered firmly. "You need to be here for Asma. We'll only be gone a few days." Saleem then swiftly steered the conversation away from the subject, reminiscing about how, when they travelled as children with their parents to Peshawar, his mother would cook and take food for the whole week. She was laughing now and joining in the journey down memory lane, distracted, thankfully.

I helped to collect the dishes and, together with Nazya, took them through to the kitchen.

"You'll be lucky if she lets you go to Lahore," she said. "She won't let her sons do anything. If she could, she'd even sleep with them!"

Her comments stung and I felt hurt that she'd take this approach, rather than offer me support.

The following day, Saleem took off again for Lahore, leaving me at the mercy of his family. Truth be told, he wasn't there much for me when he was at home, but his presence did, at least, take the edge off my loneliness and keep his mother in check a little.

With newfound confidence, buoyed by Saleem's change of attitude, I'd decided that our trip to Lahore would be a good time to discuss attending Fahad's wedding in England. Perhaps this was a new beginning and, with the baby on its way, Saleem had turned over a new leaf, I thought.

In the days leading up to the trip, I roamed around the house with greater ease, even in Saleem's absence, feeling more assured than I had done before, knowing he'd stood firm about taking me with him to Lahore.

When Saleem finally arrived home, I was truly excited to see him. His cousins, Laila and Adam, had come from the village to see him and were waiting on the veranda. I brought them all drinks and sat with them whilst his mother finished praying.

When she joined them, I left to go and pack my bag. Suddenly, just a few minutes later, I heard Saleem scream out in my direction, addressing me with the same insults he'd used in the past. "*Kutey kee bachee!*" he screeched. "Get in here now! Why didn't you look after my mother while I was gone? She said she had to wake up every morning and make breakfast for the both of you?"

I was shaking, unable to take in what was happening. I couldn't believe he was talking to me in this way and using this language, especially in front of his cousins. Then everything went blank.

Next thing I knew, water was being splashed on my face. It seemed I'd fainted, but Saleem was still shouting at me, leaning over my shoulder. "You stupid woman," he spat. "What the hell are you doing? You're poison for us." I realized with horror that he was kicking my leg.

"What are you doing? She isn't in a fit state," Adam said, clearly concerned.

Here was my husband abusing me and taking pleasure from doing so, whilst I was semi-conscious, in front of guests. Once again, I was on the floor, being humiliated by someone I could hardly think of as human, but now also worried about a life other than my own.

Adam pushed Saleem away, saying "*Bhai*, what are you doing?"

Saleem snapped back, "She deserves it! How dare she treat my mother like a servant? How could she do this?"

Even while still coming round, I was incensed, knowing that I'd done no such thing. How dare his mother lie and cause this scene…and how dare my husband explode in this way without even hearing my side of things.

I decided at that moment that he was truly mad. While I'd seen his temper before, I never thought he'd act like this in front of visitors and while I was pregnant. I felt embarrassed and worthless. Perhaps most depressingly, I'd also just begun to think things were improving.

Leila grabbed me and helped me up off the floor, away from Saleem. We shuffled to the bedroom and she went off to fetch me a glass of water. I could tell that she was upset on my behalf.

As I sat there, I suddenly felt a searing pain shoot across my lower abdomen. Instinctively, I ran to the bathroom, only to look down and find I was bleeding again. Petrified, I began to panic. I knew that however bad things were, they'd only get worse if I lost the baby. I'd lose my status in the family, low as it was already and Saleem would reject me or take his anger out on me. What was I going to do?

Leila knocked quietly on the door, asking whether she could come in.

"I'm fine," I answered, although I knew she could tell I was crying.

"*Bhabi*, please open the door and let me see if you're okay," she begged.

Fearing the drama might generate interest from the others, I let her in. As soon as she saw the blood, she took me by the shoulders.

"What happened?" she asked, horrified.

"I don't know, I'm scared," was all I could manage.

Leila ran off, calling for Saleem. "*Bhai, bhai*, you need to come!"

Saleem came running and, on seeing the blood, told me to get changed so he could take me to the hospital. Feeling weak and faint, I struggled to dress, prompting Saleem to become impatient.

"Look what you've done now. Is there no end to your dramas?" he asked, pacing up and down restlessly as I looked for clean clothes. "I'm getting sick of you and your behaviour."

By now I was at breaking point and began sobbing uncontrollably. "Please, just stop it. I can't take any more," I wept.

It seemed to work and he shut up, perhaps surprised by my reaction or worried I might faint again in front of him.

We made the journey to the hospital in silence. I couldn't help replaying the evening in my mind, thinking about how quickly things had gone from preparing for our planned trip to Lahore to another hospital dash, thanks to Saleem's mother and her poisonous lies. Something stirred within me and I suddenly knew that if I lost my baby, I would never forgive either of them.

Fortunately, the same members of staff were on duty at the hospital and remembered me from my visit just over a week ago.

"Did you rest as we advised?" the doctor asked.

Before I could answer, Saleem cut in. "Yes, she's done nothing strenuous and my mother even cooked and cleaned for her," he said.

If he was expecting praise for his mother, he wasn't getting it from this doctor.

"Well, it's a small price to pay for the health of her grandchild, isn't it?" she answered, eyeing him frostily with a small smile.

I was told to undress and put on a hospital gown so that the doctor and consultant could examine me. A nurse began setting up the equipment to do an ultrasound and listen for a heartbeat. As I undressed, I noticed there were bruises on my leg, which I presumed were from when I collapsed on the floor or while Saleem was kicking me. The doctor had also spotted them and tactfully suggested Saleem leave the room whilst she examined me.

"How did you get those bruises?" she asked me, gently.

"I think I fell when I was feeling faint. That's when the bleeding started as well," I answered, unable to meet her eyes.

There was a pause, during which the doctor appeared to be thinking what to say next or how to say it.

"Listen," she said, eventually. "We get a lot of cases like this here, but now you're pregnant, you've got to look after your baby and that means telling the truth."

As I turned my face away from her, the tears began flowing and I yearned to be in my mother's arms, for her to comfort me and stroke my hair, gestures I had taken for granted over the years. When was the last time anyone had shown me genuine love on that scale?

I decided that although this doctor wasn't a relative, she was, at least, someone I could trust and came clean about the events of the evening. She listened patiently as I explained that I'd fainted after Saleem had screamed and sworn at me because his mother said she'd had to cook and clean.

She digested this information and then looked me straight in the eye.

"Listen, it's not my job to give out advice, but it's worth bearing in mind that many mothers-in-law are reluctant to let go of their sons," she said, softly. "You have no family here, so you need to be a bit clever in front of your husband and his mother."

I told her we were on our way to Lahore and that everything had been fine until his mother-in-law opened her mouth. She seemed to take this in, although made no comment.

"Your baby is fine and the bleeding is nothing to worry about. It's due to the umbilical cord issue that we noted before," she said. "Just be careful, continue to rest and try to avoid becoming stressed. I'll give you an injection and some medication, which will help."

The doctor called Saleem back in and told him that she'd examined me and that the baby was fine. "It's important that your wife avoids becoming anxious or she risks losing the baby," she told him. "Taking her to Lahore would be good for both of them."

As she finished talking, Saleem's mother rushed into the room, sobbing, followed by Adam.

"What's happened? How is my daughter? I was so worried," she said, tears streaming down her face.

All for the benefit of the doctor and her son, I thought grimly.

Luckily, I knew one of them wouldn't be taken in by her theatrics.

"Your daughter-in-law's fine," the doctor said. "But she must rest and avoid any stress. I've advised your son to take her to Lahore."

14
Perfected in Pain

We travelled to Lahore on a packed coach, with Saleem and I barely speaking. The journey took over two hours, but air conditioning and a TV screen showing Indian movies helped pass the time.

My head was still reeling from events of the week just gone, making it difficult to focus on anything else. As the coach entered Lahore and the huge, red-bricked Badshahi Mosque came into view, I forgot my problems for a few minutes, transfixed, imagining myself back in the era of the Mughal Empire.

Lahore had a different ambience that I'd been keen to revisit for some time. The prospect of a week away from my in-laws had lifted my spirits, although inevitably I was worried about Saleem's temper and how he was going to treat me during our trip.

Eventually, the coach came to a halt and we all made our way down the steps while the driver jumped down and began taking the luggage from the hold and putting it on the ground for us to collect. I stood back and waited for Saleem to find our bags, relieved to be in the open air. The heat that greeted me though was made worse by the large shawl Saleem expected me to wear over my head and shoulders when we were out. I was conscious that my mother and sisters had never covered their hair at home, but thought that perhaps in Pakistan this requirement to look 'respectful' was taken more seriously. I wasn't prepared to risk disobeying Saleem, having witnessed his temper tantrums becoming more frequent of late, so thought it best to assume the role of obedient wife in the circumstances.

Saleem waved down a taxi to take us to Lahore Cantonment, a garrison where one of his friends had arranged for us to stay. The room in the army mess was smaller than I would've liked and we were sharing a bathroom and kitchenette with other people, but I decided these were a small price to pay for a week away from my husband's family. Saleem told me that he was going out for 10 minutes to catch up with his friends, leaving me to unpack and find my way around.

Exhausted and thirsty, I was desperate for a cold drink, but unable to find a fridge, I eventually decided to freshen up and rest.

Before I knew it, fatigue took over and I fell into a deep sleep, only to be woken a couple of hours later by a loud clattering. Saleem had stumbled into the room and was trying to catch his balance, laughing to himself. To my horror, I realized he was drunk. Slurring his words, he told me he'd been drinking whisky with his friends along the corridor.

"We just got carried away," he said, shrugging his shoulders and fixing me with glassy, blood-shot eyes and a lop-sided smile. "I've been drinking since I was 17 and I guess I find it hard to stop."

I decided that now wasn't the time to discuss his drinking, even though I was upset.

"Saleem, I need water and something to eat. I'm really thirsty and hungry," I said.

Saleem telephoned through to the mess kitchen and asked for some food and water to be brought to our room. While we waited for it to arrive, I went to the bathroom, performed my ablutions and prepared to read my *Maghrib* prayers. Knowing my husband was sinning and drunk heightened my need to connect with God.

With these thoughts making my head spin, I performed my prayers, bowing down before God. Tearfully, I asked Him what I'd done wrong to find myself in this situation, since my belief at that time was that God would give you a life partner who was a reflection of yourself.

My religious knowledge was limited, although I was able to pray and read in Arabic, but on that particular day I cried out to Him, opening myself up completely. I remembered a passage from the Qur'an.

And of His signs is that He created for you from yourselves mates that you may find tranquillity in them; and He placed between you affection and mercy. Indeed in that are signs for a people who give thought…

It made me think that here I was, with a man who was nothing like me, someone who drank and hit a woman. *How has it come to this?* I mused. *Why must I be married to this man and face these challenges? And why are You making me suffer, God?*

Just at that moment Rumi's words floated into my mind – 'Maybe you're searching from the branches for what only appears in the root' – but before I could reflect on it further, the cook arrived with vegetable curry, fresh chapatis, fruit and water. Ravenous, I sat down and ate whilst Saleem listened to music with a glass of whisky in his hand. He seemed absorbed in the songs, eyes closed and shaking his head to the rhythm. The gulf between us had never been wider; we were both hungry, but for such different things.

The next day, I woke up and washed, keen to get out of the room and do some sight-seeing. Saleem said we'd have breakfast and then visit Shalimar Gardens, before doing a site tour of Mughal history, which he knew I loved.

While we were eating breakfast in the mess, his mother called. I could tell from his responses that she was asking how I was.

"*Ami jaan* wants to speak to you and find out how you are," he said, handing me the phone.

"*Assalam alaikum,*" I said.

"How are you, my dear? Are you well?" she asked. "Is my son taking good care of you? When are you coming back?"

We'd barely left and she was already asking when we'd be home.

I was digesting the questions she was firing at me when I realized she'd already moved on to another subject.

"A sensible wife and daughter doesn't share her problems with her family, especially her parents, since they'll only get upset and there's not much they can do," she said.

I knew that she was sending me a message, warning me not to discuss what was happening within my marriage and at her house with my family. Even though I'd put some distance between us, she'd still managed to cast a shadow over our trip and dampen my first day, I thought, bitterly.

I finished my breakfast, which was a delicious spicy omelette and went to get my bag, checking off everything I needed for the day: wet wipes, mineral water, mosquito repellent and sunscreen. Saleem put on his sunglasses and we walked outside, where his friend's driver was waiting to give us a lift. I knew not to mention Saleem's drinking from the previous night and instead allowed him to start talking about Akbar the Great and the Mughal Empire, which was founded in the Indian subcontinent in 1526. I adored this part of history and listened intently as Saleem talked me through the era, from the days of the first emperor, Babur, who reigned from 1526 until 1530 and onwards to his successors, including Humayun, Akbar, Jahangir, Shah Jahan and Aurangzeb. My favourite was Shah Jahan because of his incredible architecture, especially his contribution in the form of the Taj Mahal, which was built for his beloved wife, Mumtaz Mahal. I saw this as the epitome of romantic gestures. No wonder his reign was regarded as the Golden Age of the Mughal Empire, I thought.

I felt as if I was stepping back in history, not only to a time that fascinated me, but also a period not so long ago in my own life – my time at university, when I studied the Mughals as part of my art research. I'd loved my university course and knew that this trip was now giving me a welcome boost of creative energy.

As we moved along the congested roads of Lahore, under its polluted skies and past the huge buildings, I became increasingly aware of the scale of this huge city, which eclipsed Faisalabad so easily. The influence of the British Rule in India was heavily in evidence, while the architecture of buildings such as Punjab University, Lahore Museum and the Aitchison College was outstanding.

I took photo after photo of these glorious landmarks as we drove past them, thankful that we had Saleem's late father's camera with us to capture the scenes. As the driver parked by Shalimar Gardens, I jumped out of the car like an excited child, desperate to get my first glimpse of the scenes I'd seen in countless articles when researching the influence of Persian gardens for my studies.

The Shalimar Gardens were laid out as a Persian paradise, with the aim of creating a representation of utopia on earth, where humans could coexist in perfect harmony with nature. Work began on them in 1641, during the reign of Shah Jahan and was completed the following year. In 1981 the gardens were made a UNESCO World Heritage Site, in recognition of their part in exemplifying a Mughal garden design at its best.

Saleem's friend had arranged for a guide to take us around. As we toured the site and talked about the gardens and their place in history, I realized that Saleem was surprised at how much I knew and the passion I felt for this subject. Perhaps this day would serve as a reminder that I had some intellect and wasn't just his wife and a mother-to-be, I thought.

We began making our way through the various terraces, with the tour guide talking us through the features and characteristics of each one. The Shalimar Gardens contain the most elaborate waterworks of any Mughal garden, featuring 410 fountains that are showcased in wide, marble pools known as *hauz*. They are also home to five glorious water cascades, including the Sawan Bhadon. Aside from their beauty, the gardens are also delightfully cool, thanks to the dense foliage and water they contain, meaning they provide welcome respite from the city's blistering summer temperatures, which can easily edge toward 49 degrees Celsius.

I was thankful for the *chadar*, a large cotton shawl, that I'd draped over my head, which was protecting me from the fierce sun, even though I was still getting used to the idea of dressing so modestly.

The guide's English was excellent and I found the tour fascinating, especially when we came to the famous fountain with marble candleholders behind it.

After we'd finished looking around, Saleem and I sat in the shade and had our lunch. I felt more relaxed than I had for weeks and was reluctant to break the spell. Yet, before long, Saleem said we'd need to make a move, since we were expected for dinner later at the home of one of his distant cousins.

When we got back to the mess, I thanked Saleem for making an effort to give me such an amazing day. "Welcome," he replied, with a smile. "Rest and get ready for the evening while I go and play cards with the guys."

Feeling content, I went off for a nap, hoping that perhaps my life was getting back on track and that maybe God had answered my prayers in my time of need. I woke from my nap and took my time getting ready, choosing a pretty outfit, pinning up my hair and putting on some makeup.

Eventually, Saleem came back to get changed. Once he'd washed and put on the clothes I'd got ready for him, we left for his cousin's house. The family were incredibly welcoming and couldn't do enough for us. Saleem's aunt went out of her way to make sure I was comfortable – nothing at all like my in-laws, I thought, grimly.

I calculated that her children were of a similar age to me and once we started chatting, we found that we got on really well.

"You are so lucky," they said to Saleem. "Shama is amazing, so lovely and beautiful."

"I thought she was the lucky one to have me," Saleem replied with a smile.

Laughter filled the room and, once again, I thought what a delightful family. As we left, they showered us with gifts and goodbyes, telling us to come again soon.

"Weren't they lovely, making such an effort and fussing over us?" I said to Saleem, as we made our way back to the mess.

"Why are you bothering about them?" he snapped back.

"I'm just saying I appreciated the trouble they went to for us," I replied, surprised at his reaction.

"Well, don't get too friendly with them," he answered. "Listen, in this country they want to make friends with you because they know you're from England and have sisters. They just want their sons to marry your sisters."

"What?" I exclaimed. "They never asked about my family or told me about their sons! What are you talking about?" But I could tell from his expression that the subject was closed.

Our second day in Lahore involved more sight-seeing, including visits to Jahanghir's Tomb and Hiran Minar, much to my delight and dinner out. Saleem seemed to be making a special effort to be the husband I'd hoped for – attentive and communicative. In the evening, we went to a park, walking and talking. The conversation inevitably turned to the baby and possible names. He chatted animatedly about boys' names, but seemed less interested when I suggested what to call the baby if it was a girl. Having time alone as a couple also allowed us to get to know more about each other. It was in Lahore that I discovered my husband was allergic to cheese, not too keen on fish and that black was his favourite colour for clothes. I didn't have him all to myself though. Every morning, at 8am on the dot, his mother would phone.

The wound on my chest was healed, but had left a prominent red scar. Looking at it on our second day Saleem asked, "Is it healing? Does it still hurt you?"

"Not on the outside, but in my heart, yes," I answered, surprised he'd broached the subject. "I mean I was hurt, devastated, in fact, that you could behave in that way," I continued.

"This is why I drink, to take my mind off everything," he replied, after a pause. "And there's something else." His voice faded and I turned to him, expectantly. "I'm not well," he continued. "I don't have long to live."

There was a silence as I tried to make sense of what he was saying.

"What do you mean?" I asked him.

"I'm telling you I won't be around forever, but I can't bear to talk about it…" came the answer.

Once again, Saleem had sent my head reeling. I didn't know whether to ask more questions or let him be. Did he have cancer or another serious illness? Or could it be that he was being manipulative, trying to make me feel sorry for him?

I knew I was out of my depth, trying to make sense of it all and yet, above all, I felt an obligation to do my best to make my marriage work.

Enjoying some privacy and quality time together meant that I'd made some progress in learning to understand my husband's ways and character traits. I recalled what the doctor had said to me about being diplomatic and wondered if there was any way that I could bring up the issue of going to my brother Fahad's wedding in the UK. I was desperate to go, but couldn't think how to ask. I also wanted to confide in Saleem about my unhappiness in Faisalabad, even when he came back from Lahore at the weekends. I yearned to tell him that I felt he was a son and brother first and a husband second and that his behaviour changed when he was with his family. But I knew I needed to find the right moment to bring up these sensitive issues.

On our final day, we paid a visit to one of my favourite parts of Lahore, the Badshahi Mosque. Red-bricked and huge in scale, the mosque was a truly formidable sight to behold, Staring at it, I found it incredible to think that people were able to accomplish such a feat by building this towering place of worship hundreds of years ago. Everything about this and the other glorious buildings we visited, from the Sheesh Mahal and Diwan-i-Am to the Mughals' rooms, seemed to transport me back in time.

My wonderful week in Lahore was drawing to an end and as we made the journey back to Faisalabad, I felt like Cinderella just before the clock strikes midnight, with my return to servant duty. Sadness engulfed me as we drew nearer to Saleem's house. As if sensing that something was amiss, he turned to me and asked me how I was feeling and whether the sickness and bleeding had stopped.

I told him everything was fine and that I was feeling much healthier, having eaten well throughout the week in Lahore. I was prepared to put to one side the awful things Saleem had done to me because he'd been decent for a few days. Deep down, I knew this wasn't good enough and wondered why I was being so accepting of his behaviour. Was it vulnerability or desperation? Or was it because I felt committed to the man I'd married, having made my marriage vows? I simply didn't know.

As we entered the house, we were greeted by Saleem's mother, who hugged her son as if he'd been away for years. She even greeted me with respect, which was a surprise.

"The house felt so empty without you both, we really missed you," she said. "I've cooked your favourite biryani and for my daughter her favourite kebabs."

Her reactions seemed over the top and she was being suspiciously nice. Saleem gave her an account of what we did in Lahore, telling her how much I'd enjoyed it and how healthy I felt. Hearing him share our news with me by his side made me feel comfortable and content, like a proper wife, I thought.

We spent the next day at Saleem's ancestral village, where we met some more of his relatives, who were also hospitable and kind, like his family had been in Lahore. Saleem liked to visit the graves of his father and grandparents and pay his respects when he went to the village, which I found touching.

Then came the day I dreaded. Saleem had returned to Lahore alone to look for work and, sure enough, early in the morning, there was a loud knock on my door.

"Why aren't you getting up?" came my mother-in-law's voice.

With Saleem gone, she was back to her best.

I walked slowly to the door and opened it. "I've taken some medication and it's made me drowsy. I was resting," I answered.

"You have to be up for your prayers and then there's the milk to boil," she replied, sharply.

The milk was delivered regularly, fresh from the buffalo, so needed to be boiled, cooled and chilled before we could use it. Wearily, I showered and started my daily chores, which ranged from cleaning the floors and cooking to washing and ironing the clothes. We were back to the old routine, except now I was five months' pregnant and struggling more than before with the heavy workload.

A routine visit to the clinic a few weeks on indicated that I wasn't gaining weight and that the baby wasn't growing at a satisfactory rate, with the result that I was immediately sent to the hospital for a check-up. There, Saleem and I were told in no uncertain terms that I needed bed rest and that if I didn't take better care of myself, I'd be admitted again.

The journey home was awful, with Saleem shouting and swearing at me for not looking after myself. As soon as we entered the house, he called his mother over.

"Look at this woman, Mother," he said, gesturing wildly at me. "She is nothing more than a burden, trying to make us look bad. She won't take the doctor's advice and rest in bed, so now the baby is suffering."

As he spoke, he grabbed my upper arm in a tight, clamp-like grip. Hesitantly, I began to answer. "But, your mother wakes me up every day at half five in the morning to pray and begin the housework," I said, looking at him. "How am I supposed to rest?"

His face darkened with anger. "Are you are saying this is my mother's fault?" he spat.

"Are you that stupid?"

His hand flew across my cheek, with a slap hard enough to send me to the floor.

"Saleem, what are you doing?" I heard his mother's voice above me. "She is going to blame you, are you stupid? Not her face."

I was lying on my side, curled around my stomach to best protect my baby. As the tears began to fall, I realized that no one was coming to help me. Slowly, I rose and, without looking at either of them, I took myself off to the bathroom to wash my face. I looked at my reflection in the mirror, my cheek an angry red where I'd been hit. I curled up in a ball on the bathroom floor, crying uncontrollably, desperately trying to think about what I could do. Ideas whirled through my head. Maybe I could try to get hold of my brother Sajjad, but I had no idea how to put such a plan into action. My only solace at that moment was

Rumi, whose words 'Just as clay needs to go through intense heat to be strong, love can only be perfected in pain' came to my mind.

While I was in the bathroom, the kindly woman from next door had popped in to visit. Saleem's mother shouted out to me to come and prepare the tea, pulling me out of my musings. Wearily, I made my way to the kitchen, prepared the tea and took it through to the veranda, together with a plate of biscuits.

The neighbour, or Aunty as we called her, stared at me in shock. "Oh my! What happened to her face? How did she get those marks?" she asked Saleem's mother.

"Oh, she stood on a chair to clean the fans and fell. We told her not to, but she insisted. Saleem was so worried, but she refused to go to hospital," Saleem's mother said, shrugging, with a fake smile of concern. Turning to me, she continued, "*Beta*, you really must be careful in your condition, you know you can easily hurt your baby."

I went back into the kitchen, unable to listen anymore and certainly not prepared to play along with this woman's charade. As I washed up, I realized I'd never been around anyone who was able to lie so blatantly and as easily as my mother-in-law.

While I was cleaning up in the kitchen, Aunty brought the tray into the kitchen. "You should have left it, it's fine," I said, taking it from her with a small smile.

"*Beta*, you must put some cream on your face or go to the doctor," she said, kindly. Then she lowered her voice and moved closer to me. "There are many stories about your in-laws in the neighbourhood and how they treat their daughters-in-law," she whispered. "The first one left and divorced her husband after he burnt her with a cigarette."

At that point, I made a decision. "Aunty, listen," I whispered urgently. "I'm going to write a letter to my brother, put it in a bag and throw it onto your roof. Will you post it for me? I can't ask these people to post a letter for me. They don't even let me breathe."

"Of course," she replied, concern etched on her face. "Your parents should have found out more about this family before they arranged your marriage. They might be my neighbours, but they're not good people."

A mix of emotions washed over me; relief that I'd found a kind, sympathetic ear and hope that I might find a way out of this unbearable situation.

"Aunty what does '*khanzeer*' mean?" I asked.

She looked at me, shocked. "Why are you asking?" she said. "It's a terrible word."

"My husband uses it a lot when he's speaking to me, so I wondered…" I trailed off, miserably.

"It is so bad, *beta*, it means whore," she said, embarrassed.

Later that evening, Saleem came into the room and looked at my bruised and swollen face, yet made no apology. Any idea I'd had that he could change was naivete on my part. He told me he'd be getting the coach for Lahore in the early hours of the morning. Where once I'd have been sorry to see him go, my thoughts were different this time. *Good,* I thought. *I don't want to be around you and this will give me time to write to my brother.*

My heart was thumping and the adrenalin was rushing through my body, but I knew that sending a letter home was what I needed to do. I managed to sneak a roll of toilet paper into my room and, using my eyeliner, since I didn't have a pen to hand, began writing.

'Sajjad, please get me out of this hell. These people will kill my baby and me. I don't want Mum and Dad to know, but please help me. I can't answer the phone or call... HELP!'

On a separate card, ripped from a tissue box, I wrote the address for Aunty and then I put them both in a small carrier bag, together with a stone to weigh everything down.

Later on in the day, when everyone napped, I went to the roof and looked down onto Aunty's veranda. First, I threw a few stones, to catch her attention, followed by the bag containing the letter and address.

Three days passed, with no sign of Aunty, leaving me unsure whether she'd done anything with my letter or even received it safely. By now, my brother Fahad's wedding had taken place without me, a miserable reminder of just how cut off I was from my family. Finally, six days after I threw the bag onto her veranda, Aunty paid us a visit.

I served tea and waited patiently, in the hope that we might grab a moment together alone in the kitchen. However, I didn't need to wait.

"You know, I can't believe how many things get blown onto our veranda when it's windy," she said, casting me a quick look.

"Yes," I murmured, joining in the conversation. "It must get really dirty when the weather's like that."

"Oh yes, but sometimes it's interesting what we find; clothes and even shopping bags!"

I started to laugh politely, delighted that she'd received my letter, but nervous that my mother-in-law might become suspicious if she said too much. Saleem's mother kept her chatting for half an hour, but finally the moment came when I was asked to see Aunty to the door. "You got my letter, then?" I whispered.

"Yes, I was trying to tell you. My husband posted it yesterday."

"OK, thank God, thank God. Just seven days for it to reach the UK and my brother will know what's happening," I whispered, trying to hold back the emotion I felt.

The next week was pure torture, waiting to hear from Sajjad and working under the watchful eye of my mother-in-law. My health was deteriorating and I was in pain much of the time. One afternoon, I began bleeding again. Saleem was away, so I went to find his mother.

"I need to go to the hospital," I told her, panicking.

"Oh, come on, please, not more of these dramas," she answered.

"It's not a drama. I'm bleeding. The baby – your grandchild – is at risk," I replied, distraught.

She ignored me, leaving me feeling helpless and unable to do anything until Saleem arrived that evening. It seemed that every time he came through the door, there was a problem, I thought bitterly, but at that point I couldn't worry about anyone other than myself.

"Saleem, I'm sick. I need to go to the doctor's," I told him immediately. "I'm in pain and bleeding again. I'm also feeling dizzy. I really need to go right now."

Before I could say anything else, his mother had interrupted me.

"My son has barely put his foot in the door and this drama queen is trying to stress him out," she shouted angrily to no one in particular.

"It's his baby. He needs to know," I retorted, concern for my baby overriding any fear I had of her. "I've been telling you all day, I'm bleeding." I turned to Saleem, desperate. "She didn't understand or listen," I said. "I need to go." It appeared that I'd won, for once and we left for the doctor.

The message there was the same. "Sir, I told you that your wife must have bed rest," the doctor said, resignedly. "The skin on her hands and feet are rough, indicating that she's been working, not resting. I told you last time that she needed to relax and be stress-free." He informed Saleem that they were going to admit me on and off until delivery to monitor me and warned him they could be forced to perform a caesarean section if the dizziness and blackouts continued.

"Doctor, are you sure?" Saleem asked.

"Sir, I'm a doctor. I know my job," the doctor answered, politely. "All this could have been avoided if your wife had rested. I don't pretend to know what's going on at home, but it's clear your wife hasn't been doing that."

Saleem then called his mother and told her that I was being admitted for two weeks. While I could only catch parts of the conversation, I realized they were discussing hospital fees and what a burden I'd become. I imagined they were also considering that the bill was likely to rise from now on.

We popped home, so I could pack. I put my essentials in a bag as quickly as possible, desperate to leave again and get back to the hospital, away from my mother-in-law, who sat in her chair cursing me under her breath.

When Saleem came to visit me in hospital that evening, he said his mother was unable to join him because his sisters were visiting. Of course, I was delighted that she hadn't come, but also felt sure that she and her daughters were plotting something.

The doctor came to chat to us and asked Saleem to sit down. He had a serious look on his face. "Sir, do you really not care about the wellbeing of your wife and baby?" he asked. "Her health is very fragile. She needs to look after herself. There are risks to both your wife's health and that of the baby. I cannot let her go home until her blood pressure and protein levels are stable. We also need to check to see if she has symptoms of preeclampsia."

"What's that?" Saleem asked, looking alarmed.

"It's when the levels of protein in the urine are too high, but let's not worry about that until we know more," the doctor answered. He then told Saleem where to go to pick up his bill and the prescription for my medication.

I already knew that the medical fees were a contentious issue and was acutely aware that Saleem wasn't working at present, but I put all this to the back of my mind. As far as I was concerned, I was his wife and we'd made vows to be there for each other in sickness and in health.

Saleem came into the room with the medication and I decided that now was the moment to tell him some home truths. "I wish you'd listen to me. I don't play games. With people from England, what you see is what you get," I said. "I'm back in hospital again and if anything happens to my baby, I will never forgive you."

With that, I turned on my side, hoping that he'd decide against conversation. Saleem was pacing up and down the room, silently. After a while, he came toward me. "Please, just rest and look after yourself," he begged. "I'm going to go home to get my things. I've left some money for you to get food from the canteen." For once, he looked confused and lost, very different from the charming, well-spoken handsome man who'd swept me off my feet when I first met him.

After he left, I dozed off and was delighted to wake up ravenous. Dinner soon arrived and I was enjoying the privilege of eating in peace, when the doctor arrived. This time, he had a team of colleagues with him. "Where's your husband?" the doctor asked.

"Is everything okay?" I asked, fear welling up inside me. "You can talk to me, its fine."

"Madam, we prefer to wait for your husband," the doctor insisted, gently.

"Is the baby okay? Please tell me," I begged, distraught.

"The baby is fine for now and you are stable, but the tests show you have preeclampsia," he began explaining.

At that moment, Saleem walked in, followed by his mother and sisters.

"Is everything okay?" he asked, looking at the group of medics.

"Could your family stay in the waiting room?" the doctor asked.

There was concern on my mother-in-law's face as she took in the scene. "Is everything OK or not?" she asked Saleem.

"Mother, you need to wait outside," he said firmly. "Once I know, I'll tell you."

When the family had been ushered out, the doctor turned to Saleem. "Sir, your wife has preeclampsia," he said. "It's very serious and is putting her health at risk." They went through the details and Saleem, looking concerned, asked one question after another. "It's not clear what causes preeclampsia, but your wife's wellbeing and the development of the baby are our priority," the doctor told him. "It's important we keep your wife in hospital for now."

After they'd left, Saleem turned to me. "I think its best if you stay in hospital," he said, finally, patting my shoulder. "The doctors know what they're doing. Your health and that of the baby are what's important." He left to get his family and, almost immediately, his mother came rushing toward me, crying and hugging me as if I was at death's door.

"My poor *beta*. May *Allah* be with you. I think people have put the evil eye on you," she exclaimed. She took 10 rupees out of her bag and began swirling them over my head, saying it was my *Sadaqah*, a voluntary act of charity she would donate on my behalf.

All these theatrics for her son's benefit, I thought. Behind her, Saleem's sisters were praying for me and the baby, as if we were unlikely to survive. They stayed for a few hours and then went home, while Saleem remained behind, telling his mother that the doctors needed to see us both in the morning.

When I woke, Saleem was sitting nearby. Realizing I'd stirred, he turned to me. "We were thinking. You still have the open ticket from when your brother was getting married, but you never used it," he said. "Why don't you go to England to have the baby?"

I couldn't believe what I was hearing. Then it dawned on me. Of course, Sajjad must have received my letter and acted on it.

"Your brother called," Saleem continued, as if reading my mind. "He said he planned to visit, but we told him it might be better if you went to England to give birth. We remembered that you said treatment is free there and my mother is worried that they may give you a caesarean section here just to make money. Unfortunately, it happens. Having babies is big business."

There was a pause while I let this wonderful news sink in. "You should go soon," Saleem continued. "After all, you can't fly once you reach the seven-month mark."

15
Love Is a Mirror

My family had sent an open ticket for Fahad's wedding, so all we needed to do was to set a date for me to fly. I'd been distraught at not being allowed to attend the celebration, but now the ticket was my means of escape back to England. Saleem made the necessary arrangements and told me I was booked to fly back on February 21st. He called my parents and told them. As expected, they were overjoyed that I'd be with them soon and would remain in the UK for the birth of their first grandchild. I felt the same, but still couldn't quite believe it was going to happen.

I was so homesick. I had no sense of belonging at Saleem's house and had never accepted it as my home. The sense of foreboding I had had from the time I'd first met Saleem had come to pass. My gut feeling that something terrible was going to happen hadn't been wrong. If only I'd just listened to myself. I'd questioned everything to do with his behaviour and that of his family right from the start, yet had been too naïve to understand the significance of what I was witnessing and experiencing. Was this my way out?

The entire plan seemed too good to be true. To reassure myself, I kept reminding myself that Saleem's family had their reasons for sending me to the UK. They weren't prepared to pay for my treatment and hospitalization and my parents had sent a free ticket, so the plan suited them. Still, I knew I wouldn't quite believe I was going until I'd boarded the plane.

I desperately wanted to buy some gifts for everyone, knowing I'd feel awful returning empty-handed, but I wasn't sure how to broach the subject with Saleem. Would he lash out at me if I asked? I knew there was no point whatsoever in approaching his mother, but maybe I could try a different tactic with my husband.

I chose my moment carefully, waiting until we were alone. "Saleem, you know how highly my family think of you and respect you?" I began. "I was thinking I could take them some gifts and say you sent them."

"That's a good idea," he replied, thoughtfully. "They'd feel pleased that I gave them something and I'd score some points with them for sure." I couldn't believe that I was learning to be clever with my husband, as the doctor had diplomatically called it, but here it was in action, working very well!

The next day Saleem took me to the Ghanta Ghar Bazaar. Built during the British rule, the shopping hub was dominated by a central clock tower, with the bazaars divided around it in the shape of the Union Jack flag. I bought some traditional outfits for my sisters and brothers, together with jewellery and other accessories. Feeling the heat, I asked Saleem if we could head back.

When we arrived home with the shopping, Saleem's mother immediately wanted to know what we'd bought and how much everything had cost. I was desperate to go and lie down and didn't feel up to handling her questions, but was resigned to answering them when Saleem stepped in. "Mom, I think Shama's tired," he said, gently. "Maybe she can show you everything after she's had a rest?"

Wow, I thought, my husband had finally stood up for me in front of his mother! I tactfully left the room and went for a lie down. Later, revived and unable to control my excitement, I decided to begin packing. Saleem's mother said I couldn't take the jewellery that my parents gave me because the UK wasn't safe and, since I was pregnant, it was better to be cautious. It didn't occur to me to question this or ask where my jewellery was. All I cared about was going home – nothing else mattered.

Everything I was taking went into my case, including my gifts, which I decided, in a moment of rebellion, not to show my mother-in-law. I was desperately counting the days, hours and minutes until I could leave this hellhole. Although I was travelling thousands of miles from Saleem's family, I'd be taking some mental scars with me to the UK. Perhaps I'd have the opportunity to bury them there, I thought, hopefully.

Saleem and I went on to the veranda, where I tried to keep us cool with a hand fan made from dried grass. *It would be good to get away from the heat for the last few months of my pregnancy,* I thought.

After what seemed an eternity, the day of my departure arrived. Saleem came back from Lahore the night before to a house in a state of flux, with me trying to contain my excitement and his mother agitated about my departure. Saleem took my case for me and called a taxi. While I fetched my shawl, his uncle, who was a fisherman, arrived with a cooler containing prawns and fish. These were the finest from his catch, he told me proudly and he'd be delighted if I'd take them with me to the UK. I didn't want to tell him that we could buy great seafood in the UK and my heart sank at the thought of having to carry them the whole way there.

Rumi's poem, titled *The Song of the Reed* kept entering my mind. My brother had once explained to me how a reed had been taken from the flower bed and attached to a stringed instrument, but yearned to return home, hence its sound was always melancholy. I was the string at this moment, desperate to go home.

When it was time to leave, I walked quickly down the steps of my mother-in-law's house and headed to the car without a backward glance. I was so happy that even Saleem's lecture on the way to the airport couldn't dampen my mood.

"You know this is your home now, right? You're going to England only to visit. It's not your home – home is where your husband is," he said. "So, go. Take care of your health, have the baby, and come back."

"Aren't you coming for the delivery?" I asked, shocked. I'd assumed Saleem would join me near my due date.

"How can we afford for me to come too?"

"But my parents sent you a ticket as well, didn't they?"

There was a silence while Saleem gave this some thought. "I'll see if I can get a visa, but I'm not sure," he said. "My mother will need me here." I was relieved rather than upset that Saleem was unsure about following me to the UK. More often than not, I felt on edge in his presence.

At the airport, my luggage was checked in and my ticket and passport were in my hand, alongside the cumbersome cooler containing the seafood. Saleem turned to me. "OK, then, I hope you have a safe flight," he said, a little awkwardly, "call me when you arrive." With that, somewhat bizarrely, he shook my hand. He was sending me across the world and hadn't even asked me if I needed anything or given me any money.

The porters took the cooler from me, thank goodness, so that I only had my handbag to carry. I breezed through passport control and up the steps of the plane. Once in my seat, I took a long, deep breath. "Thank you, God...thank you," I whispered, as the plane took off, overwhelmed with relief, "*Alhamdullilah*!"

Luckily, the plane wasn't full, so I had room to make myself comfortable for the flight. I wasn't keen on flying, and my nervousness usually kept me on edge, but overcome with exhaustion I soon fell into a deep sleep and only woke up when we were about to land.

Once we touched down in Manchester, I couldn't wait to disembark. As I stepped onto the tarmac, my emotions got the better of me and I collapsed to the ground with relief, assuming a *sujood* position, as if in prayer, and kissed the concrete, before bursting into tears. The security guard ran up to me, concerned.

"Madam, what are you doing?" he asked.

I gazed up at him, tears rolling down my face. "I'm so lucky to be home and I'm so, so, so happy..." I said, between sobs.

"Madam, you can't stop like this," he said, gently, "there are still people who need to disembark. Please move along."

I dragged myself up and shakily began walking towards passport control. It was still sinking in that I was finally back and would have my baby in England, surrounded by my family. Bit by bit, my spirits were lifting.

I collected my case and navigated my trolley, complete with the cooler, into the arrivals hall. I immediately spotted my sisters and my extended family, including aunts, uncles, and cousins, all of whom had come to meet me. Frantically waving and armed with flowers, they came running toward me. I was engulfed in a group hug, with my sisters whispering into my hair, and no one wanting to let go. It was all too much, and I burst into tears, sobbing uncontrollably.

When we finally moved apart, my sisters stepped back and looked at me. Their smiles quickly gave way to looks of concern and my aunt took my hand.

"You're so weak, my dear, and you've lost so much weight," she said, putting her arm around my bony shoulder.

It was true. I'd lost two stone since they'd last seen me, despite being six months' pregnant.

"Yes, I've had terrible morning sickness," I said. Now wasn't the time to talk about the other problems that had contributed to my poor health and left me barely weighing seven stone.

We got into the car and headed onto the motorway. I greedily soaked in the English countryside, as if seeing it for the first time, while my family talked over each other, excitedly. My sisters commented on the fact that I was quiet, asking if I was tired, probably because I'd always been the family chatterbox. Granted, I felt exhausted, but I was also reflecting on the fact that I'd escaped and that each mile on the motorway, past the fields and housing estates and service stations, was taking me closer to my parents' house, my old home.

My mother had stayed behind, busily preparing food and getting my room ready, excited that I would be giving birth in the UK and bringing their first grandchild into the family home.

We parked in the drive and there was Mom, standing at the gate, her red cheeks and nose signalling that she'd been crying. I climbed out of the car as quickly as I could and we embraced, both of us in tears and unwilling to let the other go.

"Thank God, you're home," she said, stroking my face.

I wasn't sure at this point who knew about the letter I'd sent to Sajjad, so I didn't reply, simply smiled and said how lovely it was to see her.

It was 7pm UK time, so we all piled into the lounge and Mum brought drinks in, after which Dad called everyone to the table to eat. I was desperate to change and asked Mum if I could go upstairs to freshen up.

"Of course," she answered. "You're in the master bedroom."

I climbed the stairs, followed by my little cousin, Anum, and as we entered the room I breathed in sharply. My parents had decorated the entire room and put a beautiful crib in the corner, complete with baby toys. Tears rolled down my face once again. I couldn't help but compare this luxury to what I'd left back in Pakistan. Mum had put pyjamas and all my favourite things in the drawers. Guiltily, I saw that she'd put photos from my wedding on the dresser, probably thinking I'd be pleased. I moved away from them quickly and went to the attached bathroom, washed and changed into my new pyjamas.

"Hurry up, they're are all waiting for you in the dining room," Anum said.

Our dining room was my mother's favourite place to gather us all together. She loved nothing better than having everyone seated around the table to eat and spend quality time as a family. However, this time it was different for me, as I was the guest of honour. The meal was a celebration of my return, complete with

VIP treatment and my favourite dishes. As soon as my mother brought the food out, the memories of her wonderful cooking overtook me and I grabbed the food with my hands, like someone who has been starved for weeks. I piled my plate with chicken, kebabs and lamb chops, savouring the smell and sight of this mountain of food.

For the entire duration of my stay at Saleem's house, I hadn't touched meat. Even though I'd been instructed to take lamb and chicken from the freezer and cook it, there was only ever enough for Saleem and his brother. At the beginning, I'd asked what we would eat and was told to make some *daal*. But now, here I was, the VIP visitor, back with my family as a wife and pregnant.

I was replaying those meal-time-preparation scenes in Faisalabad in my head while stuffing food into my mouth and gulping it down when I realized that all eyes around the table were on me. Feeling compelled to explain my behaviour, I apologized and started to cry.

"I'm so sorry, it's just that I haven't eaten meat for eight months," I said, trailing off, with my eyes fixed on the mound of food in front of me.

There was a silence around the room, broken only by my stifled sobs, as my family digested this news and my mother and sisters stared at me, horrified.

"Are you okay?" my father asked, eventually.

Waves of nausea engulfed me. "I can't eat, I think I might be sick, I'm so sorry," I answered, standing up, shakily. Immediately, my sisters came to my aid and helped me upstairs to bed.

I could tell that my family sensed I was not the bubbly daughter and sister that had left all those months ago. I knew I'd been traumatized by my in-laws, but perhaps my family thought the changes they were witnessing were simply down to difficulties in adjusting to my new life abroad as a wife, a daughter-in-law and now a mother-to-be. I climbed into bed, still reflecting, but as soon as my head touched the pillow, I fell into a deep sleep.

My mother had arranged for a doctor to come and visit me first thing in the morning. I heard the knock at my bedroom door as I began to wake and jumped, thinking I was back in Faisalabad, being summoned to wake up, pray and begin cleaning.

"Shama, are you awake?" came my sister Amina's voice. "Dr Fleming has come to check you over."

I opened my eyes to find my sisters Amina and Fatima both sat on my bed, smiling. I smiled back, reassured and comforted by the care and attention I was being given by my loving family. My mum walked in with the doctor, her nose and cheeks red from crying again. The doctor examined me and said he thought it was best if I went straight to the maternity wing of the local hospital for further tests and a scan as they held no data on my pregnancy. As he was writing a referral letter, Mum said she'd take me there and began dashing around putting a bag together for me. I looked on, dazed, struggling to take everything in.

Just as we were about to leave, Saleem called. "Why didn't you call me when you arrived? My mother waited all night for you to call," he exploded. "Women like you are a waste of space."

I didn't answer back as my sisters and mother were looking on and could see the expression on my face. "I'm on my way to the hospital, Saleem," I said, quietly. "The doctor has just visited. I don't feel so good…"

"What? Why didn't you say? You…"

"I have to go. I'll call you later," I said, not wanting to hear any more, before handing the phone to my mother, who I knew would talk politely to both Saleem and his mother in the manner expected.

My father drove us to the hospital in Burnley, where a team of consultants were expecting me. They asked me questions about my pregnancy and then sent me for an ultrasound and scan. The decision was made to keep me in overnight. I was given an intravenous drip and glucose, since I was underweight.

My aunt Suraya said she would stay overnight with me. During the evening she chatted away and I could see she was doing her best to cheer me up. Deep down though, I could sense she was concerned at the huge change in her bubbly, outgoing niece. Aside from feeling the effects of the life I'd escaped from, I was also worried that she or my mother would see my scar. I knew it would destroy my mum to discover that her daughter's husband could do such a thing to his wife.

The following morning, the consultant came over with two other doctors to tell me that I might have preeclampsia, confirming the concerns of the medics in Pakistan. They said it was best if I stayed in hospital until my protein levels had normalized but reassured me that the baby was fine and growing, which lifted my mood.

I'd found time to read up a bit more about preeclampsia and knew it could be life-threatening. Characterized by high blood pressure, it usually manifested itself in or around the 20th week of pregnancy and could damage the vital organs, including the liver and kidneys. It was essential that I was carefully monitored in the last three months of my pregnancy. On the plus side, I knew I'd now be able to rest in comfort, with the support and care of my family.

That evening, while dozing in hospital, I overheard my parents mention Saleem's name, saying they thought he should be here with me. Ever the conciliator, my father was telling my mother that Saleem couldn't be expected to simply leave work, but my mother interrupted him, angrily.

"He isn't working anyway, he's just looking for a job," she retorted. "We should get him a visa to visit so at least he can fly over if need be. We can sponsor him."

I didn't speak to Saleem much over the next few weeks. Returning home, heavily pregnant, managing the complications and thinking about my married life back in Faisalabad, it was all simply too much to compute. Instead, I remained in a bubble, in my lovely room, surrounded by my family, feeling cared for, but still finding it difficult to smile, even though there were plenty of visitors, keen to catch up with me.

I soon slipped into the new routine, enveloped in the warmth of my loved ones. One day, towards the beginning of the eighth month of my pregnancy, I suddenly felt dizzy. Clinging on to the edge of my bed to keep my balance, I called out for my mother. She took one look at me and announced that she was taking me to the hospital. As we made our way there, I began to feel frightened and, for the first time since arriving in the UK, wanted Saleem by my side. My parents had applied for Saleem's visa, which he had been granted thanks to my father's sponsorship, meaning he could travel to the UK at any time.

The last time we'd spoken and I'd raised the subject, he'd said that it wasn't important in his culture for the husband to be present during a baby's birth and he'd travel over afterwards. Stunned, I couldn't understand this. Did he really not mind missing the moment our child came into the world? Apparently not.

After a few days in hospital, my blood pressure normalized and I was allowed to return home. The final few weeks of the pregnancy would prove to be difficult, not so much physically, since my weight had increased thanks to my mother's cooking and care, but rather due to my mental state. It was almost as if, now I was being looked after and feeling stronger, I felt compelled to repeatedly revisit those terrible months in Pakistan in my mind. At night I tossed and turned, experiencing one nightmare after another of my time in Faisalabad. The slightest reminder of my time there, whether a noise, smell, or vision, triggered flashbacks. I still hadn't told my mother what had happened, not wanting to burden her, but this had just made me feel worse.

I tried to focus on the birth and the excitement of preparing for the new arrival. My mother and sisters had decorated the room in neutral colours, since we didn't know whether the baby was a boy or girl, but that didn't stop my sisters and I from speculating.

As April came to an end, the familiar dizziness returned and I found myself back in hospital undergoing tests. With both my blood pressure and protein levels creeping up, the doctors decided to admit me on May 1st for a planned birth. I was to be induced and as a high-risk patient had been allocated a private room with a nurse.

The plan was for a natural birth with an epidural. While the sight of the needle was terrifying, the nurse reassured me that I'd feel no contractions and that given my condition, pain relief was the best option.

Sure enough, even though the monitor showed each contraction and my stomach tensing, I felt no pain and even began to relax, watching Eastenders with my mother and sisters. Mum made me a drink of castor oil and milk, which she said would help with the delivery. The doctors popped in from time to time and said that when I had dilated to 10cm, they'd tell me to begin pushing.

At 2pm the next day, May 2nd, my daughter came into the world. Holding her and looking at her face, I was overwhelmed and incredulous, unable to take in that Saleem and I had created this perfect little person, complete with tiny face, hands and feet. Scrutinizing her closely and smiling wryly, I realized the baby looked exactly like my in-laws. They were still managing to haunt me, despite the geographical distance between us.

My mother and sisters were jumping up and down with joy, but I simply wanted to rest. I slept from mid-afternoon until the evening, when a steady stream of visitors began arriving, bringing flowers, cuddly toys, fruit and gifts.

Mum arrived again, this time with a special nightgown for me to put on and a nightie for the baby, since everyone wanted to take photos. I wanted to call the baby Zoya, a name that perfectly reflected her cuteness and tiny features.

My mother called my mother-in-law from the hospital to share the news that Saleem was now the father of a baby girl and congratulated them.

"*Mubarak*," Mum said.

Instead of the reciprocal congratulations, my mum was met with a short silence. "We don't say *mubarak* if it's a girl. We only distribute alms and give *mubarak* for sons," I overheard my mother-in-law answering, flatly. "My son is only young and now he has aged because he has a daughter!"

My mother hung up, astounded at my mother-in-law's reaction. Perhaps, I thought, she was seeing my in-laws' true colours at last. I could hear her talking to my father in a low voice about such levels of ignorance. Around me, they forced their smiles, but I could see they were saddened by the reaction to such joyful news and trying to hide it from me.

After three days, I was allowed home and my mother told me to call Saleem and speak to him.

"How are you?" he said.

"I'm fine, how are you? When are you coming?"

"I'll see. How's everything in England?"

"Everything's good," I replied.

I wanted to tell him about the baby and how she looked, but he showed no interest, asking nothing about the birth or his daughter. Was it the shock of becoming a father, I wondered?

"Anyway, I'm really tired, the baby's up at night and I'm breastfeeding her," I said finally. "What do you think of the name Zoya?"

"Call her whatever you like," he said, flatly.

Then I realized that, just like his mother, he was disappointed that I'd given birth to a girl.

One week later, my brother Sajjad went to Manchester airport to collect Saleem, who'd finally decided to visit. Despite the past, I was excited to see him, convinced that he would change and begin respecting me more now that I was the mother of his child. I dressed Zoya in a little Kenzo outfit and bonnet my sister Neelam, who loved pretty designer dresses, had bought. The dress was too big, but still looked cute.

Mum was preparing a banquet of food to welcome her son-in-law. My family had even had a cake made saying 'Welcome Saleem to our family.' What kind and generous people they were, I thought, warmly, making such an effort for his arrival and first-ever visit to the UK. How different, I thought, to the welcome I'd been given at his house.

Stepping through the door, he was given a rapturous greeting, which he reciprocated by launching his own charm offensive, delighting everyone and conversing with my family, just as he'd done before the wedding.

16
Reason Is Powerless

As I woke Saleem the next morning, I wondered how he viewed life here, when the contrasts were so marked. Here he was, free from the power cuts that plagued daily life in Pakistan, enjoying clean air and water and looking out on a view of the beautiful English countryside. I could tell that my mother had made a huge effort to ensure he was comfortable as well. The bedroom with bath was fully equipped with everything he could need, from toiletries to clothes. I knew she'd look upon him as a son, which made the memories of how my mother-in-law had treated me even more painful.

That morning, I sat on a chair feeding Zoya, feeling relaxed and calm, as I always did during these bonding moments. Saleem came over and my heart soared. He was finally taking an interest in our daughter, I thought. I soon realized there was something else on his mind.

"Shama, your body's changed," he said, unable to meet my eyes. "It looks completely different. It's a bit of a shock, to be honest."

How could he be so insensitive?

"I've just had a baby!" I responded, incredulous. "What did you expect? That I'd look like a supermodel?"

"No," he said quickly. "I just meant that it feels strange looking at your body, like it's not you. And touching it would feel even more weird."

"Which bit of my body looks strange exactly?" I retorted. "Are the effects of having a baby worse than the scar you've left on my body?"

Being at my parents had given me newfound confidence. We were on my territory now. I turned away from him to focus again on Zoya while he watched silently. I had more important things to think about than him.

"I need to feed Zoya and her nappy needs changing," I said, matter-of-factly. "Can you help? Everything I need is over there, in the nappy drawer."

Saleem turned to me, aghast. "No way! I'm not doing anything of the sort!" he spluttered. "That's not a man's job. Changing nappies and feeding babies is for women!"

"What?!" I asked. "Are you for real? Seriously, Saleem, I need you to help me! I've just delivered a baby and am still recovering! I've had stitches and it's really difficult to move around. The midwife and the health worker will be here soon. Please, just give me a hand."

"Listen, I'll leave the room when they come and then you can sort yourself out, OK?"

I couldn't believe what I was hearing, so I tried a different approach. "What will everyone think?" I asked him.

"Why do you always worry about what other people are thinking?" he replied, irritably.

I could tell he was becoming annoyed now, but so was I.

"Well, I'm sorry, but in this country, fathers help with the care of their children!" I snapped back. "This is your child, as well as mine and we're meant to support each other, that's part of what being married is about. And right now, I need your help to change our baby."

With a sinking heart, I realized that Saleem wasn't going to budge. After an uncomfortable silence during which we both stared at each other, waiting for the other to back down, he simply turned and left the room.

I looked at Zoya as I fed her; her perfect little head, which was smaller than my breast and her tiny, fragile hands. Saleem didn't deserve such a beautiful creature in his life. Was I being disloyal or unreasonable? No, I thought. He had no sense of wonder at the living, breathing miracle we'd made together. Where was the appreciation or gratitude at how lucky and blessed we both were?

Remembering that the midwife was on her way, I pushed these thoughts to one side and gingerly moved across to the changing table, where the nappies and other bits and pieces were piled up. Once Zoya was changed, I dressed her in a cute, mint-green baby-grow and matching, hand-knitted cardigan. It drowned her, but she still looked adorable. Then, I added a hat to keep her warm and mittens to stop her from scratching herself.

As I gazed at her in my arms, my heart almost burst with love. *There is nothing I want but your presence,* I thought to myself, remembering Rumi's wonderful words. But I was also exhausted. My legs were still weak from the epidural and my stomach still bloated with the after-effect of giving birth. I'd read stories about how breastfeeding helped the womb to contract, but as I waited for this to happen I couldn't help thinking how strange it felt, to have this void where my baby had grown over the months, connecting with me and letting me know she was there with her sudden movements. It was as if I'd lost something, something I now had to share with the outside world.

These contemplative moments alone with Zoya were incredibly special, providing important time for us to form the bond that would last a lifetime. I knew Saleem was missing out on not connecting emotionally with his daughter and losing the opportunity to create once-in-a-lifetime memories, but I decided that this was his loss. I had more important things to worry about.

When I was younger, I'd heard the women in my extended family say that a child brings you closer together as a couple. This might be true in some cases, I thought sadly, but it certainly hadn't helped me and Saleem in our relationship. He was as cold as ever, blocking me out and now he seemed to be doing the same with little Zoya. I had no idea why.

I was about to try and make my way downstairs when my mum shouted that the midwife and health visitor had arrived. Saleem brought them upstairs and then left the room, just as he'd said he would. The midwife checked my stitches and my breasts to see if I was producing milk without a problem. Then, the health visitor handed me a red book, which she said would be used to record key information about Zoya, including her growth and weight, alongside updates on her vaccinations. By this time, Saleem had reappeared and was busy charming the women, who were asking him if he was excited about meeting his daughter. I could see that the two of them were both falling under his spell, just as I had done once.

I watched him walk the midwife and health visitor down the stairs, complimenting them on their professionalism and thanking them for the care they'd given his wife and daughter. After they'd gone, Saleem asked me how much the treatment was costing. "It's all free," I said, "it's a government service."

"Wow, that's amazing and they're so good and thorough," he replied. Saleem had realized how different the ante- and post-natal care offered in the UK were from the services available in Pakistan. Perhaps he could now understand why I was so shocked at the level of care I'd received in Pakistan, I thought.

We went into the lounge, where Mum took Zoya from me and reminded me not to walk around too much; I was still weak and my ankles were swollen. Always thoughtful, she'd arranged for a masseuse to come daily for the next week or so. She kept reminding me of the foods and drinks to avoid while breastfeeding. In the past, I might have thought she was fussing, but now I knew she simply cared and wanted what was best for me and the baby.

That day, the house was full of family and friends trooping in, one after another, wanting to see the baby and meet Saleem. By the time the last guest had left, I was exhausted. I realized that Saleem still expected me to unpack his things and put them away. As I emptied his suitcase, I spotted a cheap and cheerful outfit for a baby girl, alongside a little gift box with a dummy, milk bottle and bib for the baby.

"Oh, I forgot, my mother and sister sent those," he said, dismissively. He hadn't even remembered to give Zoya her gifts and now, I realized he hadn't even bothered to buy anything for me – his wife and the mother of his child. Surely this wasn't normal behaviour? Or was I being over-emotional? If I was being honest, it didn't surprise me; my expectations were falling by the day.

Weeks passed in a flurry of activity that was inevitably centred on Zoya. I became more confident as a mother and Zoya was thriving, enveloped in the love of my family. I thought Saleem might decide to return to Pakistan, but he told me he'd changed his mind and felt we should settle in the UK. I was delighted, but I also couldn't believe he hadn't considered such a huge decision to be worthy of discussion.

"I've realized there's quite a lot of openings for someone with a computer science degree. I think this could be a new start," he told me.

I wondered how his mother and siblings had taken the news. He was certainly in touch with them regularly, phoning them daily, sometimes talking to them for hours and also writing long letters. Saleem might have decided the UK had something to offer him, but his mindset remained firmly in Pakistan. At times he would be quite rude towards my family, as if being the son-in-law made him superior. I had seen this time and again during my months in Pakistan, especially in households where the families were uneducated. My parents, on the other hand, had always brought us up to be mindful that we were guests in someone else's house and remember our manners.

Saleem was so entrenched in Pakistani culture that he had no understanding of UK values or interest in them. He had no desire to learn about the concept of gender equality or adapt in any way, even though I tried to explain how beneficial it could be all round. I cited the example of my parents, who had worked together their entire married life, for the good of the whole family.

Mum and Dad didn't criticize Saleem once, but I felt for them, given the effort they made, cooking his favourite foods and entertaining him. He would be particularly rude whenever he came off the phone to his mother and sister. Sometimes I overheard their words of wisdom from the other side of the room: "Don't let your in-laws walk all over you. Remember, they're not your parents. Don't sell out like all those other guys who got married and went to the UK."

A few weeks into Saleem's stay, his brother Imran called to say he, his wife and kids were travelling to Canada and planned to visit the UK for a couple of days en route. Saleem was so excited that I felt for him, remembering he was separated from his family. My mother noticed too and she immediately offered to put them up. She enjoyed entertaining and was very good at it, always making people feel welcome.

"Be sure to tell me what they like to eat and we'll also arrange for you all to go out sight-seeing," she said.

Mum and my sisters busied themselves readying the spare room in preparation for the guests. I watched my mother with affection as she added the final touches that were a tradition of hers: flowers and even a little hamper, containing chocolates, perfume, soap, tissues, sweets and nuts, topped with a note saying 'Welcome to the Mughal residence.'

Since Saleem had always refused to drive in the UK, my father drove him to the airport to collect his brother and family. When they arrived, my mum welcomed Imran's wife, Farzana, with a bouquet of flowers and we all went into the lounge. I noticed anew how hospitable my family were, always greeting guests with so much warmth, whoever they were.

After dinner we all went upstairs. Imran let out a whistle: "Wow, you are really living the life! It's like a five-star hotel here, isn't it?"

"Yes," Saleem replied, smugly. "My in-laws are really making me feel at home. They're even trying to help me find a job and are great at helping Shama with the baby."

Zoya, I wanted to scream, *she's called Zoya. Use her name!*

"Wow, man, you're really lucky. You've got all of this! And you can change your life completely," Imran continued. "We're planning to go to Canada, because we think it's a better prospect for the kids. You have to look ahead and think of them."

As we showed them round the rest of the house, Imran was quiet. "How on earth did Shama manage to live in Pakistan when she was used to all of this, especially with you away so much of the week?" he said to Saleem.

I could see that Saleem was digesting his brother's comments and mulling them over, as if for the first time. "Well, now you know why I wanted to marry her," he answered, finally. "She's a genuine woman, humble and well brought up."

What a phony! I thought. The words simply rolled off his tongue, one cliché after another, simply to keep things smooth with his brother!

The next evening my parents held a special dinner for their guests. My father gave a speech, in which he formally welcomed Saleem's brother and his family. He paid tribute to their father, saying that he and my mother were honoured to have handed their daughter over to Saleem's family. If only they knew.

At least Imran had a different perspective. I heard him on the phone to my mother-in-law and her daughter praising me and my family. They'd hate that, I thought. Before Imran left for Canada, he gave Saleem some money to buy something for Zoya. I was touched by the gesture that was lost on my husband.

***

The weeks turned into months and still Saleem seemed unable to find a job, although I wasn't convinced he was putting that much effort into looking. He was also nipping out to the pubs and drinking, unaware that I knew. Not only was he failing to help with Zoya, he was missing all her milestones, from sitting up and holding things to her delightful smiles. Thankfully, I had my family to help celebrate these magical moments and lend a hand. My mum and sisters loved taking Zoya to the park to feed the ducks, giving me a welcome rest, but it saddened me that Saleem wasn't interested in getting involved.

Before we knew it, my six-month check-up had come around and it was time to set off for the health clinic. The doctor who checked me over seemed satisfied with how I looked, given the difficult pregnancy.

"So, how's everything else going? Have you had a period since giving birth?" she asked.

"No, but that's not uncommon if you're breastfeeding, is it?" I answered.

"What about birth control?" she asked.

"Well, we're not using any, I thought you couldn't get pregnant if you're breastfeeding."

Panic was beginning to well up inside me, which the doctor could sense.

"It's OK. Look, just leave a urine sample with us and we'll book you in for a scan," she said.

We returned home and I put the test to the back of my mind until the following morning, when the hospital phoned asking me to go back in to discuss the results as soon as possible.

My father drove me and Zoya to the hospital with my aunt Suraya, who also had an appointment there that morning.

As we made our way to the ultrasound department, my nerves were in shreds. I knew that the call asking me to come in quickly was a cause for concern and, on top of that, Zoya was teething, which had left me sleep-deprived and exhausted.

Once the ultrasound was done, the doctor came in and took me through a list of questions, such as whether my monthly cycle was regular and how my first pregnancy went.

"Is your husband here with you?" he asked.

I shook my head. He then asked the nurse to restart the ultrasound and, once the scanner was in place, asked me to look at the screen.

"Congratulations are in order and doubly so," he said, smiling. "You're approximately three months pregnant with non-identical twins."

He began explaining how, if I looked, I'd see there were two placentas on the screen, but I was unable to take anything in. Pregnant again? And with twins? While I had a baby that was teething and had me up all night?

"But I've been breastfeeding and thought that was a reliable form of contraception?" I managed to say.

"Well, Mrs Mughal, the ultrasound doesn't lie," the doctor answered.

Once outside in the waiting room, I was relieved to find that Dad and my aunt had taken Zoya outside for a breath of fresh air, leaving me with a moment to digest the news I'd just received. How had my life spiralled out of control and changed so dramatically in such a short space of time? As I pondered these and other questions, the tears began to flow and, even as my dad and aunt brought a chuckling Zoya back into view, I was powerless to stop them.

"Shama, what is it?" my aunt asked, her voice full of concern.

"Nothing, everything's fine, I was just feeling emotional and missing Zoya," I replied.

"Silly girl, we're all here for you," she answered, laughing and ruffling my hair.

When we arrived back at the house, I took Zoya straight up to my bedroom to feed her. Saleem was sprawled on the bed on the phone to his mother, chatting about life in Pakistan, oblivious to the impact that motherhood was having on me and the new turn things were about to take. Eventually he got off the phone and looked at me.

"Why are you crying?" he asked. "Can't you cope with the fact that I'm calling my mother? Is that your problem? You really are a pathetic creature."

"You really don't care, do you?" I answered, between sobs. "I had to go to the hospital alone because you're so uninterested in everything to do with me and our family. The doctor even asked me where my husband was."

"Well, just because I'm in England, don't expect me to become your slave," he answered, with a shrug.

"What's that got to do with being there for your wife and daughter?" I hit back. "Isn't that your duty?"

"What do you want me to do? Hold your hand all the time?" he snarled.

Exhausted and in emotional turmoil, I'd lost any desire to talk civilly to my husband by now.

"Anyway," I said, matter-of-factly, "just to let you know I'm pregnant and the doctor says I'm expecting twins. Are you happy now? You weren't even there to see them on the screen for the first time."

"What the hell? Are you bullshitting me? Don't play games with me, Shama," Saleem replied, menacingly.

"I'm not. Look, here's the scan, just for your information," I retorted, thrusting the picture into his hand. Saleem was silent, absorbing the news.

There, I thought, *think about that instead of your non-news from Pakistan.*

Before I could put my thoughts into words, there was a knock and my mother popped her head around the door. "I'm just back from the supermarket and thought you might want your nappies," she said. Her smile was bright, but I was sure she could sense the tension in the room and had caught the tail end of our exchange.

"How was your appointment, Shama?" she asked. "You and Saleem were home quickly."

"Saleem didn't go, Mom. I went with Aunty Suraya and Dad," I replied, miserably. "I've got some news as well. The doctor did an ultrasound and told me I'm three months' pregnant with twins. I was just explaining everything to Saleem."

My mother's face went pale as she absorbed my words.

"Shama," she said, slowly. "Did you say you're expecting twins?"

"Yes. That's why Dr Barker asked me to go back to the hospital quickly," I said, flatly.

I was aware that my mother would detect nothing in the way of excitement in my voice. To be fair to her, she rallied immediately.

"Well, what a lovely surprise!" she said, a little too brightly. "Just the most wonderful news! A brother or sister for Zoya and so soon!"

"Two, Mom, maybe one of each, it's twins," I corrected, still unable to mirror her enthusiasm.

"It's shocking news, isn't it?" Saleem said to my mother, as if expecting her to agree with him.

"I think it's fantastic news," my mother replied, frowning. "We haven't got twins in our family, which makes it even more exciting. I'm going downstairs to let Shama's father know."

"Why are you so horrified?" I asked Saleem, once she'd left. "It's not like you'll be looking after them, is it?" Wrecked from a lack of sleep and distraught at the news I'd been given, I ploughed on. "I guess if it's boys, you'll become even more big-headed and if it's girls, you'll think about throwing yourself down a well."

With Zoya fed and dropping off to sleep in my arms, I decided I'd nap with her. Saleem was back on the phone to Pakistan, sharing the news with his family. In his typical Jekyll and Hyde manner, he spoke excitedly to his mom, telling her how blessed he was. As I dozed off, he was voicing his hope that we'd be granted a son this time around.

When I woke up a few hours later and headed downstairs to the lounge, I was greeted by shouts of congratulations and hugs from my family, who'd been told the news by my mother. They were all delighted at the prospect of having twins in the family, but I wasn't quite able to share their enthusiasm. Saleem's attitude toward me and Zoya cast a shadow over the celebration, as did the prospect of looking after two babies and a one-year-old at the same time.

Though free from the health scares I'd experienced the first time around, other than a touch of anaemia, my second pregnancy still proved to be exhausting, even though Mum did her best to help me, especially when it came to looking after and entertaining Zoya. I napped and put my feet up when the opportunity arose. Thank goodness for my family, I thought, especially since Saleem barely contributed.

One day, after coming back from a trip to the park with Zoya and almost five months' pregnant, I decided to lie down on the sofa while Mum prepared tea. Just as I was dozing off something hit me hard on the back of my head. Startled and wincing with pain, I opened my eyes and jumped up to find Saleem reaching to hit me again with hardback books held in his hand.

"Ow! What are you doing? That really hurt!" I said, moving away.

"*Kutey kee bachee*! Why haven't you written to my sisters since you left Pakistan?" he shouted at me, his face in mine. "They're complaining that you're ignoring them."

My aunt rushed into the room, concern etched across her face.

"Saleem, what's the matter? Why are you shouting? I thought I heard a bang," she said, her eyes falling on the books that were now in a pile between the two of us.

"Yes, it was me," he replied, clearly still furious, "I told Shama to write to my sisters when she came back to the UK. She hasn't even bothered and now they're complaining to me."

"And that's the reason you banged those books?" Aunty asked in a measured voice.

"Yes, Aunty," I interjected, tearfully, unable to keep quiet, "and they hurt, too."

"What do you mean, they hurt?" she asked. When I didn't answer, she repeated, gently, "What do you mean, child?"

"Nothing," I answered, miserably.

There was a pause during which I could sense that my aunt was assessing the situation.

"Saleem, I hope you didn't hit Shama with those books," she said, eventually. "I might not be her mother, but I will be straight with you and give you my honest opinion on that sort of behaviour. Surely you can see she doesn't need stress or trauma right now?"

She left the room, biting her lip and visibly upset. "I'm going upstairs to feed Zoya," I told Saleem, quickly stepping toward the door. As I walked out leaving Saleem alone, he looked both scared and agitated.

Upstairs, alone with Zoya, I tried to put what happened out of my mind, but before long, Saleem stormed in, slamming the door behind him.

"Are you happy now? Acting out your dramas to your family?" he shouted, pacing up and down. "And look how your aunt spoke to me! It's a disgrace!"

I decided against retaliating. I knew all too well my husband couldn't be trusted when angry. I stayed quiet, trying to not catch his eye and just focused on feeding Zoya. But my lack of response fuelled Saleem's rage instead of calming him down.

"You…you nasty piece of work. You just don't care, do you?" he said, through gritted teeth and before I could move out of the way, his hand was around my face, claw-like, gripping my cheeks so tightly that I couldn't open my mouth to shout.

Just as I thought I was about to faint, he pushed my face away and slapped me across my left cheek with such force that my head was thrown back, hitting the wall behind me.

For a split second, the room swam and then everything went black. Confused and only semi-conscious, I could hear Zoya screaming. She was still in my arms though. Instinctively, I pulled her further toward me to comfort her, but noticed with horror that she had an angry red mark on her face that could only have come from Saleem. His hand must have caught her face when he struck me. As red-hot anger surged through me, I was hit with dizziness again and I stumbled.

I woke to find I was lying on a bed in a cubicle that was closed off with green curtains. As I tried to get my bearings, I frantically began looking for Zoya and saw a doctor standing by the side of my bed.

"You're awake. That's good news," she said smiling. "The police want to ask you some questions, but I'm only giving them a few minutes. You really need to rest."

As if on cue, a policewoman stepped in from around the curtain, smiling sympathetically. "Hello, Shama. I won't stay long," she promised. "I know you're still feeling fragile, but we do need to talk to you about how you got those injuries to your face."

Instinctively, I raised my fingers to my cheek and flinched at how tender it was to the touch. Then I remembered Saleem striking my face and Zoya's cries. Zoya! Was she safe and well? I needed to know.

"I fell while feeding my baby," I said, my eyes remaining fixed on the bedsheet.

"How did you fall, Shama?" the policewoman continued, calmly.

"I just lost my balance," I said, miserably.

"Are you sure that's what happened?" she asked, gently. "It's just that your injuries aren't compatible with a fall. You know, Shama, you've got nothing to be ashamed of. Nothing that happened was your fault."

"I'm certain that I fell," I answered, more confidently, desperate to get home.

"Well, here's my number if you decide you want to talk to me," she said with a sigh, handing me a card.

As soon as she'd left, I swung my legs to the side, stood up gingerly and poked my head out of the curtain, searching for the bathroom. Once inside, I headed for the basin to wash my hands and splash some water on my face. Catching sight of my reflection in the mirror, I gripped the counter to steady myself. My left cheek was aflame and swollen under the eye, where bruising was beginning to appear and dried blood had gathered at the corner of my mouth. I looked a mess. Saleem had overstepped the mark; he had hit me under my parents' roof.

As I made my way back to my bed, my mother and father were being shown through to my cubicle by a nurse. I was desperate to ask them about Zoya, but I couldn't speak. Dad looked more upset than I'd ever seen him and Mum was dabbing her eyes with a tissue, unbidden tears silently falling. I wanted to comfort them, but through my pain and exhaustion I couldn't think of anything to say that would help. In the end, it was my father who spoke.

"Shama, I have never laid a finger on your mother since the day I met her," he said, "I am truly ashamed when I hear about any man hitting a woman, but to discover that my son-in-law has hit my daughter horrifies me."

"And with you pregnant, carrying his twin babies?" my mother managed to add. "We had to call an ambulance when we came into the room and found you out cold on the sofa, with Zoya still in your arms. He simply stormed out of the house."

I couldn't look at either of them, horribly embarrassed that they'd unearthed the truth about Saleem in such a traumatic way. Where was he, anyway? Was he sorry? And more importantly, where was Zoya?

"Zoya's with Aunty Suraya, don't worry, darling," Mum said soothingly, as if reading my mind. I managed a feeble smile and grasped her hand, at which point the doctor arrived.

"Tests show that the babies are fine, Mrs Mughal, but we believe your jaw is fractured, though we'll need to do an x-ray to confirm that, and you've got some nasty bruising," she said, sympathetically. "We'll keep you in for a couple of days as a precaution, since your pregnancy has risks associated with it, but there are no other major concerns."

After she'd left, my parents went to get a coffee, leaving me wondering how on earth I'd ended up in this position. How had I gone from a strong, independent, fun-loving girl who lived life to the full to this pathetic, passive person that allowed a tyrannous control freak to abuse her physically and mentally and even put their child at risk? If only I could turn the clock back to when I was simply a daughter, rather than wife, daughter-in-law, mother and, yes, mother-to-be.

Just as my own tears began to fall, my sister Neelam came rushing in, armed with flowers and chocolates.

"How dare that bastard do this to you! I hate him, Shams, I hate him!" she burst out, before I had the chance to say hello.

"Neelu, don't get involved. You don't know what happened," I pleaded half-heartedly, struggling to speak through my aching jaw.

"I know enough! Aunty Suraya told us all that he hit you with a book and then beat you up. He's a pig!" she said, her face distorted with emotion.

"Please, stop it," I begged.

"Sorry, but I can't," continued Neelam. "How could you let him treat you like this? Look at your face and think of your babies...he nearly killed them!"

Neelam's anger was exhausting, but I knew it was only because she cared. And she was right, in every way. When she saw how painful it was for me to converse, she moved across the bed and wrapped her arms around me.

"Please, don't let him do this to you, please!" she begged, hugging me tightly and sobbing. "He can't treat you like this! You were always the strong one, the one who taught us not to tolerate violence or other unreasonable behaviour. That's one of the reasons we're so upset."

Her words rang true, but part of me also knew this was something I had to address by myself with my husband.

"So, where's Saleem?" I asked.

"Hopefully dead somewhere," Neelam replied, through gritted teeth.

"Enough, Neelu. Where is he?" I pleaded.

She sighed. "Mainly sitting in your room," she answered. "Mum calls him down to eat, not that I would, but you know what she's like. Dad wants to have it out with him, but he refuses to talk to anyone. Aunty Suraya wants to tell him to come and visit you, but it's as if he's switched off and is alienating himself from us all."

Had it really taken so long for me to realize that this man didn't give a damn about me or our children, born and unborn? That he had no regard for me and my family and that his main concern was looking after number one now that he'd lost the respect of my kind and caring parents, who'd welcomed him and shown him such hospitality?

As I let these thoughts sink in, I became aware that Neelam was talking to me.

"Shama, you know, I heard Mum knock on Saleem's door earlier on and when he came out, she asked him what happened," she was saying. "He said he didn't know and that you simply fell and began making a scene."

I smiled, despite myself, at his ability to lie and defend himself to the hilt.

"Wait, there's more," Neelam said, tearfully. "I heard her telling Saleem that this crisis was affecting the whole family. She explained that the stress was making her ill and that her blood pressure was up, causing dizziness and nosebleeds. Then I heard her say 'Your wife is critical in hospital. She has one child here with us that you never ask about and two on the way.' And do you know what his response to Mum was? 'Never mind, everyone gets nosebleeds.' That's the kind of animal he is!"

The thought of my mother having to talk to Saleem in this way heightened my misery. I couldn't help feeling guilty. Should I have said more about my time in Pakistan to them when I first arrived? About his behaviour back home? But how could I have broached this subject when they were so delighted to see me and Saleem had won their hearts? My head was reeling and I was struggling to keep my eyes open. Noticing this, Neelam gave me a hug, blew me a kiss and said she'd come back in the morning.

When, eventually, it was time for me to go home, Mum and Dad came to collect me, while Saleem remained conspicuous by his absence. "Your head, neck and back will be sore for a few days, so it's probably best to avoid stairs," the doctor said as she signed my discharge papers.

Mum was trying to suppress her tears, but I remained numb, asking myself over and again how my life had spiralled downward in such a short time. I was weighed down by responsibilities, an education cut short, marriage over the other side of the world to a man who went from Prince Charming to a monster in a matter of days, pregnancy, babies and now health scares, all before my 21st birthday.

As we went into the house, Aunty Suraya placed Zoya in my arms. "I've missed you so much," I whispered into Zoya's tufts of hair, hugging her tightly. I was relieved to see that the red mark on her cheek was fading, but still felt horrified that she'd been the victim of Saleem's anger.

Mum and Aunty Suraya began making up a bed for me downstairs while I made up for lost time with Zoya. I wasn't particularly surprised that Saleem hadn't come downstairs, despite knowing I was back.

I discovered from my sister Amina that my parents had called his family and told them what had happened, only to hear his mother defend her son. My family had not only seen Saleem's true colours, but had learned some home truths about his mother and sisters, I thought.

Weak and still in pain, I was conscious that my parents were having to decide how to deal with the situation, since Saleem remained a guest in their house. Neelam told me a couple of days later that Dad had decided to enlist the help of a mutual friend that we affectionately called Uncle, thinking that perhaps having an outsider talk to Saleem might help.

In the afternoon, I heard the doorbell ring and footsteps on the stairs as my fair and kind-hearted father took Uncle and Saleem upstairs. The chat didn't last long and, before I knew it, all three men came into the lounge, where I was sat with Zoya and the rest of my family, including my brothers, who'd been summoned for the day. Saleem was furious as he marched through the doorway.

"OK, OK, yes, I hit your daughter and you know what? She deserved it," he said.

There was a stunned silence as everyone stared at Saleem, digesting his outburst. My father was first to speak. "You should never hit a woman, but doing that to my daughter and in our house where we welcomed you?" he said, his face pale with rage.

I closed my eyes and let out a sigh, wanting nothing other than this man to leave the room, even better, the house. I had allowed him to hurt me physically and mentally and now he was inflicting harm on my family too.

"What's the matter with you all?" he asked, eyes blazing and lips twisted in a smirk. "Why are you making such a big deal out of it? She's just looking for attention! She's a drama queen, I'll give you that!"

Now it was my mother's turn to intervene. "You think those bruises and that broken jaw are play-acting?" she asked, calmly. "Let me tell you now that no man hits a woman in this house. Perhaps things are different where you were raised, but it certainly doesn't happen here!"

"Why are you bringing my family into this?" he hissed.

"Because from what you've said, it sounds as if it's seen as acceptable amongst your family," she replied. Then she turned abruptly to my brothers. "Shama needs to rest now. Please take Saleem back to his room," she said.

The tension was palpable as Fahad and Sajjad guided Saleem out of the lounge and back up the stairs, clearly tempted to punch rather than escort him.

I knew Mum and Dad had begun discussing the best way forward, whether my marriage could or should be saved, or if the best course of action would be to send Saleem back to Pakistan, even though I had Zoya and was pregnant. I felt awful knowing that I was contributing to my parents' suffering. I'd inadvertently become a major source of worry to them, even if I wasn't directly to blame. Rumi once said that reason is powerless in the expression of love. If only it were love that had made Saleem lose all reason, I thought to myself.

17
The Way Appears

Four days passed. I stayed downstairs convalescing and saw nothing of Saleem. My mother and sisters took it in turns to bring my meals, sit with me and entertain Zoya, as I gradually grew stronger. On the morning of the fifth day, Saleem poked his head around the door. Still half asleep, I hoisted myself up on my pillow.

"How are you?" he said without emotion, walking into the room. "The marks on your face have faded, so I guess you're feeling better now?"

Was he expecting me to answer him or give some reassurance? And there was I thinking he'd come to apologize and tell me that he loved me!

Saleem moved awkwardly closer and perched himself on the edge of the bed. He gave a small smile and it occurred to me that perhaps he needed something. That would make sense, I thought, with a sinking heart.

"I was thinking, what with everything that's happened, I mean, I know your parents have been great and everything..." he trailed off and took a breath. "Maybe it's time for a new start, just us. I need my own space, Shama."

I had to suppress a smile at the absurdity of this suggestion.

"Saleem, how on earth would we manage to do that?" I asked. "You have no money and you're not even working!"

"I know, I know and I'll keep trying to find a job, but I think it's really important," he answered.

"What about Zoya?" I asked. "My mum has been a huge help and I'll need her even more as my due date gets nearer."

I was fully aware now that Saleem would do little to help with our children and I'd be left to struggle alone if we moved away from my family. Luckily, Zoya woke up at that moment, providing a welcome opportunity for me to avoid further conversation. Saleem went to pick her up from her cot, but she recoiled and began to cry. Did it occur to him that he was a stranger to her? The man who had hurt her?

"What happened to her face?" he asked me, spotting the red mark on her cheek as he handed her to me.

"It was when you hit me, you caught Zoya's face too," I replied. If I expected any remorse, I was disappointed. Sadly, I saw his expression remained completely unchanged. His own daughter's pain had no impact on him at all. He simply put our daughter in my arms and left the room, announcing over his shoulder that he was going to telephone Pakistan.

Another couple of days passed and I was well enough to move back upstairs to my bedroom. The relief of having sufficiently recovered to climb the stairs was overshadowed by the enormity of what had happened to put me in hospital and the fact that nothing had yet been resolved. Tension in the household remained high and relations between Saleem and my family were strained. With Zoya resting her head on my chest gurgling happily, I begged God to tell me what I'd done to be punished in this way.

The days turned into weeks and my pregnancy entered its third trimester. We fell into a routine in which my mum and sisters helped to look after Zoya when I needed to rest, while Saleem spent as much time out of the house as possible, supposedly looking for work. Once or twice I suggested firms that were hiring and handed him job adverts from the local papers, but he reacted with such anger, asking me if I was accusing him of not trying hard enough, that I decided to back off. Truth be told, I was suspicious about his lack of success and wondered where he was all day, but knew better than to ask.

The atmosphere had begun to thaw at home, although I knew things would never be quite the same again. My parents were civil to Saleem, but their characteristic warmth had disappeared. How could I blame them? I knew Saleem had noticed a change in their attitude, but at least he hadn't mentioned moving out again – an idea I prayed he'd put to one side.

Around this time, Sajjad came to visit. He'd been away on business and the last time I'd seen him was when he'd guided Saleem up to our room after our family confrontation. After we'd hugged and got past the pleasantries, I could tell Sajjad wanted to talk to me about my marriage, so I asked Mum if she'd take Zoya to the park.

Sajjad smiled and squeezed my hand. "How are you, Shama?" he said, gently. "Be honest with me, anything you say will stay between us, I promise."

I let out a long sigh and closed my eyes. "Truthfully? My life's a nightmare," I answered. "I'm a nervous wreck, thanks to Saleem's temper and moods. I never know what will set him off, and, what with the pregnancy, I'm exhausted."

"I understand, and I really feel for you," he answered. "Of course, it's difficult for you and everyone else too. I'm sure you've noticed that the situation is affecting the whole family, especially Mum and Dad."

"Yes, I know. I feel really bad about it, but what can I do?" I asked him.

There was a silence. "I've been thinking, maybe part of the problem is that Saleem needs to be given more responsibility, especially with the twins on the way," he said. "Here, he has everything done for him. Perhaps if you had your own place, nearby mind, his behaviour would improve. What do you think?"

My immediate reaction was to protest, but then I began to think of my poor parents and the effect of recent events on their health, not to mention the stress of having Saleem living in their house. There was also the future of my marriage to consider. Was I prepared to give things another try with Saleem? If so, perhaps a fresh start in our own home was what we needed. I could see that Sajjad was trying to read my mind as I thought through the pros and cons of his suggestion.

"Shama, I'll be honest with you, I've talked it through with Mum and Dad and Mum isn't keen on the idea, you know how she worries," he admitted, "but Dad and I have assured her that one of us will visit every day. We'll get the house through one of Dad's friends, so you can live rent-free, at least to begin with, until you're financially more secure."

"Give me a bit of time to think about it, can you? Before I talk it over with Saleem?" I asked, although I knew he'd jump at the opportunity to have his own place.

"Sure, Shama, I know how much you have on your plate," he said, giving me another hug, "and there's no rush either. We all feel you shouldn't do anything until the twins are born."

I waited until the next day before discussing my family's proposal with Saleem and, as predicted, he was thrilled. "It's a new start for us, but you'll have to find a job," I stressed. "We get our own space, but there'll be bills to pay and more mouths to feed."

"I know, I know, I will," he replied. "I have been trying, but my qualifications don't seem to match with what people are looking for here and I haven't worked for a while, which seems to be going against me." I suspected that Saleem was turning down work he felt was beneath him, but chose not to mention this.

The precious weeks leading up to the birth of the twins were spent with my mother and sisters. I was going to miss them terribly, even if I moved close by. I could tell Mum was worried about whether this was the right decision, but I did my best to put her mind at rest.

"I'll only be a few streets away, Mom and Saleem has talked about wanting his space, so this could be just what we all need, especially once there's five of us," I said. "And I know you'll come and help with the children – we'll still see each other all the time."

Saleem divided his time between looking for work and helping my brothers prepare the house, which kept him busy. His mood improved, prompting me to think that maybe he really did need a project, something to focus on.

Mum and my sisters were busy buying double of everything for the babies and taking me to my hospital visits, while Dad did whatever he could to help with lifts and errands. It was on one such day when we were driving along a particularly bumpy road, on our way to look at the house that he'd chosen for me and Saleem, when I began to feel a nagging ache and familiar tightness in my back.

"Dad, I think the babies might be coming," I said, panic beginning to rise inside me. My mind began racing as I tried to remember whether I had everything

I needed in my bag for the hospital. The prospect of giving birth to two babies filled me with fear. What if something went wrong? Who would take care of Zoya if I was taken ill or worse? Would the twins both survive if there were complications?

Caught up in my thoughts, I'd hardly noticed that Dad had done a U-turn and driven back home. He jumped out of the car and ran round the other side to help me out and up to the front door. Instinctively, Mum was there and guiding me to a chair.

"My waters have broken, Mom," I said.

"Everything's fine, Neelam is upstairs getting your bag. She'll stay here with Zoya," she said, with a reassuring smile. "I'm going to call Saleem and we'll make our way to the hospital."

I could tell that she knew I was panicking and gave her a hug of gratitude. Dad put my bag in the boot while Mum and Saleem walked me to the car. Perhaps his presence at the hospital this time would help him bond better with the babies, I thought.

The staff at the maternity wing had notes detailing the preeclampsia from my first pregnancy. My contractions were becoming increasingly painful and I was trying to take deep breaths but struggling to do so. I was wired up so the midwife and consultant could monitor me, with Mum by my side and squeezing my hand, while Saleem and Dad sat outside in the waiting room.

"It's all so exciting," Mum said, with a smile. I tried to smile back, but out of the corner of my eye I could see the consultant in deep conversation with the midwife. The two of them then approached the bed.

"Mrs Mughal, one of the babies has opened their bowels during the early stages of labour," the consultant explained. "There's a risk of complication if the baby swallows that fluid, so we're just going to carry out some tests to ensure everything is satisfactory."

"OK," I said, feeling anything but. I could feel my mother's breathing quicken as well, but she continued to smile and hold my hand, as the doctor explained the process involved.

My feet were placed in stirrups to enable the consultant to access the baby's head. I knew this lack of dignity was necessary and that childbirth is nothing short of a miracle, resulting in a new life, or two in my case, God willing, but still.

The consultant disappeared to examine the results while Mum went outside to update Saleem and my father. When he reappeared, he asked Mum to fetch Saleem.

"While everything is satisfactory at the moment, Mrs Mughal, the babies' oxygen levels are dropping slightly. We'll carry on monitoring you closely for now, but if they continue to drop, we might have to consider performing a caesarean. Either way, we think it's better if we give you an epidural, in case an operation is needed."

"OK," I said, trying to stay calm.

A nurse took Saleem to one side and asked him to put on a gown, hat and mask, while I was wheeled into a room that resembled a small operating theatre. Despite the concerns I had, I couldn't help smiling to myself at the sight of Saleem gowned up and imagining what must be going through his head, given his opinions about the husband's role in childbirth and parenthood. The nurse then came round and explained that because of the epidural I wouldn't feel the contractions, so she'd tell me when to push. "You have a little way to go yet, as you're not fully dilated, so I'll talk you through it," she said with a smile. She turned her face to Saleem. "Your wife's doing really well, Mr Mirza," she said.

I followed her gaze, hoping for some words of encouragement from Saleem, but he appeared speechless. His face was a sickly yellow colour and he was gripping the side of the bed for support. Anyone would think he was about to give birth, I thought grimly. For a split second I wished it was my mother in his place – she'd certainly be more useful in the circumstances. The nurse's voice brought me back to the present.

"OK, big push, Mrs Mughal," she said.

"Push, Shama!"

Was that Saleem joining in or did I imagine it? There was no time for analysis – I gave a mighty push, despite being unable to feel anything and out slithered the first of the twins, closely followed by the second. The nurse whisked them away to check them over, before handing them to me. "Congratulations, two beautiful, healthy babies, a boy and a girl," she said, smiling.

I cradled them both, one on each side, as they wriggled and quickly began suckling. Saleem was ecstatic that he'd got his prized heir, looking adoringly at our son, before rushing out to break the news to my parents. I hoped that he'd take a greater interest in all three of his children from now on.

I was taken back to the ward, where my parents were waiting, excitedly. "Neelam will come up later with Zoya, so these adorable babies can meet their big sister," my mum said, happily.

Saleem went off to find a coffee machine, leaving me with my parents.

"He seems happy, my child. Perhaps this really will be a new start," Mum whispered.

"I hope so," I answered.

After we'd carefully put the twins in their cots next to me, I drifted off to sleep. Later that evening, a friend of my father's from the local community came to the ward and recited the *adhan* call to prayer in the right ear of each baby and then "*Allahu akbar*" in the left, in keeping with tradition.

Arriving home with the babies, newly named Adam and Sara, I was catapulted into a whirlwind of activity, in which I had no concept of day or night. The routine of everyday life was replaced by a constant round of feeding, nappy-changing, bathing and soothing the twins to sleep while also trying to find time for little Zoya, who was now a year old. Thank goodness we'd decided to stay at my parents for a little longer, I thought, as Mum appeared at the bedroom door with a pile of clean baby-grows.

One afternoon, when Adam and Sara were about four weeks old and just waking up from their afternoon nap, Saleem burst in with a smile on his face.

"The house is ready, we can move in," he said.

On moving-in day, Dad made endless journeys back and forth, ferrying our baby items and belongings to the house. He, Saleem and my brothers traipsed in and out with our things while Mum began putting her special touches to the rooms, unfolding new bed linen, rolling out rugs and scattering cushions. I knew that she still had concerns deep down about the move, but she put on a smile and said how nice it would be for us to have our own space.

After the final boxes had been brought in from the car and the twins were settled in their cots, my parents and brothers gave me a hug and, somewhat coolly shook Saleem's hand.

"Good luck, my child. I'm just a phone call away if you need me. Call any time," Mum said, holding me tightly.

I watched them go with tears in my eyes, but tried to focus on Saleem, who looked more upbeat than I'd seen him for months. I prayed, not for the first time, that this new phase in our lives would be a change for the better.

"Here's to us in our new home," he said, taking my hand and smiling.

We soon fell into a routine, with Saleem leaving the house in the daytime to go to the library and job centre to look for work. I suspected that sometimes he was going to the pub, since he came back smelling of alcohol, but I decided not to confront him and risk being on the receiving end of his temper.

I was too tired to argue with him, looking after two babies and a one-year-old. Mum popped in most days and brought food, luckily, but the everyday routine was still exhausting.

I began missing the company of adults my own age. Being back in the UK had reminded me of my student days, my university friends, my career hopes – my former life. Could I possibly resurrect it? The thought niggled away at me as I went about my daily routine. Perhaps I didn't have to wave goodbye to my hopes and dreams after all. Deep down, I knew, too, that returning to university and gaining the qualifications I'd been so close to obtaining before could be my 'Plan B' if my marriage failed, a shot at independence, although I wasn't yet ready to discuss this with my family.

I sent off for university syllabuses, ensuring I hid them from Saleem and pored over them while the children napped. The next step was to fill in the application forms. Could I bring myself to take the plunge? Was I ready?

Sat at the table, with the papers sprawled out in front of me, I thought about my life. Saleem and I were living under the same roof, but were either of us really happy? There'd been no repeats of the violence that took place at my parents' house, but he was cold and distant, taking very little interest in family life. He was also coy about his whereabouts during the daytime, getting annoyed if I pressed him on the subject, though he still hadn't found a job.

I decided I had nothing to lose by applying and that I'd worry about telling Saleem later if I was accepted. On a warm July morning, I pushed the twins down the high street in their double buggy, Zoya now toddling by my side. With trembling hands, I slipped the envelopes containing my application forms in the post box. There, it was done. No going back now!

With a smile, I turned to the children, feeling happier than I'd done for months, if not years. It was a beautiful bright morning and I didn't feel like going home yet. "How about feeding the ducks?" I asked them.

After a wonderful hour in the park, during which Zoya played on the swings and slide, we headed back. Once indoors, I fed and bathed all three children and settled them in bed. They fell asleep almost instantly, exhausted from the day, leaving me free to focus on dinner. Saleem expected fresh food daily when he came in, even though he knew how busy I was with the children and that my mother couldn't be expected to help me cook all the time.

From the kitchen, I heard the click of the front door, telling me he was home. I turned to say hello, but something about Saleem's face warned me that there was a problem. His eyes were glassy and he was swaying. Was he drunk or under the influence of something else? I had no idea and didn't really care.

"Why isn't my food ready yet?" he barked.

"It won't be long, I've been out with the children. We wanted to make the most of the lovely day," I answered, quietly.

He threw his jacket onto the sofa.

"You're always taking the kids out. Can't you just stay at home so I don't have to come home to chaos?" he said, raising his voice.

"What do you mean?" I asked. "I take them to the park to feed the ducks and so that Zoya can run around. It's good for them."

"I don't want you to go out more than you need to. Do you understand?" he shouted. I decided against arguing, given the mood he was in and knowing that the children were sleeping upstairs. Instead, I handed him his dinner and returned to the kitchen. I could see him through the doorway and watched him as he ate and flicked through the television channels, settling on a news channel. How on earth had I wound up with a husband who didn't even want me to take his children to the park, I thought miserably.

"Where's the salt when I need it?" he bellowed, shattering my musings. Sighing, I took the salt in to him, but as I turned to go, he pulled the sleeve of my top.

"Why didn't your parents give you a house and car in the dowry?" he asked. "They should have!"

"Pardon?" I said, furious. "Why should they? Haven't they done enough to start us off in life? Now it's time for you to show some responsibility as a father and husband!"

"Why don't you ask them?" he persisted. This was his response to being unable or unwilling to find work to pay the bills that had already begun piling up?

"No way, Saleem," I answered. "My children are not a begging bowl. I will work and provide them with everything if need be. I will go back to university. You always said your father wanted his daughters-in-law to be educated."

The words were out before I could stop myself. There was silence and then, as I walked back towards the kitchen, the sound of smashing glass. Reeling around, I saw Saleem's glass in smithereens across the fireplace. The wall behind it, which only recently had been freshly painted by my brothers, was splattered with orange juice.

"Understand this, I will cut you up into tiny pieces, get rid of them, and then call your family and tell them you've disappeared," he snarled, spittle appearing at the sides of his mouth. He jumped to his feet, charging toward me as I backed into the kitchen. He grabbed a rolling pin that was on the work surface and pushed me onto the floor, standing over me with it.

"Stop it, Saleem, the kids are sleeping," I begged, hoping this would make him see sense.

"I'm serious," he said, ignoring my pleas and repeatedly kicking my legs violently. "I really will kill you and chop you up."

Finally spent of his rage, he turned and stomped upstairs. I stayed exactly as I was, cradling my bruised legs, until I heard the sound of our bedroom door opening and the creak of our bed, telling me he was lying down. I waited a few minutes more, hoping he'd fallen asleep. Then I crept on all fours into the lounge and grabbed the phone. With trembling hands, I dialled Sajjad's number. Thank goodness he was in.

"He's threatened to kill me and been violent again," I whispered, "please call the police."

"Are you safe?" he asked, urgently.

"I think so, for now. He's asleep."

The police arrived in a matter of minutes and took Saleem to the station for questioning. As he was put into a car, Sajjad arrived, his face pinched with worry.

"Are you OK, Shama? The children?" he asked, hugging me.

"They're asleep, they're fine. I've told the police I don't want him back," I said.

The next few days were difficult. I heard from Sajjad that Saleem had gone to stay with a friend, but he phoned me constantly. I refused to take his calls. Then his sister Shazia telephoned from Pakistan. "You should let your husband back in the house," she said, tersely. "Your husband is irreplaceable. You should put him above your own family." I hung up.

Over the days that followed, there were many visits from officials. Saleem was being charged with assault, so I had to make a statement. Social services wanted reassurance that I didn't plan to take Saleem back, which I was happy to give. I was also advised to contact the local domestic violence unit.

Saleem pleaded guilty and was given a caution. He agreed to seek help for his anger, which I genuinely hoped he'd do. Measures were also put in place, at my request, to prevent him from taking the children out of the country.

One week after Saleem's admission of guilt, Sajjad came to visit me with the news that Saleem had apparently returned to Pakistan.

"To be honest, I'm not that surprised," I said.

"Come round this evening for dinner. Mum is expecting you," he said, scooping up the twins and giving Zoya a cuddle. I waved him off, still digesting the news and wondering what life had in store for me next. As worries of my future whirled in my mind, I heard the sound of the post arrive.

Bills, I thought grimly, making my way to the mat, where the envelopes lay. My parents had been helping me with them, aware that Saleem wasn't working, but I hated asking them for money repeatedly when they'd done so much already.

Three brown envelopes that looked like they contained reminders lay on the mat. Sighing, I scooped them up, but then spotted a fourth envelope beneath them with the Manchester University logo stamped on the front. I breathed in sharply. Could this be the news I'd been waiting for? I ripped open the envelope.

Dear Mrs Mughal,

With reference to your application...we would like to offer you a place...on the...BA Literature and Arts course in the academic year 1999/00, beginning September...

I'd been accepted! My prayers had been answered! I was going back to university to complete the last two years of my degree, two years after having to abandon it.

I knew that there would be a huge amount of organizing to do and I'd need support and help from my family, but I'd taken that all-important first step. The tears began to fall, but for the first time they were tears of relief. A phase of my life was over, but another was about to begin. I performed my ablutions and prayed the prayer of thanks, reciting over and over one of my favourite verses from the Qur'an:

Indeed Allah is with those who patiently endure.
[Qur'an 8:46]

18
Seeking

September arrived and with it the first day of term – not for the children, but for me. I was going to drop Zoya, Adam and Sara off at my parents' house and walk to the train station. I'd timed the journey to the campus and, although it was tight, I could get there on time for my first lecture, as long as the handover went smoothly.

But predictably, it didn't. Zoya had sensed that something was going on and began playing up, refusing to eat her breakfast or get dressed. The twins picked up that the routine was different, so decided that they too would cause some disruption, grizzling and making it impossible for me to get myself ready.

As the clock ticked and my precious plans fell apart, I sat down, my bag on the floor with my books carefully packed inside and wept with despair. How on earth did I think I could manage to return to university with three children and no husband to support me?

The phone rang. Mom's concerned voice greeted me with,

"Shama, child? Where are you?" She'd been expecting me to drop off the children 20 minutes ago. My dear mother had offered to help with childcare as soon as she heard I'd been accepted on my course, so I could return to my studies.

"I can't do it, Mom, everything's gone wrong this morning," I said miserably, between sobs.

"Dad will come over and fetch you all. Just get your things together and don't worry," she said.

He was there in 10 minutes. I was red-eyed and still feeling sorry for myself, but the children were suddenly jumping up and down, delighted at the sight of their grandfather, all signs of their earlier tantrums gone.

"Go, Shama, they'll be fine," he said. "Just get the later train and don't worry."

I kissed the children and hugged him, closing the front door behind me and headed for the station. Forced to now rush, I was soon out of breath and my legs felt like jelly, but I soldiered on, focused on how much I wanted to make this work and create a better life for my children.

I arrived at the campus too late for the first lecture, so I decided to wait and speak to my tutor afterwards. I was shaking as I waited for him to call me in, stomach churning. What kind of student would he think I was, not even managing to make the first lecture? Possible excuses were running through my head, but as the clock ticked I decided that perhaps it was best just to be honest.

"Come in, Shama," he called, eventually.

"I'm so sorry I was late," I said, bursting in and rushing to get the words out. "I recently had twins and my marriage has broken down. I'm determined to finish my degree and support my children, but I know it's going to be tough…" my voice trailed off.

I closed my eyes and sighed deeply. This wasn't how my second chance here was supposed to start was all I could think. My tutor pulled out a chair and offered me a glass of water.

"You've had a difficult first day, but I'm sure it will get easier. Give it time," he said gently, "there'll be plenty of support for you here." His smile and manner provided just the reassurance I needed. I knew my children were happy with my parents, who loved them dearly. I had support at home and here as well.

Everyone was on my side, but everyday life was both stressful and exhausting. As soon as my alarm went off at six in the morning, I stumbled out of bed, quickly getting myself ready and then waking the children up, washing and dressing them, making and feeding them breakfast while trying to make sure I didn't forget any of my own books and notes.

Once I'd put the kids to sleep each night, I prepared their bags for the next day, with milk formula, nappies, changes of clothes and toys. The twins were not too much trouble. They were comfortable in their routine, which consisted largely of eating and sleeping, but Zoya was a bright and bubbly toddler who needed entertaining.

After a few false starts, we eventually got a routine going and things began to fall into place. We were still always tight for time and more often than not I was still racing around frantically when my father's car pulled up outside. We'd decided that he'd collect the four of us and drop the children with my mother before taking me to the station. I was acutely aware of the commitment my parents had agreed to make so that I could finish my education and knew that I'd never be able to repay them for what they were doing.

As I watched Dad pull up outside the house, punctual as always, it occurred to me that in my earlier student days I'd taken my parents for granted, failing to appreciate everything they'd done for me. Was this a sign that I was growing up? The fact that I was now able to recognize just how much they were doing to help me? Especially Dad, so reliable and happy to help, driving us from A to B.

As I waved goodbye to him at the station, I thought of how I'd always relied on others to drive me around. Even though I was back at college and bringing up my children on my own, I was far from independent. Much as I loved my parents dearly and was indebted to them, I didn't want to rely on their support open-endedly.

The decision to get my degree was an important step forward. On the days when it all felt too much and I thought of giving up, I'd remind myself that I was increasing my chances of a career, a means of supporting my children, but also doing something for myself. When had I last thought of myself? Even before I'd finished my teens, my life had been taken up first by a demanding husband and then, very quickly, by my beloved children.

Having no partner present to share the highs and lows of my busy and demanding life made things tougher. Since he'd returned to Pakistan, Saleem hadn't phoned once, which upset me more than I'd expected. Despite everything that had happened, I'd assumed he'd contact me to ask about the children at least and keep up-to-date on their progress. I'd never wanted Zoya and the twins to be deprived of a father and my heart bled for them, knowing they'd soon start questioning Saleem's absence.

I was so angry at him and his entire family, I knew they had a lot to do with the lack of contact. Still, I sent him photos and letters regularly, documenting each new milestone of his children's development. The irony of this wasn't lost on me. Now I was the one writing letters to a man who, just a few years earlier, penned me page after page of words declaring his excitement at spending the rest of his life with me; words that had caused my heart to pound and convinced me I was madly in love. Now, there was nothing, not a word nor a penny from the man who was a husband and father and, supposedly, the breadwinner. After all, according to Islam, the man should be responsible for providing shelter and food for his family.

I did my best to push these thoughts and my resentment to one side and focus on the positives. Most of the time the practicalities took over anyway, through necessity. My train journeys were spent planning meals for the children and how I'd manage to fit in the housework and other chores in the house, right down to the details of bedtime reading with the children. I wanted to make the most of the precious time I had with them, but there was so much to fit in. When I could, I'd try to combine helping them with their development with jobs around the house, like asking Zoya to count the pasta shapes and put them in sets while I was cooking and cleaning.

Sometimes I'd doze off or become lost in thought on the train and wake with a start as we approached my station. My life was no different to these journeys, hurtling along so quickly that I couldn't keep up. Nothing stood still, not even for a second; the clock simply kept on ticking. *Just a pause for breath would be good once in a while,* I thought.

There were highs and lows and at times I felt empty. When I felt down, I reminded myself that there were people in the world much worse off than me and I forced myself to count my blessings; a loving family that included three wonderful children who would always be a part of me. Nobody could take that away from me, whatever happened in the years ahead. The children were the only positive thing to have come out of my marriage, a welcome diversion when

I began dwelling on my wedding, the horrendous months I spent in Pakistan and the more recent dramas at my parents' house. Similarly, university was an escape from my domestic routine, which I knew I'd earned. Mother, daughter, student…so many roles to play.

My tutors were pleased with my progress and I did my best to meet the deadlines on assignments. Night after night, I sat at the table once the children were asleep, books in front of me, sipping one cup of coffee after another, partly to help me stay awake and partly for warmth in the chilly Lancashire evenings. Hands curled around my mug, I smiled as I remembered the casual coffees of yesteryear in cafes with friends, laughing and chatting. Here I was, a world away, hardly able to stay awake and trying to keep my heating bill down. Dinners and lunches consisted of leftovers or something quick and simple. Right now, as long as the children were eating well, I was happy.

One day, out of the blue, Saleem phoned. I tried to rally, assuming he'd want to hear our news and began telling him about what the children had been up to and about my university studies. As I paused for breath, I realized he hadn't really said much and, before I knew it, he'd hung up, saying he'd call again soon. I rubbed my eyes, tired and now also preoccupied. What was behind this unexpected call? Could it be that he wanted something?

Saleem began calling regularly. I did my best to bring him up-to-date on all the milestones he'd missed; Zoya's first words, Adam and Sara sitting, crawling and giggling, what they all liked to eat and how each had their own personality. With each call, the conversation became easier and less tense. Perhaps distance and time spent apart had made Saleem realize what he'd lost and brought him to his senses. Perhaps he'd finally changed and really wanted to make our marriage work. Part of me was desperate to broach the subject, but with my course at such a critical point, I held back from asking him if he planned to come back. I wasn't prepared to risk his mood swings and aggression when I was so near to qualifying, even though I wanted the children to see their father.

My greater concern was that unless I mentioned the children, he rarely asked about them. Even when I gave him details of what they'd been doing, he didn't sound interested. He never once asked how I was supporting myself or mentioned money. In fact, he still said very little during the conversations, other than telling me about life in Pakistan.

At the point when my finals were approaching, I decided against dwelling on Saleem and what the future may or may not hold. My thesis was completed and the practical work I'd done in hours snatched here and there, sometimes in the dead of night, was ready to be exhibited. I was exhausted and relieved in equal measure. After two years of hard work, what a privilege to have some free time – time I could spend with my children and give my parents back their freedom!

As results day drew closer, my nerves were on edge, keeping me awake at night. I knew I'd done my best, but what if all my hard work and the favours I'd asked of Mum and Dad were for nothing? What was my Plan B this time?

Eventually, the moment of truth arrived. I had waited in agony for the letter that would determine my future to come through the letterbox; when it finally did, with hands trembling, I ripped open the envelope – its familiar crest on the outside – and skimmed through the notes. I'd been awarded a degree with first-class honours! Success! Shrieking for joy, I gathered my children into a bear hug as tears of happiness ran down my cheeks – they'd kept me going when I came close to giving up. I'd done it! I'd qualified! Whatever happened, nobody could take that away from me. All the hard work and pain had been worthwhile.

I rang my parents, who were ecstatic.

"Congratulations, Shama, my child, I'm so proud of you. I always knew you'd do it," Mum said, before passing the phone to Dad, her voice wavering with emotion.

"Well done, that's fantastic. We'll go out for dinner tonight to celebrate," Dad added.

After I'd hung up, I thought I'd call Saleem to let him know. He was still my husband and I'd kept him up-to-date on the ups and downs of my studies since we'd been back in touch. When he answered immediately, I thought he may have been waiting for my results too, but evidently results day was not at the top of his thoughts.

"I received my results. I got a first-class honours," I told him, excitedly.

"That's good, it was all worth it then. You must be pleased that I allowed you to go to university now," he said.

I took a deep breath and counted to 10 as I'd taught myself to do when I didn't trust myself to speak. Then, I let it all out.

"Seriously? You allowed? When I applied in secret and had to rely on my parents for help with the children because you, my husband, were back in Pakistan?" Then, deciding, I wouldn't rise any further to the comment, I added, "Will you be coming for my graduation?"

But this was clearly the wrong thing to say.

"How can you ask that? You know I haven't got any money for a ticket," came Saleem's surly reply.

"But it's important and it's an occasion we should celebrate as a family," I insisted.

"Sorry, Shama, but it's out of the question," he said firmly, closing the chance of any further conversation.

After he'd hung up, I kicked myself for asking him. When would I learn to expect nothing and stop asking? And did I really want him there? Well, maybe. I was thinking about the children, who hadn't seen their father for months, but I'd done my best to put that right.

I had no intention of allowing Saleem's reaction to cast a cloud over my impending graduation. My parents, siblings and children were all coming to watch me receive my degree and join in the celebrations.

"I'll come round and help you with your hair and makeup," my sister Fatima had said on the phone the night before.

As we discussed styles and went through the products we'd use, memories of getting ready for my wedding came flooding back. I'd been so naïve then. Today was a different kind of celebration, a milestone that had been achieved through sheer hard work and sacrifice, on my part, but also on the part of my parents. I was delighted that they'd be there to share the moment.

As I took my place amongst the other, younger students, I felt prouder than I'd ever done before. I was a mother of three, wife and daughter, but now I was also a graduate. Walking up to collect my degree from the Dean and shaking his hand, I couldn't help thanking him for allowing me to return and finish my course.

"You did the hard work, Shama, never forget that," he said, smiling.

The afternoon celebrations were followed by a wonderful meal out, at which we laughed and talked in a way we hadn't for almost two years. The pressure was off, for me and also my parents. They hadn't complained once, but I knew they'd found looking after the children tiring at times.

With no university lectures to fill my days, I made the most of spending quality time with the kids. Thoughts of what I was going to do next were never far from my mind. I knew I wanted to work in the art world, but I hadn't gotten much further than that.

"We can still help with childcare, Shama. I love having the children," Mum said, when I told her about my plans.

"But not all the time, Mom, I should be able to afford some nursery fees once I'm working," I replied.

I knew childcare wouldn't be cheap, but I'd get help from the government with childcare fees and I desperately wanted to give my mum some of her free time back. After researching vacancies and opportunities, I began sending off applications and eventually secured a position at the Spinning 1 Gallery in Manchester. Finally, I was doing something professional. It was an entry-level post, helping to arrange exhibitions and process sales, but the work was fascinating. Not only were the shows wide-ranging, covering photography and visual art, but the gallery was also involved in local education, bringing schoolchildren in for talks on certain days of the week, which I really enjoyed.

I loved my job, but the commute by train was expensive and made the day long. I was still frantic in the mornings, sometimes falling asleep on the train, often planning meals on my journeys and then once home packing bags for the next day, just as I had been in my university days.

A car would be good, I thought. I'd passed my test before leaving for Pakistan, but never driven since. Could I get behind the wheel after so many years of just being a passenger? Where would I find the money to buy a car? I didn't want to ask my parents for money when they'd done so much for me already and I thought it unlikely that the bank would lend me anything, since I'd been in my job for just a few weeks. What else could I do?

Sitting at my dressing table, getting ready for work, I opened my jewellery box. My mother had given me a beautiful set of gold bangles as a gift when Zoya was born. I already had plenty of other jewellery that she'd gifted me over the years. Could I perhaps sell some of them? Gathering the bangles into a pouch, I took them into one of the jewellery shops in town for a valuation on the way back from work. "I can offer you £2,500 for the lot," the jeweller said.

I was about to protest, suspecting they were worth more, but knew I had little in the way of bargaining power. That would be enough to buy a second-hand car and pay the insurance, I thought. "Done," I answered.

The next stop was the newsagent, where I picked up a local paper and began trawling through the second-hand car adverts. I circled in blue pen anything under £2000. Once I'd narrowed the list down, the choice was limited, but one particular car sounded like it might be suitable and affordable: a white Nissan Sunny.

I phoned the number in the advert. "It's nothing special, I'll tell you know, but it's always been reliable," the seller said.

"Can I come and have a look at it on Saturday morning?" I asked, unabashed.

"Sure," came the answer.

When Saturday arrived, I dropped the children off at my neighbour's and walked round to the address I'd been given. Nothing special proved to mean rust on one of the doors, several scratches and a dent in the boot. However, it was within my budget and would be good on petrol.

"I'll take it," I told the guy.

"But do you know where I could get some second-hand car seats for my kids?"

"Why don't you try the charity shop on the high street?" he suggested.

The next day was Sunday and, feeling on cloud nine, I put the children in their second-hand car seats and drove round to my parents, desperate for them to share in what I felt was a massive achievement. As I parked outside their house, Fahad's wife, Kulsoom, opened the front door and came toward me, laughing.

"What on earth are you driving, Shama?" she said. "Don't park it too near the house, will you? It really lowers the tone!" She turned and walked back to the house as I fought back tears. Granted, my car certainly wasn't flash, but I'd bought it with my own money and, for the first time in my life, I hadn't had to ask my dad for a lift. Of course, this would be lost on my sister-in-law, who was traveling in rickshaws until she'd married my brother Fahad and begun a new life in the UK.

But the reaction from my father and brother cut even deeper. No pats on the back or approving smiles.

"Shama, why didn't you let us know you were thinking of buying a car? We'd have given you some advice," was all Sajjad said.

I knew he had my best interests at heart, but just a 'well done' would have been appreciated that day. Even within my lovely family there was an expectation that male advice should be given and received.

Still, the car proved to be reliable, despite its age and my lack of research on it and was indeed life-changing. I was able to drive myself to the supermarket and commute to work. Life as a single parent working full-time was still exhausting, but definitely more manageable with a car. Most importantly, it had given me more independence.

The children benefited too, since we were able to travel farther afield to explore parks and museums. Weekends were especially enjoyable, since I no longer had to pack in university studies, which freed up time to relax and spend precious hours with them.

Life was tiring, but fulfilling and I felt incredibly proud of what I'd achieved, although sometimes in the evening I wondered about Saleem. His calls had tailed off after he'd told me he couldn't make my graduation and it had now been over two years since he'd returned to Pakistan. He'd be a stranger to his children if they saw him, I thought. Didn't that bother him? Or were we simply not a priority?

Then, one Saturday early afternoon, when the children were having a nap and I was in the kitchen preparing dinner, the doorbell rang. I quickly put down the knife I'd been using to peel onions and rinsed my hands under the tap. I opened the door with a huge smile, expecting it to be my parents or sisters, but then pulled back, confused. Standing there was a stranger with a familiar face. It was too much to take in.

"Saleem?" I said, as more of a question than a statement.

"*Assalam alaikum.* Are you going to leave me standing on the doorstep? Aren't you happy to see me?" he replied.

"It's just a shock. I wasn't expecting you. Why didn't you call and let me know you were coming?" I said, trying to gather my thoughts. My mother's training in hospitality kicked in and I automatically stepped aside, saying, "Come in."

Saleem walked through into the lounge carrying a suitcase. With no hug or kiss, he took off his sunglasses and sat down on the sofa. He'd shaved off his moustache, I noticed, and was wearing jeans and a blue check shirt, one I thought I'd have been washing by hand if I was still living in Pakistan.

I stared at him, waiting for him to say something, but then heard a noise on the stairs. Zoya had woken up and was on her way down. Appearing at the door, holding Barney, her favourite soft toy, she greeted me sleepily.

"Mommy," she said as I scooped her up in my arms. Pointing to Saleem, she added, "Who's that man?"

"It's your *baba*, your daddy, he's come to visit. Isn't that nice?" I said, desperately trying to find the right words.

"No, Mommy, *Baba* went on airplane, he's in Pakistan," she corrected.

I winced, heartbroken for her. Could Saleem see the impact of his actions on his children? Zoya didn't even know him. She regarded my parents, siblings and me as her close family. Saleem had played no part in her life and now, here he was, a stranger sitting on the sofa, who'd simply turned up out of the blue.

"Yes, he was, sweetie, but he's come to visit. It's *Baba*. See?" I said, forcing a smile.

I was also willing Saleem to come over and give his daughter a reassuring hug and talk to her, but he made no movement; instead he looked at her for the first time, annoyed.

"That's not a very nice way for a little girl to talk to her *baba*," he said.

Luckily, Zoya found this amusing rather than upsetting, assuming Saleem was playing a game with her in the way my dad and brothers sometimes did. She turned to me again.

"Is this *Baba* we sometimes speak to on the phone, Mommy?"

"Yes, darling."

"But he's got a big moustache. I saw it in the photos."

"Well, he did, but he's changed a bit now, like when your uncle had a haircut," I explained.

This seemed to satisfy her and she ran over to join him on the sofa, grinning. Saleem tried to make conversation, asking her about Barney and her favourite games, but I could see he was struggling. Sighing, I went into the kitchen to make us all a drink. Bringing the tray in, I tried to help him by getting Zoya to sing the nursery rhymes I knew she'd learnt. I waited for him to ask about the twins, but he seemed more interested in looking round the room, asking about the furniture and television that I'd saved hard to buy.

"Haven't you forgotten something?" I asked. He looked puzzled.

"I don't think so, everything's in my case," he answered.

"I meant here, in this house."

"Shama, don't talk in riddles, I'm tired, I've been travelling for hours," he cut in, irritably.

"The twins – you haven't even asked about them!"

"Oh yes, I guess it's because they're not around," he said, shrugging.

There was a pause as I let his words sink in. How could he take so little interest in his own flesh and blood, I wondered. And he still hadn't asked about them now!

"I'll go upstairs and see if they're awake, shall I?" I said, finally.

The day continued in a surreal way, with the children tentative around Saleem, eyeing him warily to begin with, but gradually edging closer to him and involving him in their conversations as the hours ticked by. Over dinner, I tried to ask him how long he planned to stay, but he was vague in his response and seemed to find the question insulting.

"Anyone would think you weren't pleased to see your husband!" he sniped.

By Sunday, the children seemed to have accepted Saleem and were delighted at the idea of having their father around. I enjoyed seeing their happy faces, but was also worried. What if he left as suddenly as he'd arrived? I'd be the one picking up the pieces. My parents were also concerned about Saleem's unexpected visit. I'd phoned them on Saturday night while he was in the shower to explain his surprise appearance.

"Of course, we'll have you all over for a meal as soon as he's settled, but please be careful, child and phone us immediately if you need anything," Mum had said.

Monday was a working day for me, something that I imagined hadn't occurred to Saleem. I left him in bed early in the morning, deciding that it was still best to take the children to nursery, even though he was in the house. Yes, he was their dad, I thought, but how could I leave them in his care when he'd played such a small part in their lives and never been hands-on even when we were together?

The subject of how long Saleem planned to stay and the reasons for his sudden arrival remained a mystery. I decided against asking further, after he'd snapped when I raised the subject the first time around. As the days passed, we fell into some sort of routine. I'd drive off to work with the children, leaving Saleem asleep and come home later, after stopping off either at the nursery or my parents' house.

Saleem had raised his eyebrows when he realized I now owned a car, but said nothing. He hadn't driven when in the UK before, so at least I knew he'd be unlikely to ask to use my trusty wheels.

Even though Saleem was at home all day, he still expected me to cook and clean. The cultural differences were as wide as ever and I found his expectations even more difficult to accept, having lived without him for so long. Life as a single parent was tiring yet rewarding, but life with a husband who expected you to do everything was both exhausting and demoralizing.

I was concerned about how Saleem was spending his days. He told me he'd begun searching for work, but sometimes he'd roll in late in the evening smelling of alcohol and more than once I found bottles of whisky hidden at the back of the kitchen cupboard.

Whenever I tried to ask him how the job search was going, he would snap that it was none of my business and the familiar name-calling began. I told myself to give it time. After all, hadn't Rumi once said that patience is the way out of anxiety? I began to stay longer at my parents after work when collecting the children, acutely aware that they had witnessed more than once the angry exchanges and heard the insults that Saleem was hurling in my direction.

One night, after accepting my mother's invitation to stay for dinner, I made my way home and as I pulled up outside our front door, I spotted Saleem hovering menacingly at the window.

"Children, why don't you go up to your rooms and play for a bit? I need to speak to *Baba*," I told them instinctively, as I unlocked the front door.

As they ran upstairs, Saleem barged into the hall.

"Where's my dinner? It's gone seven," he barked.

"I'll fix it now," I said, eager to appease him. "We've already eaten at my parents."

"You spend too much time there, it's not right. I'm your family and this is your home," he shouted back.

"What?" I replied, unable to believe what I was hearing. "They're my parents and they help with the kids! The children love seeing them as well!"

"I mean it!" he growled. "You stop spending so much time there, do you understand? Pick them up and get yourself home or there'll be trouble."

19
The Water of Life

Saleem had come back into our lives, but there was little in the way of happiness at this turn of events. I was unable to draw a line under the past and the scars caused by his behaviour, both physical and mental, ran deep, as did my own internal conflicts. I wanted the children to have a relationship with their father and marriage was something you worked hard to preserve in our culture, but his unpredictable moods were a major cause of tension. And now he was driving a wedge between me and my family. I struggled to reconcile the wisdom of Rumi with my situation. One quote remained stuck in my mind: "Plant the love of the holy ones within your spirit; don't give your heart to anything, but the love of those whose hearts are glad."

Having only recently gotten my self-confidence back, I was once again questioning myself. How should I deal with the dilemma I faced? What would a good mother do? Saleem was the father of my children, after all…didn't he deserve another chance to change? Perhaps I needed to be more understanding and think about the traumas that he, too, had faced, such as the death of his father. Maybe counselling would help him, if I could persuade him to go. Yet his behaviour made it difficult for me to be sympathetic and supportive.

Every evening, I took myself off to bed, exhausted, in the knowledge that my husband was sat downstairs in the lounge filling a glass with whisky and listening to *ghazal* poetry set to music. As I dozed off alone, night after night, any hope I had of him coming upstairs and showing me the affection that I craved disappeared.

After a few weeks, Saleem was offered a packing job in a local factory. It wasn't what he'd hoped for, but I was secretly relieved, grateful for the extra income and also convinced that it was better for him to be occupied than sitting at home or out who knew where.

Going to work was something of a shock for him, after doing next to nothing for so long. On the first day, he came home in a foul mood, complaining about how tired he felt and badmouthing his colleagues. In some ways I felt sorry for him, since he'd found himself forced to do unskilled work because his qualifications weren't recognized in the UK. But what were the alternatives? I was working hard to keep the family afloat and we needed the extra income.

Saleem stuck the job out, but his resentment was evident. "This country's a joke. I've got no life, there's nothing to do. I don't know why you want to stay here," he grumbled as he slumped on the sofa.

I did my best to make our life enjoyable, but I was also feeling the strain of combining work, family and household chores. The twins were becoming more demanding, as was Zoya and Saleem showed no desire to help around the house, even though his working day was shorter than mine.

As his moods worsened, once again I began to feel that I'd failed as a wife and mother. Mom's words were never far from my mind: 'Remember that your family and husband come first, everything else comes second.' Should I be giving my husband more attention? And if so, what should I sacrifice? I was already stretched to breaking point.

The decisions I faced were not helped by the fact that Saleem's moods were having a negative effect on the children. I always made time to play with them whenever I could, even if I was struggling to keep my eyes open, drawing and making Lego models in their rooms, which were full of toys, games and books.

Zoya was quite independent and would happily play on her own, but when she heard Saleem shouting, she'd run into the toilet and shut herself in there. I wondered if she viewed this small room with a lock on the door as her safe space and remembered, with a pang of anguish, how I'd often locked myself in the bathroom in the early days to escape my husband.

I began to notice that Zoya's lips were pale when she emerged from the bathroom and she'd also developed a stutter. Yet, she also adored her father, running to him for cuddles and asking him to look at pictures she'd drawn. If he was in a good mood, he'd give her a smile and admire her colouring, but at other times he simply ignored her or brushed her off, at which point my heart bled for my daughter.

My favourite part of the day was reading to the children at bedtime. My mother had kept my favourite childhood books, like *Topsy and Tim* and the Beatrix Potter stories. The children loved being read to. We'd all cuddle up and look at the pictures together, after which I'd switch off the light and give them a kiss goodnight. Once they'd settled, I'd traipse downstairs, tired but content and make myself a cup of tea or coffee whilst Saleem sat sipping his whisky and listening to his music.

These evenings together, which could have been so precious, were awkward and stilted. Instead of talking as a couple or planning as a team, we were two individuals leading separate lives, with Saleem making his requests for food and drink from the sofa in front of the television and me scurrying around waiting on him or ironing his clothes.

Yet, I still strived to be a good wife and make Saleem happy, hoping that by doing so I could help to lighten his moods and improve his temperament. As I prepared him a snack and went through the shopping for the next day in my head,

I wondered whether the other wives and mothers in my town and farther afield were feeling the same as me. Were they happy in their lives or did they also regret some of their decisions? Were they feeling weighed down by responsibilities and the monotony of their daily routines or did they think it was all worthwhile? And maybe if they did, it was because they made those sacrifices and did those exhausting chores knowing that the love they felt for their husband was reciprocated. As for me, I felt like my life was passing me by, each day the *drip, drip, drip* from a tap – drops of water simply lost down the plughole.

"Shama!" Saleem's voice brought me out of my daydream with a jolt. "Are you stupid? Why did you put my clothes on the hanger when you know I'm about to put them on?"

"I didn't want them to crease after I'd ironed them," I replied.

Too late, I realized that Saleem was not in the mood for what he saw as retaliation. Before I could step away his face was in mine and I could smell his hot whisky breath.

"Stupid woman," he hissed, gripping both my cheeks with one hand and squeezing them.

Why hadn't I just kept quiet, I asked myself. And were the children fully asleep? I didn't want them disturbed.

"I'm going to bed," I said calmly, freeing myself and walking upstairs, hoping desperately that he wouldn't follow me. Thankfully, I heard him slump back on the sofa.

That weekend, Sajjad was coming over to take the children out. All three were excited, as Sajjad had been working abroad at that time and rarely got the chance to treat his nieces and nephew. I was upstairs getting them ready when the doorbell rang and Saleem answered it.

"Uncle's here!" Zoya said, jigging up and down, impatiently. "Can we go down, Mommy, please?"

"Of course, I'll bring your bags," I said, with a smile.

I followed them down the stairs as they counted each step, something I'd encouraged them to do to help them learn their numbers. "One, two, three…" Sara and Adam tailed off as we neared 10, but Zoya proudly chanted her numbers up to the final stair. "Twenty!" she said proudly, turning to me for a clap and then followed her younger brother and sister into the lounge. If only Saleem could also find it in him to give his children a bit of praise from time to time!

Stopping to check the children's bags, I could already hear their shrieks of delight and giggles as they greeted their uncle. It was wonderful to listen to the sound of happy children, something I realized was missing a lot of the time from our house. As I entered the room, Sajjad was swinging each of them round in turn, causing them to erupt in giggles. I smiled, but my happiness at the scene was tainted by the knowledge that my children never ran to their father in this way.

"Sajjad," I said, running to him and allowing myself to be given a bear hug. "It's wonderful to see you."

"You too, Shama!"

Sajjad had brought Zoya a huge teddy bear and the twins a rocking horse to share.

"Look, look, Mommy!" said Zoya, ecstatically cuddling her toy.

"What lucky children you are!" I said.

The twins were jumping up and down, impatiently.

"Okay, let's get you up in the saddle, but one at a time, guys!" Sajjad told them.

"Me first, Uncle Sajjad!" they pleaded in unison.

"Hmm, how are we going to decide this?" he said, making a funny face at them. "Maybe I'd better have the first ride to be fair!"

The twins both squealed with laughter and I joined in, full of love for my brother, the happiness he'd brought into our home and the way he interacted with my children, in a display of unconditional love.

"Does anyone want a drink?" I asked.

Saleem instantly handed me his empty mug without a word while my brother looked on, shocked.

"No, thanks, I'm fine, but I'll come into the kitchen with you," he said.

"Shama," he said, quietly, once I'd filled the kettle. "Are you OK? You look sad."

"Sure, I'm fine, just a bit tired, can't you see?" I replied, with a bright smile.

"Yes, I can see, that's why I asked," he answered, seriously.

His words were lost on me until later, when I had time to think about them. But at that moment, the children were running around in circles, over-excited and keen to get going. I waved them off and wished I was going too. Other couples would relish some precious time together alone, I thought sadly, but here I was, thinking I'd rather spend the day with my brother and my children than with my husband. With a heavy heart I began filling a bucket to clean the kitchen floor, when I heard Saleem call out.

"Are you busy?"

No term of endearment or pet name, in fact, no name at all!

"Yes, I'm cleaning the kitchen."

"I want you to come in here and sit beside me."

I stopped midway filling the bucket, my spirits rising. Perhaps Saleem just needed more peaceful, child-free surroundings to talk to me. I could understand that.

"Coming," I called back, turning off the tap.

"Listen," he said, as I sat down next to him. "You need to stop doing things that make me want to punish you. You deserve to be punished for what you do. You really are stupid and dumb, a genuine idiot."

I stared at him, unable to take in his words.

"What do you mean?" was all I could manage.

"I want you to think hard and try to stay one step ahead of me. Think what I want, so I don't have to keep asking," he continued.

"I already do that all the time and I always put you first," I answered. "But you don't show me that you care at all. In fact, you're really rude and can be scary as well."

"What?" he shouted, prompting me to shift backwards on the sofa. "You think I'm rude for telling you that you should cater to my needs and for letting you know when you're in the wrong? You deserve the treatment you get in that case."

"Listen, I need to go and clean the kitchen," I said wearily, unwilling to hear any more. But as I got up to go, Saleem wrenched my arm.

"Sit down," he snarled. "Where the hell do you think you're going? I'll tell you when you can leave."

"What have I done?" I asked, trying to hold back the tears. "Why are you doing this?"

"I hate this life!" he spat, venomously. "I hate England and the people in this country! They are all crap!"

"Well, why have you come here?" I retorted. "I left this country and came to Pakistan to get married, but you wanted me to come back here to have the children and then you came over here again."

"Shut up, I'm talking, I didn't ask you for your opinion."

With that, he gripped the hair on the back of my head and yanked it so that my head jerked back. Then he brought his face level with mine.

"I cannot stand you," he hissed.

Before I could wrestle free, he'd pushed me to the floor and was kicking me. Instinctively, I brought my arms up over my face and my knees to my chest in an attempt to protect myself. I counted to myself, a tactic I'd learned to help me get through times like these, until the kicking stopped and I heard the lounge door open and close.

I remained in that position for what seemed like hours, replaying the morning's events over and over in my mind while trying to think whether I could have prevented them. I decided that the answer was no. Nothing I'd have said or done would've made a difference. Saleem was simply hellbent on taking his bad moods out on me. When was I going to face the facts? I was a victim of domestic violence; the bruises and cuts were the evidence. I allowed a man – my husband and the father of my children – to beat me up and tried to make allowances for it, even thinking I could be to blame in some way. And then I'd simply return to our everyday routine, as if nothing had happened…until the next time.

Saleem grabbed his jacket and left before I'd got up. Once I was sure he'd gone, I picked myself up gingerly and moved across to the sofa. Unable to face doing much, I decided to catch up with the soaps on TV for the week. It occurred to me that my life was a bit like a soap opera, except the characters all seemed to be having a better time of it than me.

Eventually I got up, bruised and sore and decided I'd make some coffee, before carrying on where I'd left off with cleaning the kitchen and preparing dinner. I knew I needed to change and shower before the kids came back, but I could hardly bear the thought of undressing. As I took off my clothes and looked in the mirror, I had to grip the sink to stop myself from shaking. Was that my reflection? Horrified, I leaned in closer to inspect the red marks that told the story of how my husband had dug his fingers into my cheeks in anger. I sat, undressed, on the toilet seat, trying to digest what the reflection staring back at me meant. This wasn't the face of a working mum who'd got her life together – it was the face of a victim, an unhappy, defeated woman who'd given up on life and simply accepted her fate on a daily basis.

After I'd showered, I got dressed and went downstairs, knowing my brother would be bringing the children back soon.

A knock at the door signalled they'd arrived. I went to open up, putting on my best smile. They tumbled in, Zoya hugging me first. I pulled her toward me and bent to kiss her cheek, but as she caught sight of my eye she pulled back.

"Mommy, what happened to you? Your face is red," she said.

"Oh, don't worry about me, let's see what you've got there, you lucky girl," I said, brightly. "My, what a lovely balloon and what else have you got? Sweets, yum!"

"Uncle got them!" she said, dancing off, with the twins in tow.

"I hope you said thank you!" I called after them.

The children ran upstairs, leaving me and Sajjad alone.

"Shama, where's Saleem?" he said, quietly.

"He's gone out," I replied. I knew there was no point in trying to pretend that my injuries were caused by anything or anyone else.

"This isn't right, what he's doing to you," he said. "Why are you allowing him to treat you like this when you still have us, your family, on your side? You don't need to put up with it, Shama."

"My problem is that it's my marriage, isn't it? And marriages are for life…" My voice trailed off as the tears started falling.

"Well, if you won't think about yourself, can't you at least think of the kids?" Sajjad pleaded. "Think what this is doing to them. It's wrong and we all love them, not just you."

"I know, I know," I said, rubbing my eyes. "I know the kids are disturbed. I just don't know what to do for the best." I was sobbing by now, but also feeling humiliated. "Honestly, Sajjad, I appreciate that you care, but you have to let me figure this out by myself."

At that moment the front door opened and Saleem walked in, staggering and eyes glazed. Horrified, I realized my brother would now know that my husband was not only a wife-beater, but also a drinker. He swayed as he came toward us, sneering and reeking of alcohol.

"What's this, then?" he said, turning to Sajjad. "Are you badmouthing me, telling my wife a load of rubbish?"

There was a pause, during which I could tell my brother was trying to decide on his tactics.

"Look, Saleem," he said eventually. "You know this is wrong. Have you got no shame? Don't you have any pride? Don't you care that your wife and kids are witnessing your behaviour and that it's affecting them?"

Before he could finish, Saleem had squared up to Sajjad and pushed him in the chest with the palms of both hands, catching him by surprise so that he stumbled backward.

"What the hell are you doing? You might be my sister's husband, but don't push your luck, Saleem!" Sajjad said, recovering his balance.

But Saleem took no notice, pushing him again and grabbing him by the shoulders.

"I'm not going to give you another warning, Saleem," Sajjad said through gritted teeth. "Get the hell away from me."

"Or what?" Saleem snarled, his face just an inch or two away from my brother's. I was trying to decide whether to intervene when Zoya ran in. "Mommy, I'm hungry, can I..." she broke off, staring at her father and uncle as they glared at each other.

"Just give us a few minutes, darling and I'll sort something out. Go back up to your room for now," I whispered. But she didn't even wait to be told, turning and dashing up the stairs, fear etched across her little face.

"Saleem, for God's sake, think of the children. They know what's going on, just stop!" I pleaded.

Then, before I could move, he'd turned away from Sajjad and swung his fist in my direction, catching me on the left temple. I gasped in pain and sank to my knees, clasping my head. Out of the corner of my eye I saw my brother land a punch on Saleem's cheek and frog-march him to the front door, picking up his jacket on the way.

"Get the hell out of this house, you drunk psycho, before I kill you. I'm not going to stand here and watch you hit my sister. We've run out of patience with you, you evil nutter," he said, shoving him out onto the doorstep and shutting the door behind him.

By now I was in tears. "Sajjad, leave him be," I begged. "God knows what he'll do to me now."

My brother stared at me and sighed, his shoulders dropping.

"Stay here and look after the children, Shama," he said and with that, he picked up his car keys and went outside.

I looked out of the window to see Sajjad opening the passenger door of his car and pushing Saleem inside, before driving away. Numb, I sat on the sofa, wondering what on earth would happen next. Then I remembered about the children – they must be starving. I rushed out to the kitchen and heated up the food I'd prepared earlier, before calling them to eat. They traipsed down the stairs, subdued, sensing something was wrong and shuffled toward the table.

"I'm not hungry, Mommy," Zoya said, pushing her plate away.

"Nor am I," Sara said.

Adam, blessed with a healthy appetite, picked up his cutlery and tucked in immediately.

"Girls, please eat something," I begged.

At that moment, the doorbell rang and I rushed to the door. My father stood on the doorstep, his face lined with worry.

"Sajjad asked me to come over," he said, as I followed him through to the lounge. He was about to say more, but then he saw the children at the table.

"Shama, is it true, what your brother told me?" I looked at the floor, unable to answer. "You can't carry on like this, my child," he said quietly. "Please think of your health and the children. You look terrible. It's obvious that whatever's going on here is affecting you badly."

I was touched by his concern and knew he meant well, but neither he nor my brother seemed to understand just how torn I was, that I still felt a sense of loyalty to this man, whatever he did and however he behaved. Even now, I was worried about him.

"What has Sajjad done with Saleem, Dad?" I asked.

"He's dropped him off at a friend's, someone who works with him at the factory," my father answered. He looked at me, seemingly astonished that I cared enough to ask. No one in my family understood just how torn I was.

The next two days passed without incident. I took leave from work and stayed indoors, focusing on the children. Mum brought some food over and took away with her a bag of clothes I'd packed for Saleem, which my brother dropped at his friend's house. Then on the third day, the phone rang.

"Hi, how are you, Shama?" It was Saleem's voice. "I want to be with you. Can I come over?"

"Saleem, too much has happened," I answered, with a sigh. "I can't take it any more – you have no idea how to treat a woman. You frighten me and the children are suffering as well. I'm sorry, I can't have you back. We need to separate."

I put the phone down, but still felt confused. Deep down, I couldn't help hoping that maybe, now I was being firm, Saleem would change. Pushing these thoughts to one side, I phoned my parents and said I was on my way 'round.

"Can you ask my brothers to be there too?" I asked.

"Of course, Shama," my mother said, her voice strained with worry.

"We're going to visit your grandparents," I told the children as I put them in the car.

"What, in the evening? We don't usually do that!" Zoya said, excitedly. She didn't miss a trick!

Once we were there, my sister Fatima led the children off to her bedroom, armed with their favourite toys, so I could talk to the family.

"You should know that Saleem phoned earlier this evening," I began. "I've told him not to come back and that I need a break from him. I thought I'd let you all know." There was a sigh of relief around the room and, as I finished, my mother started to cry.

"We are so happy, child. We've been worried that one day we'll hear he's killed you," she said. "Saleem is not a good person and his family aren't supportive either."

I went out to the kitchen with my mother, leaving my father and brothers to discuss what I'd said.

"You know, child, you have given him plenty of chances," my mother said, turning to me. "You offered him a fresh start in your own place, with the opportunity to show some responsibility, but he hasn't taken it. You've had to do all of that yourself. I know you wanted the relationship to work and were trying to do the best for the children. But you must remember that you tried."

She hugged me and I wrapped my arms around her in return. My mother, who'd always told me to put my family first, was now also telling me that I didn't need to feel guilty. Perhaps this was what I needed to hear, I thought, as relief washed over me.

But there were still challenges to face. Saleem's mother called my parents, telling them that if we didn't allow Saleem back in the house, he'd divorce me. My parents refused to react to her threats, maintaining a dignified silence.

Yet, once the children were asleep and I was alone downstairs in the house, there were moments of sadness, times when I couldn't shake off the feeling that I'd failed at my marriage. I asked myself again and again whether I could have done anything differently to avoid breaking up my family and leaving my children without their father around. I'd had a wonderfully happy and privileged childhood and had desperately wanted my children to have the same start in life.

I'd been a single parent before, but somehow it felt lonelier this time 'round, perhaps because Saleem had become part of our lives for a while. I was also fearful at the thought of being on my own. At just 25 years old, I was already mother to three children and felt much older, thanks to the physical and mental abuse I'd suffered.

Perhaps it was just as well that there wasn't much time to dwell on things. Everyday life resumed quickly enough, with work, the children and household chores taking up the bulk of the day. My parents rallied once again, helping with the children and offering to give me some time to myself, but I knew the latest episode with Saleem had taken its toll on them. I was also acutely aware that, despite their loyalty, the prospect of having a divorce in the family – the first – would be a source of embarrassment to them. *I've failed,* I told myself, *as a daughter, a wife, and, if I don't manage to provide for Zoya, Sara and Adam, as a mother too.*

20
Safe Havens

Although life as a single mum wasn't easy, I decided it was best to keep Saleem out of our lives. Soon enough, I was relieved and not surprised to hear from my brother that he'd returned to Pakistan. Watching the children reach their milestones and sharing in their ups and downs was incredibly fulfilling, but there was always a niggling feeling inside that I'd failed as a wife. On the rare occasions I had time to reflect on things, I felt anxious and hollow, but unable to identify the cause of this deep unhappiness. Pushing these thoughts to one side, I tried hard to focus on the positives and count my blessings. Yet, each time I looked at the children I felt I'd done them an injustice by breaking up their home. Deep down, I knew it hadn't been a happy place, but that didn't stop me yearning for the ideal family unit and the stability I thought that brought with it.

Work was my me time, away from the home, the family and my local community, a place where I was Shama, rather than a mom, sister, or daughter. I loved the opportunity that my work gave me to be myself and relished using the skills I'd worked so hard to acquire. At the gallery I was treated like an adult and taken seriously, with those around me valuing my opinion. I was happy to throw myself into my job and as I did so my confidence grew, with the result that when my initial contract came to an end, I was offered the position of co-curator of exhibitions.

Was it luck? Was I simply in the right place at the right time? Or had my hard work paid off? Self-belief continued to elude me, even as my boss congratulated me on my promotion. Still, I welcomed the extra money after struggling to buy even the basics for so long.

Reliant on my parents for years, I was determined to become more independent and, in turn, raise my children to adopt the same approach. Buying a place of my own seemed a good place to start. I'd begun squirrelling away money for a deposit from the time of my first salary and then had been able to increase the amount once I was promoted. The time had come to start looking at what I could afford and how much the bank was prepared to lend me. Excitedly,

I began searching through the property pages of the local papers and made an appointment with a mortgage advisor at the bank. The options were narrow, but I'd be able to buy something modest with three bedrooms with what the bank was prepared to lend me. It was the news I was desperate to hear. Four walls of my very own!

Truth be told, my knowledge of the property market was basic to say the least, but I decided the best thing to do was to follow my heart. I traipsed around one generic property after the other, with none really jumping out at me, when the estate agent rang to tell me about a cosy, two-bedroomed, terraced house located on the other side of town.

Perhaps it was the sight of two young boys playing together as their mom, a single mother, watched them with a tired smile, but something just clicked as we were shown round the house. I felt an affinity with this family, with a mum who was doing her best for her boisterous kids. Somehow, the energy felt right. The price was within my range as well and I liked the fact that the property was the other side of town, within driving distance of my family, but far enough away for me to feel independent. I applied for a mortgage without telling anyone and, once approved, made an offer on the house.

Throughout this part of the process, I still couldn't quite believe that I was on my way to becoming a homeowner, but on the day that the formal letter arrived from the solicitor to say the vendor had accepted my offer, the excitement began to set in.

The weeks leading up to completion were spent packing and putting our belongings in boxes. I involved the children as much as I could, although they were better at taking things out of cases than putting them in. They flatly refused to throw away any of their toys, even those gathering dust in the cupboards. Finally, the day of the move came and we drove round to the estate agent to collect the keys. As we unlocked the door for the first time, the woman next door called across from her front garden to say hello.

"We wondered who bought Anna's house," she said across the fence. "They were a lovely family, but she was down on her luck and simply couldn't afford to keep it, poor love."

Remembering the two boys and their mother's lovely smile, I felt a wave of sympathy for them. *Hopefully they'll get back on their feet,* I thought. Life was full of ups and downs, as I knew only too well.

Once we'd brought in all our boxes and the removal men had carried in the furniture, it was time to go and share the good news with my parents. I took a box of sweets with me, as was the custom in our culture when there was good news to share. I knew my parents would be shocked. Keeping the move secret from them had been a major challenge, but I'd been determined to go through the entire purchasing process alone and then tell them about it at the end. It had become a target I'd set myself and now I'd achieved it, I couldn't wait to share the news with them.

As I pulled up outside their house, the children could sense my excitement and were bouncing around in their car seats. Mum opened the front door before

I'd even rung the doorbell, holding her arms out wide to embrace her grandchildren, as was her routine. Before I had an opportunity to break the news, Zoya had done it for me.

"Nano, Zoya's got a new house, I've got a new room," she was saying, clutching her yellow Teletubby and jumping up and down. My mother turned to me confused.

"Has she been on a sleepover?" she asked.

"No, Mom, actually, I've bought a house on Apple Street – we've just collected the keys. I didn't want to tell you until it was finalized," I said, walking indoors.

My parents turned to each other as they sat down, trying to take in the news. Their silence told me that they were finding it difficult to digest, or perhaps thought they'd misunderstood me. I knew my father would also be a little hurt that I hadn't sought his advice, just like when I'd bought my first car.

"I wanted to do this on my own, Dad," I said, gently, touching his arm. "It was important to show you that I'm becoming more independent and making a better life for my children."

"Child, I'm very proud of you," he answered, softly. "But you have nothing to prove. Your mother and I know you're an excellent mother."

Having their blessing meant a great deal to me and with the air cleared it was time to celebrate. Then came the hard work of decorating and renovating to make the house really feel like our home.

It was tiring, but also exciting and immensely satisfying. I sensed that my life was changing. Money was still tight, especially with a mortgage to pay, but I felt in greater control. My parents had noticed the change in me and were proud of what I was doing.

The children settled into their new home quickly, delighted at the fact that they had more room to play with their toys and read their books. They were growing up quickly, each with their own unique character and personality.

Saleem rarely called, but I phoned him regularly to give him updates on the children. I couldn't help wondering what would happen if I didn't take the initiative and call him. Didn't he want to know how his children were getting on? I wanted him to have a relationship with them and hear about their milestones, but sometimes even when I called, he didn't sound especially interested or even concerned about the welfare of his kids. Could it be because of the distance? I sent him photos, but I knew that they were no substitute for seeing the children on a daily basis.

Although I appeared confident and upbeat on the outside, the failure of my marriage and Saleem's absence, both as a husband and as a father, gnawed away at me. After the children had gone to bed, the house seemed unnaturally quiet and there was an emptiness I couldn't get rid of. Sometimes I panicked about the dangers of living alone, putting a chair in front of the front door in case of a break-in when I heard a strange noise or read about a burglary in the local paper.

One weekend, Pauline, an old schoolfriend, came over and we got chatting about jobs abroad and life as a single parent. She had taught English as a foreign language in Asia and still received notifications about jobs in the region. Pauline also knew that I was torn about whether to let Saleem back into our lives.

"You know, if you're really worried about the kids not having a relationship with their father, you could always move back to Pakistan, but take a job there, so you'd have more control and power," she said. "The balance would be completely different this time around."

Pauline had seen an advert for a job as chief curator of the British Embassy's art gallery in Karachi. "Look at the package, it's fantastic," she said. "The salary's great, but you'll also get loads of perks, like accommodation, security and an education at a top international school for the children. I'll drop the application forms over if you want."

"I'll have a look at it," I said, with a smile. "And thanks for thinking of me."

Was this the answer? To return to Pakistan – a place that held such terrible memories – so that my children would know their father better? Could I make that sacrifice? I wasn't convinced Saleem deserved this opportunity, but I kept reminding myself that I was considering all options for the children, not for him.

That weekend, the children were spending some time at my parents while I waited for a new sofa and carpet fitters to arrive. I took the information pack that Pauline had dropped through my letterbox out of the drawer and started looking through it. She'd been right – it was an attractive package. Pakistan was keen to attract British Pakistanis to work there, opening doors to people like myself.

I began filling in the forms. I could always bring the process to a halt at any point, if I wanted. The carpet fitters had been and the new sofa was in place – a beautiful, fluffy, woollen, off-white pile carpet and cream leather sofa. Impractical perhaps, I thought with a smile, making a mental note that the children would have to be told no food or shoes in this room. But, importantly, it was my choice and would be paid for by myself.

I looked at the almost-completed application form and felt wrenched. Here I was, making a beautiful home for my children and applying for a job thousands of miles away just so they could be near a father who hardly ever phoned them. Was it the right thing to do? Surely it had to be worth a try, I thought, as I finished the paperwork and sealed the envelope. Now to post it!

Monday morning came round with the usual routine of waking early, making breakfast, preparing lunches, getting Zoya into her school uniform and ensuring the twins had everything they needed for the day at nursery. While the children finished their breakfast, I showered and put on my work clothes. As I drew back the curtains, I noticed frost on the ground, so made a note to start the car to warm it up.

It was a typically hectic start – I'd dealt with countless similar days – and yet, somehow, today it all seemed too much. Having waved the kids off, I pulled over into a layby and let the tears flow. Perhaps it was the job application and thoughts of Pakistan, but I suddenly felt the need to talk to Saleem.

Later that evening, I dialled the number.

"Saleem, how are you? We haven't heard from you for ages. Why haven't you been in touch? The children keep talking about you and miss you."

"Hi, Shama, I'm good. Why haven't you called?"

"Because you're the one away from your children and wife, not me!" I could feel my patience evaporating at his blasé manner.

"You should stay in touch more," I continued. "It's your responsibility! Don't you miss them or me?"

"Of course, but what can I do?" he asked. "I have no money or time to call you regularly."

"Why not?"

"Because I'm busy these days looking for a decent job!"

"Shall I send you pictures of the twins and Zoya?" I asked, thinking it was better to change the subject.

"I do miss you, Shama," Saleem said in a quiet voice. "I miss you and I will always love you."

"But what is love, Saleem?" I asked. "I have been raising your children on my own and you hardly ever call us?"

There was a silence, as I waited for Saleem to reply, but when there was no response, my emotions got the better of me.

"You have no idea how much it hurts, knowing our children have a home with no father," I said. "I've just bought my own home because I want the children to have some security and dignity. The twins go to nursery and Zoya's even started school; they're doing well. They have a lovely room with books and toys to play with. And you don't even contribute or get to see any of this."

"I miss you, Shama. You are a good person," he answered. "I have nothing to give you, but I do miss you."

His words touched me. After all, he was missing out. But he still hadn't asked about the children. Was he not bothered? The familiar doubts began to return.

"I'll have to go. I've got to think of my phone bill," I told him, hanging up.

Barely a week later, I received a letter informing me I'd been selected for a preliminary telephone interview for the job. I was excited, but determined to keep calm, knowing competition for the post would be fierce.

I prepared as much as I could for the interview. I felt it went well, since it gave me an opportunity to showcase my experience curating exhibitions and I was able to tell them that, since I'd already lived in Pakistan, I was confident I'd be able to adjust to life there. Once it was over, I wondered if I should tell my family and Saleem about the job, but decided to wait.

That Friday afternoon, my mobile phone began ringing in the office.

"Shama Mughal?" a woman's voice asked.

"Yes, speaking."

"This is the international arts and culture team at the British Foreign Office. We were wondering if you could attend an interview on Wednesday here in London?"

"Wednesday?!"

"We know it's short notice," the woman said, apologetically. "But the person who oversees the entire project in Karachi just happens to be in the UK right now and really wants to see you. Of course, we'll reimburse your travel."

Luckily for me the gallery was shut on Wednesdays and I knew my mum would agree to have the children.

"Yes, that's fine. I'm sure I can make arrangements," I said.

"That's great," the woman said. "We've scheduled an appointment for 11am. I'll give you the details."

Once she'd explained where they were located, she told me to book my tickets, keep all the receipts and they'd reimburse me at the end of the interview. *Wow, that was quick!* I thought. The adrenalin boost was just what I needed to put practical arrangements in place and prepare for the interview.

I popped over to my parents and asked Mum if she'd be able to keep the children for longer than usual on Wednesday evening as I had a job interview in London. "Of course, Shama, but London?" she asked, concerned. "Do you really want to move there? Even if it's a great opportunity, you'll have no family support."

I certainly wasn't going to tell her at this stage that the job was in Pakistan and not London! My mum and dad were the best parents anyone could wish for, loving us unconditionally, despite and perhaps even because of our flaws. Hardworking and honest, they had set me and my siblings a great example and made us into the adults we'd become. But even though we were all grown up, they still worried unnecessarily.

The weekend was certainly going to be a busy one, prepping for the interview along with all my usual chores. As soon as I had a minute to myself, I called Pauline to tell her that I'd been shortlisted and asked to attend an interview in London.

"That's fantastic news, Shama. I knew you'd get through!" she said. "I'll pop over tomorrow and we can have a real catch-up!"

The weekend passed in a haze of researching the project, roleplaying the interview with Pauline and the usual rounds of shopping, cooking, cleaning and playing with the children.

Before I knew it, Wednesday morning had come around and I was sitting on the train on my way to London. As I stared out of the window, taking in the scenery, I reflected on how life was also hurtling by at a similar pace. Opportunities like the one I had today were rare. Perhaps this was my chance to change not only my life but those of others around me.

I arrived at Euston just as my nerves began to kick in. Breathing deeply, I steadied myself; I was well prepared and determined to make the most of this opportunity to reunite my family.

The embassy was just a short walk away from the station, giving me time to mentally recap my preparation. Once I'd gone through security, I was asked to wait in a reception room decorated with posters of the UK's arts and culture projects abroad. I smiled at a scene of an art show in Karachi, memories of my happier times in Pakistan flooding back.

The door opened and a smartly dressed woman entered with a welcoming smile. "Good morning, Shama," she said, holding out her hand. "Thanks so much for coming at such short notice. I'm Annabel Cardin, head of overseas human resources for arts and culture."

She guided me along a corridor and into a small room, where she invited me to take a seat.

"I hope your journey down from Lancashire was OK," she said with a smile. "It's a beautiful part of the world, I believe."

"Yes, it is," I answered.

Once we were both settled and I'd been offered coffee, Annabel told me a little about the role and asked me why I'd applied for a post in Pakistan. I explained that my husband was over there and that having lived there when first married, I believed I understood the country's cultural ethos and values. I also told her that given the progress that was taking place there, these were exciting times to return to Pakistan and be part of its transformation. Annabel was welcoming and made me feel at ease. I felt calm, making my points confidently, without feeling that I sounded arrogant. The conversation moved on to the art scene in both the UK and Pakistan, up-and-coming artists from the regions and other related topics. Glancing at the clock, I realized to my surprise that we'd been talking for over an hour. As she stood up to see me out, Annabel said I was welcome to stay and look around.

"We have three other candidates to interview, but we'll be able to let you know before the end of the week," she said.

As I left, I thought the interview had gone well, but wondered how the organization would feel about my domestic situation. Would they think that a single candidate would be a safer bet than a mother taking her entire family to Karachi? On the train going home, I decided the best course of action was to put the interview to the back of my mind until I heard from Annabel.

That week Zoya's school was holding a daytime concert and the parents were invited to come and watch, a great way of taking my mind off the job and interview. Zoya had been having singing lessons that term and loved performing.

In the evening, as we read our customary bedtime story, Zoya chatted excitedly, telling me how much she was looking forward to me coming to watch her.

"I wouldn't miss it for the world," I said, with a smile.

I'd arranged to leave work early for the performance and after dashing to the school from the gallery I took my place in the hall with the other parents. As she began singing, tears came to my eyes and I thought my heart would burst with pride. Here was my beautiful, talented daughter, singing in front of all these people! I managed a little wave and smile as I watched her and took photos. *What a shame that her father isn't here to see this too,* I thought sadly.

I took the kids to Pizza Hut to celebrate after the performance. What a wonderful afternoon we had, laughing and eating while Zoya talked us through the concert, imitating her teacher and one of the students who was almost too nervous to perform her piece. We laughed and ate as one happy family. I knew I would always treasure this very special day.

The rest of the week passed at its usual frantic pace and, before I knew it, Saturday had arrived. I was dressed for work and waiting for Sajjad to come and collect the children, when Zoya came into my bedroom with the post.

"Mommy, you've got a letter," she announced.

My heart rose in my chest. Could it be news about the job? Or was it just a boring bill? There was no time to open it as the doorbell rang.

"That'll be Uncle," I told the children. "Come on, coats and bags!"

Saturdays were always busy at work, since the weekend brought more window shoppers and browsers to the gallery. The morning passed quickly as I welcomed customers through the door and talked them through the artworks that had caught their eye. It was during a rare break when I dashed to the kitchen to make a coffee that I remembered the letter in my bag.

I filled the kettle, left it to boil and took the letter to the toilet.

Dear Ms Mughal…it began.

I started skim-reading the following paragraph and the first words that jumped out at me were 'sorry' and 'unfortunately.' Of course, it was a rejection. How could I have expected otherwise? Halfway down the page, I caught sight of the words 'relocation expenses' and my breath caught in my throat. I willed myself to go back to the beginning and read the letter slowly.

There were a couple of lines about how much they'd enjoyed meeting me and then…I began skimming again and, as I did so, I could feel my heart racing.

We are sorry that this offer comes at such short notice…
We're delighted to offer you the role of…
…unfortunately, the position was vacated at extremely short notice…

They were offering me the job!

I read and reread the letter, my hands shaking, aware that my colleagues in the gallery would be wondering where I'd got to. Further on, there was a mention of a tentative start date – five weeks' time! And an offer to pay all removal, transportation and initial accommodation costs. It was too much to take in during a coffee break. As I folded the letter and put it back in my bag, my emotions got the better of me and I began to cry. It had never occurred to me that things could progress so quickly, but here I was, a single mother of three in the UK, being asked to relocate to Pakistan in just a few weeks.

Other thoughts now raced through my head. What about my mortgage, my parents, giving notice? *First things first,* I thought, *let's just get through the day at work.*

Once the gallery was closed, I picked up the children and headed home, planning to spend Sunday going through my current employment contract. The embassy had given me five days to make a decision and, as I'd thought, I was obliged to give my current employer one month's notice, so time was tight. I wrote my resignation letter, making sure I thanked the gallery for the opportunities they'd given me and explaining that I'd decided to move overseas to be with my husband.

Writing these words made me think of Saleem and I had a sudden desire to share the news with him. After all, he was a pivotal player in this. I dialled his number and got his answer machine, so left a message.

With hungry children expecting dinner, their baths and bedtime reading still to do, there was little time to dwell on where he could be. I'd just said goodnight to the twins and left Zoya looking at a book when the phone rang. It was Saleem.

"Shama? Is everything OK?" he asked.

I took a deep breath and told him that I'd be over in a month's time. I was about to explain about the job, when he interrupted me: "How can you afford the tickets and where will we all stay?"

"It's all sorted. You don't need to worry," I replied. "I thought you'd be happy. Saleem, I want us to be a proper family, living together. Don't you get it?"

"Yes, of course, but you're making snap decisions. This needs careful thought," he said.

"You haven't given me a chance to explain," I said. "I've been offered a job in Karachi, with a full package of expenses."

There was another silence. "What do you mean? You've got a job?" he asked. I was about to explain when he interrupted again: "I have to go. Call me later."

"No, you can call me back when you're free," I answered, nonplussed.

As I tidied up and prepared my things for the following day, I waited on tenterhooks for Saleem to call back. It had been impossible to gauge how he felt at the news that we would be joining him in Pakistan in just over a month. I was disappointed at his reaction. I had secretly hoped he'd be ecstatic at the thought of finally having his wife and children with him, but I consoled myself by thinking he had just been overwhelmed. It was, after all, a lot for him to take in.

My emotions were all over the place. Sharing the news with Saleem had been something of a reality check. Until that day, the decision to move had seemed little more than a dream. I pushed Saleem's lukewarm reaction to one side, feeling sure he'd be overjoyed once the news had sunk in properly. I was convinced that this move would benefit us all, providing the children with an opportunity to be part of a family unit and have a loving father around. Hopefully, it would also allow me to try to develop a relationship with my husband again too. In different circumstances and with time having healed some of the old wounds, perhaps Saleem and I could give our marriage another go, I thought.

Thinking of Saleem reminded me that he hadn't yet called back. I was impatient to give him more details about the job. In the meantime, I set about making a to-do list to help ease the nerves I now felt. It included practicalities, but also my motivation for going.

- *Tell Mum and Dad*
- *Rent out house*
- *Travel and other documents*

— *Start packing*
— *Box up big items*
— *Arrive in Pakistan*
— *United at last as a family*
— *A new chapter and a new start*

On Monday, I gave my notice at work and was surprised at how emotional I'd become. My colleagues were upset I was leaving, but happy for me, wishing me luck in my new role and confident I'd do well.

I knew that telling my parents would be far less straightforward. I'd settled on the coming Saturday to speak to them and arrived at the large Victorian house of my childhood in the mid-afternoon. The children ran up to their grandparents for hugs, always delighted to see them, before running off to find Sajjad. We sat in the lounge and Mum brought in tea and snacks. After we'd talked about the kids, always the first topic of conversation, Dad asked how the interview in London had gone.

"I really enjoyed the trip and, in fact, I wanted to tell you actually, they've offered me the job," I said. My parents exchanged a look, waiting for me to elaborate. "I need to explain something to you both," I said. "The job's not local, which means I have to move."

"Yes, Shama, as I said the other day, that's what worries us," Mum began. "You won't have any support in London."

"Mom, I'm not going to be in London," I interrupted. "And I will have support for the children, they're going to be with their father."

"What do you mean?" Mum asked, confused.

"The job is in Karachi," I continued. "It's managing the British Embassy's art gallery there."

There was a silence while my parents took in the significance of what I was saying. "Surely you're not serious?" Mum said.

As she put down her cup, I could see her hands were shaking. I waited for my father to say something, but he simply stared at the floor. I could see by his furrowed brow that he was deep in thought.

"Shama, this is crazy," Mum said, finally. "You're not thinking straight. You're going to uproot your children – our grandchildren – and take them to Karachi to be near their dad - that idiot who caused you so much pain?" Her voice trailed off. She didn't trust herself to say anything else.

"Mom, I know Saleem behaved badly and made mistakes, but he's their father and the children need him in their lives," I said, gently. "They don't understand why they haven't got a dad like their friends."

Dad spoke for the first time, cutting in sharply. "You think a man like him can be a proper father, Shama?" he said.

"Yes, Dad, I do, if he is given the chance to learn from the past," I replied. "And also, if he has no option but to step up to his responsibilities."

Tension filled the room as we all sat staring at each other. Mum spoke first. "I must see to the food," she said, getting up and going to the kitchen, her place of refuge.

With the kids at the table, we avoided the topic of Karachi over dinner, although the conversation was strained. Even the children sensed the tension, playing up more than usual. Before leaving, I told my parents that I needed to start packing and planning and that I would be busy after work. "It would be great if you could have the children for longer, Mom, but if not…" I said, before trailing off.

"You know you don't even have to ask, Shama," Mum said, hesitating and then embracing me. "We're just worried and it's such a huge step after everything."

"I know, Mom. I have thought it through," I said. "But thanks." I hugged her back and rounded up the children to leave. No going back now!

My next step was to contact a local shipping company to find out about transporting my belongings over and then to begin sorting through which belongings we wanted to take and what to put in storage.

Tuesday evening, while I was packing up the children's old toys and preparing boxes to give some of them to charity, the telephone rang. It was Saleem.

"Shama? Hi. Sorry about the other day, I had the chance to go and find out about some work, plus I can't really afford long phone calls right now," he said.

The same excuses as always and still Saleem didn't seem able to hold down a secure job. Memories of him supposedly looking for work, sitting in front of the television, and coming back drunk from our local pubs flashed through my mind, but I brushed them aside. Those were difficult times for all of us and things would be different. I had a good job waiting for me in Karachi and had matured since then.

Realizing that I was serious about going to Pakistan, my family supported me in my preparations, but I knew that inside they were heartbroken at the prospect of their beloved daughter and grandchildren being so far away. I could also tell that they had doubts about whether Saleem would step up to his responsibilities and especially whether he'd learned to control his temper.

In a moment of confidence, my sister Fatima told me Mum had been crying when she thought no one else could hear or see. She'd also heard Mum say to Dad that she thought Saleem was going to kill me and take the children away.

"She's bound to worry, but I think she's letting her imagination run wild because it's such a big step," I said. "You know, we're all going to miss them too, but I have to think of the importance of the children building a relationship with their father. That has to be a priority and this is a great way to do it."

"Shama, please, don't forget what it was like before," Fatima said. "Just be careful and go in with your eyes open, OK?" My parents weren't the only ones worried, I thought.

The next two weeks passed in a whirlwind of packing and organizing. My family looked on, bewildered, helping whenever they could, but seemingly unsure as to whether I would actually go through with my plans.

Most of my belongings and those of the children had been sent on to the accommodation that the embassy had found for us and our furniture had been put in storage. The local estate agent had found a tenant for the house and, before I knew it, we were left with just our travel luggage.

We'd arranged to spend the last week at my parents' house so that they could have some quality time with the children before we left. All three kids were excited about going to see their father, but I knew they'd miss their grandparents dreadfully.

The mood was a little lighter now that Mum and Dad had accepted my decision. I did my best to acknowledge that they would always have concerns for their child and grandchildren, even though they knew I wanted to become more independent. "We'll come and visit you, but please take care of my grandchildren out there, won't you?" Mum begged.

"Of course, Mom," I answered, hugging her. "But remember, I won't be on my own. I'll have the full support and security of the embassy."

A few days before we were due to travel, Saleem called again. "You know I don't have the money to come over and help you travel?" he said.

"It's OK, the embassy is dealing with everything," I said.

I knew Saleem was still adjusting to the prospect of having his family with him, but it would have been nice to hear a bit more enthusiasm in his voice. Still, there was plenty to be excited about: a new chapter in my life, a new job, getting to know my husband again, this time on a more equal footing and the children forming a relationship with their father.

What I hadn't told my parents was that for me this was the final throw of the dice. Yes, I owed it to the kids to give their father a chance to be involved in their lives, but that was where my part ended. I could only give him the opportunity – it was something I wanted to do, to have peace of mind and the satisfaction of knowing I'd tried one last time. The rest was down to him.

I was reminded of Rumi's wise words:

Some human beings are safe havens
Be companions with them.

Was the great poet telling me something?

21
The Darkest Clouds

On the day of our departure, emotions were running high on all fronts. The kids were excited at the prospect of boarding a plane, while my parents, who had driven us to the airport, watched on, trying to hide their tears and smile for the sake of their grandchildren. After we'd checked in, the time came for us to make our way airside. I tried to wipe my own tears away, but not before Adam spotted me.

"Mama, why are you crying?" he asked. "We're going on an airplane. You should be very excited. We're flying for the first time in the sky."

None of the children mentioned that they were looking forward to seeing their father, even though I'd explained that he would be waiting for us in Pakistan.

"Yes, that's right, darling and I am excited," I said, gently, with a smile. "I'm just a bit sad because we're saying goodbye to people we love, too."

We said our final goodbyes to my parents and siblings, all of whom had come to wave us off, with everybody hugging each other until I almost had to pull them apart. Mum and my sisters were crying openly, while my dad did his best to comfort Mum and hold back his own tears.

I scooped up the children's colouring books and crayons, zipping them inside their rucksacks and hoisting the bags onto their backs. All three of them were chatting excitedly, asking questions about the plane, but not really understanding the significance of the trip or that they wouldn't see their beloved grandparents for some time.

"Wave to everyone, a big final wave!" I said to them as we stood at the top of the escalators before going through security. They turned and grinned at my parents, blowing kisses, oblivious to the pain and anguish of the people we were leaving behind.

Before long, we were queuing with our fellow passengers to board the plane. As I stood there, shuffling along, answering the children's endless questions, I had a sudden flashback to travelling to Pakistan, excitement vying with mixed emotions at my fast-approaching wedding and surrounded by my sisters.

On that occasion, we'd been met by my father's relatives, but this time there'd be an embassy car waiting for us, although I hoped Saleem would be there too. I'd given him the flight details and the address of where we'd be staying. I was hoping he'd travel from his mother's house to Karachi to meet us.

Once we were airborne, the novelty of flying soon wore off for the children and they fell asleep for most of the seven-hour journey, giving me an opportunity to prepare for our arrival. Taking the job and moving to another country was a huge step, but I was also relishing the opportunity of a new challenge. It felt like the next natural step in my journey to independence, although I knew I'd miss my family terribly.

When we arrived in Karachi, we retrieved our luggage and made our way through the arrivals hall. We were greeted by an embassy representative and armed security guard. The children clung to me frantically, still sleepy from the flight and frightened by the sight of armed guards and the chaotic noise of the airport. "Don't worry, it's just a bit busy and this man is here to keep us safe," I said, as they rubbed their eyes and leaned against each other. I craned my neck looking for Saleem in the bustling crowd, unable to spot him. While I was searching for one face in a sea of many, a small man appeared in front of me and, with a smile, introduced himself as Dr Andrew Robertson, my new boss.

"Welcome to Karachi, Shama. I hope you had a good flight," he said, handing me some flowers. "You must be Zoya, Adam and Sara," he added, bending down to speak to the children at their level. "Welcome, all of you, too!" He handed the children a toy each, which they accepted shyly, with a small thank you.

Dr Robertson's assistant, Rana, introduced herself, before giving instructions to the staff who were taking our luggage outside and asking us to follow her to the cars. I had one final glance around for Saleem and decided I couldn't ask these new colleagues to wait. I'd given him details of our flight, I thought, and he hadn't turned up. That was his choice. Pushing my disappointment to one side, I smiled at Rana and answered her questions about our flight and my family as we walked through the car park. Once we were en route, Dr Robertson began telling me about our accommodation and its location.

"It sounds lovely, we can't wait to see it, can we?" I asked the children. "I don't suppose my husband or his family have been in touch, have they?"

"No, no one from this end has contacted us," he replied. Then, lowering his voice, he added, "Our staff in London have of course made us aware of your personal situation, Mrs Mughal. We take the safety and security of our people very seriously."

He needn't have worried about the children overhearing anything, since they were transfixed by the passing scenery and keeping Rana busy with their endless questions. Our house was near a grand palace called the Arabic Mahal in Khayaban-e-Badar Street.

"Is it a real palace, Mommy?" Zoya asked, looking at the imposing, tall grey walls that surrounded the building opposite as we got out of the car.

"Yes, I believe so," I answered, fairly impressed myself. "Isn't that exciting?"

Dr Robertson rang the doorbell for us as our suitcases were taken out of the trunk and brought to the doorstep. "You'll have two members of staff with you – a housekeeper and a maid," he said.

The housekeeper opened the door with a smile, introducing himself as Shafiq and welcomed us in.

"Wow, look at all this space," said Zoya, running on ahead and sliding across the marble floors.

"I'll show you around, madam," Shafiq said.

Dr Robertson walked by my side as Shafiq showed me each room in turn, before taking us out into the huge garden, which included a swimming pool.

"Over there are the staff's quarters, at the back of the house," he explained. "The fridge is full to start you off. There are other necessities on the table, including a sim card and some rupees for necessities. I'll let you settle in and call later to discuss tomorrow's arrangements."

"That all sounds great, thank you!" I answered, unable to take in much of what he was saying.

The maid, who was called Maha, made me a cup of tea and poured the children some juice.

"Can we carry on exploring the house, Mama?" they pleaded. "Please?"

I'd planned for them to have a nap, but relented, telling myself that at least they hadn't asked why their father wasn't at the airport to meet them. We went room to room, marvelling at the spaciousness of the villa and the facilities, compared to our cosy house in Nelson.

"Look, you've even got your own attached bathrooms – one for each bedroom!" I said. "And all this space for your toys, too!"

The beds were already made up, so all the children needed to do was to put their toys and books away. After dinner, which had been prepared in advance for us, all three were finally flagging, so I suggested showers and beds. None of them argued, which I knew meant they were exhausted.

"Mommy, will you sleep in here tonight?" Zoya asked as I tucked her in.

"Of course, I will. Don't you like your room, sweetheart?" I asked, stroking her hair.

"I do. It's just that it's new. I'm not used to it yet and I miss my old room," she answered sleepily.

"Me too, but it will all be fine. This is a new adventure, that's all," I said, giving her a cuddle.

I woke in the morning to the smell of breakfast being cooked. The children were already stirring, so I rallied them and got them dressed. Dr Robertson had told me the night before that a driver would be coming to collect us all at around 9am. First, we would be going to the international school to enrol the children and then on to the gallery, where I'd be meeting my new colleagues.

While the children were having their breakfast I tried to call Saleem from my mobile phone, but there was no reply. Frustrated, I decided that I wasn't going to try again for now. I had to make my new job and settling the children my priority.

Before long, the driver arrived and it was time to set off. The kindergarten and school were linked, which meant the children would be next door to each other. I knew all three of them were feeling a little nervous about starting a new school, so I did my best to put them at ease.

"Doesn't it look lovely? Look at all these pictures on the walls! And the playthings!" I said as we walked through the hall. The head teacher came out to meet us and we were taken through to her office, where she introduced the children to their teachers. "I'm sure you'll be very happy here, Zoya, Adam and Sara," she said with a smile.

I could tell that they were feeling more at ease, so I waved them off with a kiss, assuring them that I'd be back to collect them later. As I completed the paperwork to enrol them and ordered their uniforms, I knew how lucky I was to have such resilient, confident kids, especially given the absence of their father.

Next stop was the gallery. As the driver stopped outside and opened the car door for me, I paused in awe of the spectacular building. Even from the outside, it was evident that the space was huge. The team had gathered at the entrance to meet me, with welcoming smiles on their faces.

Inside was equally impressive, with the main space given over to an exhibition of work by a Portuguese artist that filled the gallery with vibrancy and colour, while the corridors led off to workshops and a lecture room.

"What a fantastic layout," I said to a woman named Jo, who introduced herself as my assistant.

"We love it here. I'm sure you'll feel the same," she replied. As she handed me a coffee, I was convinced the decision to move here was the right one.

The morning was spent settling in at my office, meeting the team and being brought up-to-speed on the current projects, alongside others in the pipeline.

Dr Robertson had arranged for the entire team to have lunch at a restaurant called ZamZama nearby, which specialized in grilled chicken. As we sat on ZamZama's terrace in the warm sunshine, enjoying the gentle breeze, the team asked me about my family, the work I was doing before and my links with Pakistan. I could tell from their questions and responses that they were genuinely interested in me and keen to welcome me on board.

Dr Robertson told me to go home and rest after lunch, saying he'd see me in the morning. Before heading home, I stopped off at the school to collect the children. Standing at the entrance, I waited anxiously to hear whether they'd enjoyed their first day, but I needn't have worried. They came running out, delighted to see me, but also keen to tell me about their teachers and new friends and what they'd done.

Relieved, I gave them a kiss. "Let's get you home and give you something to eat then," I said, happily.

Later, while they napped, I began unpacking properly and going through the boxes of things that had been shipped over ahead of our arrival, when my new mobile phone rang. Answering, I recognized Saleem's voice.

"Saleem, where the hell are you? Why weren't you at the airport and why haven't you answered my calls before now?" I asked. "The children were expecting to see you when we arrived."

"I wanted to come, but I needed to wrap up a few things first," he said. "And anyway, I couldn't really afford a flight to Karachi, but I've managed to get the money together now, so I'll be with you tomorrow."

I decided not to argue. I was angry that he'd let us all down, but chose to focus instead on the fact that he was now, finally, on his way.

"Guess what?" I said to the children, gathering them round when they were getting ready for bed. "*Baba's* coming to Karachi. He'll be here tomorrow."

There was little in the way of reaction. They were much more excited when my parents called 10 minutes later, squabbling over taking turns to talk to my mum and dad and describing the villa and their school. I promised to send my parents photos of the house and surroundings and, in return, Mum told me they planned to visit us as soon as possible.

The following morning, I waved the children off to school, reassured when they rushed in without a backward glance, keen to catch up with their new friends. As the driver took me to the office, I thought how lucky I was to be on my way to a job I could tell I'd love and with my husband arriving that evening.

The day was spent in one-to-one meetings with members of the team. Before I knew it, it was time to collect the children from school. I'd wanted to make sure all three were settled before handing this duty over to my staff, but I needn't have worried, according to the head, who beckoned me in when she saw me at the door and took me to one side. "Zoya, Adam and Sara all seem to be getting along fine," she said with a smile. "I think they're adjusting very well to the change – they're playing with the other children as if they've known them for months."

Relieved, I gave them all a big hug as they came dashing out of their classrooms. One less thing to worry about!

Saleem's flight was scheduled to arrive at 7pm. I'd asked the driver if he was able to do the airport run, since this was a busy time for me with the children and he'd agreed. I'd told all three that they could stay up a bit later as a special treat to see their *Baba*, although once again, they seemed indifferent to news of Saleem's arrival. Perhaps it would be different when he came through the door, I thought.

They were sitting on the sofa in their dressing gowns when the car pulled up outside and the doorbell rang.

"*Baba's* here!" I said to them, with a smile. "Shall we go and let him in?"

I thought they'd rush to the door, but instead they followed me slowly and shyly, hanging back as I opened it.

"Hey, kids! How about this?" he said, with his arms outstretched. "Aren't you happy your *baba's* here?"

"We're always happy," Adam replied, clinging onto my leg, while the girls held back on the other side of me, looking at him cautiously.

Zoya chewed her nails, a nervous habit I'd tried to break and eyed Saleem.

"Mommy, have we really got a *baba*?" she asked, turning to me. "Because we've never seen this man before. I think he's a stranger in disguise."

"Of course he's your *baba*. It's just that you haven't seen him for a long time," I said with a bright laugh, although I was distraught inside. "It's fine to go and give him a hug, children."

A little reluctantly they stepped up to Saleem and put their arms round him, before rushing off, keen to get back to their toys.

"They just need time," I said to Saleem, giving him a hug myself. "Anyway, it's great to see you and for all of us to be together, isn't it? Come through!"

I showed Saleem where to put his bags and called the kids down again.

"Why don't you give *Baba* a tour of the house?" I said, thinking it might help to break the ice. I could tell that he was taken aback by the size of the villa and the standard of the accommodation.

"Let's go and eat," I said. "The maid has prepared a special dinner."

"You have staff too?" he asked, impressed. What a difference, I thought, to when I was at Saleem's family's house and being treated worse than staff myself.

The next day, Saleem accompanied the driver as he drove the children to school and dropped me off at work. He could see how quickly we'd all adapted to our new life and settled in. Being in an expat community helped tremendously, as did having staff to help me at home.

I hoped Saleem would realize how lucky we all were and what a wonderful opportunity we'd been given to have another go at family life, but also the sacrifice I'd made by leaving my loved ones to come over to Pakistan.

I had another plan in the back of my mind to encourage Saleem to look for work via the embassy, which supported the partners of its staff in finding employment. That evening, we took the children to our local park. Finally, on neutral territory and watching the kids play, the time felt right to talk.

"Saleem, I did this for us and for the children, so that we can work together on our family and ensure the kids have both their parents around," I began. "Things will be completely different. We won't have any financial problems or worries about schools and work here."

I'd expected a positive response, but my words were met with silence.

"This wasn't an easy or small decision, you know," I continued, frustrated. "I'd just bought a house in the UK, I left a job I loved, uprooted the children and had to say goodbye to my family, who love their grandchildren dearly and did a lot to help me."

But before I'd finished, Saleem cut in. "Shama, I never told you to come. You made this choice," he said.

"Yes," I acknowledged, "but I made it for us. Aren't you happy about it?"

"Of course, I'm happy," he answered, hesitantly. "I want us to be together and I studied in this city, so I'm more than happy to be here."

"Can we please try, for the sake of the family? For the kids?" I pleaded. "I didn't think I'd get this job and my parents were so upset about us leaving. But now we're here, I really think we have an opportunity to make things work. Let's make the most of our time together and enjoy watching the children grow into healthy, happy adults."

He turned to me with a smile and took my hand and in a flash, I remembered how handsome and charming my husband could be.

"I'll see if the embassy can find you a post too." I said. "Part of my contract is to support the spouse with relocating, so there's a good chance they will. We'll get annual flights too. And Mum and Dad will come to visit in a few months. Everything will be great."

"I want my mother to come and join us here too," Saleem said, suddenly.

"Yes, why not? We have loads of room," I said brightly, although inside my heart sank. Saleem's mother was the last person I wanted in my house. Still, knowing I was in control counted for something and I was already counting down the days until my parents were due to fly over.

As we began to settle into a routine, I felt that, finally, our attempt to create a happy family life was succeeding. The children were thriving at school and beginning to forge a relationship with Saleem, while I adored my job.

One evening, as we sat down to dinner, Saleem announced that he was considering taking a job in Multan.

"But why there?" I asked, in despair. "The idea was that we'd all be together in Karachi!"

Saleem simply shrugged, as though it wasn't even important for him to be with his wife and children.

Ramadan was approaching – an important time of family get-togethers, fasting and communal prayers. I knew I'd really miss my family during the holy month and the Eid celebration when it came afterwards, even though they'd send gifts and call. I tried to stay positive, telling myself that it would be exciting to experience Ramadan in Pakistan, but my heart was heavy. Getting calls from home didn't make things easier. I could tell my mother was crying during her calls, even though she tried to conceal it.

Slowly, other more serious problems had begun to arise, problems I didn't dare talk to her or anyone else about. Since the beginning of Ramadan, Saleem had become much moodier and more short-tempered, snapping at the children and criticizing me. I tried to gloss over it initially, telling myself that the Holy Month was always challenging and that he was also finding it difficult to adapt to life in Karachi. But he had started drinking again and taking himself off to the drawing room to listen to *ghazals*, saying they brought back memories of his father and childhood.

One evening, when he didn't join me for *iftar* to break the fast, I went storming in and told him I'd had enough.

"We are your family. Your children don't understand what you're doing," I began.

He turned to face me, eyes glazed, breath stinking of whisky.

"What do you know? Spoilt bitch, with everything you want!" he snarled and slapped me across the face.

Instinctively, I put my hand to my cheek, turned and fled, before realizing, to my horror that the children had been woken by the shouting and were standing in the doorway.

"Come on, back to bed, Daddy and Mommy were just a bit upset about something," I said, trying to hold back the tears.

Later, looking in the mirror at the red mark across my cheek, I thought about what had happened. Here we were, supposedly making a fresh start, but Saleem's moods and behaviour were depressingly familiar. Could it be that the change of location and circumstances weren't, after all, enough to make him happier?

We continued in this way through the first part of Ramadan, with a couple of good days followed by a bad one, during which Saleem would be verbally abusive and at times lash out. I thought I'd done a good job of shielding the children from their father's temper until, one Saturday morning, while tidying away their toys, I found a piece of paper covered in numbers and lines. I was about to call them in and ask what they'd been working on when, to my horror, I spotted the scrawl at the top of the page in Zoya's writing: 'How many times *Baba* has hit Mama.' The lines underneath were a tally that the kids had been keeping.

I wept silently. Who was I trying to convince that my children didn't know what was going on? I was trying to protect the kids and keep my family together, but all I was really doing was allowing them to witness the same violence I'd eradicated years earlier and showing them how to make excuses for the violence of others. They were suffering, on the other side of the world from their loving extended family.

I did my best to keep the children apart from Saleem, made easier by the size of the house, but my hopes of strengthening their relationship with him were fading. Meanwhile, the end of the calendar month was fast approaching and it was almost payday for our staff.

"Did you sort out the salaries?" Saleem asked irritably, striding into the lounge, where I was relaxing after putting the children to bed.

"No, not yet. I need to go to the bank and take care of it with my card," I answered, noting his mood and deciding against asking him why he was so interested.

That same day, Nargis, the maid of a colleague of mine named Hannah, had come over to help us since Maha was sick. Nargis came in with a smile and once again I marvelled at how lucky I was to have colleagues in Karachi like Hannah that had become firm friends; people who cared and were willing to help out in an emergency.

I chatted to Nargis for a few minutes, letting her know where everything was and suggested that she begin with a pile of ironing, before returning to the lounge. As I made my way to the sofa, Saleem came into the room, staggering toward me with that familiar glassy look I'd come to dread.

"Shama, why didn't you pay the staff?" he said, his breath reeking of whisky.

"I told you, Saleem, it's not the end of the month until tomorrow, so it's not urgent and I need to go to the bank," I said with a sigh. "Just leave it, OK?"

I got up to go back to the kitchen, unwilling to get embroiled in an argument when I could see he'd been drinking, but he followed me grabbing a handful of my hair and pulling me back.

"*Kutey kee bachee,* don't you know…didn't you hear me?" he shouted.

"Ow, get off me! What do you mean?" I yelled. I looked around, embarrassed that Nargis would hear my husband hurling insults at me, but the noise on the stairs told me that she was taking the ironing up to the bedrooms.

I turned to tell Saleem to leave me alone just as I felt a sharp pain across my forehead. Letting out a piercing scream, I opened my eyes to find Saleem preparing to swing the iron at me for what must be a second time. I crouched down, dazed, hands to my forehead, blood seeping through my fingers. Luckily, the second blow missed me as Saleem drunkenly lurched.

Hearing the commotion, Nargis came rushing into the kitchen, followed closely by the children, who'd followed her down the stairs.

"Mommy, Mommy! You're bleeding," screamed Zoya, rushing toward me, while Nargis ran past me to wrench the iron out of Saleem's hands.

"*Sahib*, what are you doing? Give me that, please," she begged, shock and bewilderment etched across her face.

Zoya stood crying beside me, while Adam and Sara hugged each other in the doorway, petrified. Having taken the iron from Saleem, who was too drunk to put up much of a fight, Nargis ran to get a towel from the bathroom and wrapped it around my head. Once it was secure, she poured me a glass of water.

Ignoring her efforts with me, Saleem stumbled out of the room and into the drawing room, closing the door behind him. Nargis phoned Hannah, who immediately sent a driver over to take me to the hospital.

"Mommy, I want to come, don't leave me here," Zoya begged between sobs. How could I refuse? I gathered all three of them together and we sped off. Once there, I was seen quickly by a doctor, who told me I needed three stitches across my forehead. I winced as he worked, but the pain was nothing compared to the agony of knowing that Saleem had yet again humiliated me and resorted to violence in front of our children.

"Look, see? Mama's fine, it's just like a plaster," I said to the kids, smiling wanly as we made our way back to the car to go home.

"But it's not, Mommy. It wasn't an accident," Zoya whispered. "It was Daddy."

When we arrived back, I took some painkillers and staggered upstairs to put the children to bed. As I expected, they refused to go into their separate rooms and begged me to sleep with them. Exhausted and guilt-ridden, I couldn't bring myself to refuse, so we all huddled up together on Zoya's bed. There was no sign of Saleem.

The next morning, my head was pounding, but I was determined to go into work. I brushed my hair over the stitches and told the children that there'd be a special treat after school if they were good today. Would they mention anything to their teacher? I had no idea.

Hannah gave me a small smile across the office when I arrived and I could tell from the look that she had no intention of mentioning the incident. I returned her smile gratefully, knowing that I owed her my privacy, dignity and respect.

A week or so later, my stitches had dissolved and I was feeling a little stronger and more positive. Saleem was keeping out of my way at home, ashamed perhaps. My parents were due to visit soon and I was busy curating a new show for Eid – my first major project – when Jo, my assistant, put through a call.

"It's your sister Fatima, from the UK. She says it's urgent," she said.

"Shama?" my sister's voice was trembling and I could tell she was crying. "I'm sorry to have to call you like this, but I have some bad news."

"What is it, Fatima?" I said, slumping back in my chair.

"It's Mum and Dad. They've been involved in a car crash. They're in hospital and are unconscious."

I was struggling to take anything in.

"What are you talking about? I was chatting to Mum on the phone last night," I said. "She was fine, she's really excited about coming over. You must have made a mistake."

I hung up and immediately called my brother Sajjad, knowing I'd get more sense out of him.

"Hi, Sajjad. Fatima just called me about Mum and Dad. She says they've been in a car crash, but I spoke to them yesterday evening," I began.

"Shama, it's true," he said gently. "We don't know much, only that they were on their way to an *iftar* dinner in Manchester, when the car seems to have hit something on the motorway and spun out of control," he said. "They're in hospital and we're waiting for news. Dad seems to have taken the brunt of it but we don't know much yet."

"No! You're lying! It's not true!" I answered, distraught.

"Shama, please. We didn't want to tell you like this, but we had to because you're so far away," he said. "We're all upset…"

I couldn't bear to hear any more and hung up. I pulled down the blinds in my office, so I wouldn't be disturbed, and cried quietly for a few minutes. What was I doing here in Karachi, far away from my parents, sacrificing the close relationship I had with them for a man who didn't even treat his family well? And now this.

As the terrible news began to sink in, I tried calling home again, but the line was engaged. Nobody at work knew my parents, which made the situation much worse. But Saleem knew them; they had helped us both and supported him in the past.

I dialled his number. "Saleem, something terrible has happened. It's my parents," I began, between sobs. "They've been badly injured in a car crash. I don't know what to do."

There was a pause, during which I imagined Saleem was digesting this news, but his reaction, when it came, threw me completely.

"Shama, are you that idiotic and so easily taken in?" he said, almost laughing. "I don't believe that's the case for one minute. It's bullshit! It's just some sort of plan your family have made up to persuade you to go back to England!"

"Saleem!" I screamed. "Are you mad? This is my parents we're talking about! Nobody in my family would ever stoop so low to lie about their health. I have to go to England as soon as possible and see them."

"What you need to do is to calm down, rather than overreacting," he said. "Personally, I don't believe it's true, but let me call my friends and ask them."

I hung up and sat back down, shaking. There was a tentative knock on the door, and Jo appeared with a glass of water, having realized something was very wrong. I began explaining what had happened, and Jo immediately phoned Dr Robertson and sent for the driver to take me home.

In the car on the way back to the villa I had visions of my mother sobbing as she said goodbye to us at the airport. I pictured her face when I announced that we were moving to Pakistan. I'd left my parents, taking their beloved grandchildren, and now they were in hospital. Somehow, I felt as if I was to blame.

Once I was home, Dr Robertson called. He was both sympathetic and supportive, just what I needed. He assured me that the embassy would arrange our tickets and transportation home. Saleem, however, was anything but, flitting between begging me not to go and throwing temper tantrums, insulting my family. In a fit of rage, he threw his biggest bombshell.

"Well, you're not taking the kids!" he snarled.

Adam and Sara started crying and Zoya ran up to her room. I'd noticed that she'd become much more anxious of late and that her nail-biting was growing worse.

"Don't be ridiculous, the children have to be with me!" I retorted. How could I tell him that they didn't want to be around their father any more than was absolutely necessary? Instead, I tried a different tack. "We can all go," I said. "It would be much easier if you're there to help with the children. The embassy will look after the house here – there's nothing to worry about."

The doorbell rang, cutting our conversation off, and I went to answer it. It was Dr Robertson, who'd come over to run through the practical arrangements. I could tell from his face that he'd overheard at least some of the exchange between Saleem and myself. "Let's go through the paperwork, if that's OK, Shama," he said. Looking up at Saleem who was roaming around the room menacingly, he added, quietly, "This is a very difficult time for you all and you're fasting too, which makes things more challenging. Please let's try to stay calm." Turning to me, he added, "Shama, why don't you try calling your family again to get an update and give them your flight details?"

I rang the home number and this time Fatima answered immediately. She told me that they were taking it in turns to go to the hospital.

The rest of the day dragged on endlessly, as I packed a bag and waited until it was time to go to the airport. Saleem remained cold and uncommunicative, offering none of the support that I so badly needed. Luckily, a couple of moms from the school popped in to express sympathy and give the children a hug.

I knew I was lucky to have built up a support network in such a short space of time. Dr Robertson, in particular, had sorted the paperwork, travel documents and emergency leave with minimum fuss and great efficiency. Everyone had been great, except Saleem. My husband was still sulking and stomping about, offering nothing in the way of support to me or the children in this time of need. I wondered if Saleem had even considered how they felt about their grandparents being so poorly. Since he hadn't yet indicated whether he planned to come, I'd also had to inform Dr Robertson that it was only me and the children travelling. The matter had been taken out of his hands.

It was autumn in the UK, so I knew we'd need warm clothes, but couldn't really focus on what to pack. Fortunately, Maha took over and rooted out our jumpers and coats, many of which were at the back of our cupboards.

I told the staff at our villa that since it was almost Eid, they could all go home to their families for the holidays. Saleem said he would stay and take care of the house, rather than head back to his family.

Once the car was loaded up for the journey to the airport, he turned to me and said, "Let me know when you arrive and how your parents are."

"Aren't you even coming to the airport?" I asked.

"Shama, it's better if I don't," he said. "There'll be a lot of traffic at this time and you are with your staff – you'll be fine!"

I couldn't believe what I was hearing. "Saleem, are you for real?" I said, despairingly. "I need you with me – you're my husband – you're meant to support me in difficult times like this!"

But he wasn't budging. Finally, the driver wound down the window, an embarrassed look on his face at witnessing this public argument.

"Mrs Mughal, we need to get going," he said, awkwardly.

I turned resignedly and got into the car, where the children sat, looking puzzled and upset. The embassy had arranged for us to be fast-tracked through check-in, although the entire process still seemed to take an eternity. All I could think of was getting to the hospital and seeing my poor, injured parents.

I was still trying to come to terms with the fact that Saleem hadn't offered to come with me. What kind of husband leaves his wife to face such a terrible crisis alone, offering no support to his family? I knew my parents weren't his blood relatives, but surely he could understand how much they meant to me? Couldn't he put himself in my place and imagine how he'd feel if it was his mother?

I tried to sleep during the flight, but worry and stress made it impossible. The children were also jumpy and, sensing my anxiety, only napped in fits and starts. We arrived in Manchester to a dull, wet day, which somehow suited our mood. I raced through baggage reclaim and with the children running alongside searched frantically for Sajjad, who had come to meet us. Spotting him in the crowd, I was taken aback at how tired and thin he looked.

"Shall we go straight to the hospital?" I asked him, after we'd hugged.

"Let's take the children home, Shama. They look exhausted," he replied, averting his gaze.

Something didn't feel right, but I was too tired and worried to think about it. When we arrived at my parents' house, I was surprised to see the driveway full of cars. Fatima opened the front door, having seen us pull up and I watched the bittersweet moment of her hugging my children, delighted to see them, but also distraught about the circumstances which had prompted our return.

Finally, she looked up at me and I could see that her eyes were red raw from crying. She hugged me as if not wanting to let me go. The children clung to me as we walked into the house, exhausted and overwhelmed at the number of relatives that had gathered. As I entered the dining area, I noticed that it was full of prayer beads, white sheets had been placed on the lounge floor and the room had been emptied. The women rose, one by one, proceeding to hug me and cry. One began singing a song in Punjabi that told the story of how I'd left my parents to travel to Karachi and how much Mum and Dad were looking forward to seeing my face again. As I moved along the row of women, I finally arrived at my mother's best friend, Aunty Nasreen, who hugged me so tightly that I struggled to breathe. "Whatever was *Allah's* will, Shama," she whispered.

I was struggling to make sense of the scene. Why were all these people here rather than at the hospital?

"Aunty, what do you mean?" I asked.

The women continued to sob while the Qur'an played in the background, signalling morning prayers and suddenly the fog in my head began to clear. October 29th, 2004 would forever stay etched in my mind.

"We are so sorry that your father has gone," Aunty Nasreen said, her voice trembling with emotion.

"Now is the time to think of your mother. She is on life support – she needs our prayers."

I felt the floor shift under my feet and struggled to keep upright, holding on to Aunty in case I fell. The last time we'd had a death in the family was when my uncle had a brain haemorrhage and passed away. I'd been too young to comprehend what was happening and had invited the girls at the mosque to our house, telling them we were having a party and that there was plenty of food for everyone.

Sensing that Aunty Nasreen had spoken to me before my brothers had been able to take me to one side, Fatima came rushing over.

"Shams, we couldn't tell you on the phone, we had to see you…" she began.

"It's OK, I understand," I replied, as we embraced, though I didn't understand at all. What on earth was happening? My siblings were in pieces like me. I knew Sajjad had meant to talk to me. He'd been trying to find the right moment, but I'd been swallowed up by the household of mourners as soon as we'd opened the front door.

I couldn't tell how long we stood there, but after hugging my siblings one by one, I made my excuses and took my bags up to my old bedroom, leaving my children in the arms of their aunts and uncles. There I wept for my father, for the goodbye I didn't get to say to him, for my mother, who didn't yet know her husband was dead, for my children, who didn't understand what was happening and for myself – for losing the one man in my life who had never failed to take care of my every need and for still being married to a man who had shown nothing in the way of support, sympathy, care, or love.

I took my phone out of my bag and saw that I'd received several missed calls from Shafiq, the housekeeper. I dialled his number.

"Shafiq, why are you ringing?" I asked, impatiently. "You know I have a family emergency on my hands!"

"I'm very sorry to trouble you, Mrs Mughal, but I didn't know what else to do," he said, anxiously. "*Sahib* is indoors with Maha. She hasn't left the house to go home, as you instructed."

His voice was hesitant and I could tell he'd been reluctant to burden me with this additional crisis; that my husband was inside the house alone with our young maid. I called the landline and Maha answered.

"The Mughal residence," she said, giggling.

"Where is *Sahib*?"

"He told me to come into this room to clean, Madam. I'll fetch him, just one moment."

"*Assalam alaikum*, Saleem?"

"Yes, *Walaikum salam*. How are you?"

"What do you mean how am I?" I screamed. "I've just found out that we've lost my dad and my mother is still unconscious. How do you think I am? And to make things even worse, Shafiq informs me that my husband has kept our maid in the house, when she was supposed to leave!"

"Shama, stop being so dramatic – you're crazy, it's the stress," he began.

"Then tell me why she's still there and answering the phone, giggling!" I said.

"It's simple," he said, calmly. "She's the only other person in the house and I was in the drawing room so couldn't get to the phone."

"Oh really?" I replied, my voice heavy with sarcasm. "So how come she was able to put you on the phone straightaway?"

When there was no reply, I was sure my instincts were right.

"Saleem, don't lie to me," I sobbed. "My father has just died and all you can think of is getting this young woman into our bed? You really do pick your moments, don't you?"

Deep down, I wasn't surprised. There'd been plenty of other times when I'd suspected him of seeing other women, but he'd managed to convince me I was paranoid, telling me women who phoned or said hello in the streets were simply friends, even though their smiles hinted otherwise. But now? When he knew what I was going through? Did he have no conscience or empathy?

Despite it all, after I put the phone down, the doubts began to creep in. Was I overreacting, upset by the shock of losing my father and the exhaustion of the journey? There was no more time to think about Saleem and his antics as I was called back down to the lounge.

Some members of the family were gathering to go to view my father's body at the mortuary and pay their respects. I said I'd stay with the children as they understood little, other than that their lovely grandad had died. The adults that stayed behind were still crying and repeating their words of mourning and remembrance – '*La illaha ilAllah wahdahu la shareekallahu.*'

The children soon dozed off on my bed and I thought of trying to get some rest too, but found it impossible to sleep. Instead, memories of my father danced around in my head – the times he came in from a hard day's work exhausted, but always smiling, his fierce independence, the loving way he looked at my mother and his insistence on driving us girls everywhere, even if he'd just put his feet up.

I knew I needed to be strong now, for my mother, my children and my siblings, whose grief was as deep as mine. The call to Karachi and Saleem's attitude before I travelled, had left me steeped in self-pity. Was I doomed to this life of constant battles and challenges? I'd tried so hard to do the right thing, make a good life for my children, follow an independent path in the same way as my parents, but it felt as if no sooner had I overcome one hurdle than another appeared, blocking my path.

I prayed harder that night to God than I had for a very long time, pleading with Him in my greatest hour of need. I'd always been a believer and tried to live my life the best I could, but this was the greatest test I'd faced to date.

My father had died, my brothers were arranging the funeral and we were all praying for our mother to wake from a coma.

I remained in my old bedroom, unable to sleep, while trying to work out, not for the first time, whether there was any way I could keep my little family intact. I sought solace in noting my thoughts on paper, just as I had done in my university days.

Life is just a moment,
one in which time cannot be captured,
but life can, in the cherished moments
I search and I ask but it still doesn't unravel
The void the emptiness sits in the soul
Nothing but feelings and gut can fill it
–   She ©

22
Patience Is Key

We buried our father as soon as possible, in accordance with the rules of Islam. My siblings and I were braced for what was inevitably going to be one of the toughest days of our lives.

I had no experience of the religious requirements or what else was involved in a Muslim burial, since I'd been just a girl when uncle had died. I looked to my siblings for support. My brothers met with elders from the community whilst my sisters and I greeted the many guests who came to the house to pay their condolences. Several visitors recited sections of the Qur'an for my mother, who remained in hospital. The house felt more like a mosque than the family home, crowded with people who milled in and out against the melodious sounds of Arabic recitations and the smell of oud. This was reality, that precious life comes to an end, sometimes expected, sometimes not.

I was concerned about taking so much time off work in Karachi. I'd only recently taken up my post there, but fortunately, the gallery was now closed for the Eid holidays at the end of Ramadan. I was relieved to have some extra time to be with Mum and to come to terms with the traumatic events that had brought me back to the UK. Everything had happened so quickly that I'd been unable to digest what was happening and felt like an outsider looking in as my siblings planned Dad's funeral. I simply couldn't accept that I'd never see my dad alive again. Every now and then the realization would hit me with so much force that I found myself gasping for breath, in actual physical pain. The children had no understanding of what a funeral was, although I tried gently to explain that Granddad was no longer with us and had left to go to a better place. Crouched down next to them, I had no idea whether I was making a good job of this conversation, but what else could I do?

As they stared at me, wide-eyed and confused, with tears rolling down their faces, I felt drained of emotion and energy. Time passed in a blur. The children were restless and wandered aimlessly round the house. There was no routine and none of us had any appetite.

On the day of the burial, my brothers walked in, together with a man I knew from the local florist, carrying two wreaths which spelled Grandfather and Dad. I'd seen similar ones in funeral processions on TV, but how different it felt, knowing that these were for our own father and my children's grandfather. I could tell from the sobbing around me that the floral tributes were having the same effect on everyone in the house.

We had arranged for the burial to take place locally in a cemetery near to the family home. My parents had always told us that they wanted to be buried nearby, so that family members could visit their graves easily. Sajjad had tried to persuade the doctors to allow Mum to leave hospital for the burial but, while sympathetic, they refused, saying that although she was beginning to recover, she was still too weak.

Before long, someone called across the room to say that the funeral cars had arrived. I walked over to the window to see three black cars making their way slowly and sedately along the road, before pulling up outside our house. The first was the hearse, carrying my father's body in a coffin; my dad, in a closed box – the thought was unbearable. The coffin was brought into the house, carried from the car on the shoulders of my brothers and other male members of the family and friends, so that we could all pay our final respects.

I still couldn't quite believe that this was my own father's burial. I kept imagining I was attending the funeral of a distant relative and my parents would walk in to pay their respects at any moment. Tears rolled down my face again as I caught the pained expression on my brother's face. Sajjad was trying to be brave, but I knew that, like me, he was eaten up with grief, reflecting on how quickly and brutally a life can be snatched away. In this case, that of a beautiful soul, a loving husband, father, brother, grandfather and friend to many.

My brothers placed my father's coffin on several stands and removed the lid. His face had been turned in order to face the *Kaaba* in his grave, the holiest site on Earth for us Muslims and he was wrapped in a white cloth. The sight of him was breath-taking. He looked so peaceful, content and handsome and for a wild moment I thought he was simply sleeping. I had to hold myself back from rushing over and trying to wake him up and had to remind myself that this was not my father – there was no life, no breath – it was only his shell. *Oh, how we take each other for granted, assuming we have as much time as we want with our loved ones,* I thought, as my heart ached.

We gathered around the coffin, reciting words from the Qur'an, asking God to forgive my father's sins and to grant him paradise. My siblings were in pieces, like me, but I had my children to comfort, which forced me to keep myself together, at least a little. The children were upset and doing their best to understand what was happening.

I lost all sense of time, but all too soon, my brothers and the Imam were placing the lid back on my father's coffin, signalling the moment had come for his body to be taken away. It dawned on me that I would never see that kind, selfless, loving face again and I turned to my sister Neelam, screaming in anguish. We held each other in a vice-like grip, our bodies heaving as we sobbed in unison.

The rest of the day passed in a blur of talking to relatives and comforting each other. I woke the next day, exhausted after a night of tossing and turning, to the sound of my children chatting downstairs and realized that Fatima was making them breakfast. Clearly, I had eventually dozed off in the early hours and then overslept.

"Sorry, Fatima," I said, racing downstairs.

"Don't worry, Shama, it's a good way of keeping my mind off things," she said with a tired smile. "Listen, you go and see Mum today. I'll stay here with the kids."

"OK, thanks," I said, with a grateful smile.

Sajjad drove me to the hospital and said he'd come and pick me up later. I made my way to Mom's room, pulled up a chair next to her bed and began telling her about what her grandchildren had been up to back at the house. Although Mum had gained consciousness, she was still very weak. She had always been a tough woman – the anchor of the family – and we were relying on that mental strength she always showed to help her recover physically. My poor mother had only recently been told that her beloved husband was no longer with us. Sajjad had been forced to give her this heart-wrenching news and we were all terrified it would affect her recovery, but we also knew that she was in the best hands. Mum tried to ask about Saleem, but I cut her short, telling her that she needed to focus on herself.

"Get better, Mom, and then you can come and stay with me and the children in Karachi," I said. I was desperate to ensure my mother had some company when she came out of hospital. I knew she would feel the loss of my father terribly – her husband and best friend for so many years – but here she was, trying to put all of us first. What a brave and wonderful woman.

I asked the consultant, Dr Nabeel, how long my mother was likely to remain in hospital, so I could plan whether to return to Pakistan. Understandably, he didn't want to be drawn on a timescale. "Recovery times vary. If I were you, I'd go back to Karachi, now she's out of danger," he said. "I'm sure your brothers and sisters can keep you updated."

Sajjad had already told me that he understood I couldn't stay indefinitely.

"You also need to think of the children, Shama," he said, in the car on the way back to the house. "They need their routine, school and friends. Go back and we'll let you know as soon as there's any news."

"Thank you for understanding," I whispered.

I telephoned the gallery and told them I could fly back in a couple of days' time and then went to explain my plans to the children. Fatima came to help me pack and cuddle the children while I sorted out their things. How different from the last time I was preparing to go to Pakistan, I thought, when my parents came to wave us off at the airport and were planning to visit as soon as they could.

Sajjad offered to take us to the airport, but I told him we'd get a taxi, since I knew he was exhausted from the daily hospital visits to see Mum and the trauma of losing our father. Once we were on the plane back to Karachi, I was overcome by a sense of sadness and loneliness. I knew my work colleagues would be understanding, but they hadn't known my mother and father personally in the way Saleem had. I hoped he would step up to the mark and offer the support I so desperately needed at such a difficult time.

I reflected on my conversations with Saleem while I was in the UK. I realized he had hardly contacted me during the entire time. I'd been so overcome with grief while supporting my siblings, looking after the children and visiting Mum that I hadn't noticed while there. On the rare occasions we'd spoken, I'd called him and he'd been distant. In fact, he hadn't once asked how I was coping or how my family were. Perhaps he was resentful about the argument we'd had about the maid when I'd first arrived, but then, that was his fault, not mine, I thought. Or was it that he simply found it difficult to talk about his feelings like so many men?

Deep down, I knew I'd fallen back into the familiar pattern of making excuses for his behaviour and defending his faults. I had to face the fact that I'd probably be trying to cope with my grief alone, without the support of my siblings back in the UK, who at least had each other. For a second, I yearned to be back with them, rather than flying to a foreign country and a cold, inconsiderate husband. But I pushed this thought to one side, telling myself I was grieving.

Saleem had our flight details, so I desperately hoped he'd be at the airport to meet us, although I hadn't forgotten that he'd failed to turn up when we first arrived all those weeks ago. I felt tears pricking my eyes, but knew I had to stay strong for the children. What was it my mother had said to me when I told her about the job in Karachi?

"Be strong in life, never compromise on anything at all and follow your dreams. Live your life as it is."

Mum was going to find it incredibly difficult to continue her life without my father – the love of her life – but I knew that, in time, she'd take comfort from the years they'd had together. She'd been blessed with a good marriage, which had left her with many happy memories, more than I had, I thought to myself.

Once we'd landed in Karachi, the reality of having no siblings to support me in my grief hit home. I'd have to be brave and get on with life, even while feeling this fragile. As we walked through the airport, I remembered the phone call I'd had with Shafiq when I first arrived in the UK. I'd suspected Saleem of flirting with Maha or worse at that time, even though he'd denied it and accused me of being paranoid. Traditionally, in our culture, fathers would tackle these situations with sons-in-law, but I didn't have that option now. We reached the arrivals area and I stopped the trolley, took the children's hands and looked around for Saleem. All three were exhausted and far less enthusiastic than when we'd arrived here the first time. I knew my father's death and the traumatic visit to the UK had affected them too.

"Can we have McDonald's, Mommy?" Zoya asked, tugging on my sleeve and pointing to the fast-food outlet, famous for being the chain's first halal branch.

"Let me just look for *Baba*, darling, then we can have something to eat at home," I said, searching for Saleem's face in the crowds. It was then that the driver came running up to me. "Madam, welcome back. Please accept my condolences on your loss. I hope your mother is making a recovery," he said, taking the trolley.

"Thank you," I said, as Shafiq joined us. "Did *Sahib* not come to the airport?"

"No, he is not here, madam," the driver answered, avoiding my gaze. "He went to see his family."

I kept quiet, but inside I was seething with rage. Saleem had gone to spend time with his family, when he knew I was coming back, having just buried my father and left my mother in hospital.

As soon as we were home, I gave the children something to eat and put them to bed. I came downstairs to phone Saleem.

"*Assalamalaikum*. Where are you?" I asked, pretending not to know.

"I'm in the village with my sister," he replied, casually.

"But you knew we were coming back today? I needed you here, Saleem, to support me."

"Why do you need me there?" he answered, brusquely.

"How can you even ask that with everything that's just happened?" I shouted, frustrated. "Don't you get it? You're my husband and you're all I have here."

"Shama, you're a woman and a mother," he answered, impatiently. "You have to grow up and get on with life. You're being pathetic – people die all the time."

I couldn't believe what I was hearing. "What do you mean? We're supposed to be there for each other, to support each other emotionally..."

"Anyway, I can't speak, I'm with my sister," he interrupted and hung up.

Over the weekend, the parents of my children's friends came to the house to offer their condolences. Concerned and very supportive, their visits helped quell some of my isolation and I was grateful that I had been welcomed into the community so readily. One mother, Layla, spent more time than the others at the house and confided over tea that she'd gone through a similar experience.

"Let me take the children for a few hours so you get some time to yourself, even just to grieve," she said. "They can come and play or swim. I will drive them to their taekwondo class, it's no problem."

I was particularly grateful, given that Saleem had not yet returned and I was due back to work on Monday.

It was two weeks before he came back to the house, walking in one night, after the children had gone to bed. In spite of everything, I rushed over to him and gave him a hug, but there was no response.

"Saleem, it's been two weeks. I thought you'd come back sooner," I said, drawing away from him.

"I wanted to spend some time with my sister," he said, shrugging. "I'm tired, we'll talk tomorrow. Is there anything to eat? I'm starving."

"Maha's asleep, but I can make something for you," I said, getting up, pleased to have the company. I went to the kitchen and started preparing the food. But as I was chopping the ingredients, his lack of concern increasingly gnawed at me. He still hadn't asked how I was coping after Dad's death or whether my mum was recovering. I fought back tears at his selfishness, knowing they'd only make him angry and instead put the food on a tray and carried it in to him.

"Here," I said, handing him the fresh chapatis and spinach and chicken curry I'd made.

Saleem took the plate without a word and tucked in. I sat down next to him whilst he ate, waiting for him to ask about the accident and my parents once he'd finished. But he just reached for the remote and switched the television on, handing me his plate without even making eye contact.

As I walked out to the kitchen, I could hear the sound of Bollywood music coming from the television and Saleem turning up the volume. I put the plate down and breathed a huge sigh of disbelief. My father had died, my mother was seriously injured and my husband, who hadn't even asked after them or shown me any sympathy, was playing music – something he knew was entirely inappropriate in our culture so soon after a tragedy.

Exhausted and broken, I didn't even have the heart to confront him about the incident with Maha. It had knocked my confidence, knowing he had turned to this girl in my absence. She was uneducated, unattractive and not even hygienic, I thought bitterly. I felt totally demoralized and belittled, unable to understand his actions. I was heartbroken, coming to terms with the fact that I was married to a selfish, weak womanizer. But I was also vulnerable, emotional and isolated from my family, craving attention and love from my husband. Rumi said, "Love is not an emotion, it is your very existence." And this was my existence. I'd read about women who were treated appallingly by their husbands and I had never understood why they didn't leave. Now I was one of them and had realized it wasn't that straightforward.

With nobody to confide in, I headed upstairs, leaving Saleem watching television, oblivious to the pain I was in. I closed the bedroom door behind me and walked into the bathroom, put the toilet seat down and collapsed on top of it, finally allowing myself to break down in body-wrenching sobs, for my parents and for myself. Spent, all cried out, I stood to wash my face and stared at my reflection in the mirror.

"*Ya Allah*, of all the men in the world, you gave me this one?" I said out loud. "You say preserve yourself for one man and this is what I was given? Someone who isn't even there for me in my time of need?"

I remained heavy-hearted and tearful over the next few days, although I learned to disguise it as we fell back into our routine. The children began school again, which seemed to do them good and I returned to work, where my colleagues were both sympathetic and supportive.

Work was my escape and diversion, yet it upset me that I preferred to throw myself into my job than spend time with my husband. I needed to face up to the fact that my father's death had proved beyond doubt that Saleem was unlikely to change. This was the reality, that I'd never really had a husband and my children had never really had a father.

Back in England, Mum was making a slow but steady recovery. My siblings updated me regularly until she was strong enough to speak to me on the phone herself. When we did chat for the first time, I was shocked at how fragile she sounded. I knew that while her physical injuries were healing, the trauma of losing her life partner in such horrific circumstances would stay with her forever.

I could tell she was putting on a brave voice, brushing aside my questions about her recovery and asking instead about her beloved grandchildren. I was wracked with guilt that I couldn't be there for her physically and pictured myself at her bedside, holding her hand. Knowing how much she'd done for me in the past, the example she'd set us of having a work ethic, focusing on education, being humble, respectful and kind and her words of wisdom, always uttered calmly and patiently, added to my frustration that I couldn't give her something back in her time of need.

As our routine returned, my focus shifted to Saleem's womanizing ways, which I'd chosen to ignore in my grief. Now anger rose within me and I railed against my husband, but also against the God I was raised to believe in, asking Him time and again why He had given me this man, from all those I could've had, for a husband. I was incensed that He had failed to look after me. I had tried to follow His Word and live a good life, so why was I being punished in this way?

"Why are my children and I being made to suffer?" I asked Him, out loud. Having sharpened my focus on my husband's behaviour, I realized that the tell-tale signs of his womanizing had always been there. While he'd try to tell me I was suspicious and paranoid and that he was simply out drinking whisky and reminiscing about his father, I could see the guilt in his eyes. I certainly hadn't imagined the late-night calls that we received, when women would tell me they'd called a wrong number after I'd answered. Knowing that I would never be unfaithful to my husband made the hurt and pain even harder to bear.

A sixth sense told me I'd been right to think he'd slept with Maha while I'd been away and now what? Random women? But what could I do? I was working hard with three children to support on the other side of the world from my family. With this barrier of deception and infidelity standing between us, Saleem became increasingly cold and unaffectionate. Although my job kept me busy, I found my thoughts turning to my father whenever I had a spare moment, revisiting the anguish of his funeral and knowing that if he were still alive, he'd have guided me through these difficult times.

I felt as if I'd left my heart in the UK when Dad died and I was now uprooted, simply floating. I wanted my home, my siblings, the familiar walls of the family house and I desperately needed the comfort of my mother. My siblings wanted Mum to visit me to help with her recuperation and take her mind off the pain of losing her husband. Even though Mum was putting on a brave face, Fatima said, she was a shadow of her former self. She still soldiered on and I couldn't help but think that perhaps women cope better than men in these crises and that Dad would have fallen to bits if he'd been the one left alone. A few weeks on, Sajjad called to say the doctor had said Mum was well enough to make the journey to Karachi. I was thrilled, even in sadness. I knew that we could help each other with our grieving and healing.

23
Between Worlds

I spent hours on the phone with my siblings to ensure I'd have everything Mum would need for her impending trip to Karachi, from special pillows and the toiletries she loved to new towels. As her visit drew closer, I was almost as excited as the children, who couldn't wait to see their grandma after such a lengthy wait.

Although it was a long journey for Mum to make, the family all agreed that a change of scenery would do her good and help her with her own recovery. Spending time with her grandchildren, well away from the scene of the crash, could be the best therapy available, we decided.

I was also hoping that having her with us would help me deal with a growing feeling of homesickness.

"Not long now," I said to the children with a smile. "Let's begin counting down the days!"

While I discussed Mom's health down to the very last detail with Fatima, I'd given up talking to Saleem about our plans all together. He'd shown little or no interest since the time of the accident. It was hurtful, especially since he found the time to talk to his own mother and siblings almost daily.

However, I did need to talk to Saleem about my mom's visit. Given her health problems and fragile state of mind, I wanted to be sure that we wouldn't give her any reasons to worry about our marriage. It wasn't a conversation I looked forward to having, but I felt it was necessary. I chose my time carefully, waiting for the evening, when the children were asleep and Saleem was in the lounge listening to music, whisky glass in hand, looking relaxed.

"Saleem," I began, "you know Mom's arriving on Friday? She's still very delicate, so please, it's really important we don't argue when she's around. And you can't drink alcohol in front of her either, as she won't be able to handle it."

I waited for his response, unsure what form it would take, but my words were met with a stony silence. When he still hadn't replied a few minutes later, I decided to try again.

"Saleem, please," I begged. "My mother has been through a huge amount and is making this long trip to recover with us. I need to know I'll have your support, please!"

He turned to look at me, his face showing no emotion. "I'm not stupid," he said, coldly. "I know how to handle people." With that, he got up and walked out of the room, his typically ambiguous answer leaving me feeling far from reassured.

I tried to shrug off my concerns about how Saleem would behave during my mother's trip and, instead, focus on how much I was looking forward to seeing her. The children were finding it difficult to believe she was actually coming to Karachi and asked me repeatedly whether it was true.

"You'll see, when we're at the airport and she comes through to meet us!" I said, with a smile, as they asked yet again.

When the day finally arrived, Saleem announced that he was too busy to come to the airport with us. In the past, I would've been upset, but now I wasn't surprised or even bothered. The children were so excited that they more than compensated for my selfish husband's attitude.

"It's fine, the driver will take us," I responded, dismissively. Nothing was going to spoil that day.

We stood in the arrivals lounge, bouquet of flowers in hand, anxiously looking for my mother as the other passengers wandered past. I knew she'd be having assistance, so was braced for how frail she'd look and was acutely aware that, like me, she'd be thinking that this visit was meant to have been made with my father. As my thoughts threatened to spill over into tears, I focused on the children who were jumping up and down in excitement.

"Look, there she is!" yelled Zoya. I followed her gaze and, sure enough, in came my mother, helped on both sides by airport staff, but looking as elegant as ever in a crisp white shirt and *salwar*, accessorized with a beautiful turquoise scarf wrapped around her neck. She looked thin and delicate but serene. There was something innocent and angelic about her and I was filled with gratitude to God for bringing her safely to us. I'd found myself thinking about God a great deal since Dad's passing.

As Mum slowly made her way toward us, I noticed her lips twitching, as if she was trying not to cry. I knew she'd be thinking that my father should be there too and that the delight she felt at seeing us all reminded her how cruelly he'd been taken away. I felt a sudden rush of love for this brave woman who'd made such a long journey to see her daughter and grandchildren while still battling ill health. It had taken until today for me to really appreciate everything she'd done; leaving her own parents to come to the UK and working hard, while raising her children and supporting my father, only to now find herself a widow.

I knew I needed to focus on the positives to help Mom, which I could do by showing her what a good life we had in Karachi, the wonderful school that the children were attending and the satisfaction I was getting from my work. Saleem was as good as his word, at least, when we arrived back at the house, playing the role of doting dad and husband, turning on the charm and entertaining my mother with an Oscar-worthy performance. Once we were alone, he reverted to his usual cold self, making jibes and hurling insults, but I'd become resigned to how he was and was determined not to let it upset me during Mom's visit.

When I wasn't working, I took Mum out to eat and to the shops. I also took her to the Golf Club, so that the children could run around and let off steam after school. It was rewarding to see Mum begin to improve and smile a little more often. Although she often had a wistful look in her eyes, there was more colour in her cheeks and I was pleased to see she'd put on some weight. She was also a great help with the children and would often accompany the driver and Maha to their after-school activities. Mum spoke to the kids in Urdu and they responded in the same language, which made me smile. They spoke only English at home and at school, so I was so happy to hear them speaking Urdu comfortably, this language that was such an important part of their heritage.

In the evenings, we'd sit and watch television or go for a walk in the nearby Hilal Park. It was during these peaceful walks that my mother opened up about my father, talking about their relationship and the wonderful times they'd had together.

"But now he's in heaven and I have been blessed with this precious time with you and my gorgeous grandchildren," she said, smiling bravely as I hugged her.

I'd seen a huge improvement in Mom's health, both mental and physical, since she'd arrived in Karachi, but sadly, her stay with us was drawing to an end.

"These three weeks have been fantastic, Shama, and it's given me great peace of mind to see you so well-settled," she said. I noticed that she tactfully said little about Saleem.

I waved her off at the airport with a heavy heart, already missing her terribly. Rumi's words came to my mind at that moment.

But listen to me
For one moment quit
Being sad
Hear blessings
Dropping their blossoms
Around you.

Before long, we'd settled back into our routine and Mum was once again a voice on the other end of the phone. Work and the children kept me busy, while Saleem did his own thing. I'd drop the children off at school on my way to work and then my day was a whirlwind of inviting clients for show previews, promoting the gallery and meetings with staff, followed by writing up reports. In the afternoons, when our time was our own, the children played with their friends or attended after-school activities.

By April, the temperature began creeping up and no one could work without the air conditioning on. We spent our weekends at the local Park Towers mall and cooled down with ice cream. I was pleased that the children had made plenty of friends and were often invited out to other events, especially when it became too warm to do much at home.

As the months rolled on, we began planning our summer holidays. The gallery gave me four weeks off, while the children's school was closed for two months over the summer. The embassy would pay for flights back to the UK for the entire family, including Saleem. I wasn't surprised when he announced that he wouldn't be joining us.

"I can't leave my mother for a month, Shama," he began.

"It's OK, you don't need to explain," I cut in. I realized, to my surprise, that I didn't mind in the least. In fact, I was relieved that he wouldn't be joining us.

I found myself once again counting down the days until I'd see my family and the beautiful English countryside. My last visit following my parents' accident had been so traumatic that I hadn't really been able to spend any quality time with my siblings. Now we were preparing to fly over to England for a stay in my hometown when it was at its prettiest. I was looking forward to taking the children round my favourite spots: Haworth, home of the brilliant Bronte sisters; Blackpool, with its bright lights and Eureka! The National Children's Museum in Halifax. I was also looking forward to catching up with my family and friends in better circumstances.

Sajjad was at the airport to meet us and, after exchanging plenty of hugs, we were on our way back to the family home. The car journey reminded me of why I loved England so much, especially its countryside, with its trees in full bloom, green fields stretching for miles and the British wildlife quietly and occasionally making an appearance. As we passed the small cafes and farms, I felt a sense of elation. How different from Karachi, with its gridlocked roads and pollution, I thought. Stepping out of the car on the driveway, I breathed in the fresh air and closed my eyes, savouring it and remembering the happy days of my childhood. For the next few weeks, the kids would get to experience something of those times too.

Mum and the rest of the family were all waiting excitedly in the doorway and came rushing out to hug us, dragging us in and talking over each other in the way they always did when guests arrived. I was relieved to see that my mother looked even healthier than when she'd stayed with us, signalling that her recovery was going well. Looking around the room at my mum and Fatima chatting happily to my children, I knew the next few weeks would be really special. Undoubtedly, the most difficult part of the trip would be visiting my father's grave. It was something I needed to do before I could relax properly, but plucking up the courage would be difficult.

After a wonderful evening of food and conversation, followed by a good sleep, the next morning I called Sajjad , who'd offered to take me to Dad's grave and told him I was ready to make the trip. I covered my head as a traditional sign of respect, took my Qur'an and asked God to give me the strength and bravery I'd need to get through the day.

We drove to the burial site in silence, and, as we got nearer, I felt the grief from the days after the accident return. After parking, Sajjad came around to the passenger's side, opened the door and gently took my arm. We walked slowly toward the grave and before long the tears began to fall. I felt weighed down with grief for my beautiful father, who had given so much of himself for me and my siblings.

"Thank you, Dad," I whispered. "Maybe I never told you how much I loved you or let you know how much I appreciated you. You worked so hard to give us the best you possibly could and I hope I can live a life worthy of that and make you proud."

Knowing I'd never hear my father's voice again brought another wave of grief and more tears. I recited the Qur'an and asked almighty God to forgive my father's sins and allow him to rest in peace in the highest heavens. The morning was upsetting but special too and I knew I'd take away new precious memories to look back on in time.

Before I could relax, there were practical issues that needed seeing to, such as ensuring the tenant in my house was happy and that the rent was up-to-date. Once these were sorted, I could relax with Mom, Fatima and Aunty Suraya. What a time we had, eating together, relaxing at home and taking the children for fun days out in the parks and countryside.

The weeks flew by and before we knew it, the trip was coming to an end. Since our last day coincided with Fatima's birthday, we had a huge family dinner, complete with a magnificent birthday cake prepared by my loving mother.

"I want a cake too," Zoya wailed, as she watched my mother icing it.

"Tell you what, come with me to the supermarket and you can choose a little cake just for you!" Fatima said, taking her hand. I smiled as Zoya's face lit up, thinking how innocent children were and how easily pleased.

I expected Saleem to phone to wish his sister-in-law a happy birthday, but there was no call on that, our final, day. I wasn't overly surprised, since communication between us had been occasional and brief, limited to pleasantries and practical arrangements with the staff. I always asked after his family, although he rarely reciprocated and most of the calls were made by me.

Before we knew it, it was time for Sajjad to drive us to the airport. Mum was sobbing. The emptiness of the house would be stifling now her beloved grandchildren and I were leaving. As we hugged goodbye, I questioned once again my decision to take the job in Karachi.

Shepherding the children on to the plane, I took my seat with a heavy heart and, as we took off, tears flowed. Was it leaving my loving family or going back to a cold, uncaring husband that upset me the most? I had no idea.

I realized that I was dreading seeing Saleem and had no desire to share news of my time in England with him. I wanted to keep those happy times separate and certainly didn't want him tainting them.

Before leaving the UK, I'd arranged for the driver to collect us in Karachi without even asking Saleem, remembering how disappointed the children had been before when their father had failed to turn up at the airport. But to my surprise, Saleem was there, waiting for us.

"Hi, kids! How was your holiday? Did you have fun with your mom's family?" he asked, with a smile.

I was speechless. His behaviour was so out of character. Maybe he'd genuinely missed us and I'd underestimated him. Experience had made me cynical, but for now I decided to let things be, especially since the children were so happy to see their father.

On the journey home, Saleem asked the children what they'd done in England and they did their best to tell him about their adventures, although they were still shy, having had so little contact with their father on a day-to-day basis.

We arrived at the house and the staff welcomed us home and took our bags inside. After freshening up, we sat down for lunch – McDonald's for the kids, at their request and a delicious meal prepared by Maha for me and Saleem. Even though Saleem was making an effort to be friendly, I realized I hadn't missed him at all during my time in the UK. If anything, I'd been relieved to get away from the negative environment and recuperate after the trauma of not only losing my father and coping with Mom's injuries but also receiving no emotional support from my husband.

Rumi once said that love is a mirror and that 'In it you seen nothing except your reflection. You see nothing except your real face.' I knew that the way Saleem had treated me in our years together had robbed me of my self-esteem, so much so that I refused to have a mirror in my room. After having so many insults thrown at me over the years, I couldn't bear to look at my face. I'd been brought up to believe that we were all God's creatures and as beautiful as we were individual, irrespective of gender, race, or colour. But after being called all the names under the sun, I had no confidence left. I was Shama to my family and friends, but whenever I happened to catch sight of myself in a mirror, all I could think of was Saleem shouting *"Kutey kee bachee"* at me.

I didn't see a much-loved daughter, sister and mother; just a failed wife who'd been unable to earn love and respect from her husband. Thinking back to my days as a happy, confident teenage girl, checking her appearance in a mirror, I wondered how on earth I'd arrived at this point. My friends from those days would never have believed it.

Once I was back at work and the children began a new academic year at school, daily life took over. I noticed that the kids needed less from me now, whether it was reading to themselves or putting on their clothes. I felt wistful, but also immensely proud that I'd brought them up to be independent. They were thinking for themselves, noticing things and expressing their opinions freely.

As we headed into autumn, Zoya decided one day that she wanted to switch from her sandals to her winter shoes. "I'm going to polish them, Mom, all by myself," she said, proudly. "I'll go and get the polish from *Baba's* cupboard."

She marched into my bedroom and pulled open the door of Saleem's wardrobe, where he kept his knick-knacks, including the shoe polish. As she rummaged through the boxes and cloths, she pulled out a bottle of whisky. Turning to me, she held it up, a horrified look on her face.

"Mom, look! Oh, my word! There's a *sharab* bottle in *Baba's* cupboard!" she exclaimed.

"Don't be silly Zoya, it's just juice!" I said, rushing over and trying to snatch the bottle back, but Zoya was well beyond the age when I could fool her.

"No, Mom, it's not," she said firmly. "Look, it says whisky here on the label and it's not the colour of juice."

"Well, maybe it's apple juice," I answered, desperately. She looked at me, confused and hurt and I silently cursed her father for putting me in this position. Zoya was well aware that as Muslims we weren't allowed to consume alcohol.

"Actually, I think it belongs to the part-time gardener, who's not Muslim," I said quickly. "Let's give it back to him."

I would have willingly left Saleem to explain himself, but he was on one of the many visits he made to his mother, so I waited until the children were asleep and then rang him.

"Your own daughter found your whisky while looking for the shoe polish," I said, seething. "Are you proud of yourself? Is this what you want to teach your children?"

"Don't blame me, Shama," he retorted. "It's your fault for allowing her to go rooting through my things. I blame you, *kutey kee bachee*!"

"How can you blame me?" I answered, furious now. "Do I drink? Do I? How dare you! You hide things, keep secrets and then your kids discover stuff about you. Why do you do them in the first place?"

I was convinced that Zoya's discovery would permanently scar her and taint her views of her father even more. I realized that the older they became, the more they were noticing, from the lack of time he made for them and the little interest he took in their lives to his inability to show them any affection. Yet, life continued. I persevered at what there was of my marriage and making a home, with a busy routine keeping me going and providing little time for me to dwell on my failed relationship. Life was a cycle of breakfast, school drop-offs, work, school pick-ups, activities, dinner and much-needed sleep. Time at work and with the children was fulfilling and rewarding, but there was nothing between me and Saleem as a couple, not even any pretence any more. Saleem spent more and more time in Punjab, where he said it was easier to find work and visiting his family. I kept my focus firmly on the upcoming summer, when, once again, I could visit my family and breathe in the fresh, country air of England, my home.

24
Holding On and Letting Go

As we moved into the new year, I began to notice a difference in Saleem, although I couldn't quite put my finger on what it was. I'd find him pacing up and down restlessly outside. When I tried to talk to him about it, he'd tell me that he needed this time alone to reminisce about his childhood. I always tried to be supportive when he was in these moods and certainly never gave him a hard time, but still, I felt sad that he was shutting me out.

Surprisingly, he'd also become more thoughtful and caring around me and the children, which was great. One Saturday in spring, Saleem decided to take us to the Golf Club, where the children could play in the park before we all sat down to have dinner. I was thrilled, since it was so rare for us all to go out together. Usually, it was just me and the children for days out, with Saleem showing no interest. Maybe, just maybe, God has listened to my prayers, I thought. I'd always secretly hoped that He wouldn't let me down. *Life certainly moves in a mysterious way,* I said to myself, smiling, as we watched the children running around the park to their heart's content.

That day at the Golf Club seemed to be the start of a new phase in our lives. Each weekend, we'd go for walks or for something to eat. Saleem began spending more time with the children in the evenings, helping them with their homework and reading to them. My spirits rose as I watched them huddled together on the sofa. The children adored him, soaking up his words like little sponges and Saleem's intelligence shone through. He was more than capable of getting the kids to understand the principles they were learning, whether fractions or words in the stories they were reading. We were becoming a close family unit at last, I thought, closing my eyes and smiling to myself. My dream was finally coming true.

Spring was marching on and the evenings were becoming lighter, meaning we could spend more time outdoors. One evening, as we walked in Hilal Park and the kids ran on ahead of us, Saleem took my hand.

"Shama, I need to get a proper job and earn some decent money for the children and you. You're working too hard, you need to rest," he said, looking straight at me. "I really think we should go back to the UK so that I can study for some better qualifications. You've done your bit, now I should do the same."

I was touched by his words and his concern. For the first time, my husband seemed worried about how hard I was working and wanted to improve his prospects for the sake of his family. God was finally answering my prayers!

"Let me think about it. Let's just be happy for now," I answered, taking his hand.

It wasn't all plain sailing. Saleem still sloped off to the study with a bottle of whisky in the evenings from time to time, a signal for me to stay out of his way. He'd often stagger into the bedroom toward the end of the night determined to pick a fight.

One time, when we were due to go out to friends, he exploded with rage because I hadn't ensured his shirt was ironed, lashing out and punching me in the face. His temper was so out of control that he didn't care who saw my bruises and cuts. It was almost as if he was proud of what he'd done.

I did my best to cover up the marks with makeup when going in to work, but they were often noticeable. When colleagues at the gallery or other moms asked me what had happened, I'd pretend I'd fallen over, but I could tell from their reactions that they were sceptical.

One afternoon, when I was collecting the children from school, nursing a black eye and a cut lip, Laura, the mother of a boy in Zoya's class, touched my arm gently.

"You know, women should never feel ashamed of what they're going through," she whispered, "and don't ever think it's your fault. I'm here if you need to talk."

I smiled through tears, feeling as though I'd found a friend that I could confide in. Laura and I began spending time together when we could. I found her to be a good listener and non-judgmental, perhaps because she was older than me. She'd also met my mother when she came to stay and may well have sensed that I was missing Mom's words of wisdom. I'd thought God was listening to me at last, but then felt that maybe I'd got that wrong. At the very least though it seemed that now He'd sent me an angel to unload on.

Saleem was becoming increasingly frustrated about the lack of job opportunities and had begun pressing me to make a decision on moving back to the UK.

"I can do a master's in computer-aided design and that will open loads more doors," he said. "I'll be happier and then we'll all be happier."

He was also keen to get a British passport and nationality, convinced that this would improve his chances of getting a well-paid job. I was unsure whether things would work out for Saleem in England, as his problems went far deeper than a qualification, but I was also desperately missing my family. Perhaps the time was right to move back, I thought. I'd held down a difficult job, proved I could be independent and would have a good reference now. I was keen to spend more time with Mom, but had concerns as well, such as whether another move would unsettle the children. Although they missed their family, they loved their life in Karachi and they were all doing well at school. I also appreciated the help I had around the house, as it made my day-to-day life so much easier.

Still, if Saleem's anger stemmed in part from his frustration at not being able to find a job that would allow him to support his family, this could be the answer. I reminded myself that I'd seen another, much nicer, side to him in recent months. Perhaps I'd get to see more of that if he was happier. I told Saleem that I agreed with his proposal to return to the UK and he was genuinely delighted.

"Things will be different this time, you'll see," he said.

Once again, we began preparing for a move, slowly packing up our belongings, working out where we'd stay and applying for school places. Saleem began looking for courses for himself. The plan was for us to move in with my mother initially, since my house was still being rented out.

We hired a company to deal with the packing and shipping so that I could focus on finishing the projects I was involved in at work and make a smooth handover. My work colleagues were sad to hear that I was going, but understood the reasons for my decision, especially after my father's death.

The next few weeks passed in a whirlwind of activity. Once word was out that we were leaving, everyone we knew invited us round for meals and social gatherings to say goodbye. Adam played football for the mini Karachi United team, so had a huge group of friends, while both the girls were popular at school. As the invitations flooded in and people said their farewells and wished us luck, it occurred to me that our Karachi friends really were like a big family. We'd probably taken this companionship for granted, I thought and were unlikely to find such a large group of friends in the UK.

It was the week before our departure and we were left with just the suitcases that would go with us on the plane. The children ran around a now-empty house as I reflected on the time we'd spent there. I'd be taking fond memories back with me, but also sadness that Dad never got to see the life I'd made in Karachi.

Once we'd said our final goodbyes and were on the plane home, all thoughts were on seeing my family, especially Mom, who was ecstatic that we were coming home. In time-honoured tradition, she'd prepared a huge welcome meal and all my siblings were there to greet us.

She'd taken a great deal of care to make us feel at home by redecorating our rooms and adding details, such as soft toys, new pyjamas and slippers, all to ensure the children felt settled. There were also photos of us all, including some from our wedding day, on the dressing table.

There was a lot of adjusting to do. I'd been lucky enough to get the children places at a good school, but there were no house staff to help me with the routine now. Luckily, my mum and Fatima were there to support me, delighted at the chance to spend time with the kids. I was also in a state of limbo about my own career, having returned to the UK without a job. I'd hoped that these few weeks would give Saleem and me some valuable time together, but, to my disappointment, I quickly realized that he'd already rediscovered the local pubs and was spending more and more time in them.

"Please, Saleem, don't fall back into those old ways," I begged. "This is a small town and everyone knows everyone else. You'll be bringing my family into disrepute." But my words fell on deaf ears.

A week or so after we'd moved back, I asked Saleem if he'd completed his application for the post-graduate course he'd seen at Sheffield University.

"Yes, it's all taken care of. You don't need to nag. I'll be starting in September," he replied, abruptly. I didn't care that he was annoyed I was hassling him. The main thing was that he'd applied, which left me clear to make my own plans. I called around the galleries I knew from my time in Manchester, including the space that I'd worked at before leaving for Karachi.

My old boss, Linda, was delighted to hear I was back and invited me along for coffee. After catching up on each other's news and hearing about the new projects under way at the gallery, we got onto the subject of work.

"As it happens, Shama, your successor will be going on maternity leave soon. How would you like to cover her?" Linda asked.

"I'd love to!" I answered quickly, thrilled. "Thanks so much for the opportunity!"

Things are falling into place, I thought. At least I'd have some money of my own to contribute to our upkeep. Saleem decided it would make more sense to study away from home, saying he needed the peace and quiet to focus. "That way, you and the children can stay with your mother," he explained. "It makes sense for now, Shama. We need to keep our expenses down."

The idea seemed to be a good one. Saleem's studies were costly, since he was applying as an overseas student. I'd been trying to work out how we were going to be able to finance them and had decided that the only way was to take out a loan against the house I'd bought. I had concerns, but Saleem persuaded me it was the right decision.

"Shama, don't worry I'll pay you back," he said. "You know I'm doing this for you and the children."

"OK, but please, come and visit whenever you can," I said.

"Of course, I will," he replied.

September quickly came around and I was immersed in preparing the children for the new school year while also ensuring Saleem had everything he needed for life as a mature student. We waved him off, calling out to him to promise to come back that weekend. Saleem called the following evening, telling us about his first lectures and room, which he laughed about, comparing it to a shoe box. "I'll see you all on Friday," he said.

As Friday rolled around, I let the children stay up later than usual waiting for their *baba*, but Saleem didn't turn up.

"I don't think *Baba's* coming," Zoya said sadly.

"Maybe he's been held up," I said, inwardly seething.

The next day, Saleem called. "I don't think I'm going to be able to get back as often as I'd hoped," he said. "There's much more work than I thought."

"The kids miss you, Saleem. At the very least you could have let us know yesterday," I said. "Please try to make an effort."

Things were tough. With Saleem away and work keeping me busy, the children began playing up and were taking time to settle at their new school. I missed the little luxuries of life in Karachi. There were precious moments too, such as cuddling up with the children after school and hearing about their day, but I was worried that Saleem was becoming distant again. His calls had become less frequent.

Sad and exhausted, I'd make coffee and sit with Mum in the evenings whilst she watched the news. I knew she could sense I was unhappy and was concerned about me, which made me feel guilty, since I was desperate not to give her anything to worry about. While happy to have us there, the car crash and loss of my father had taken their toll on her health and she looked much more delicate than before.

One morning in October, I was sifting through my inbox and scanning artists' biographies at work when a strange feeling came over me, as if something was wrong. My first thought was that one of the children was hurt or sick. Instinctively, I checked my phone, but there were no new messages or missed calls. Returning to my work, I ploughed on but felt distracted. Getting up to make a cup of tea, I took another glance at my phone and saw that Sajjad had tried to call me. I phoned him back immediately.

"Shama, can you leave work and come home?" he said, urgently. "It's Mom, she's fallen ill."

"What is it, what's happened?" I said, panic rising inside.

"Just come home, Shama," he said.

I began shaking and could feel my heart beating against my ribcage. I struggled to breathe, remembering the phone call about the crash that killed my father and the room began to spin.

"What's happened? Tell me!" I screamed, prompting Linda to come running over. "She's never ill. I don't understand!"

Eventually, Linda persuaded me to hang up and took me off to the kitchen, where she gave me a glass of water.

"Shama, are you sure you're OK to drive home?" she said gently. "We can arrange a lift if you want."

"No, I'll be fine, I just need to get back. Thank you," I said, grabbing my jacket.

I'd tried to call Fatima and Aunty Suraya, but no one had picked up, further elevating my anxiety. On the way home, I called Sajjad again, although I knew I shouldn't be using my mobile while driving.

This time he picked up. "I'm on my way. Is Mum at the hospital?" I asked.

"No, she's here. Come home," he said quickly. "We're waiting for the doctor to do the paperwork and then they'll take her in."

As I drove home, I recalled that this was the second time in as many years that I'd been given bad news on the telephone about a loved one. First Dad and now Mom, I thought, brushing away the tears as I turned off the main road towards Mom's house. It was too much to cope with. Pulling up outside the house, I saw that several familiar cars were already parked nearby, their presence reflecting the seriousness of Mom's condition.

I parked and ran inside, bumping into my sisters who were hugging each other and crying. I tried to ask them what was happening, my voice now an unrecognizable shriek. Aunty Suraya rushed to me and gently ushered me to one side.

"It was her time, Shama. She had to go," she said, holding me close.

Nothing was registering. "What do you mean? Go where?" I asked, confused. The dizziness and nausea had returned and I held on to my aunt to keep my balance.

"Mom's fine," I continued. "She's frailer than she used to be but still, for her age…" I trailed off as I realized that my aunt, like my sisters, was sobbing silently, her body shaking with grief.

"She's gone, she's gone," she said, with tears rolling down her face. "They think it was a sudden heart attack."

"What are you talking about? I saw her this morning!" I said.

"Come, Shama," my aunt said, taking me into the lounge. I stood, transfixed, looking at my mother. She was peaceful, as if asleep, I thought. But this was so familiar, a loved one beautifully composed, laid out in the room, asleep, but not breathing, no sign of life.

"This isn't my mom, Aunty," I said, turning round, the room spinning. "Where is she?"

"Child, look at her. She is not here," she said, through tears, shaking me hard. "She has gone to be with your father."

At the mention of Dad, I collapsed on the floor and let out a piercing cry.

"Why, God, why?" I screamed, fists clenched and eyes raised skywards. "Why have you done this to me? Why are you punishing me? What have I ever done to deserve this?" Then everything went black.

I came round as Fatima splashed cold water on my face and Aunty Suraya shook my shoulders.

"Shama, pull yourself together," my aunt said, pain etched across her face. "Your mum is in a better place. She has left us. She wasn't happy. Surely you can understand that?"

"No, I don't understand it!" I yelled back, pushing my aunt away and clasping my thighs in desperation. "She cannot do this, not right now when I need her the most." Then, slumped on the chair, I raised my hands to my face and howled. "Mom! I love you!"

Holding on to Fatima, I tried to stand up, but collapsed on to the floor, my face level with Mom's body. The reality that she was gone hit me hard. As everyone around me wailed, I found myself consumed with anger at the unjustness of it all. As I sat stock still, staring at my mother, apparently emotionless, the women around me began to stare.

"Shama, share your feelings and cry," they urged. "Tell your mum you forgive her for everything as she has gone."

I ignored them, venting my rage at God inside, but keeping quiet. I suddenly remembered that the children would need collecting from school and mentioned it to Fatima. I was too numb to think that she was in the same state of shock as me, but valiantly she crossed the room to speak to our neighbour Liz from two doors along.

"Liz will go and get them," she said, "But you need to call the school to give authorization."

As I phoned the school, I was hit with the thought that my mother would never collect my children from there again. How would I explain to them that their darling grandmother had died?

"Why, why, why?" I screamed, turning to Aunty Suraya for support. Finally, my grief took over, and we stood, holding each other as we sobbed, our bodies shaking with grief as we mourned the woman that bonded us.

Time seemed to stand still, but at some point Liz arrived with the children, who took in the scene with wide eyes and rushed over to me. Zoya was the first to spot her grandmother on the floor and turned to me, confused.

"Mom, what happened to *Nano*?" she said. "Is she...is she?"

"Yes, Zoya, darling, *Nano* has died, she's gone to be with Granddad," I said.

Her tears prompted another wave of grief and we clung to each other sobbing while Fatima cuddled the twins.

The women from the community quickly and efficiently made the necessary arrangements, removing the furniture, spreading out the white sheets for people to sit on and placing date seeds on the floor so that mourners could recite the Fatiha, the opening chapter of the Qur'an.

Bismillaah ar-Rahman ar-Raheem
Al hamdu lillaahi rabbil 'alameen
Ar-Rahman ar-Raheem Maaliki yaumid Deen
Iyyaaka na'abudu wa iyyaaka nasta'een
Ihdinas siraatal mustaqeem
Siraatal ladheena an 'amta' alaihim
Ghairil maghduubi' alaihim waladaaleen
Aameen
In the name of God, the Infinitely Compassionate and Merciful.
Praise be to God, Lord of all the worlds.
The Compassionate, the Merciful. Ruler on the Day of Reckoning.
You alone do we worship and You alone do we ask for help.
Guide us on the straight path,
the path of those who have received your grace;
not the path of those who have brought down wrath, nor of those who wander
astray.
Amen.

As the sounds of their recitation washed over me, I drowned in my grief of having lost both my parents, thinking my children were now without their grandparents. My brother's voice pulled me out of my own thoughts.

"Shama, you should call Saleem," Sajjad said.

"Yes, I will, but I need some time," I said.

"OK, but call him, Shama, you need his support, he's your husband," he insisted.

When I felt ready, I dialled the number and waited for Saleem to answer.

"Saleem? *Assalam alaikum*. How are you?" I said, and then, with a lump in my throat, did my best to explain what had happened. "I'm calling you to tell you that Mum had a heart attack," I said, between sobs. "It was very sudden, but she didn't make it."

He didn't believe me.

"What are you talking about, Shama?" he said. "Have you gone mad? Do you know what you're saying?"

"Of course, I know what I'm saying – my mother is dead, don't you get it?" I screamed, hysterically.

Sajjad quickly took the phone from my hand.

"Shama isn't in any fit state to talk right now, but it's true that our mother is no longer with us, Saleem," he said. "I think Shama and the kids need you right now."

I put my head on my brother's shoulder, grateful for his calmness and wise words. I could hear my husband on the phone and felt comforted by the anticipation that he'd soon be on his way back to us. But I should've known better.

"But what can I do?" Saleem replied. "I can't come, I'm studying."

Before I could intervene, Sajjad hung up and turned to me.

"Shama, listen, we need to be here for each other," he said, looking at me intently. He was trying to tell me something about my marriage and my husband's responsibilities. I disappeared into the bathroom and rang Saleem again.

"Saleem, are you coming home? Sheffield is only an hour and a half's drive away and this is a family emergency," I said, trying to stay calm. "I need you to come and be here for me and the children."

"I can't come. I have to study," he repeated, obstinately. "Don't you get it?"

"My mum is dead and the children have lost their grandmother, so soon after losing their grandfather. Where are your priorities?" I shouted. "We need you here." Drained and exhausted, I hung up, unwilling to listen to any more of Saleem's excuses.

Mom's funeral was scheduled to take place as soon as the post-mortem was done and the death certificate issued. The following two days passed in a daze, my sisters and I unable to function. I had no idea whether it was night or day, breakfast or dinnertime, remaining in my pyjamas and wandering aimlessly around the house. My brothers bravely did their best and even arranged for one of the neighbours to have the children until after the funeral, since it was clear I wasn't capable of taking care of them.

Sajjad called a family friend in Sheffield and asked if she'd be able to drive Saleem down with her for the funeral. She agreed without hesitation, saying it was the least she could do for us.

Saleem arrived immediately after all the flowers had been delivered, including the wreath spelling Mom. *Not so long ago, the flowers spelled Dad,* I thought. History was repeating itself in the worst possible way.

I waited for Saleem to come over and comfort me, now he was finally here, but he strode across the room and pulled me to one side in front of my siblings.

"Shama, where's my *salwar kameez*?" he said. "I need to get ready! Why haven't you seen to any of this? And I'm hungry, why haven't you prepared any food?"

Food? I hadn't eaten myself for two days! No sympathy or words of comfort, no expression of sorrow, just the same old inconsiderate man who took out his bad moods on his wife and thought only of himself, even when she was grieving.

The funeral gathering was in the main mosque community centre. As everyone made their way there, I told my siblings I'd follow and quickly rustled up an omelette and toast for Saleem. While he showered and ate I ironed his clothes and took the chance to freshen up myself. As he came out of the shower, I told him his lunch was ready, but instead of taking his shirt from me, he grabbed my arm.

"Haven't you missed me? It's been at least two months," he said, with a smile and a glint in his eye.

"What do you mean?" I asked.

"Don't pretend you don't know," he said, trying to pull me toward him.

"Get off, for God's sake. It's my mother's funeral!" I yelled.

Pushing him away, I ran to the bathroom and promptly threw up. Lifting my eyes upwards, I once again asked God what I'd done to deserve a husband like this, while my beloved parents had been cruelly taken from me.

When we arrived at the community centre, I braced myself for the sight of my brothers, uncles and family friends carrying in the coffin containing my mother's body. The room was a cacophony of wails and howls as the women expressed their grief in the only way they knew how.

Fatima and I held each other, while Zoya and the twins wrapped their arms around me, asking why Nano had died so soon after their grandfather. What could I say? I certainly didn't have any answers for them.

The tears flowed and I was unable to stop shaking, numb to the words of the Qur'an that were being recited. My mother's brother approached the coffin, bent double with grief, his voice cracking with emotion. "My beloved sister, you left me alone, far away. How will I cope on my own?" he asked.

The men covered Mom's face and closed the coffin, leaving the lid unscrewed and carried her away. Fatima, Neelam and I instinctively ran toward it and grabbed the side, unable or unwilling to let it go. I looked round for

Saleem, desperate for some emotional support, but he was nowhere to be seen. I pushed any thoughts of him to the back of my mind. Today was about my mother.

The men went to the graveyard and we followed them at a distance, still sobbing. Adam stood with the men and boys, in keeping with tradition and after the ceremony, wandered back over to me. "Mama, *Baba* never put soil on *Nano's* grave. Why not?" he asked, curiously. I held my son tightly.

"My poor darling, because it wasn't his mother who died, that's why," I answered, sadly.

25
Sorrow's Hand

The next day we all gathered at the family house to recite the Qur'an in her memory. After that, days went by in a daze. As I wandered around the rooms that Mum had worked so hard to keep looking homely and welcoming, I knew it was time for us to find a place of our own. I told Sajjad how I felt over coffee one evening and I could tell from his reaction that he understood.

"Shama, you know our cousins have a property business and have houses available that you can move into right away if you want, including newly renovated homes," he said. "Just give me the word and I'll sort something out."

"That would be great, but please, draw up an official contract, with rent due," I answered, giving him a hug. I valued my independence too much to take favours from my family and also wanted Saleem to shoulder some of the responsibility.

On the day of the move, we took our belongings to the new house bit by bit in the car to save the cost of hiring a van. As soon as we were inside, Saleem went upstairs to his computer, saying he needed to catch up on his studies while I arranged the furniture downstairs. Just as I was putting the final touches to the lounge and settling the children with a snack, Saleem came downstairs rubbing his eyes. "I've finished for now. I'm going out for a walk to get some fresh air," he announced, grabbing his coat.

As usual, no offer of help or comments about how nice the house looked. I sighed and put the kettle on, thinking that once the children had eaten, I'd settle them for their nap and get started with sorting out the bedroom. Armed with bags and other bits and pieces, I pushed the door open and looked around, deciding where to start. Saleem had left his computer on and as I reached across to switch it off the screen sprang back to life. Several chat files were still open. Boxes of conversations filled the screen, sentence after sentence written by Saleem. Sick to my stomach, I forced myself to skim through them.

Tell me what you are wearing right now…
You look so sexy…
I've been dying to chat to you again. When can we meet up?

As I scrolled down, I realized with horror that Saleem had arranged to meet up with a woman he'd been chatting to at the time of my mother's death. He'd told me he couldn't get away from Sheffield because of his studies, but all the time he was arranging a rendezvous with someone he'd been chatting to online.

The room began to spin and I grabbed the side of the bed to keep myself from collapsing on the floor. I wished to God that the ground would open and swallow me up. What was the point in carrying on? I sat on the bed exhausted, physically unable to carry out even the smallest task. All the energy and zest for life had been sucked out of me. I didn't even have the heart to confront Saleem when I heard the click of the front door. What was I going to do? I couldn't even confide in my sisters, knowing they, like me, were still grieving for our mother.

The next morning, I woke up with the remnants of a dream lingering in my mind, a white fabric had billowed daintily in the breeze to the sounds of melodious Arabic that reminded me of a recitation. I tried to remember the details, but the more I tried to hold on to it, the quicker it slipped away from me. Unlike Neelam, who was always sharing stories of her dreams, I didn't dream very often, so the experience left me a little on edge.

While preparing breakfast for the children, I knew that no matter how much I wanted to disappear and give up on life, I couldn't expect the world to stop and wait for me to emerge from the dark place I'd found myself in. I had to continue to move forward, recharge my batteries and find a new source of energy for the sake of my children. I knew I couldn't rely on Saleem for anything. He was stuck in his own selfish little world. I had to face the fact that I'd be solely responsible for the children's care and upbringing.

I fell back into my old routine, taking the children to school, going to work, collecting them from after-school club, helping them with their homework and driving them to their classes, which included kickboxing, music and Arabic lessons. I knew it was important for them to keep their hobbies going, but it was a struggle for me. Still mourning the loss of my mom, I was exhausted from having to do all the chores, school drop-offs and pick-ups and cooking, now I no longer had her help with the kids. Once the children were asleep, I'd sit and stare at the four walls around me and wonder how on earth my life had panned out as it had.

Saleem called Thursday evening to let me know that he was coming home for a few days as he'd handed in several essays and felt that he needed a break. A break! What was that? I thought to myself. Still, I was relieved to hear he'd be around, simply because I desperately needed to catch up on some sleep. Work had become a struggle after my mom's death. No matter how I persevered, I couldn't find any enthusiasm for the projects that I'd felt so passionately about just a few weeks before.

One weekend, as I was preparing the children for their kickboxing class, I heard Saleem on the phone talking to his brother Adnan in Pakistan. They would talk endlessly, with no thought of the huge bills that came from such lengthy international calls.

Before taking the children to class, I settled them in the kitchen with a dinner of fish, potato waffles and beans. I went into the lounge and stood in front of the gas heater to warm up, my house slippers and the thin georgette *salwar kameez* gifted to me by my mum giving me little warmth. Just at that moment, I heard Saleem shouting and swearing at the kids.

"This time, tell your mother '*Kutey kee bachee*, is your dead dad gonna shut the kitchen door? No!'" he shouted.

To my horror, I heard Zoya repeat his words in a shaky, hesitant voice. "Shut the door, *ku....t...ey...kee.....bach....ee*, shut the door."

I was disgusted he could bring his own innocent children down to this level. I knew that if I told him what I thought, I'd be making the situation worse for everyone.

"Come on, *kutey kee bachee*, let's drop the kids off at kickboxing," he said, eyeing me with a look of pure disdain and patronizing smile.

As I was putting the children's coats on, I spotted a bag in the corner that I didn't recognize. Saleem had brought a friend, Nazir, over the day before and I suspected it belonged to him.

"Shall we drop Nazir's bag off afterwards?" I asked.

"Whatever, *kutey kee bachee*, whatever," he said, smiling again. I could see he was enjoying playing out this scene in front of the children and I despised him for it.

"Let me just get changed," I said.

"There's no time, you should have got changed earlier, idiot, get in the car," Saleem snapped.

"But…" I began, but decided against arguing and hurried the children outside and into the car, shivering in the cold. The wind was biting and it was beginning to rain. We dropped the children off and on the way back Saleem swerved into the petrol station, without warning.

After he'd filled up the tank, it dawned on me that he was waiting for me to go into the garage and pay for the fuel, even though I was in a paper-thin outfit and slippers and the rain was now heavier than ever.

With a sigh, I reached for my bank card and dashed into the shop. Holding back tears, I decided to choose a drink for us both from the fridge, but found myself in a panic about what to choose for Saleem. Would he want juice or something fizzy? Orange or blackcurrant? Maybe he wouldn't want a cold drink after having a hot drink at home. Would he flip if I bought the wrong thing? I was shaking at the prospect of getting this decision wrong. How had it come to this?

Once we'd left the petrol station, Saleem turned toward our house. "Aren't we dropping Nazir's bag off?" I asked. He screeched to a halt, banging the steering wheel. "*Kutey kee bachee*, why didn't you remind me?" he shouted.

He turned the car round and headed for the M65, all the while continuing to barrage me with insults. "...*bachee bagarat aurat*, you're useless," he said, his insults becoming worse as his speed increased. "Go get your mother out of her grave," he spat in Punjabi. "I want to fuck her."

I could feel my heart beating faster and found I was struggling for breath. I couldn't take him speaking about my mother this way.

"Saleem, please, just leave me and my family alone," I begged, "for God's sake, my parents are dead, show them some respect."

My words seemed to add more fuel to the fire. Saleem started punching my right thigh with his left hand, banging the steering wheel with the other.

"Stop, Saleem! Stop it!" I screamed. He wasn't focusing on the road, but was continuing to accelerate. The rain and wind were already making visibility poor and the wipers were struggling to clear the windscreen against the downpour. Saleem swerved, prompting the car behind to hoot. Silence followed while he changed lane and I hoped that this would be enough to distract him, but suddenly he'd reached across, punched me in the side of the head, unclicking my seatbelt as I shook my head, trying to recover from the blow. He had pulled over onto the hard shoulder.

"What are you doing?" I shrieked. "Saleem, we're on a motorway!"

Without saying a word, he reached across further, unlocked the car door and began trying to push me out of the car. "Go on, get out, *kutey kee bachee*. Get out and die," he said, snarling.

My head was spinning as I frantically looked around for something to grab hold of to prevent myself from being pushed out of the car. The shock of the wind and the rain took my breath away. Instinctively, I tried to grab the steering wheel, but Saleem was too strong and wrenched my hand free, sending me out onto the tarmac. My head and shoulder hit the road with a whack and I rolled from the hard shoulder onto a grassy verge, suddenly becoming aware of the noise of the cars whizzing past and the rain beating down on my face. Unable to move, I opened my eyes for a second, just able to make out our car speeding off.

I had no idea how long I stayed huddled on the verge, but eventually, soaking wet and in excruciating pain, I tried to get up.

Was this the rock bottom that people spoke of, I wondered, stranded on the motorway, having been thrown out of a car like a bag of rubbish by my husband?

Inexplicably, despite the pain and cold, I felt a wonderful sense of relief that my time had now come and that I could leave this miserable existence. I looked up at the slate-grey sky, allowing the rain to beat down freely on my face and smiled.

"*La illaha illa Allah Muhammad Rasul Allah*," I recited.

"Are you OK?" said a voice out of the blue. I turned and realized that a car had pulled up on the hard shoulder and an elderly man was walking toward me. "What happened?" he asked.

"I'm not sure," I answered. "But no, I'm not OK." I found myself telling him about the death of my parents, one so close after the other and the tears fell freely, mixing with the rain on my face.

"Let's get you home, come on," he said kindly.

The man, whose name I hadn't even thought to ask, dropped me outside my house.

"Thank you," I said, turning to him.

"Good luck," he replied meekly, with a look of worry on his face.

Drenched, I walked toward the house, suddenly remembering that the children would be waiting to be picked up after kickboxing. I saw our car parked a little further along the road, meaning Saleem was back. Had he collected the children?

I unlocked the door and let myself in. I automatically began picking up the dirty dishes and taking them out to the kitchen, still in my soaking wet clothes. I had begun to plan how I was going to get the children away. What would we need? Where would we go? When would we make our escape? I climbed the stairs and found Adam wandering around on the landing.

"Mama, why you are wet?" he asked. "*Baba* said you went with your friend, but why were you out in the rain?"

I was still trying to think of an answer when Saleem marched arrogantly out of the bedroom. "Get back downstairs right now. I want to talk to you, *kutey kee bachee*," he shouted.

"Adam, go and play with your sisters, I'll come and chat to you soon, OK?" I whispered with a smile, distraught at his bewildered face.

"What do you want? A divorce?" Saleem said smugly, clearly thinking I'd never dare make this request.

I laughed, no fear left in me. "Saleem, I've been divorced for years!" I said with a cold smile. "When was I ever in a marriage?"

Saleem's face went white with rage and he started shaking with anger. "You bitch. I will line your sisters up in a row so I can fuck them – and your dead mother," he yelled.

"Enough is enough! Just leave! You're vile!" I spat.

"*Kutey kee bachee, baigarat aurat!*" came the familiar insult from Saleem's mouth.

For the first time, I gave as good as I'd been given year after year, launching my words at him with defiance: "*Kutey kah bachah!*"

Saleem's eyes opened wide in shock. "What did you say?" he hissed. With that, his fists clenched, he turned, ran to the kitchen and grabbed a knife from the rack. "You think I'm gonna let you talk to me like that?" he shouted, moving toward me with the knife out in front. Before I could get out of the way, he'd swiped at my stomach, blood flowing through my ripped top.

I looked at the blood but felt oddly detached from the wound and the red that was soaking through the beautiful white garment that my darling mother had bought for me, the same woman that my husband had spoken about · so disgustingly moments earlier.

"Its only blood, Saleem – go on kill me," I said, as if in a trance. "I don't feel any pain. You can't hurt me any more than you already have. I tolerated those words for years and today I said them back to you. I gave you a taste of your own medicine and you have the nerve to react in this way! What about me? The woman who has had to endure them time after time? Now you know how it feels and I'm glad. I'm really glad for that!"

The loss of blood was beginning to make me feel dizzy. Without thinking I bound my *dupatta* scarf around my stomach and went to get some cotton wool to clean myself up.

The shock of having stabbed me, as well as my reaction, had wrong-footed Saleem, who was unsure how to react. He turned, then began calling the children to come downstairs, falling into the vernacular he used when speaking to his family in Pakistan. "Children," he said, looking at me rather than them, as he spoke. "Your father will no longer be here. I'm divorcing your mother." With that he marched upstairs and began packing his bags. The children stared at me, confused and the girls both began to cry. Trust Saleem to use them as pawns in his game, I thought to myself. Why couldn't he just go?

"Listen, whatever happens, your father will always be your father, I promise," I whispered, willing him to get out of the house. "Now, let's get you ready for bed."

I left the children in front of the TV to tend to my cut, which to my relief wasn't deep. After cleaning myself up, I took the children upstairs and heard the front door slam shut while I was bathing them. A wave of relief swept over me. Could it be that I was finally free of this disgusting man? Rumi's words came to me and comforted me at that moment: 'Don't grieve. Anything you lose comes round in another form.'

The next two weeks passed uneventfully, with no word from Saleem. Things were calm, although I still felt jumpy every time my phone or the doorbell rang. The children were quieter than usual, but I had the impression that they, too, were enjoying the better atmosphere at home.

One morning, as we all got ready to leave the house for school and work, a letter arrived from a firm of solicitors, who said they were representing Saleem. He'd had the time to find a solicitor but not once had the time to even ask about his children. I decided to phone Laura, my friend in Karachi, to let off some steam.

"I knew, I knew what he was like, Shama," she said. "To tell you the truth, Hannah's maid Nargis told me that your husband threw an iron at your head, but that you didn't cry or say anything, even though you needed stitches. She said you must really love him to stay with him. That's why I wanted to support you, because I realized that once your mother went home, you had no one."

And now I didn't even have my mum in the UK. But I did have siblings and a wonderful extended family, I thought, and it was time they knew that I'd finally separated from Saleem! I was so relieved that I had made the decision and I wanted the announcement to take the form of a huge celebration, marking a major achievement. Like Saleem, I found myself a solicitor and instructed him to begin divorce proceedings.

"You'll need your marriage certificate," he advised. I went home and began searching through my files, realizing that Saleem had taken all of the official documents from the house.

The following week, another letter arrived in which Saleem's solicitor said he would be requesting half of everything, from savings and furnishings to the proceeds from the sale of the house. Realizing that I was going to have to do battle, I told my solicitor to go ahead and make preparations for what could be a challenging split. I decided I needed to sit the children down and explain what was happening in as gentle but honest a way as possible. They took the news much better than I anticipated.

"It's OK, Mom, we are happy about it," Zoya said. "We hated seeing you cry and hearing *Baba* shouting bad words at you."

"We don't need *Baba*," Adam chimed in.

The routine was exhausting, without Mum to help, but the atmosphere at home improved considerably. I came home ready to drop, but at least I wasn't worrying about what mood I'd find Saleem in. The only cloud hanging over us was the divorce proceedings. Eventually, I received a letter with a date to appear in court. The hearing was set to take place in Sheffield, so I called my friend Zarina to ask if I could stay overnight, determined to arrive in a calm and composed manner. I'd had my hair done specially and bought a new outfit to wear, since I was determined to look my best. I'd also been delighted to find I'd gone down a dress size, most likely because I was no longer comfort-eating through stress.

Neelam had stepped in to look after the children in my absence, since they had school. As I kissed Zoya, Adam and Sara goodbye before driving to Sheffield, Neelam gave me a hug. "Good luck, you'll be fine," she said.

After an evening catching up with Zarina and her family, followed by a restful sleep, her husband dropped me outside the court. I walked into the waiting area, feeling calmer than I expected and headed over to my solicitor to go through the paperwork. When he'd brought me up-to-date on the latest developments, I quickly scanned the room for Saleem, curious to see him after such a long time, but there was no sign of him.

Just as we were due to make our way into the courtroom, he rushed in, wearing the shirt that I'd given him as a gift and the suit that my parents had bought him. I couldn't believe the cheek, when he'd been so disrespectful about them and put my family through more stress with this court case.

We waited for proceedings to begin, seated opposite each other and were both made to swear on the Qur'an. Saleem's barrister then stood up and began speaking. "My client is requesting half of the proceeds of the sale of the house and the right to half of the furnishings and valuables inside," he said.

I couldn't resist laughing and saying out loud, "So your client doesn't want to see his kids, but wants me to give him half of what little money and assets we have?" My solicitor tried to hush me, but I noticed that even the judge raised his eyebrows as if in agreement with what I'd said.

"Your client will have to produce evidence of any assets owned or held in Pakistan and his student admission and enrolment letter," he said to Saleem's barrister. "I also want to know whether he is pursuing mediation, since there are children involved."

I breathed a sigh of relief. No matter what happened with the case, the pressure was off where Saleem was concerned and I could turn a new page in my life. My solicitor asked me to list everything we had and to be clinical, rather than emotional, about it. With a smile, I told him that that was easy.

"Honestly? Everything here belongs to me, bought with my hard-earned cash from working," I said. "And now he wants half of it all!"

I couldn't believe that Saleem was putting me and the children through this. It was difficult to think that once I'd felt loyalty to him and made so many sacrifices. Now, the thought of him made my stomach turn and the knowledge that I was incurring legal fees because of his vindictiveness filled me with anger.

Evenings were spent poring over paperwork, trying to work out our finances. Once I'd looked at the income and outgoings, I couldn't believe how much money I'd given Saleem to spend on who knew what. On top of it all, the loan for his studies was tied to the house. Since the house was in my name, I realized, with a heavy heart, that I was saddled with it.

The relief at having Saleem removed from my life remained strong, but a familiar loneliness was setting in, made worse by the fact that I no longer had my mother for company and my siblings were busy with their own lives. With the court case hanging over my head, I needed to watch every penny, while also making sure I could provide for the children, emotionally and financially. Oh, how I missed the words of wisdom that my mother used to give me and my father's kind smile.

26
Where There Is Ruin

Relief at having formally separated from Saleem was tempered by the knowledge that I was now completely alone, with no protection or support from a partner and three children that depended on me. Weighed down by this sense of responsibility and thoughts on how my life had panned out, I found myself struggling to sleep. As I tossed and turned at night, my mind constantly returned to the car crash that had killed my father, my mother's death and those miserable months spent in Pakistan at the beginning of my marriage.

One day in spring, while taking Adam and Sara for a check-up at the doctor's surgery, I told my GP that I was struggling to sleep and focus. After listening to me recount what I'd been through in recent months and before, he suggested a course of anti-depressants and sleeping tablets. I thanked him and took my prescription to the pharmacy, but once I'd collected the medication and read about the possible side effects, I decided this wasn't the answer. There must be another way of regaining my mental health and being strong for Zoya, who was now eight and the seven-year-old twins, I thought.

At night, I began putting chairs next to the doors to feel secure and towels along the bottom to block out any light or noise so I could get some sleep. I knew there was no way I could give the children the support they needed if I was exhausted. Money was incredibly tight, but I was determined to make sure that I kept my head above water when it came to finances. I had to ensure I paid my rent, follow up with my tenant since this money was needed to cover my mortgage on the house I'd bought and settle all the other bills.

One particularly difficult week a couple of days before payday, when the bills seemed endless, I broke down and told Aunty Suraya that I was going without a hot meal to ensure the children were eating properly.

"*Beta*, I am your mother. My home is open to you 24 hours a day, any time," she said, giving me a hug. "Whilst I am alive, you will come to my house whenever you need to and eat here."

My heart filled with gratitude, although I was humiliated at having to take my children to my aunt's house simply to ensure they had a hot meal inside them. The situation was made worse by the fact that since the death of my parents I saw less of my siblings. My mother had been the glue that kept our family together.

On one particular occasion, when we'd visited my aunt's house three days in one week, her daughter-in-law, Aleena, made a snide comment under her breath about uninvited guests as we sat down to eat. There was an awkward silence during which I felt my face burning red with embarrassment. Eventually I cleared my throat and looked her straight in the eye.

"I'm really sorry we come to eat at my aunt's so often at the moment," I said, "but right now, we're in a difficult place and she has offered me her support and hospitality. I really hope we'll turn a corner. But in the meantime, I can assure you I truly appreciate what your mother-in-law is doing and can't thank her enough. Please don't ever think I'm ungrateful."

Though these low points made it difficult to persevere, I drew strength from my children and tried to focus on helping them reach their goals. I had applied for a place for Zoya at Clitheroe Grammar School, so was now supporting her as she prepared for the entrance exam. I scoured the charity shops for second-hand books to keep the costs down, but still the expenses seemed to be never-ending.

I reached a point where I swallowed my pride and phoned my brother Sajjad, to ask if he could delay collecting the rent for my cousins on the house until my situation improved.

"Shama, you don't even need to explain," he said, immediately. "You know they are only taking rent because you insisted on paying when you moved in, don't you?"

"I know, I know, but I want to pay. It's just a temporary arrangement," I answered.

I began to wonder whether my determination to be independent was misguided and more about ego than anything else. Doubt began gnawing away at me and I sank further into depression. Would I ever climb out of this dark, unhappy, lonely place?

While I knew that my family were at the other end of the phone, I felt incredibly isolated, devoid of love and the nourishment I needed to flower and live my life to the best of my ability. When alone, I found it impossible to stop going over and over how I'd ended up in such a challenging situation, haunted by my failures and the misfortunes I'd experienced that had led to me existing rather than thriving. Rumi's words seemed to taunt me at that time: 'Don't you know yet? It's your light that lights the world.'

I prayed to God to give me enough strength to see my kids through their childhood until they could stand on their own two feet. I was determined to make sure that they wouldn't be reliant on anyone. There were times when I felt a little more positive, when I reminded myself that I had my health and was physically able to work and support my children. For much of the time I felt full of anger. I would channel my rage at God, asking him why he'd taken my parents away at the point when my marriage was falling apart, when I needed them the most.

When it got too much, I'd remind myself of the verses from the Qur'an that Mum used to say to us. Reflecting on these passages that had meant so much to her, I started to think about the words for the first time. Could the Qur'an, this holiest of books, offer me the hope and light I so desperately needed? I searched for the *Ayat al-Baqarah* to refresh my memory of its words.

On no soul doth Allah place a burden greater than it can bear. It gets every good that it earns and it suffers every ill that it earns. (Pray:) "Our Lord! Condemn us not if we forget or fall into error; our Lord! Lay not on us a burden like that which Thou didst lay on those before us; Our Lord! Lay not on us a burden greater than we have strength to bear. Blot out our sins and grant us forgiveness. Have mercy on us. Thou art our Protector; Help us against those who stand against faith." [Qur'an 2:286][1]

This verse of the Qur'an, in particular, reflected my situation. This book, which I'd read and reread many times throughout my life, a book that had taken 25 years of the Prophet's life to compile, was still a mystery to me. I'd never understood its meaning in Arabic. I'd never really tried. Faith meant having hope. I'd questioned many things in the past, from issues around the meaning of faith to the colour of my skin and my parents' origins, but hadn't turned to this book for the answers it contained. I'd tried to live a good life, one in which I didn't make judgments or discriminate against people. And yet, the more questions I asked, the more confused I felt and unclear about the direction in which I was heading. Life was like Pandora's Box, I decided, with a long list of unexpected events unfolding, one after the other. Only God knew why and I had yet to turn to Him for the answers.

The time came for Zoya to sit the exam for Clitheroe Grammar School. I knew that she would be up against hundreds of other children all competing for places and was scared that she wouldn't get in. My anxiety was heightened by my fear that I wouldn't be able to provide for her in the future, so needed her to have the best start in life. I knew it wasn't fair to transfer my fears onto my daughter, but also couldn't help feeling I'd failed as a mother.

The day of the exams came and off Zoya went. "Just do your best and remember all the hard work you've done," I said to her, with a hug. The tests included papers in English, verbal reasoning and maths. When she came out of the hall, she looked drained. "Mom, it was really hard," she said, looking dejected. My heart bled for her and my spirits sank. I had no back-up plan for her. Should I pray to God? Would He perhaps finally answer my prayers, for the sake of my daughter? Could it be that from these depths of despair, with the words of the Qur'an finally making sense, there was a ray of hope and that this was the time for me to rediscover my faith?

---

[1] Translation by Yusuf Ali.

Knowing that I wanted my daughter to do well at school because I couldn't provide for her in any other way reminded me of how lucky I'd been in my own childhood; I'd been brought up in a privileged family and my life had been idyllic – a stark contrast to my existence today.

I felt lost and confused, without direction and unsure even about what I was searching for. My anger and listlessness would often give way to guilt; I knew there were people much worse off than me. I had a roof over my head, a son and two daughters, all of whom were healthy. What else did I need?

Wallowing in self-pity wasn't doing me any good. I needed to stand on my own two feet and hold my head up high. Though my instinct was to smother my children in love, with my father dead and Saleem gone, they were short of male role models.

Events had understandably made them clingy, with all three wandering out of their rooms at night and climbing into my bed, fighting over who would sleep with me. I didn't mind as, truth be told, I loved their company and welcomed any chance I had to make them feel secure. My life had become a routine of work, housework and looking after the children. I lost count of how many cups of tea and coffee got cold and were tipped down the sink because I was too busy to drink them. Only after all the chores were done and the kids were fed, bathed and in bed did I think about myself. I'd given up taking pride in my appearance and knew that I'd let myself go, still choosing to avoid mirrors whenever possible.

A few weeks later, as I was getting ready for work, a letter arrived confirming that Zoya had been awarded a place at the grammar school. Finally, some good news. In a state of shock, I quickly performed my ablutions and settled on my prayer mat to thank God. He had listened to me. I knew I still faced several huge challenges, but at least I had been rewarded on this issue. Nothing felt more important than trying to secure a good future for my children. My tears fell as I gave thanks.

When I collected the kids from after-school club, I told them that we were going to Pizza Hut as a special celebration. Everyone ordered their favourite pizzas and tucked in happily. Once we'd finished, I looked across at them all and smiled.

"Do you know why you're having a treat today?" I asked.

"No, Mama, it's no one's birthday," Sara said with a shrug.

"Is it because *Nano* is coming back, Mama?" Adam asked.

"Don't be silly, dead people don't come back," Zoya scolded. "*Nano* is in heaven with Grandad."

My heart ached for my children and the void that their grandparents had left.

"Don't worry, kids, I'm crying with happiness," I said, brushing tears away. "We're here because Zoya got accepted into grammar school!"

"I got in? I passed the exam?" Zoya asked, leaping out of her chair.

"Yes, Zoya! You passed, my darling! I'm so proud of you! In fact, I'm proud of you all – you make me happier than I could ever have imagined was possible!" I pulled them into a group hug. "I want you all to remember that Zoya's success today is down to hard work," I said. "Work hard and be good, kind people. Never lie and live your own lives!"

"Yes, Mama," they said back in unison.

"OK!" I answered, with a laugh, signalling for the bill. "Lecture over!"

The waitress brought the card machine and I entered my pin number, waiting for my receipt. "Come on kids, coats on," I said, standing up.

"I'm sorry," the waitress said, looking embarrassed, "but I'm afraid your card has been declined." My head was reeling. I'd purposefully made sure enough money was in the account for this treat. Could a payment have come out unexpectedly? This was the trouble with living so close to the edge! "Could you try it again?" I asked, blushing.

Just as I was frantically trying to decide what to do, I spotted Mom's best friend Aunty Nasreen waiting to be seated.

"Aunty!" I waved. She came rushing over.

"Hi, Shama. Hello, children! How are you all?" she said with a smile.

"Aunty, something embarrassing has happened," I whispered. "There's been a mix up with my card. Could I possibly borrow some cash? I can pay you back tomorrow."

"Of course, *Beta*, don't worry, it's no problem at all," she said, fishing notes out of her purse.

"Thank you so much. I promise I'll pop round with the money after work," I said, hugging her.

"You know you don't need to do that," she said, patting my arm.

Miserable and depressed, I rounded up the children. "Can we go to the Ice Cream Factory too?" Adam asked. Zoya caught my eye and I realized she'd understood what the conversation with Aunty Nasreen had been about.

"It's just pizza today, Adam," she said, squeezing my arm. My daughter was supporting me.

I pushed the problem with the bill to the back of my mind, making a mental note to deal with it later. Today was about celebrating Zoya's achievement. I was ecstatic that she had secured a place at a good school, giving her a strong start in her education. "There's ice cream at home. We'll make our own special sundaes," I said to them all, smiling.

The following morning, when I was rushing around making packed lunches, there was a knock at the door.

"Recorded delivery, miss," the postman said. I signed and took the envelope in through to the kitchen. Opening it, I pulled out what I could see was my final divorce settlement – more good news; one year from today I would have my decree nisi and my divorce would be final! I took a deep breath and slowly exhaled, thanking God as I did. Things were finally falling into place.

I was a little sad and remorseful that I'd failed in my marriage and deep down was thankful that Mum and Dad weren't around to witness my divorce. I knew they'd be relieved that I'd left Saleem for good, but I'd still have felt guilty and ashamed about the effect that the break-up would have on them, given that mine was the first divorce in the family.

While there was some sadness, however, I felt relieved more than anything else that I could prepare for a new chapter in my life. I had been awarded full custody of the children, since it seemed Saleem hadn't even expressed an interest in sharing this responsibility or asked to visit them. Though disappointing, I knew deep down that they'd be better off away from him in a peaceful environment, with no swearing or violence. I was also certain that I would not receive a penny in maintenance from him. Just like Rumi advised, I decided to 'Be like a tree and let the dead leaves drop.' I had come to terms with his selfishness and ability to use people only for what he wanted. I'd watched TV shows where fathers would come on and fight for their rights to be with their children. Saleem certainly wasn't in that category.

After signing the divorce papers, I would notice happy couples and perfect-looking families wherever I went, heightening my sense of failure. Exhausted, isolated and depressed, I would take one day at a time, occasionally asking myself whether this was not only my present but my future too.

27
Hidden Depths

Childcare drop-offs and pick-ups, school runs and commutes were exhausting, as was keeping on top of my finances, from the big bills like the mortgage, insurance payments and food shopping, to ensuring the kids had money for school lunches. There were times when I wasn't sure I had enough petrol to make it through to the next payday and couldn't even top up my mobile phone.

At times, the stress became too much and I found myself waking up in the middle of the night with palpitations and drenched in sweat. I still hadn't got over the deaths of my parents and knew nobody would understand the level of grief I was dealing with unless they'd been through a similar experience themselves. On the rare occasion I would catch sight of myself in the mirror, I didn't recognize the exhausted, overweight, aged woman who stared back.

I was desperate to find a way out of the dark hole I'd fallen into for the sake of my children. Feeling that there was no one I could confide in, I found myself drawn once again to God, the one constant in my life who'd been there through all my ups and downs, even when I'd been filled with so much rage and despair that I couldn't bring myself to open the Qur'an. I desperately wanted my life to be full of peace and happiness and for my dreams to come true. God was a listener; someone I could talk to without fear of being judged. I trusted Him, truly believing that He'd given me life for a reason, whatever that may be. Perhaps it was time to make that reconnection.

The children were thriving at school. I read to them, washed their clothes, made their lunches and packed their bags. On cold, crisp mornings, I would start the car to let it warm up so that they stayed snug for the journey. En route, we sang songs and I taught them the Islamic prayer recitation. I loved these precious moments in the car, when we were all together and I could feed their curiosity and add to their knowledge. I knew I was privileged to be responsible for them. As their mother, it was my duty to give them the best start in life and guide them toward a brighter future. Life might not always turn out how you'd planned, I thought, but the journey still revealed plenty of wonderful moments if you simply allowed them to happen and tried not to worry too much.

Love was a case in point. It was the unconditional love I felt for my children and parents that kept me motivated on dark days. Love, I decided, had to be pure and come from deep within. I knew that it would be very difficult for me to open up to another man after what I'd experienced with Saleem, but I was also aware that I was a deeply emotive person, capable of giving myself fully to the right person.

Still, for now, the children had my undivided attention. Once a week, I'd collect them from school and take them to the mosque, where they went to learn Arabic. "Come on, you need to get showered and changed," I said, sending them upstairs while I prepared their fruit and snacks. I usually cooked dinner while they were at the mosque, but opening the fridge, I realized I didn't have the ingredients I needed or the cash to go shopping.

With a heavy heart, I knew I'd have to borrow some money to get me by until payday. I'd never got to this point before. Somehow, I'd always just scraped by. This was a new low for me.

I decided to text my friend Tara.

Hi, Tara, how are you? Any chance you could lend me £2.50? Had a bit of a difficult month and need to buy some bits of food. Thanks, love Shama x.

The response was swift:

Hi, Shama, long time no speak! Sure, but did you mean £25?

I was trying to work out how to reply without humiliating myself further when the phone rang.

"Shama? Are you OK? I thought you made a mistake!"

Tara's singsong voice came down the line. Oh, to be happy and carefree like my old friend!

"Hi, Tara. Yes, I'm fine," I answered, sounding anything but. "I'm just a bit short of cash. Sorry to ask, but I wondered if you could lend me £2.50 to buy a chicken."

"What?" she said with a laugh. "Are you winding me up, Shams? Is this a joke?" I couldn't bring myself to reply. "Are you OK?" she continued, the pause telling her this was not a laughing matter.

"No, I'm not!" I said miserably.

"I can't even afford to feed my kids. Don't you get it? This isn't a joke, OK?"

"OK, Shama. Calm down," she said. "I'm on my way over."

Within 15 minutes Tara was at my door, thoughtfully carrying a bag of food. Once I'd made some coffee and sat her down, the tears began falling.

"Tara, I've run out of money. I'm broke," I said, relieved at having someone to tell. She squeezed my hand and I noticed tears were forming in her eyes too.

"It will be OK, Shams. You're strong. You'll work it out. This is just a blip," she said.

It was only after she'd gone that I realized the envelope she'd left contained £25 and she'd made no mention of when she'd need it back. I felt grateful, but also humiliated and certainly not as strong as my friend had suggested, but weak and wilting. I lost count of the times I'd had to pawn my jewellery to make ends meet. Would I ever land on my feet?

On dark days I tried to remind myself of my blessings and tell myself that God didn't give us all everything. There were people who couldn't have children, I reminded myself, while I'd been lucky enough to have three. Now that Zoya had started at grammar school, I could drop her off on my way to work much more easily and she then caught the bus home. The twins would do the entrance exam for the grammar school in the spring.

Work was going well, too. I'd been asked to curate an art show titled 'Influence of Heritage,' featuring the work of several local and international artists. The project was exciting and the challenge a major one for me since it was the first exhibition I'd curated by myself since returning to the Spinning 1 Gallery.

Linda, my boss, was pushing me to make contact with the artists to ensure we had their work in on time and check they'd be present for the opening of the show. Two of them had agreed to deliver workshops and attend, but a third, Saman Daghestani, was proving difficult to track down. After plenty of chasing, I received an email from him apologizing and explaining that he'd been in Dubai at an exhibition. "Please feel free to text me on the following mobile number," he wrote.

"Dear Mr Saman, this is Shama from the Spinning 1 Gallery in Manchester regarding the exhibition. Please could you let me know your availability on the 28th of April for the opening of the exhibition?"

"Hi how r u? I think it will be okay for me to come and send my work to you."

"Great. I'll send you an email. Can you send the sizes and images of the work?"

"OK."

Afterward, I emailed him and asked for a profile picture. Saman's English wasn't great, since he'd come to the UK from Syria as an asylum-seeker and been granted a British passport. However, his work was truly impressive, especially some pieces he'd done on Syrian doors and I knew they'd fit brilliantly with our 'Influence of Heritage' theme.

There was plenty for me to do for the show, from working closely with the artists to get their work in time for it to be framed, to preparing a catalogue and sending out invitations. Linda reassured me that I'd be paid overtime, which was very welcome.

Saman kept in regular contact by text and email, asking how his work looked and whether I needed more information on the art that we would be displaying. Around this time, I had to leave work urgently after receiving a call from the school to say Adam had fallen during a football match and needed to have his leg checked out at hospital. Saman had texted me in the morning, but I hadn't got round to replying.

The next morning, I messaged him back:

Sorry for not replying to your messages. I wasn't at work. My son fell over at school and I had to take him to hospital.

His reply came immediately:

Hi, Shama. Thanks for your text. I was worried. You have a son?? How is he?

I typed back:

He's OK now, but had to have stitches, so still sore. Yes, I have a son and two daughters.

Again, the reply came immediately:

Wow, I didn't think you look old enough from your photo on the gallery website! Masha'Allah!

As the exhibition drew closer, the artists began coming in to drop off their work. I hadn't met any of them in person before, so it was exciting to greet them and look at their art first-hand. I was just putting one of the pieces of art in the back room when I heard the door open.

"Hi, is Shama here?"

"Yes, that's me," I answered coming out of the backroom.

A man stood there holding carrier bags brimming with rolled up pieces of paper and smiling.

"I'm Saman. How are you? You look even better in real life," he said smiling.

Unsure of how to react, I quickly took his bag, taking a mental note of his black shirt with dragon motif and the way his glasses dangled around his neck.

"Thanks! I'll get these off to the framers," I said, stepping away quickly. As I turned, I sensed a whiff of Calvin Klein aftershave and my breath caught at the heady scent.

The next day was a busy one communicating with the framer and checking I was happy with the catalogue. We were under pressure to ensure all the work would be ready in time. I was in the kitchen putting on the kettle when my phone beeped. It was a message from Saman.

Hey, dude. How are you?

"Dude?!" I wondered whether Saman's message had been meant for someone else and sent a reply saying just this. Back came his answer: *Lol! Hey, Shama, what does your husband do?*

Pardon? That's a very personal question and not one you should be asking! I typed indignantly.

Sorry! came the reply, followed by mine: *I should think so!*

The launch of the show grew closer and I was increasingly busy, although enjoying rising to the challenge too. Management's expectations were high and, although I was nervous, I felt confident that I could make a success of the project. I felt like I could embody Rumi's wise words and repeated to myself, 'Let the beauty of what you love, be what you do.' I'd arranged for Fatima and Neelam to come to my house and look after the kids while I'd be staying at the Britannia Hotel in central Manchester along with the artists in the week leading up to the opening. We'd secured sponsorships for the accommodation and hospitality so there were no expenses to worry about, although I was slightly apprehensive, given that this would be my first time away from home alone.

I knew I'd be expected to host dinner and show the artists around, but I needn't have worried since everyone was friendly and excited about the show. All the artists had brought their partners, except for Saman, who told me he was single. I felt obliged to spend a bit more time with him since he'd travelled from Hull and was unfamiliar with Manchester, while the couples were happy to go sight-seeing on their own.

Saman spent the evening smiling and joking and, though half the time I didn't get his jokes, he managed to cheer me up whenever I became preoccupied with the stress of the show. I thoroughly enjoyed his company. One evening when we'd had dinner and had decided to walk around the hotel garden, he turned to me and asked, "How come your husband isn't here with you and allowed you to come alone?"

"I'm sorry, Saman, but you keep asking personal questions," I answered quickly. "My husband and my private life are none of your business. Have I ever asked you about your private life, about your wife or kids?"

"Well, no, but you know I'm single, since I've already told you!"

"Anyway, just for your information, it's ex-husband and please don't ever mention him again!"

Saman's face fell and he turned away, deeply embarrassed. "I'm really sorry, Shama, I didn't realize. I shouldn't have asked," he said quietly.

"Yes, you're right, you shouldn't have! Goodnight and enjoy your evening!" I said and went back to my room.

I called Fatima to see how the children were. Zoya told me about the homework she'd done with Aunty Neelam and that they were now doing some baking. I could tell they were all having a great time, so at least there was nothing to worry about there. As soon as I'd hung up, my phone beeped and a message came through from Saman.

Hey, you up?
Why?
Can we talk? Can I call you?
Why?
I just want to!

Before I could think how to reply, the phone in my room began ringing. "Hi, Shama," he said "Look, I'm really sorry about earlier. I shouldn't have said anything I feel really bad," he began.

"Saman, I have a long day tomorrow and you shouldn't be calling my room," I interrupted.

"But I wanted to hear your voice," he continued.

A strange sensation came over me. "What? Why?" I asked, confused.

"I just like listening to your voice. It makes me happy, it's attractive," he said.

"Well, it's late, I have to go," I said, flustered.

"Shama, it's 9pm, it's early," he said with a laugh.

"Well, I'm tired. Goodnight, Saman," I said and hung up.

My heart was beating faster than usual, but I had no idea why. Why was Saman texting me and asking me so many questions? I pushed the thought to the back of my mind, all too aware that I needed to be entirely focused on the opening of the exhibition the next day. Our VIP guests included the Mayor of Manchester and I would be responsible for ensuring the evening, including his tour, ran smoothly.

In the morning, I showered, dressed, blow-dried my hair and quickly called the kids. "Good luck today, Mommy," they said down the phone, on Fatima's instructions.

"Thanks, all of you. I love you!" I replied and then dashed down to host the artists for breakfast.

Saman was already downstairs, with a black blazer over his dragon shirt. Once again, I caught a whiff of Calvin Klein.

"Good morning, madam. You look lovely this morning," he said with a smile. I tried to ignore him, but the strange sensation in my stomach was back.

As the other guests arrived, we went to the buffet to get our breakfast. One of the artists, Arnold, from Finland, was telling me how much he and his wife Kate had enjoyed sight-seeing around Manchester. They'd told me earlier that they'd just celebrated their 30th wedding anniversary, so had decided to make this a special trip to the UK.

"We're so happy we came," he said, smiling at his wife. As she returned his smile, I thought how wonderful it was that they were so happy together, after three decades of marriage. How come some marriages could stand the test of time and yet others, like mine, fell apart so quickly?

Still, this wasn't a day for feeling sorry for myself. I shrugged these thoughts off and once everyone had finished eating, I prepared to give the group their instructions. "The day is your own, but we need to meet at the gallery at 4pm, well ahead of the launch at 5pm," I said briskly. "There'll be group and solo photos, then at 5pm we'll be introducing the exhibition and saying a few words about you all and your work. You'll be collected from the hotel lobby at 3.30pm. Please be ready!"

I waved them all off and turned to gather my things before heading off to a full day at the gallery. Saman hovered near me.

"Can I come with you to the gallery?" he asked. "I haven't really got anything else to do."

"What are you going to do there?" I replied.

"Well, I can watch you," he said with a smile. I was too preoccupied to come up with an excuse.

"OK, but hurry up, it's a busy day and don't get in my way!" I answered.

When we arrived at the gallery, the assistants were already placing all the labels on the artworks and the photographers had begun taking photos, while Linda hovered, checking everything over. My spirits rose; the display looked fantastic. I could see that Saman was also impressed. The refreshments and flowers soon arrived. We were expecting about 50 people and had ensured there'd be plenty to cater to all our guests. I went over to see Linda and could feel Saman's eyes on me or was I imagining it? Apparently not! Linda turned to me.

"It looks great, Shama. Well done," she said. "And by the way, you seem to have a fan! He's a bit keen, isn't he?!"

"Well. I've got other things on my mind today!" I said, wanting to bring the conversation to an end.

Before I knew it, it was 5pm and the guests were arriving. The atmosphere was lively, with attendees milling around and chatting, helping themselves to drinks and canapés. I was in my element, keen to ensure the evening was memorable for all the right reasons. As I caught sight of myself passing by a mirror, my heart sank for a fleeting second. Although I looked smart in my scarlet outfit, I'd been unable to shift the weight I'd put on since having the twins and knew that, under my shift dress, my stomach was covered in stretch marks, not to mention the scar on my chest from when Saleem had poured boiling water on me. Yet, perhaps it was time I learned to love myself for who I was and view the marks I bore as badges of honour – of motherhood and survival.

I knew deep down that, as my mother had always said, a woman should be proud of how she looked and never feel ashamed or try to improve her appearance for others, but putting that into practice wasn't always easy. I suspected that men didn't have this issue, whereas women were all too aware of how easy it was to neglect themselves when caught up with looking after the house and children while holding down a job. Even though I was finding my feet with my work again, my self-confidence was still lacking, I realized. I knew I had to start valuing myself more highly.

The evening was a resounding success, with Linda and the gallery partners coming up to praise me. The VIPs had all come along, media coverage was set to be extensive and well-known collectors had already expressed their interest in several pieces. I was packing up on a high when Saman came over to offer his congratulations.

"How about dinner to celebrate?" he asked.

"Saman, I'm really tired and need to go home to my kids tomorrow," I said. "It's been lovely meeting you. Have a safe trip back to Hull."

"Are you sure you can't come? I'd like to spend some time with you before we all go," he said.

I felt a familiar tingling down my spine as our eyes met, but I stood firm.

"I need to help the team pack up, Saman, but thanks for the offer," I said with a smile.

I called taxis for the artists and kicked off my heels as the final guests left. Linda brought me over a coffee which I gratefully accepted.

"Well done, Shama. That was an amazing event, one of our best," she said. "The effort you put in really paid off. The feedback was amazing and the mayor was really impressed with the quality of art and artists we brought to Manchester."

"Thanks, here's to next year!" I said, delighted.

We closed up the gallery and I called a taxi to take me back to the hotel. As I sat in my room and reflected on the exhibition, I felt prouder of myself than I had done for a very long time. With work going well and the children happy and healthy, I promised myself that I'd focus on the positives in my life.

Weeks passed and there was more good news – the twins had secured places at the grammar school and would be joining Zoya there in September. There was much celebrating, with Fatima and Neelam joining us for pizza to mark the occasion.

As spring moved into summer, I could sense that the children were becoming increasingly independent, making their own snacks and drinks when they were hungry or thirsty and helping with the chores. With Adam and Sara joining Zoya at senior school in the autumn they wouldn't need me around nearly as much as before. While this brought some relief, it also served as a reminder that they were already forging their own paths in life – something I'd encouraged them to do. But what did this mean for me? Would I now be watching them move forward from the wings on my own? Was I destined for a life alone?

28
Everything Is Music

With the children settled at senior school and Linda happy to give me more responsibility on the back of the successful exhibition, we fell into a new routine. Bit by bit, I became more confident and self-assured, proud of what I'd achieved, both in my work and as a mother. As the weeks and months flew by, I wondered if my scars were beginning to heal. I certainly thought less about my marriage and the unhappy years spent with Saleem, but the physical reminders remained and at times dragged me into a dark place. My feelings about my past were also conflicted. I missed Karachi, even though I'd yearned for my family when working there. The lifestyle had been wonderful and at times I was desperate to return to it.

I knew deep down that my work was an escape from the traumas I hadn't yet dealt with, from grieving for both my parents to the breakdown of my marriage and the way I'd had to keep my family together through so much turmoil while struggling for money. I'd kept us going but ended up in my own bubble while doing so, unaware of how I'd got there. As I began to think about where I'd arrived to, I found myself reconnecting with Rumi and God. I had come to think of both as my only true friends in life. I talked to God about the many issues that were worrying me. Having been born and brought up a Muslim, it came naturally to me to turn to God in times of need and it felt that now was definitely a moment when I needed Him to hold my hand. My faith told me that He wouldn't let me down and that I could rely on Him to help me along the path to a better life and happiness.

I was reminded of the book *Faith in Divine Unity and Trust in Divine Providence* by Abu Hamid Al-Ghazali, in which he spoke about how faith wasn't a choice. Was he speaking only about Muslims? Was it the same for Christians and Jews? Was this our destiny rather than a choice? Perhaps I still hadn't learned to trust in God completely, in the way a child does with their mother, knowing that if they cry, someone will always comfort them.

Although my heart was yearning and my soul felt unnourished, I knew deep down inside me that I had plenty of love to give. But I was also aware that the clock was ticking; life was passing me by. My loneliness was heightened by the fact that the kids were becoming increasingly independent. I revelled in their development, proud of the way they asked challenging questions and worked hard at school, keen to compete. But what was my role now?

Sometimes the feelings of loneliness were almost unbearable; I'd never felt so isolated or in need of emotional support. At night, I'd often try to console myself with Rumi's words: 'The wound is the place where the light enters.' At least my career was going from strength to strength. Networking through the gallery brought fantastic opportunities, which included some part-time consultancy work for the United Nations, with one project that involved looking at creativity and the empowerment of women in the communities proving to be hugely satisfying. Alongside this, a friend who was an editor invited me to work on a community journal about the arts.

These additional projects awoke something new in me: a desire to break away from everyone and everything for a while and embark on a personal voyage of discovery. As an art student, I'd yearned to go to Istanbul to see the whirling dervishes and now I found that dream returning ever stronger. With flights becoming increasingly cheaper, I found I could afford to make a four-day trip and asked my sister Fatima if she'd like to come along to share the cost of the hotel. The children were the least of my worries as they needed less and less from me nowadays and would be happy to stay with Neelam, with help from my brother Sajjad while Fatima and I went away.

Fatima found a good deal with Turkish Airlines, complete with a twin-bed hotel room. We were set to go in October and, as the date approached, I felt my excitement growing. There was so much to look forward to; not just getting away and seeing somewhere new, but specifically feeling the magic of Istanbul and allowing Rumi into my soul.

Rumi gave me breath, inspiration, hope, enlightenment and strength. I connected with his words and related to them in so many ways. He was my muse, his wise thoughts supporting and comforting me in my darkest hours, those words penetrating deep inside where nothing else seemed able to reach.

For some reason as I read up on Istanbul one day, I thought about Saman and where he might be, having not seen him since the art exhibition. I recalled him telling me how he often went to Istanbul for art shows and lectures. I wondered if he might be able to give me some information about places to visit and tips on exploring the city. Unsure whether I still had his number, I scrolled through my work address book and found an old message. On a whim, I decided to text him.

Hi, Saman. It's Shama. I'm travelling to Istanbul and was wondering if you could suggest some places to visit? I'm really keen to see the whirling dervishes! Any ideas gratefully received! Thanks!

I sent the message off, although wasn't sure whether there'd be a reply. The thought occurred to me that he might have even changed his number by now. Over the next few days, all thoughts turned to our holiday. Both Fatima and I were incredibly excited at the prospect of just the two of us travelling overseas together. We discussed every possible aspect of the trip, from what to wear to how much luggage and spending money to take. I would've loved a new holiday wardrobe, but knew it was out of the question and told myself that I was lucky enough to be going away. Then, on Friday morning I spotted a message on my phone from Saman.

Hi, stranger – u soon forgot about me!

I smiled. Trust Saman to ignore my questions, change the subject and make it all about him! I typed my response:
Was I supposed to remember you?!

Back came the answer:

Of course! The good-looking guy from the art show! Anyway, just wanted to let u know, I'll be in Istanbul when ur due to be there ☺

I caught my breath and my heart skipped a beat. Saman was in Istanbul? I was curious to know more and continued texting.

Why are you there?

I have an exhibition and took a studio here for the show. When do u arrive?

October 28th

Looking forward! U must be excited to see me ☺. *How are ur children?*

All good, thanks. Can you tell me where I should go while there?

Yes, don't worry, I'll show you around.

I don't want you to show me around! I can go around with my sister!

Oh! Ur sister is coming? So, you're ashamed of me?!

No! But surely you didn't think I was travelling alone?!

Hahahahhahaha! I'll send you some details about Istanbul! Keep in touch!

The day arrived and Fatima and I were all packed and ready to go, super-excited like young girls. I had a fleeting memory of how similar our emotions were on the day we set off for Pakistan ahead of my wedding. What a lot had happened in the intervening years, I thought, so much turmoil! But today was a happy day, I reminded myself.

The taxi arrived to take us to Manchester Airport. Hearing the doorbell, we turned to the children and gave them bear hugs. "Be good for your aunty and uncle," I said, wrapping my arms around each of them in turn.

"Go, Mom!" Zoya said. "We'll be fine! And have a wonderful time! Take care of Aunty Fattie!"

With that we were off. As we entered the airport pushing our luggage trolleys, we chatted about what we'd see and do, naming the places that had caught our eye on TripAdvisor and the food we wanted to try. The queue at the check-in counter for Turkish Airlines was long, but nothing could dampen our spirits. At least, that's what we thought…

"Would Fatima Mughal please come over here?" the official behind the counter asked, as we waited for our boarding passes.

"Yes?" said Fatima, stepping forward.

"Sorry, Madam," said the official, "but your passport expires tomorrow. We cannot let you fly."

Fatima and I both looked at each other in shock. What?

"Fatima, didn't you check your passport?" I asked her, in disbelief.

Fatima went pale.

"Let me see," she said.

The Turkish Airlines representative handed the passport to her.

"Can't I renew it in Turkey?" she asked.

"No, Madam, I'm sorry, we can't allow you to board the plane," the representative said, apologetically.

We moved to the side, dumbfounded, to let the other passengers check in. "This means we can't go. We might as well call a taxi right now!" I said, looking at Fatima, tears in my eyes.

"Shama, I'm so, so sorry," Fatima said, hugging me.

"Listen," she said, eventually. "You can still go."

The suggestion shocked me. "What? On my own? How can I go to Istanbul alone?!"

"Seriously! Why not?" Fatima said.

"Go! I'll get my passport renewed today and join you. I'll be there by tomorrow."

It was too much for me to take in. "I don't know," I said, slowly.

"Seriously, Shama! You need to get going!" Fatima urged. "The gates will close soon! I'll do my passport and get my ticket changed."

"How will you get back?"

"Don't worry about me. I'll grab a taxi and sort everything. Just don't miss the flight!"

We hugged and I watched her leave as I went up the escalator to the departure lounge. This wasn't how it was supposed to be, me travelling alone to Istanbul. But I was still desperate to go, hoping to find some answers and I consoled myself that Fatima would eventually join me.

I wandered around the shops before boarding and then, just as I settled into my plane seat, my phone vibrated. I quickly pulled it out of my bag, thinking that Fatima had texted me with an update. But instead there was one from Saman: *Hi! What time are you landing? If you want, I can meet you guys at the airport as I am nearby!*

I was about to explain, but then remembered I hadn't texted my family, which I always did before travelling. After sending a text filled with kisses to the kids, I went back to Saman's message to tell him about the morning's drama. Just then, an air hostess approached.

"Madam, we are preparing for take-off, please switch off your phone," she said.

I already felt jittery about flying alone and now I'd missed the opportunity to have Saman meet me at the airport! I closed my eyes, trying to shrug off my fears and anxiety and surprisingly fell asleep.

Before I knew it, the captain's voice brought me out of my doze to tell us we were preparing to land. I sat up and tried to gather my thoughts. In a panic, I realized I didn't know our arrangements since Fatima had taken care of most of them. Did we have a pick-up at the airport? Much as I'd tried to be understanding, I couldn't help but feel frustrated that my sister had been so careless as to let her passport expire.

I went through immigration and while searching for the baggage reclaim belt I remembered I could switch my phone back on now. *Ping!* A message from Saman appeared in my inbox:

What time are you landing? Why are you not answering?

Too late to text a reply to Saman now, I thought. I headed out of the airport thinking I'd best get a taxi to the hotel, which I'd calculated should be about £20. I was checking my money to make sure I had enough local currency when I realized with horror that Fatima had all our spending money! We'd been in such a panic at the airport that we hadn't sorted anything out! I was trying to think what on earth to do when a voice interrupted my thoughts with the words "Welcome to Istanbul, Ms Shama."

Still disorientated from the flight I struggled to place the voice and half-turned round, suddenly realizing that it was Saman!

"I texted you to say I was coming to the airport, but you didn't reply, so I checked the flights from Manchester and here I am!" he said with a beaming smile.

The aroma of Calvin Klein brought back memories of the art show and then I saw he had a bouquet of flowers in his hand. "What are you doing here?" I asked, then regretted my tone. How rude! He'd come to the airport to meet me!

"Where's your sister? Is she still waiting for her case?" he asked. I started to explain what had happened and Saman smiled sympathetically.

"That's a shame, Shama, I know you were looking forward to seeing Istanbul together," he said. "But at least you have me now!"

I managed a smile and pushed my annoyance with Fatima and the circumstances I'd found myself to the back of my mind. "Is that a good thing or a bad thing?" I joked.

"Come on, let's get you to your hotel. I have a car and driver," he said, taking my case.

Nerves were kicking in and my stomach felt jittery. None of this was in our original plans! As we sat in the back of the car, Saman looked straight into my eyes. "Are you wearing contact lenses?" he asked.

"What a strange question!" I answered, with a nervous laugh. "Why are you asking?"

His reply took me by surprise: "Because your eyes are glowing, they look lighter and brighter."

I looked away, aware that I was blushing and overcome with shyness. I could also feel my hands becoming clammy. Saman smiled and his eyes dropped to my hands.

"That's a beautiful ring," he said, his fingers brushing against mine, "really unique." His touch sent a shiver down my spine and I realized I had goosebumps. What was going on? But it was a nice feeling, one that made me feel good inside. "Wow, look at the design," he said, edging closer. Our bodies were touching and I moved away as subtly as I could, flustered now and uncomfortable.

"So," he said, smiling at me, "aren't you pleased that I'm here and that you have my company for the day?"

I opened my mouth to reply but found myself tongue-tied.

What an idiot he must think I am, I thought, but I wasn't used to conversing with men other than Saleem and my male relatives.

Saman laughed, filling an awkward silence.

"Come on, chill out and relax, you're on holiday!" he said.

I laughed and did my best to put my nerves to one side. "It's been a long day!" I answered.

Saman was good-looking and funny, with a great personality, which helped to ease my embarrassment and make the journey go quicker. We arrived at the hotel and he jumped out to open the door for me, the perfect gentleman. He also took my bag, smiling as he did so. I couldn't help but smile back.

I checked in and handed the receptionist my passport, before making my way up to the room, Saman walking alongside me. "Shall we drop off your stuff and go for lunch or do you want to go later and freshen up first?" he asked.

"I think we can go straight away. I'll just drop my things off," I mumbled.

I felt out of my depth. Was he going to come into my room? How had I ended up in this situation?

I unlocked the door and Saman came in behind me, putting my hold-all on the floor.

"I'll wait here till you're ready," he said, flopping on the sofa.

Flustered, I grabbed my sponge bag and went to the bathroom to freshen up. As I washed my face and touched up my makeup, I could see what Saman had meant. I looked radiant and my eyes were sparkling. Maybe this trip was just what I needed! Or did Saman have something to do with it? Whatever the reason, I stared at my reflection for a few seconds longer, wanting to hold on to the moment and the face that smiled back at me.

"OK, Saman, let's go," I said.

"You look nice," he said.

"Ha ha, very funny," I retorted.

For a second, he looked confused and hurt. "Thanks, though," I said quickly.

When did anyone last pay me a compliment? It was so long ago that I'd forgotten how to accept them. Turning to apologize as we headed for the door, I bumped into him and smiled.

"It's OK, Shama. Come on, I'll show you Istanbul," he said with a smile, taking my hand to guide me toward the lift. The thrill I felt was undeniable and suddenly I thought of Rumi's words:

Let yourself be drawn
By the stronger pull
Of that which you can truly love.

As we strolled along Istiklal Street, the main shopping thoroughfare of Istanbul, I soaked up the atmosphere, the sights, sounds and aromas. It was everything I'd hoped for and more. We later passed the famous Blue Mosque and I was delighted to realize that our hotel's location in Sultanahmet was walking distance from all the sights. Fatima had got something right!

I felt energized in a way I couldn't explain. Was it the city or my companion, this man I'd met in the UK who was now showing me around Istanbul, a place I'd dreamt of visiting? Or was it a combination of the two and fate bringing us together here? Was this my destiny? I felt strongly that life was all about seeking love, following a path that had been mapped out for you. And here I was, on the next stage of my journey.

Saman chose a restaurant and we went in. As I looked through the menu, my nerves began to dissolve and I found myself laughing at his jokes. As well as recounting amusing stories, he also told me about his family and culture, showing a tender and insightful side that I hadn't seen before. I realized that I felt happier than I had for years. But each time he asked a question and I answered it, I reminded myself to be cautious. After all, in my eyes I was an overweight, ugly divorcee with children – not exactly a great catch for this handsome, funny artist!

Lunch was lovely. "I couldn't eat another thing!" I said, smiling.

"But you must try these Turkish sweets! You can't come to Istanbul and not try the baklava!" he exclaimed, calling the waiter over.

"I couldn't!" I protested.

"Don't worry, we'll share dessert," he insisted. More intimacy! And again, I felt out of my depth.

After we'd eaten, Saman asked me what I wanted to do. "Could we go to the Blue Mosque?" I asked.

"Of course!" he said, guiding me out of the restaurant and back along the street.

As we approached the majestic building, I was overcome with emotion and found myself transported back to my childhood, a time of innocence and happiness, but with the cynicism of adulthood changing the perspective of my thoughts.

'Once upon a time I thought I would grow up and wear fairy-tale dresses, marry a prince, live in a castle and always be happy.

Once upon a time I realized that nothing is ours and that everything ends.

Once upon a time I met the big bad wolf, but then escaped from him.

Once upon a time I struggled within to find myself and detached myself, solely to find myself again.

Once upon a time I yearned to go to Turkey, to search for the greatest love of all.

Once upon a time I realized that life is simply a journey for us as individuals.

Once upon a time I could see myself in my world, happily living for today with hope for tomorrow.

Once upon a time I realized that love is more powerful than pain.

Once upon a time I realized pain is good, as it keeps you alive and the soul nourished.'

With all these words dancing around in my head, I closed my eyes and reached out to the wall for support, visibly shaking. Saman looked at me intently and, saying nothing, simply leaned forward and put his hand on my shoulder.

"It's OK," he said gently. "When I first came here as a refugee from Syria, the mosque, its architecture and atmosphere really moved me. I felt its historical significance. Here was this amazing structure, while in my country we were destroying buildings and their legacy. This country offered me an opening to England, Shama. From here I managed to escape and settle in the UK."

I smiled and wiped stray tears from my eyes, taking in his story.

"What happened to you? You're an amazing woman," he continued. "How come you're divorced? How could any man let you go?"

"Saman, please," I interrupted him. "I am nothing special. I had to end the relationship for my children's sake. It was hard as I thought I was in love, but now I'm just relieved and wish I'd left him years ago. He was a womanizing drinker who used to beat me up."

I paused, but, rather than intervening, Saman waited patiently for me to collect my breath and continue. "I tolerated all of that, but the last straw was that he was no kind of a father to my children. I would die for them, they're my life and that's what did it for me," I said. "My parents would be over the moon to know that I left him and that I am enjoying my life without him. I'm glad I left but sad as well, because I believed love and marriage were for life."

Saman smiled. "Well, let's not go there. It's the past, Shama," he said, guiding me toward the gardens nearby. "Live your life. You only have one life, Shama. Please live it! I want to see you happy."

As we made our way back into the main street, Saman turned to me with a smile. "I have a surprise for you tonight!" he said. "Be ready at 6.30pm. Have a nap and I will bring my things over."

"Your things?" I asked, not knowing what on earth he could mean.

"I thought it would be good if I stayed in the same hotel as you are on your own and I have to check out of where I am anyway. Is that okay?" he said, with a look that was hard to refuse.

"I suppose so," came my answer.

The familiar butterflies were fluttering in my stomach and excitement rose inside me, along with a sprinkling of fear. We walked back to the hotel in a comfortable silence, the conversation in the mosque having somehow brought us closer.

Saman dropped me off at my room and I went inside to shower and rest. I quickly fell into a deep sleep, woken only by the phone ringing at 5.25pm.

"Hello?" I said, still drowsy.

"Hey, Shama, I'm here! I've checked in! Let me know when you're ready!"

"Oh, OK!"

I put the phone down and tried to gather my thoughts. I felt anxious knowing we were under the same roof. Still, it was time to get ready! I splashed some water on my face and applied my makeup, but then hesitated about what to wear. I wanted to look my best, to create a different exterior, one that relayed confidence and self-assuredness.

I made sure I was down in reception at 6.30pm sharp so Saman wouldn't need to come to my room. I was admiring the décor when I heard a voice.

"Hi, Shama."

Saman was sitting in the small one-seater chair, smiling – he'd been there all along! I caught my breath at how handsome he looked, having changed into a beautifully tailored dark brown jacket with a soft camel-coloured jumper underneath. "Are you excited about your surprise?" he asked.

I'd forgotten about it but smiled back at him nervously.

"I bought you this shawl because it gets chilly here in the evenings," he said, handing me the garment. I was touched – here was a man who not only said the right things at the right time to me but was also thoughtful and considerate.

"Thank you, that's really sweet," I said, placing the shawl around my shoulders. "I am a bit curious about my surprise, actually."

"We'll walk there and then you'll know what it is soon enough," he said. "Don't worry, it's something good. I'm not planning to kill you!"

I laughed at his excitement, which reminded me of my kids when they were younger. We walked for about 20 minutes at a leisurely stroll, chatting about Istanbul while Saman shared his stories of how he'd lived in the city for a month before making his way to Europe. He was funny and lively. I could see how he'd adapted to British lifestyle so easily.

By now, we'd reached the main street and I realized we'd joined a queue outside a theatre.

"Shama, this is a gift for you to thank you for what you did for me back in Manchester," he said. "Tonight, you will fulfil your dream of seeing the whirling dervishes performing the *Sema*."

I was speechless. My dream, in which I saw a whirling dervish spinning, his white robe catching the wind and flapping, as if it had a life of its own, danced into my mind, poised to become a reality, thanks to this man who was almost a stranger. A wonderful gesture and gift for me – Shama – someone of little significance, just an ordinary person, but maybe, just maybe, someone who deserved a little happiness in her life.

I looked at Saman with astonishment, ready to embrace him with gratitude, but then checked myself. Why was he doing this? Perhaps the time had come to banish the self-doubt, I told myself. Here was someone who was genuinely kind and thoughtful, who'd simply gone out of his way to do something for me, winning my heart in the process. "Thank you, this means everything to me," I said, wiping away a tear.

We went in and took our seats on the floor. I was full of anticipation and delighted to see that Saman had brought his camera with him. "Here," he said, handing it to me with a smile. Suddenly, there was a rustle of movement from a row of black cloaks and the performance began. I looked up and for the next 20 minutes remained transfixed, as if I was hypnotized, mesmerized by the spectacle in front of me.

Out of the corner of my eye, I could see Saman glancing at me every now and then, smiling at my reaction. As I turned to look at him and saw his face, it dawned on me that his delight came from seeing me so happy. These selfless acts were something I had only experienced from my parents many years ago.

The dervishes whirled on incessantly and, caught up in the moment, I felt the tears run down my face. The entire experience felt cathartic, as though I was releasing all the inner feelings that had been holding me back. I turned to Saman and noticed that he was crying too.

After the performance, we walked slowly down the street in silence. I was so exhausted that I found it hard to put one foot in front of the other, yet somehow felt cleansed, although I couldn't explain how or why.

We came to the Blue Mosque area and decided to sit awhile outside, admiring its beauty. The silence was loaded; we didn't need to exchange words to communicate with each other. After a while I pulled myself out of the stupor I was in.

"Can we leave, Saman? I need to find out if my sister is coming tomorrow and call my children," I said.

"Yes, of course!" He jumped up and adjusted the shawl around my shoulders from where it had slipped, ever the gentleman.

When we reached the hotel, I thanked him for a wonderful evening.

"You're welcome, Shama. You deserve to be happy!" he said with a smile, turning back toward the lift.

Once in my room, I Skyped Fatima, who explained that she'd got her passport and was arriving at 6pm the following day. Next the kids appeared, chatting away and telling me their stories.

"Can't you stay longer, Mama?" they asked. "We're having such fun here with Aunty and Uncle."

"Night-night and be good," I said with a smile.

Exhausted, I brushed my teeth, washed my face and headed for bed. I was about to do some reading when I looked at my phone and saw four messages from Saman.

Thanks for a lovely day – I miss u!

U have a special impact on me, Shama!

I want to be around u all the time!

Miss you!

Reading the texts produced mixed emotions in me, a combination of happiness and fear. Here I was, away from home, alone in Istanbul, with a man I hardly knew telling me how he felt about me. *God, are you playing games with me?* I asked.

Saman kept texting:

Do u want to go out for a walk by the sea, Shama? Answer me! I know ur looking at the messages!

Before long, the phone next to the bed rang. I picked it up and heard Saman's voice, saying, "Hey, how are you? Stop ignoring me!"

"Listen, Saman, I had a great day, but it's late and my sister arrives tomorrow," I said, as politely as I could.

"Why are you worried? She'll get collected and brought to the hotel and I'll leave in the morning," came his reply. There was a pause while I tried to think how to respond.

"Look, Shama, I just want to be with you before I go. It's as simple as that," Saman said eventually. "Let's go out, sit by the sea through the night and watch the sunrise. It's a truly beautiful time of the day in Istanbul. How often will you get to experience that, Shama? Stop being boring. And I know you're not sleeping! Come on, do something spontaneous!"

I was confused, desperate to see the sunrise, but still holding back. In the end, I caved in.

"OK," I said eventually. "Give me ten minutes and I'll meet you in reception."

"Thanks, Shama," he said, quietly. "Remember, we only live once. Let's just enjoy it. You deserve to be happy! But bring a jacket, it will be nippy!"

We walked to the seafront and found a spot that Saman said would give us a perfect view of the sunrise. It was still dark, but as we sat in a comfortable silence, communicating without words, the inky skies cleared, signalling the dawn of a new day. Seated beside each other, but without touching, I could smell Saman's fragrance and feel the energy that emanated from him. He had a special aura about him and it drew me to him like a magnet. The atmosphere was charged, electric. I knew he was feeling it too.

"Look, Shama," he whispered, leaning in toward me. "The sun just peeked at us."

I followed his gaze and sat mesmerized as the grey expanse in front of us gave way to a magical mix of colours, illuminating both the sky and the waters below while bringing the cityscape around us to life. The birth of a new day that would stay etched in my memory, like a favourite film, forever.

Neither of us wanted to spoil the moment by moving or talking, but finally Saman broke the silence and said we needed to head back. We stood up, exchanging no words, both holding on to what we knew was a truly intimate moment between us.

Saman dropped me off at my room and I headed straight for my bed, where I immediately fell into a deep sleep, drained mentally and physically by the intense 24 hours that had gone before, yet feeling happier than I had done for as long as I could remember. The mix of emotions was complex: not only joy but a spark of hope and a peaceful contentment.

As I dozed off, it occurred to me that I'd spent a great deal of time and energy unnecessarily trying to explain myself in words to the people around me. In the past 24 hours, I'd realized that in some situations, there was no need for words. My thoughts could remain where they were, a part of me, but not needing to be dissected or to define me. I would let myself be guided by what was in my soul as much as by what was in my mind. I felt enlightened. A new day had dawned. Something told me that the next sunrise would bring another fresh start, as would the one after that. The sun wouldn't always be bright, but there would always be another dawn.

As for Saman, as he disappeared over the horizon, I somehow knew that whether he returned with the sunrise or faded with the sunset, I'd always be grateful for the beautiful dawn that he'd shown me. Realizing that sleep was unlikely to come any time soon, I pulled out my notebook. By chance, the pages fell open at an earlier entry: *I search from horizon to horizon to find the greatest love of all.* On this same page I began writing:

Oh, my beloved…
I sail to you in the ocean of my dreams
To a far-away distant place
Of great beauty and tranquillity
Where pain and suffering do not exist,
Where we give praise to God for our joy and happiness,
Where our love intertwines with a love for all things.

Oh, beloved keeper of my heart
The companion of my soul
You have reached out and touched the essence of my being
And shown me the way to a higher plane

Your love has awakened me from my years of slumber
A beckoning call to the spiritual world
Where my body is mist in the mountains
This is where our hearts belong
This is where our souls live…
Oh, beloved the keeper of my heart
come now and reclaim me…
Forever yours.

— *She* ©